EMPIRE
OF IRON

A NOVEL OF
✦THE VESTAL VIRGINS✦

EMPIRE
OF IRON

DEBRA MAY MACLEOD

**BLACK
STONE**
PUBLISHING

Copyright © 2022 by Debra May Macleod
Published in 2022 by Blackstone Publishing
Cover and book design by Alenka Vdovič Linaschke
Forum Romanum illustration by Ana Rey
Book logo by Jeanine Henning

Any historical figures and events referenced in this book
are depicted in a fictitious manner. All other characters
and events are products of the author's imagination, and
any similarity to real persons, living or dead, is coincidental.

Printed in the United States of America

First edition: 2022
ISBN 978-1-0940-0030-5
Fiction / Historical / Ancient

Version 1

CIP data for this book is available
from the Library of Congress

Blackstone Publishing
31 Mistletoe Rd.
Ashland, OR 97520

www.BlackstonePublishing.com

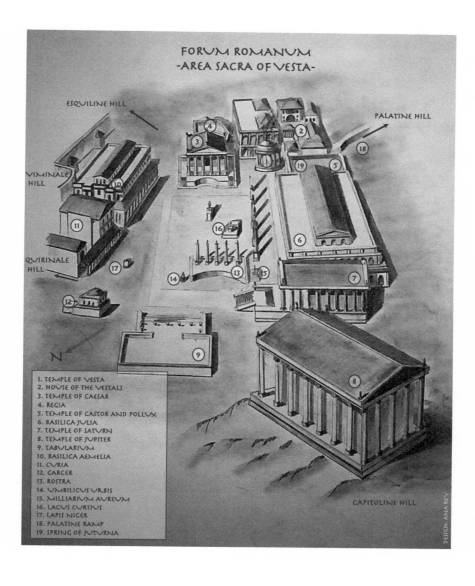

FORUM ROMANUM
-AREA SACRA OF VESTA-

ESQUILINE HILL

PALATINE HILL

VIMINALE HILL

QUIRINALE HILL

CAPITOLINE HILL

N

1. TEMPLE OF VESTA
2. HOUSE OF THE VESTALS
3. TEMPLE OF CAESAR
4. REGIA
5. TEMPLE OF CASTOR AND POLLUX
6. BASILICA JULIA
7. TEMPLE OF SATURN
8. TEMPLE OF JUPITER
9. TABULARIUM
10. BASILICA AEMELIA
11. CURIA
12. CARCER
13. ROSTRA
14. UMBILICUS URBIS
15. MILLIARIUM AUREUM
16. LACUS CURTIUS
17. LAPIS NIGER
18. PALATINE RAMP
19. SPRING OF JUTURNA

DESIGN: ANA REY

AUTHOR'S NOTE

At the front of this book, you'll find a simplified illustration of the Roman Forum and the structures mentioned in the story.

At the back, I have included a dramatis personae, or cast of characters. You'll also find other reader-friendly resources there, including the names of the gods and mythical figures mentioned in the series, a glossary of Latin and other important terms, and a couple of illustrations that tie into the storyline and that I think you'll find fascinating.

Thank you for reading.

PROLOGUE

The Vestal Tacita versus the Gaul

ROME, 390 BCE

The young Vestal Virgin Tacita dropped to her knees at the edge of the Lacus Curtius, the ominous deep pit located between the Temple of Vesta and the Senate house in the Roman Forum. As she looked down into the black void, the fabric of her white veil brushed against her cheek, and she hastily pulled the veil off, dropping it onto the ground beside her.

She looked at the rolled-up lead curse tablet in her hand, kissed the cool metal, and pushed it through the bars of the iron grating that covered the pit. After a long moment, she heard a faint splash far below.

The priestess placed her palms on the grating and bent over until her nose was touching it. She saw nothing but blackness as she looked down but soon felt the cool, clammy air of the pit creep up to cling to her face like the legs of an unseen insect.

"Gods of the underworld," she said, trying to keep her voice steady and unhurried. "I am Tacita, unsullied priestess of Vesta. I call upon you to curse our enemies. I call upon you, Pluto, black-hearted brother of Vesta, to destroy the—"

An earsplitting shout followed by a heavy crash made her jump, and she looked up at the Capitoline Hill before her. Even in the muted orange light of the early morning, she could make out the wild figures of the invading Gauls surrounding the Temple of Jupiter, slashing their way

through the disorganized Roman soldiers and banging on the great bronze
doors with the hilts of their swords. Her heart pounded, although she
wasn't sure whether from fear or rage.

Another shout, this one closer.

"Priestess Tacita!"

The Vestal turned her head to the right to see a toga-clad figure rushing toward her on the Via Sacra. She stood and ran to meet him. "Senator
Fabius," she called out, "you should be at your home, fortified!"

"It is too late for that, Priestess." Either forgetting or not caring about
protocol, he gripped the young Vestal by her elbows. "Why have you not
fled Rome with the sacred objects? Vesta's flame, the Palladium—"

"They are safe, Senator," she said. "Lucius Albinius and his sons took
the Palladium, the wills, and as many of the scrolls as we could pack to the
flamen's estate and buried them in the vineyards."

The old senator looked past the Vestal, to the circular Temple of Vesta.
Only wisps of smoke rose from the opening in the domed roof. It was like
looking at the last breaths of the goddess herself.

"Where are the other priestesses?" he asked.

"They escaped with Albinius. He will take them and the sacred embers
to Caere. There is a Temple of Vesta there. The flame will not die."

"No," said the senator. "But we shall." He kissed the Vestal on the
cheek and then held her face in his hands. Tacita could feel his hands
trembling. There were tears in his eyes. "I remember you as a child," he
said, "trying to catch lizards crawling up the side of the Rostra."

A long, loud shriek of terror prompted the senator to look over his
shoulder at the Capitoline Hill. Tacita followed his wide-eyed stare,
and they both caught sight of a woman's body tumbling down the hill,
thrown from above, her bloodied *stola* falling off to reveal an even blood-
ier nakedness.

Senator Fabius put his hand on the hilt of the dagger at his side. "Dear
girl," he said, "give me the last honor of sparing you."

She smiled sadly at him. "You need no more honor, Senator. I must
finish my duty to the goddess."

They held hands for a long moment, the old Roman senator and the young Vestal priestess. Tacita did not want to let him go. She did not want to pull her eyes away from his. He was strong. Familiar. He represented the life she knew, the world she knew.

Yet, even as she held his gaze, she knew that world was being torn down around her, torn down by barbarian men who could never have dreamed of building such things themselves.

The shouting and screaming from the top of the Capitoline grew louder, more undeniable. The Gauls still hadn't broken through the doors of Jupiter's temple, but they now clearly outnumbered the Roman soldiers and citizens defending it.

Movement behind the senator caught the Vestal's eye: his colleagues were emerging from the Senate house. They walked slowly, defiantly, until they stood in a single row before it.

Only moments later, a horde of Gauls, their swords out and their eyes mad, appeared from the back of the Senate house and stood in front of the statesmen like beasts sizing up their prey, wondering when to go in for the kill.

"*Vesta Mater viam tuam luminabit*," Tacita said to the senator. Mother Vesta will light your way. She felt him squeeze her hands tightly and then pull his away.

Tacita watched him walk back to the Senate house to join his colleagues as the Gauls surrounded them on all sides.

Slowly, she began to walk backward, back to the Temple of Vesta, the Gauls now streaming into the Forum from every direction. To the priestess, they looked like animals newly unleashed, running into this building and that, chasing people out, and then howling in pursuit.

A particularly hideous Gaul with a long mustache, ratty bearskin cloak, and ridiculously pointed helmet jabbed at Senator Fabius with the tip of his sword. When the senator didn't react, the Gaul jabbed harder, and a stream of red began to run down his chest. The Gaul turned to look at his companions. They didn't know what to make of these men who, knowing they were beaten, refused to act beaten.

Tacita saw the Gaul raise his sword and, not wanting to see the senator's head fly from his body, gathered the bottom of her *tunica* and turned to run as fast as she could, barefoot, along the cobblestone back to the temple. Behind her, she could hear the *whoosh* of flames as the invading barbarians began to set Rome ablaze.

As she ran by the great meeting hall, she saw a young nobleman named Lucius Sergius and his wife embracing under one of the arches in the colonnade. Their tiny son was standing between them, clutching his mother's stola, even as clouds of thick black smoke filled the air and floated heavily toward them. Tacita knew the orange flames were close behind. Tacita knew how fire worked.

She watched Lucius as she ran past the hall. All at once—and it happened so fast she could barely comprehend it—he stepped back and swept the blade of his dagger across his son's throat. He gripped the back of the child's tunica and lowered him to the floor. And then, in what seemed like the same motion, he thrust the dagger into his wife's chest. She clutched his shoulders and slid down his body.

Lucius had no sooner lowered his wife's limp body to the floor when a group of eight or ten Gauls charged at him from farther down the colonnade, bursting out of the black smoke like nightmare embers of a fire. Lucius took two steps back and unsheathed a long sword from his side.

Tacita cleared the hall before she could see any more—but not before one of the Gauls had seen her. He broke away from his companions and ran after her.

Tacita sprinted up the steps of the circular Temple of Vesta, pulled open the doors, and fell inside, tumbling onto the floor and scrambling to the hearth, where the last embers of the sacred fire burned.

With the fire almost out and the sun barely risen, it was unusually cool inside the temple's inner sanctum, and a chill ran over the Vestal's bare arms. She clutched the marble hearth and pulled herself to her feet. Despite her fear and panic, she had a sudden realization: she had never before been in the temple alone but had always been accompanied by at least one other Vestal on watch, and perhaps a novice or two.

The doors to the temple swung open, and the Gaul stood in the doorway, his bulky form blocking out the light. He wore the same peaked, dull helmet as the others Tacita had seen, with long, reddish hair sprouting out from under it. Instead of a sword or a spear, he held an ax. It dripped blood. Pieces of flesh and hair were stuck to the curved blade.

Tacita remembered how the senators had stood, and she straightened her back as he entered the holy space of Vesta's temple and closed the doors behind him, shutting out all the light except that which managed to filter in from the hole in the temple's domed roof.

His eyes moved up and down her, and he dropped the ax to the floor. He parted his lips in what Tacita interpreted as a smug smile—although the few teeth he had were black and rotten—and began to move closer, licking his lips and unfastening his belt.

Tacita met his smug smile with her own. "You stinking godless pig," she said. "I would sodomize myself on Priapus before I'd let you lay hands on me."

As the Gaul opened his mouth to laugh at whatever the girl had said in her Roman tongue, Tacita clutched a handful of hot ash from the hearth and threw it into his eyes. He laughed out loud and brought his hands up to wipe the ash from his eyes—he had broken through the gates of Rome and massacred a hundred armed men; a little ash was amusing.

Less amusing was the split-second realization that the girl had struck him on the side of the head with something very hard—something sharp. He blinked.

Tacita swung the iron stoker again, harder this time, hitting the same spot on his skull. He shook his head. She swung again.

He slumped to his knees. She raised the iron stoker over her head and brought it down on his skull, over and over, not stopping until he collapsed onto his belly and whatever was supposed to be inside his head was spreading across the goddess's floor in a viscous pool of red, white, and gray.

Tacita gripped the stoker and stared down at the dead Gaul, her chest heaving from her efforts. The temple's sanctum was eerily quiet. Gone were the familiar voices of her sister Vestals, gone was the comforting *snap* of Vesta's fire. Her throat tightened to know that she would never hear them again.

Outside the temple's doors, she could hear the war cries of the invaders growing closer, growing bolder, growing wilder.

She could hear the shrieks of women calling for their husbands, screaming for their children, and then the shouts of Roman men looking for their families in the chaos, calling out to other men, trying to mount whatever last desperate defense they could.

She could hear the roar of the growing fire as it consumed the nearby meeting hall, that sound soon made even more dreadful by the swarming, heavy footfalls of the enemy and the sputter of the torches they carried. And then loud voices on the steps of the temple. Foreign voices. Men's voices.

As the doors to the temple opened once again to the enemy, Tacita slipped her hand under the last burning embers of the hearth fire and pulled out the dagger hiding underneath. The ash swirled around her and fell to the floor, flyaway gray pieces clinging to her white tunica.

"*Vesta Sancta, permitte hanc actionem*," she whispered, crushing the last embers with the palm of her hand to extinguish the fire and ignoring the heat that singed her flesh. "*Meam viam illumina.*"

Tacita pressed the tip of the dagger's blade under her left breast—as she had been taught to do to protect her purity—and thrust upward, feeling the heat and pain sear through her chest. She gasped but could not feel any air enter her lungs.

She fell on her back beside the Gaul and looked up through the hole in the temple's roof, seeing the last of the orange sunrise give way to a clear blue sky and then, strangely, a black one.

CHAPTER I

Nemo in Amore Videt
No one sees when in love.

—PROPERTIUS

ROME, 18 BCE

372 years later

Tacita awoke. She could tell by the throaty gasps between cries that her daughter, Calidia, had been crying for some time. She lifted herself off the couch in Soren's triclinium to find a house slave, a light-skinned woman with an annoyingly angular face and horse teeth, staring at her from an uncomfortably close distance. She was instantly irritated.

"Can you not hear Calidia crying?" she asked the slave. "Why are you not tending to her?"

"Master Soren told me not to."

Tacita rubbed her eyes.

"A message came for you earlier today, Domina. From the House of the Vestals." The slave pointed to a scroll sitting on a handsomely carved wooden shelf on the other side of the dining room.

"Leave me alone," said Tacita.

"Yes, Domina."

The slave left, and Tacita straightened her back, trying to stretch the long sleep out of her stiff spine and cramped legs. She stood and wobbled on her feet for a moment before crossing the room to pick the scroll up off the shelf. She examined it. Quintina's Vestal seal was unbroken. That meant Soren hadn't yet seen it.

Tacita brushed her thumb over the hardened wax. She thought about breaking it and reading the scroll before Soren could but then quickly thought better of it. The house slaves all spied on her, including the horse-toothed one who was always trying to catch Soren's eye. She set the scroll back down on the table and started toward Calidia's nursery.

The sound of Soren's snoring echoed off the walls, and she paused by the door to their bedchamber. His afternoon naps were growing longer these days. That was just as well. They improved his mood. She peeked in at him: he was sprawled naked on the bed, and a slave was fanning him with a large *flabellum* made of feathers.

She imagined herself strolling to the side of the bed, stripping off her dress, letting her hair fall over her shoulders, and then climbing on top of him before he was fully awake. These days, it was easier that way. She could have him in his half wakefulness, when he was most receptive to her, before he could grab hold of whatever penetrable slave was within reach to satisfy himself.

Soren groaned and turned onto his side, and Tacita's stomach fluttered with desire for him. It was the same desire she'd felt the first time she had ever seen him. It was at the amphitheater, when his renegade charioteer, Scorpus, had lost a big race.

She could still see the rage in Soren's face. The power. At that moment, she knew she had to have him, and she'd spent every social event in Rome after that flitting in front of him, trying to make him notice her, using whatever boy or man she was with—from her sister's crush, Septimus, to Caesar himself—to make him jealous.

In the end, she had done better than make him jealous. She had made him need her—well, her and the baby. Mostly the baby. But she wore his wedding ring and shared his bed. His politics and feuds were of no concern to her.

As Calidia's cries turned into wails, Tacita pulled her eyes away from Soren and walked quickly into the nursery. She peered down into the baby's cradle to see Calidia grasping the hand of her little wooden doll, the one the Vestal Cossinia had given to her on their last visit to the House of the Vestals.

"Your cries could wake Hypnos," Tacita said as she swooped the infant up in a bundle of blankets and slipped the strap off her dress to expose her breast. Calidia latched on while Tacita wiped a tiny tear off her smooth cheek.

A sound caught her attention, and she turned her head to find Soren standing naked in the doorway. She had a sudden feeling of self-consciousness and thought about asking for a wet nurse again, but she knew what the answer would be. No.

Soren stepped closer until his bare chest was near hers. Tacita giggled and reached out to stroke his chest with her fingertips. "You are the only father in the world who sleeps through his child's cries and wakes at her silence."

He stepped away without responding, but Tacita could read his mind. *I am not her father.* He left the nursery and disappeared down the colonnaded hallway.

That's fine, she thought. *You will soon learn to love the baby as you love me.*

For his part, Soren could not read Tacita's mind. It was not because her mind was complex or her thoughts inscrutable—he doubted she had the capacity for serious thought—but rather because he could not have cared less what she was thinking about.

He returned to his bedchamber, where a teenage boy was retrieving a tunica and belt from the wardrobe. Soren eyed the boy; while he had always preferred women, the release he had experienced with the slave Anchises had stayed with him. These days, his male slaves had almost as much reason to avoid him as his female slaves did.

The teenage boy had an escape plan, though. "Domine," he said, "a message came from the House of the Vestals. It is on the shelf in the triclinium."

Soren grinned while the slave dressed him, then walked quickly toward the triclinium as the boy followed carrying a pair of sandals.

Reaching the wooden shelf, Soren picked up the scroll and felt just a little deflated. It was from Priestess Quintina, not High Priestess Pomponia.

Pomponia didn't write to him often but rather sent brief replies to the letters he sent her—letters inquiring about Tuccia's residual estate or property, or lingering tax matters from the purchase of Anchises and Thracius. None of the letters were necessary, and they both knew it, but he liked writing them, and even more, he liked that she was obliged to respond.

The scroll in his hand was marked private and addressed to Tacita. It was held together by the Vestal's red wax seal: an image of Vesta's temple with the Roman Eagle on top and the abbreviated inscription s SAC QUIN-TINA—for *Sancta Sacerdos*, or Holy Priestess, Quintina—below.

He broke the seal and uncurled the papyrus, reading while the slave busied himself putting the sandals on his master's feet.

Dear sister,

The empress recently had a lovely canopy added to the terrace atop our house. There is not a better place in all of Rome to lunch. I am hoping you might come by tomorrow and bring my niece, Calidia. I have not seen either of you in almost two weeks and miss you terribly.

Please let me know if you require any assistance in your private life, sister. There is little I am not empowered to do, should you offi-cially request my help in any matter.

With great affection,
Your sister Quintina

Soren curled the scroll back up. Sighing impatiently as the boy strug-gled to finish tying the second sandal, he handed him the scroll. "Put this in my office," he said. "With the others."

"Yes, Domine."

Soren ran his fingers through his short dark hair and let his lips curl into a half smile. *Please let me know if you require any assistance in your pri-vate life, sister.* He snorted.

The only person who seemed oblivious to how much he hated Tacita was Tacita herself.

CHAPTER II

Alea Iacta Est
The die is cast.

—JULIUS CAESAR

Ankhu couldn't hide his disgust any more than he could hide his opinion that his mistress had made a terrible error in judgment. He scowled and looked at the Titan who stood in front of him wearing only a loincloth, piles of sticky black hair at his feet, scraps from his freshly shaven head.

Scorpus scratched his bald scalp. "I managed to hide in Rome for months with a full head of hair," he said. "One day with you, and I'm bald as an egg."

"We're leaving Rome."

"Why?"

"Because the priestess said so. I'm taking you to her villa in Tivoli. We're taking the horses now. I'm to keep you quiet there until she can decide what to do with you."

Although I know what to do with you, thought Ankhu. *Let you ride a horse's length ahead, throw a blade at the back of your head, and bury your body on the side of the Via Tiburtina.*

Ankhu had asked his mistress to let him do it. Rather, he had pleaded with her. But she had refused. Ankhu had even tried invoking the memory of the Roman man she had loved, the one who had once—it seemed another life ago—owned him.

Master Quintus would never have permitted this, Priestess, Ankhu had told her. *The man is a runaway slave, and a murderous one. If he is caught and tortured, he may implicate you. Master Quintus would have killed Scorpus without a second thought.*

But the priestess hadn't listened, and Ankhu felt a twinge of the frustration his former master had so often displayed at the Vestal's stubbornness. Still, he would do as instructed. He had served her for over ten years now and would do whatever the priestess asked of him. She knew it as well as he did.

"The sun will be up soon," Ankhu said to Scorpus. "I want to be on horseback before the streets are full. Pile your old clothes over there and then clean up this hair—bloody Osiris, look at the lice! But first put this on." The Egyptian freedman held out a long white linen skirt to the charioteer.

"If I put that on, I'll look like you," said Scorpus.

"You're already as brown as me."

"The sun made me so, not the gods."

Ankhu threw the skirt at Scorpus's head. "Thank the sun when you pray, then. Your gods have done you no favors." He looked at Scorpus's wrist. "Take that off."

Scorpus removed the leather cuff from around his wrist, its scorpion medallion being the last remnant of his identity, and dropped it onto the pile of his old clothes. He wrapped the skirt around his waist and bent down to pick up the clumps of matted hair from the pristine marble floor—Pomponius's floor—and toss them into a basket. When Ankhu's back was turned, he quickly retrieved his leather cuff and tucked it into his loincloth. Standing, he noted the colorful frescoes of birds and trees painted on the deep orange walls. It was a fine home, and at one time it had been a refuge for him. He supposed it still was.

"Pomponius brought me here when I escaped my prison cart," he said.

"Oh? And how did his high-society neighbors not notice a bloody Titan marching up the Caelian Hill in broad daylight?" asked Ankhu.

"We hid behind a fish cart until sunset. And then when we reached the Caelian, Pomponius told me to walk with confidence, like I was supposed to be there. No one looked twice."

"Yes, hiding in plain sight," said Ankhu. "We will do the same." He held out a wig to Scorpus. "You are my kinsman. We are Egyptian freedmen of the Vestalis Maxima, heading to Tivoli to tend her vineyard. You must dress as I do."

"So, you shave your head, then you shave my head, only to wear a wig? No wonder your people are slaves of Rome."

"You are the only slave in this room," said Ankhu.

Scorpus put the wig on his head. "It itches."

"It's wool." The Egyptian set a wig—a finer one, made of human hair—on his own head, ignoring the charioteer's huff of indignation. He bent down to retrieve something from a satchel leaning against the orange wall. "I am going to line your eyes with kohl. You are going to remain silent while I do."

After he was finished styling Scorpus's eyes into the almond-shaped fashion of Egyptian men, Ankhu grinned smugly. "You almost look civilized. As long as you don't open your mouth, the disguise will get us out of Rome."

They packed up the rest of their gear, loaded it into leather bags on their horses, and led the animals away from Pomponius's house and in the direction of the Porta Tiburtina. Ankhu walked ahead, the clip-clopping of horse hooves echoing along the quiet, empty early-morning street.

It took less than an hour to reach the great arch of the Porta Tiburtina, the gate that would allow them to pass out of Rome and begin their day's journey to Tivoli along the well-maintained cobblestone of the Via Tiburtina.

The gate wasn't really a gate; at least, that wasn't its first function. Rather, it was the large arch of a massive aqueduct the emperor Augustus had both repaired and recommissioned. Now it served as both aqueduct and a sort of triumphal arch around which the city's border control operated. If you were headed into the countryside leading to Tivoli, or returning from that area, you had to pass through the Porta Tiburtina.

Although the sun was just coming up, there was already a backlog of travelers on foot, on horseback, or in horse-drawn litters or carts, all blinking the sleep out of their eyes and waiting with strained patience for the soldiers and city officials to either let them leave or enter Rome.

Ankhu passed the reins of his horse to Scorpus, who was doing his best to appear nonchalant despite the knot of dread forming in his gut. If his identity were to be discovered, he'd be hauled straight off to the Carcer. No doubt a very entertaining public execution would follow.

The Egyptian rummaged through one of the bags draped over his horse's hind end and pulled out a scroll and a very fine-looking clay amphora of wine. He held out his arms as he approached one of the armor-clad soldiers. The soldier smiled, and they clasped arms in greeting.

"Ankhu, you goat fucker, it's been ages."

"It has indeed," the Egyptian replied. "You were not here when I last passed through the gate."

"I was sick. Had a rotten tooth that almost killed me. Took two men to pull it out, and let me tell you, my friend, death would've been better." The soldier opened his mouth and used the tip of his *gladius* to point to the spot where the offending tooth had been. "See that there? See that gaping spot? They ripped two wrong teeth out, the bastards, before they finally wrenched the rotten one out. I have the mouth of an eighty-year-old."

"It is no matter. I have something you don't need to chew," said Ankhu. He held up the amphora of wine.

The soldier raised his eyebrows. "From your mistress's cellar?"

"Of course," said Ankhu.

The soldier took the amphora and pulled out the cork. He placed his nose to the hole. "That's nice," he critiqued. "Unique aroma."

"It is genuine Falernian wine," said Ankhu. "Not that cheap imitation stuff they sell in the market. I recommend a measured approach to consumption . . . and I wouldn't drink it next to the fire."

The soldier took a sip and then raised his eyebrows higher, surprised and impressed. "I thank you, my friend," and as an afterthought to himself, "I will hide this from my wife." He glanced casually over Ankhu's shoulder to Scorpus. "Who's that with you?"

The question sounded more curious than official. Nevertheless, Scorpus felt himself break into a cold sweat. The soldier was looking directly at him: the woolen wig, the wraparound skirt, the Egyptian cosmetics. The guise suddenly struck him as impossibly transparent.

Not knowing what else to do, Scorpus bowed his head slightly to the soldier—just a little, so as to keep the wig in place—keeping eye contact and praying to Jupiter that the man wasn't a serious fan of the chariot races. He scratched his horse's black head in an effort to appear unperturbed. The moment he stopped, the horse nudged his arm for more.

"He's my kinsman from Alexandria," Ankhu answered. "Come to help me manage the priestess's villa in Tivoli." He held out a scroll, presumably his kinsman's identification, but the soldier didn't take it. He kept looking at Scorpus. His eyes narrowed, and it seemed he might ask a follow-up question—did the man's large frame not remind him of someone?

"It is going to be a hot one," said Ankhu.

"Hotter than yesterday," the soldier replied. It was enough to divert the stream of his thoughts, and he grumbled some halfhearted complaints about the slow-pouring fountains and lack of public latrines around the Porta Tiburtina. "Wouldn't you think water would be put to better use within a stone's throw of an aqueduct?"

Ankhu nodded sympathetically.

Finally, the soldier waved his arm at a gate official to indicate that Ankhu and his companion could pass. "May Apollo protect you," he said. "Watch your backs around the Altar to Proserpina. We've had reports of marauders hiding in a herd of sheep, if you can believe it." He laughed. "Hiding under them, like Ulysses and his men escaping the Cyclops."

"We live in a strange world," replied Ankhu, "where sheep are more cunning than wolves." The soldier nodded, and Ankhu waved in parting. "*Gratias ago tibi, amice.* I thank you, my friend." He strode purposefully back to Scorpus, took his horse's reins out of the charioteer's hands, and led the way to the gate.

Scorpus followed closely behind. As he walked his horse along the cobblestone under the marble arch, he looked up at the aggrandizing inscription on the tympanum:

IMP CAESAR DIVI IULI F
AUGUSTUS PONTIFEX MAXIMUS
RIVOS AQUARUM OMNIUM REFECIT

Imperator Caesar, son of the Divine Julius, Pontifex Maximus Augustus, restored all these aqueducts.

Below the inscription, on the upper curve of the arch itself, was a carved *bucranium*, or ox skull, a symbol of the most impressive animal used in religious sacrifice. Scorpus took it as a sign and made a silent promise to offer thanks to the gods as soon as he could. For, like the hero Ulysses, an absurd covering of wool had saved him from certain death.

* * *

The deep purple of the canopy that covered the terrace of the House of the Vestals was the same royal purple of the canopy that covered the great balcony at Caesar's home. That was either a flattering gesture on the empress Livia's part or, more likely, an oversight.

Either way, it was beautiful, and the Vestalis Maxima Pomponia had immediately taken to having her regular breakfast—bread, cheese, and grapes—on the couch beneath it, protected from the glare of the morning sun.

The position gave her a bird's-eye view, quite literally, of the Forum as it came to life each morning. It also let her keep an eye on the comings and goings between the House of the Vestals and the Palatine Hill. If Caesar were on his way, or perhaps Despina's messenger, she was the first to know.

Even better, she could watch the smoke coming out of the Temple of Vesta's domed roof and assess the fire's strength: if the wind was right, she could even enjoy the mild fragrance of any incense that had been added to the hearth. The practice seemed to please the goddess and had helped to keep the contagion at bay.

She smiled at Anchises as he joined her and sat on an adjacent couch. He was sipping a strongly spiced wine, some wild beast of his own concoction, to help soothe a raw throat.

"*Salve*, Domina," he greeted her.

"Good morning, Anchises."

He squinted out at the Forum. The sound of wooden supply carts moving along the cobblestone of the Via Sacra mixed with the voices of merchants headed to the basilicas and magistrates on their way to the Senate house. In the distance was the booming voice of the newsreader making his announcements before the Rostra; Anchises and the priestess were waiting for news of a different sort, however.

"They should have passed through the Porta Tiburtina by now," said Pomponia.

"I cannot imagine two more capable men," Anchises reassured. "No doubt they are riding free to Tivoli this moment. Scorpus is insufferable, but he can be useful to us, Priestess."

"I will think on it," said Pomponia.

"Think on what, Pomponia?"

Pomponia and Anchises both turned their heads, startled by Quintina's quiet approach.

"I'm sorry. I didn't mean to intrude," she said.

"You aren't intruding," Pomponia replied. "Anchises and I were just discussing your sister. Have you received a reply to your letter?"

"Yes," said Quintina. "Written in Soren's hand, of course. Tacita regrets she cannot visit this week." She rolled her eyes.

"Soren tightens the vise until the wood cracks," said Anchises. "Never until it breaks. I wager he will let her visit next week."

"But not without him," replied Quintina. "Never without him. I would like to speak to her alone."

"That would be unwise," said Pomponia. "And pointless. She would tell Soren everything said between you, hoping her devotion would increase his love for her. Then he would speak ill of us, and she would agree with him. It is predictable. Her only purpose is to please him."

Quintina sighed in frustration. She knew it was true. She took a piece of cheese from Pomponia's plate and absently chewed it. "Lucretia has asked me to teach the novices today, so I'll be in their study if you need me. *Valete.*"

Alone again on the terrace with Anchises, Pomponia waved a small iridescent blue dragonfly off her white veil and stood up. "I'm meeting Tiberius at the Temple of Juno," she said. "He is having a special aureus struck for the emperor with Vestal priestesses on the reverse. Caesar has a vast collection of coins and often orders unique strikes for important dignitaries, so he will appreciate the gesture. While I'm gone, have the librarian file those scrolls in my office—the ones in the basket, not the ones on my desk."

"Of course, Domina. I know which ones. Take care."

Pomponia left the balcony still chewing the last of her grapes. Two young novice Vestals passed by her on the way to the study, and she patted the first, Varinia, on the head. The girl smiled up at her and ran off, trying not to trip on a tunica that was just a little too long on her.

Pomponia thought about reaching out to the second novice, Longina, but couldn't bring herself to do it. For some reason, she was developing a dislike for the girl. She was clever enough, and her performance was satisfactory, but being a priestess of Vesta wasn't just about academics or etiquette. It wasn't just about mastering the *invocationes* and *ritus*, upholding the Pax Deorum, learning the *jus divinum*, or even devoting oneself to the goddess and Rome.

Being a priestess of Vesta was also about having the ability to live in relatively close quarters with numerous other women and to do so free of conflict and competition. It was about character. And unfortunately, Lucretia and Caecilia, the two priestesses who worked most closely with the novices, had both wondered aloud to Pomponia whether Longina's character was suited to the order.

Moving into her quarters, Pomponia let her body slaves freshen her appearance and then exited the House of the Vestals to step inside the shaded but warm space of the *lectica* that awaited her on the street just outside the portico.

She busied herself reading documents, and it seemed that the litter-bearers had no sooner lifted the lectica than they were setting it down atop the Capitoline Hill in front of the Temple of Juno Moneta, the money temple. It was here that Rome's stores of gold, silver, and bronze were kept.

Caeso pulled back the curtain of her lectica, and Pomponia stepped out, her other guard, Publius, shooing away a noisy goose that had wandered over from Juno's sacred grove adjacent to the temple. It flapped at him and bit at his tunica.

Doing his best to ignore the assault, Publius stood at attention as

Tiberius approached. He greeted Pomponia with a smile, and she fell into step beside him, heading toward the temple's colonnaded portico. As they reached it, she was surprised to find the widow of Senator Pavo, a woman named Mallonia, waiting dutifully on the lowest marble step.

The woman bowed to Pomponia. "High Priestess," she said, "it is good to see you again."

"And you, Mallonia," replied Pomponia. "You're looking well."

It was partly true. The middle-aged widow had largely recovered from her senator husband's death from the contagion and looked healthy enough; however, her thin hair, blotched complexion, and tall yet round frame were features that had never done her any favors.

Yet Fortuna had been fair. Mallonia's wealth and patrician status had more than compensated for nature's thriftiness, and the woman had married well. For a Roman woman, little else mattered.

In a gesture that struck Pomponia as unusually bold, Tiberius put his hand on the small of Mallonia's back and guided both women up the steps. Two guards opened the large bronze doors, and they passed into the color and grandeur of the temple's interior.

Straight ahead in the temple's *cella*, a massive bronze statue of the goddess Juno stood holding a staff, on top of which sat the golden Eagle, the symbol of Rome and also the symbolic animal of Juno's divine husband, Jupiter.

"Senator Pavo bestowed a large quantity of gold to Caesar in his will," said Tiberius. "I am having the emperor's special-issue coins minted from that."

"Your husband is as generous in death as he was in life," Pomponia said to Mallonia.

"Caesar was good to us," said Mallonia.

"He had reason to be," Tiberius said. "Your husband helped pay Caesar and Agrippa's troops during the civil war, before the money started coming in from the proscriptions. It was men like him who created the empire."

An elderly magistrate by the name of Sepullius Macer, dressed in a very clean, ivory-colored toga, waited for Tiberius to finish speaking and then greeted his prestigious guests with a deferential bow.

"*Salvete*, Master Tiberius," he said, "and High Priestess. We are ready for your inspection."

"Very good, Sepullius," said Tiberius.

The magistrate led the trio down a long, wide colonnade. One wall was covered in a lively mural that depicted a historical scene: Juno's sacred geese attacking a horde of Gauls who were trying to scale the Capitoline Hill under the cover of night. The geese's honking had alerted the Romans to the invaders' presence.

This was why, even centuries later, the sacred geese had the honor of living undisturbed in the grand gardens of Juno's temple, their occasional attacks on citizens overlooked and indulged. In fact, killing a sacred goose was punishable by being flung off the top of the Tarpeian Rock to one's death. It was a punishment that fit the crime. Juno's geese had helped protect Rome's treasury on the citadel of the Capitoline Hill. Many believed they still did.

That was important, since Rome had a lot of bills to pay. It paid its client kings, who in turn paid even more in tribute and taxes. It paid its civil servants. It paid for a never-ending campaign of public works and infrastructure, from roads and bathhouses to medical clinics and sanitation. Most important, it paid the soldiers of the great Roman army, without whom none of it would be possible.

The magistrate led Tiberius, Pomponia, and Mallonia into the adjacent area of the temple complex that served as the city's mint, passing various *officinae*, until they arrived at the appropriate workshop; it was warm from the melting of metals, loud from the hammering of coins being struck, and alive with tunica-clad workers so preoccupied with their duties that they didn't even notice their illustrious visitors.

"To design this coin for the emperor," said Sepullius, "I commissioned the same engraver who created this intricate design on one of the dictator Julius Caesar's denarii." He held out his palm to show a coin. "On the obverse is Julius Caesar's visage." He flipped the coin over. "On the reverse is Venus holding a small Victory in her hand. As you can see, the depiction of the goddess is exceptionally detailed. It is why I chose him to design the coin. Showing the Vestal priestesses in particular required a special skill."

The old magistrate nodded to his assistant, and a young man knelt before Tiberius and Pomponia, holding up a silver tray upon which were three newly minted and identical gold coins. Pomponia took one.

On the obverse was the sharp face of Augustus, slightly more handsome in gold than in the flesh. This portrait would show people across the Roman world what their emperor looked like, so it was important that it make a strong impression. Literally.

Pomponia turned the aureus over. On the reverse was a fine depiction of the Vestal Virgins, including herself as Vestalis Maxima, offering into the hearth. An image of the temple was in the background with VESTA stamped above and the letters SC, for senatorial approval, below. Likewise, this image would travel across the empire, reassuring the masses—or at least those who could afford to have a gold piece in their purse—that Vesta's priestesses faithfully tended the eternal flame in the Caput Mundi.

"It is very fine," said Mallonia. "My husband would be honored to be associated in some small way with such a thing."

Pomponia turned to Mallonia to say something suitably gracious but stopped. Tiberius was staring at the widow, a woman some twenty years his senior, with an unmistakable look of desire in his eyes.

As if that weren't brazen enough, he moved to stand in front of her and reached out to touch one of her long emerald earrings, brushing his hand against her bare shoulder as he did. "My apologies, I thought it was falling off," he lied. Mallonia looked at him sharply and took a step back, barely able to hide her displeasure.

Tiberius maintained the closeness between them by stepping forward to compensate for her retreat. Mallonia's face hardened, and she took another step back. He advanced again. In any other situation, their dance and Tiberius's sudden lasciviousness might have been comedic, but taking place in front of the Vestalis Maxima and the entire Roman mint, it was only disturbing.

Finally, Tiberius succeeded in landing a kiss on Mallonia's lips. The widow reacted instinctively with a slap across his face. She muttered a shocked "How dare you." Her lips tightened in anger and disgust, and she wiped her mouth with the back of her hand.

Pomponia's eyes widened. In over thirty years of public service—after working alongside two Caesars and some of Rome's greatest names in the Senate, military, and religious collegia—she had never found herself faced with such indecorum on the part of an important man. Even Marc Antony would have known better. Her thoughts bounced off each other. *Should I correct him? Is Mallonia significant enough to risk my relationship with Caesar's heir?*

The magistrate looked at her, pleading for direction. Pomponia opened her mouth, still not sure of what would come out, when Tiberius seemed to check himself.

"Lady Pavo . . ."

Pomponia waited for the apology, but the incredulousness of the encounter persisted, and Tiberius did not offer one.

"Priestess Pomponia, thank you for stepping away from your duties to come today," he said. Again facing Mallonia, he quickly attempted to kiss her hand. She pulled it back at the last moment. Tiberius frowned and awkwardly departed the mint.

Pomponia turned to the magistrate. "The coin is approved," she said. "Excellent work again, Sepullius. Caesar will be pleased, and I will mention you by name."

The magistrate's face opened up. "Thank you, Priestess."

She took a small step toward him. "Not a word of this."

"Of course not, High Priestess."

"We will see ourselves out."

As the two women made their way out of the mint and back down the wide frescoed colonnade toward the temple's cella, Pomponia decided to address the obvious. "Tell me," she said to Mallonia, "if I am not intruding, is there a"—she searched for the right word—"a *familiarity* between you and Tiberius?"

"No, nothing of the sort," said Mallonia. "I cannot explain his behavior. I have known Tiberius since he was a child. My husband knew him. He has no reason to treat me with such disrespect, but this is not the first time he has done so in recent months." She licked her lips, then grimaced at the thought of Tiberius's lips on hers. "I can only think the habits of another are becoming his own."

"Oh? And who might that be?"

"My late husband's brother," Mallonia replied. "Soren."

Pomponia stopped abruptly.

Mallonia looked at her curiously. "I'm assuming you've met him," she said, "as he is married to Priestess Quintina's sister." She sniffed. "He was pleased with that connection, I can tell you."

"Yes, he visits our house on occasion," Pomponia replied casually. It was a revelation that Mallonia thought so little of her former brother-in-law. The Vestal set off again and called ahead to Caeso and Publius, who were waiting near the doors. "Have my lectica brought close."

The guards slipped outside as the two women moved through the cella and out of the cool marble temple into the warmth of the open air.

"You have Caesar's ear," said Mallonia, as they descended the steps. "Perhaps you could speak to him on my behalf. You need to—"

"I need do nothing," Pomponia asserted. Tiberius's behavior was strange and rude, but what could she say to Caesar? *Your stepson kissed a noblewoman?* It wasn't exactly treason.

Mallonia lowered her eyes. "I apologize, High Priestess."

"It is no matter," softened Pomponia. Soren's former sister-in-law could be a wellspring of information. She put her hand on the woman's shoulder. "We will speak again."

"Thank you, Priestess," said Mallonia.

Pomponia stepped into the shade of her lectica and pulled the curtain closed. *No, Mallonia,* she thought. *Thank you.*

CHAPTER III

Prosperum Scelus Virtus Vocatur
Successful crime is called virtue.

−SENECA

THE ISLAND OF PANDATERIA

All around was rock. Hard, cold fields of rock with dry patches of scrubby green brush between them. Beyond that, the sea. And beyond that—well, it didn't matter anymore.

Julia sat cross-legged on the ground near the edge of the cliff that marked the highest point of her island of exile, Pandateria. She pulled her woolen *palla* around herself. In days gone by, she'd have had a slave bring her some warm honey or lemon water and a plate of delicacies. These days, she had to fend for herself.

She had no slaves. She had no human company at all, no one except for the little ugly man who twice monthly dropped off a wooden crate of supplies—stale bread, drinkable water, bruised fruit—on shore before immediately turning back to the mainland in his small sailboat without even making eye contact.

The man had his orders, and they came from the emperor of Rome himself. *Do not speak to my daughter. Bring only bread, water, and old fruit. No meat or cheese. No sweets. And absolutely no wine.*

Julia had never imagined that such a desolate place could exist. It was colorless. It was an island of extremes: either freezing cold or burning hot; there was no in between. From what she could tell, the gods didn't even know it existed. The only one who seemed to have a presence was Vulcan, and he grumbled miserably inside the island's volcano as if he were as unhappy to be there as she was.

She tried not to obsess over the fact that the volcano was less than a ten-minute walk away. It wasn't like she could get much farther from it. She could walk the entire length of the island in less than fifteen minutes. If the thing erupted, she would be ash within moments. The gods knew the latrine-sized shack of a hut that she was forced to use as shelter wouldn't offer any protection.

A pang of sadness gripped her throat. Would her father weep at news of her death? Would he think of the days he bounced her on his knee or boasted of her cleverness in the Senate? Would he remember the tenderness between them when little Agrippa was born? She wondered.

She did not wonder whether Tiberius or Livia would weep at news of her death. They would dance on the Rostra after dark. But then, had she not done worse things on the Rostra?

Julia closed her eyes but opened them after only a moment. The silence was too overwhelming. In Rome, it was all but impossible to find a moment's silence. On Pandateria, it was all but impossible to find a moment's sound.

But then she was corrected by a cautious squawk and the soft *slap-slap* of webbed feet approaching. She turned her head to smile at the island's only other inhabitant, a worn-looking seagull whose left wing jutted out at an unnatural angle. Like her, it was in exile.

"Come and get it, Phoenix," she said. She reached out to remove a cloth that was covering a pile of bread and a shallow bowl of water, and the gull waddled toward it, downing the bread greedily and taking long draws of the fresh water.

Sated, it cocked its head, one moment looking at Julia and the next gazing up at the unreachable sky. It settled down barely an arm's length away from her, tucking its head into its good wing to sleep.

Julia lay back slowly so as not to disturb it, and then closed her eyes again, following Phoenix into sleep.

CHAPTER IV

Latet Anguis in Herba
A snake is hiding in the grass.

—VIRGIL

Octavian sat beside Livia on the marble edging of the healing Spring of Juturna, a watery shrine of sorts located in the narrow space between the House of the Vestals and the Temple of Castor and Pollux.

Like every other structure in the Forum Romanum, whether monumental or modest, the spring had a story to tell. It was believed that the divine twins Castor and Pollux let their horses drink at the spring when they had first arrived in Rome; their temple was then built only steps away, with massive marble statues of the heroes and their horses looking down at the spring from above.

Livia slipped a silver cup into the pool, filled it with clear water, and handed it to Octavian. He drank it to the bottom. Refreshed, he let his frame relax as she dipped a cloth into the spring, wrung it out, and wiped it over his brow, cheeks, and neck.

"You are much improved, husband," she said, doing her best to sound sympathetic. Octavian's constant bouts of illness were as tiring to her as they were troubling to him.

"The waters are a blessed remedy," said Octavian. He squinted at the bottom of the marble basin. "Look at all the coin down there, Livia."

"The people offer for your health, Caesar."

"I want this collected regularly. It will pay for the gilding on the Dii

Consentes by the upcoming *ludi*, and probably the marble of my Ara Pacis as well."

Livia looked into the water at the thin layer of coin below. *That is a flattering overestimate*, she thought. *Typical.* "It looks to be a great amount," she said in an agreeable tone. "I will speak to a magistrate." She trailed her fingers across the glassy surface of the water. How many times had she drunk from this spring? How many times had she drenched herself in its healing waters, praying they would bring health and life to her womb?

When it hadn't worked, when she had finally realized that it would never work, she had wrapped her piss pot in her palla, carried it to the Forum, and emptied it into the spring herself.

A rise of voices some twenty feet away caught her attention. Both she and Octavian looked over to see one of the soldiers who was guarding the street entrance to the spring—it had been cordoned off since the emperor's arrival—engaged in an increasingly vocal conversation with a woman.

Slowly, and with growing irritation, Livia recognized the woman's voice: Scribonia, Octavian's former wife.

"Let her come," Octavian called out. He met Livia's chastising eyes. "Or shall I let her continue to make a scene?"

The soldier moved aside, and Scribonia approached, dressed in a fine yellow stola with her curly brown hair tucked obediently behind the deep blue veil that hung down her back. She ignored Livia and knelt directly in front of Octavian. "Caesar," she said, "I beg you—"

Octavian bristled. "Scribonia. Stop."

"Let me visit our daughter, Caesar. I need to see that she lives."

"She lives. She has food and shelter."

"I need to see her with my own eyes."

"It is not possible."

"You are Caesar. Anything is possible." Scribonia looked up at him. "Why punish me, Octavian?" she asked, daring to dispense with his great title. "Did I not support your rise and honor you, even during our unhappy marriage? Have I not always shown dignity as your former wife? Do I not praise and kneel to Caesar in public?"

Livia held her breath. She could tell by Octavian's expression that he was affected. If he weakened his resolve, if he softened the terms of Julia's exile to permit a visitor, she knew that more concessions would follow.

As bad, she worried that Octavian might inquire about his granddaughter Agrippina, Julia's child with Agrippa, who now resided with Scribonia. Rumor had it that Agrippina was every bit as adorable as her mother had been as a child. Livia had endured Julia's baby-faced power over Octavian. She couldn't stomach it twice.

"Caesar," she interjected, "let me speak with Scribonia alone." She looked at Scribonia with compassion. "I am a mother as well."

Octavian stood, brushing Scribonia's hands away as she tried to reach for him. He strode down the narrow street, toward his guards, and out into the Forum.

Scribonia sat back on her heels. "Empress," she said, "I only wish to accompany my daughter into exile. I will bring nothing but the dress on my back and will never return to Rome, if that's what Caesar commands."

"I will speak to Caesar on your behalf," said Livia. "Do not petition him again, or you will only anger him and make matters worse for Julia. Leave it with me."

"Thank you, Lady Livia," said Scribonia.

Livia turned her head away, and Scribonia stood up. She bowed and silently walked back into the busyness of the Forum, allowing herself to feel a glimmer of hope. Perhaps her pleading had appealed to the empress's maternal nature.

What she didn't know, of course, was that she was not the first to have appealed to Caesar on Julia's behalf.

Maecenas had previously pleaded with Octavian to let him renovate the one *domus* on Pandateria—a rarely used imperial refuge—so that Julia could live in it, saying that Agrippa would have wanted it so. Maecenas had even insisted on paying for the renovation himself to remove any hint that the emperor was softening his stance on his daughter's austere banishment. After a brief show of opposition, Octavian had allowed it.

Yet, shortly after the improvements were completed, Livia had persuaded Octavian that news of such agreeable habitation would come across to the Senate and the people of Rome as capitulation. "It pains me to say it, husband," she had wept, "because of the love I have for Julia. But my first duty is to Caesar."

So the domus and its comforts were boarded up, and Julia was tossed back out onto the rock, having no recourse but to huddle in a miserable hut with a single brazier for warmth. Most slaves and freedmen in Rome lived better.

Yet Livia knew it was just a matter of time until Octavian relaxed the terms of his daughter's exile. His fatherly feelings for her may have paled when news of her abundant adulteries had surfaced, but their color was returning.

That very morning, Livia had secretly watched Octavian praying at the altar to Vesta in their home. He had laid his head on the marble altar like a child laying his head on his mother's lap and whispered a private prayer into the sacred fire. *Protect my daughter, Vesta Mater. Find a way for me to bring her home.*

His words felt like a catapult striking Livia in the chest. If Julia returned home, if she and Octavian began to communicate or reconnect at all, there was no doubt the little royal slut would eventually persuade her father to disinherit Tiberius.

"All make way for Emperor Caesar Augustus!"

The distant shout stopped Livia's descent into the dark pit of her worsening thoughts. Octavian was on the move to the Senate house.

She stood and walked away from the Spring of Juturna, past the House of the Vestals and into the Forum, where four armored soldiers awaited her.

The soldiers flanked her as she strolled past the Temple of Vesta, reminding herself that she had a scheduled meeting with the Vestalis Maxima in the Tabularium to discuss the allocation of more funds to the Vestal order. She passed by the gleaming marble columns of the Temple to the Divine Julius Caesar, glancing up at their gilded capitals, and turned to walk along the Via Sacra toward the Senate house.

Octavian was already halfway there, walking under his scarlet banner, which bore in gold letters IMP CAES AUG and SPQR. His lictors marched ahead of him while citizens scrambled to catch a glimpse of the procession.

Although the emperor could often be found in the Forum on political or religious business, his frail health meant that he usually traveled in a lectica. Seeing him walk along the cobblestone, strong and confident, was a good sign.

Livia quickened her step until she followed closely behind him, both of them arriving in front of the Senate house at nearly the same time. A gathering of senators, noblemen, and magistrates were already engaged in animated conversation with Tiberius. This included the patrician Soren, who these days seemed ever-present in the life of Caesar's heir.

Octavian looked over his shoulder and smiled approvingly at Livia. He liked it when she made an appearance at the Senate: the empress of Rome, supporting her great husband in all things. She smiled back, wishing she were anywhere else.

Three senators approached her with deep bows, asking after Caesar's health—about which she offered her reassurances—and then complimenting her on the recent improvements to numerous altars throughout the city, which had been undertaken at Livia's private expense.

After a mercifully few minutes, a scribe opened the doors to the Senate. Caesar passed through them with Tiberius and the rest of Rome's important men filing into the great Curia after him for a full day of speeches, proposed laws, appeals, and, Livia suspected, more self-serving motions than a team of scribes could document.

When the doors of the Senate house closed behind the last man, Livia found that the only remaining people of note were herself and Soren. He grinned at her and she nodded, granting him permission to approach.

"Empress Livia," he said, "what a pleasant surprise to see you here."

"But no surprise to see you here, Soren," she replied. "Only my son's guards and his favorite dog are so reliably close to him."

Soren absorbed the gibe. It was a useful insight into the empress's nature. "I mean no disrespect to your great husband, Empress," he said, "but I believe that Tiberius is destined to be an even greater Caesar than the two who came before him."

"It is not seditious to say so," Livia replied. "Perhaps I have you wrong, Soren," she said plainly. "Perhaps you are not a sycophant at all but rather a man who recognizes greatness when he sees it."

"That is a more accurate assessment," Soren replied with as much plainness. "I am committed to your son's success."

"How committed?"

"Entirely."

Livia gestured for her guards to move back, giving her and Soren more privacy. "It is hard to believe, but there are some whose commitment to my son is less whole."

"Of whom do you speak, Empress? If such men are not careful, I will strike them down myself."

"I speak of the emperor."

Soren knew she would get there. Nonetheless, the quickness of it momentarily took him off guard. He held her eyes. "It is unlike the emperor to show such poor judgment." When she did not challenge that, he pressed on. "But Tiberius remains his heir. Surely that proves Caesar's faith in him."

"*Fronti nulla fides*," said Livia. Appearances can be deceptive. She began to walk idly away from the Senate house, toward the Tabularium. Soren stayed by her side while two guards walked ahead and three more trailed behind at a watchful distance. "Tiberius was not Caesar's first choice," she continued. "If certain people have their way, he will not be Caesar's final choice either."

"Perhaps those people can be silenced."

Livia shook her head. "That would only create more noise."

"I understand," said Soren. "Then is there no way to guarantee Caesar does not change his mind?"

The empress glanced at him, then looked away. "There is only one way."

* * *

Tacita took off her sandals and stepped into the shallow pool of water in the center of the courtyard in Soren's house. The decorative orange fish within—her sister had gifted them to her from the pool in the Vestals' courtyard—darted in all directions but soon calmed, one of them even nibbling at her ankle with its soft lips on the off chance it was more edible than it appeared.

Calidia was sleeping soundly in a cradle under the shade of a nearby palm tree. Even looking at her slumbering face made Tacita sleepy, and she found herself yawning. Her mouth was still open when a house slave entered the garden from the atrium.

"Domina," he said, "there is a guest here. She says Master Soren is expecting her."

"Oh? He didn't tell me anyone was coming. Show her in."

The slave disappeared and reappeared a moment later with an attractive woman who, somewhat to Tacita's relief, was probably fifteen or even twenty years older than she was. She was dressed formally in a deep emerald gown and wore a gold tiara.

The woman smiled widely. "You must be Tacita," she said. "Soren has told me so much about you. I am Aelina."

Tacita stepped out of the pool. "How do you know my husband?" she asked, trying to sound more cavalier than she felt.

"We knew each other in Capua," said Aelina. "We were"—her smile became even wider—"good friends."

"Really? Strange he has not mentioned you."

"Oh, that fox," Aelina said with a laugh. "You know what men are like." Seeing Tacita's blank expression, Aelina bit her lip. "Forgive me. I did not mean to make you uncomfortable."

"You could never do such a thing," assured Tacita. She sat on the couch beside the pool and motioned for Aelina to sit on an adjacent chair. As she strapped her sandals back on, she peered over at Calidia, just in case Aelina had not seen the baby's cradle.

Aelina either didn't notice or didn't care. But Tacita wouldn't give up that easily. She reached into the cradle and lifted Calidia out, putting the baby to her breast as motherly as she could. Calidia made soft grunts of protest at being disturbed.

"How did you become acquainted with my husband?" she asked. *It is a reasonable question*, she thought. *No need to take it as jealousy.*

"Soren was good friends with my late husband, Mettius," replied Aelina. "I am pleased he still befriends me, especially after that debacle with the slave Scorpus. I am the one who sold Scorpus to him in the first place."

"Soren doesn't hold a grudge."

Aelina guffawed so loudly that Calidia almost jumped out of Tacita's arms. "Are we speaking of the same man?" she challenged buoyantly.

Both women heard Soren's voice in the atrium as he barked something at a slave before walking heavily into the garden. The corner of his mouth lifted in amusement at the sight of Aelina, and he permitted her to embrace him.

"What are you doing in Rome?" he asked.

"Your memory is as short as your temper," Aelina chided, her voice gentle. "You promised to take me to the amphitheater for the games this week. We wrote of it, remember? You also said that you would accompany me to my niece's wedding reception tonight. No woman wants to attend such an event alone. Tacita, you don't mind if I borrow your husband this evening, do you? I promise I will return him unscathed."

"Well, it's not really a good night," said Tacita. "Little Calidia has been fussing and—"

"Ah yes, I remember now." Soren nodded. "Fine. Let's go get it over with, then." He turned and strode out of the garden back toward the atrium, Aelina nearly breaking into a run to catch up with him.

Tacita quickly lifted Calidia onto her shoulder and shuffled after them. But it was no use. She emerged from the portico just in time to see her husband and his Capuan mistress climb into Soren's lectica and pull the curtains closed behind them.

CHAPTER V

Aut Neca aut Necare
Kill or be killed.

—A ROMAN EXPRESSION

I'm getting old, thought Pomponia as she tiredly brushed her veil off the side of her face. *All I can think about is the bath.*

Beside the seated Vestalis Maxima of Rome, the priestesses Cossinia, Quintina, and Lucasta were on their feet in the Vestals' private viewing box in the amphitheater, excitedly craning their necks to see the procession of wild beasts being let loose into the arena. Their cheers rose to join those of thousands of other spectators. It hurt Pomponia's head.

She had been working nonstop for the past several days alongside a tax quaestor; the Flamens Dialis, Martialis, and Quirinalis; and even the empress to review and allocate temple funds in Rome and the provinces. Many temples in Rome and throughout the empire acted as banks for wealthy or important citizens; they were well guarded, and it was presumed, not always wisely, that the priests who had access to the underground vaults were honest.

Under the direction of Nona and Sabina, the Temple of Vesta in Carthage was proving to be especially profitable in terms of storing and lending money—with interest, of course. Pomponia was doing her best to keep its profits within the Vestal order. So far, and with Livia's support, she had been successful in doing so; however, the victory had come at the cost of a lingering headache. Pomponia wished she could have stayed home.

Perhaps on another day it would suffice to send others. Priestesses Cossinia, Quintina, Caecilia, and Lucretia were all well-established Vestal Virgins who had developed strong political and personal friendships with Rome's elite. There were also some excellent novices at the ready.

But today's games were special, and the presence of the high priestess was expected. These were the first ludi put on and paid for by Tiberius, in honor of the emperor and in recognition of being named Caesar's heir. And Pomponia had to admit that the amphitheater's notorious administrator, Taurus, had outdone himself for the occasion.

Even the preshow beast hunts promised to be something special. Instead of simply releasing the wild beasts—an assortment of exotic big cats—onto the open floor of the oval arena, a massive wooden maze had been constructed on its sand-covered floor and the animals were channeled into that. From the seats above, they looked like huge fur-covered fish slipping into a maze of narrow streams.

But fish didn't roar.

Quintina looked down at her. "Pomponia, can you see?"

"Yes, I'm fine."

"You should stand up."

"I can see well enough, Quintina. Don't worry about me. Watch the show."

In the amphitheater below, a number of so-called hunters ran—or rather were forced at the point of swords to run—into the maze. Each wore only a loincloth and carried a dented, bloodstained shield and a gladius. Throughout the stadium, bets began to be laid.

The high wooden walls that chuted man and beast along the interconnected channels made it impossible for those within the maze to see what was coming around the next corner. The spectators above could see, though. They shouted and stamped, pointed and grabbed their heads as an unwitting and clearly unwilling hunter turned a bend to run head-on into a snarling leopard.

Although the leopard had been denied food for several days, it wasn't particularly interested in eating. Like the other big cats that slunk around corners and darted down straight parts of the maze, this one looked overwhelmed by the sounds, smells, and sights of the arena. It crouched down, hissing and spitting at the hunter. It wasn't looking to kill; it was looking to escape. The hunter seemed to feel the same way.

Yet in the arena, it was kill or be killed. The hunter let out the most courageous war cry he could muster and descended upon the animal, who, meanwhile, had decided it wasn't going to give up without a fight either.

As the snarls and shrieks from the arena floor animated the crowd, Pomponia looked for a wine slave. It was a rare occasion she could watch a beast hunt, even after all these years, and not think about Cicero and the compassion he'd shown during the spectacle of an elephant slaughter. Cicero believed such mercilessness appealed only to the worst of men, and certainly not to the gods.

He wasn't the only one who felt that way. The cruelty of the games had a growing number of critics in the Senate and other circles, and Pomponia felt it was only a matter of time until the people of Rome softened their hearts. Not all of them—that was not the nature of man—but enough to challenge the status quo.

With no slave in her immediate sight—Livia was right, they often pretended to be busy elsewhere when really they had sneaked off to watch the show—Pomponia stood up to stretch her legs and find refreshments. At the same time, Despina entered the Vestals' box, dressed in a pretty sky-blue tunica and an orange glass-bead necklace.

"High Priestess," she said, "the empress requests that you join her and Caesar on the imperial balcony. The main performance will be starting soon."

"Very well," said Pomponia. She was about to tell Quintina she was leaving, when the younger Vestal instinctively turned around and nodded in understanding. Pomponia smiled to herself. She used to keep watch over Fabiana's movements in the same way.

Walking alongside Despina and trailed by Caeso and Publius, Pomponia moved along an arched colonnade that led onto Caesar's ornate balcony.

"Anything of interest to convey?" Pomponia discreetly asked Caesar's most senior slave.

"More of the same," Despina replied under her breath. "I will send another letter in a couple of days, sooner if something noteworthy happens."

Pomponia nodded.

As they strode onto the grand balcony, Pomponia saw Octavian in his usual spot, seated on an elegant high-backed chair in the center of the front row. Tiberius was on one side of him, and a visiting dignitary—the client king of Judea, named Herod—was on the other. Although Tiberius and Herod were keenly watching the bloodbath below, Octavian was preoccupied with a scroll. Since Agrippa's death, the man rarely stopped working.

Senators, high-ranking priests, and various patrician men from Rome's oldest and most noble families filled the rest of the seats on the prestigious balcony. To Pomponia's displeasure, that included Soren; however, Tacita wasn't with him. Instead, a woman she had never met was sitting next to him, her fingers brushing his arm in a playful yet possessive way.

Pomponia smiled polite greetings to all. Soren rose from his chair in what she interpreted as mock respect. She forced the smile to stay on her face as she looked at him and then sat next to Livia on a cushioned chair on the very edge of the balcony's front row.

"Are you enjoying yourself?" Livia asked and then answered her own question. "Of course you aren't. Neither am I."

Pomponia smoothed the front of her stola. "The quaestor sent a message this morning," she said. "He has been authorized to keep the profits of the Carthage temple in the Vestal order. He wouldn't have done so without your insistence, so thank you."

"Some of the other temples can barely turn a profit," said Livia. "The priests use coin that should be marked for the treasury to gild their favorite whores. Why should they then be allowed to pilfer from better-run temples?"

The two women continued to ignore the beast hunt below and instead shared their grievances until the loud blast of a horn turned their attention back to the arena floor.

As slaves moved through the channels of the maze to pile the remains of man and beast onto carts and take them away, Taurus—wrapped in a royal-blue cloak and wearing a golden crown—took to the raised stage in the amphitheater. He was always a crowd-pleaser.

"Emperor and Empress," he said and bowed, "blessed priestesses of

Vesta, and honored friends, welcome all! It is time for today's main performance." He opened his arms wide, slowly spinning in a circle to address the masses of spectators around him. "My fellow Romans," he shouted, "you have all heard the legend"—he paused for dramatic effect—"the legend of King Minos and the Minotaur! Today, with the indulgence of our great emperor, I shall play the part of the mighty Greek king."

Taurus took a deep bow and his golden crown tumbled off, falling to the floor of the stage with perfect comedic timing. He scrambled to put it back on as the crowd erupted into laughter.

"Ah, you laugh," shouted Taurus, "but it is not as easy as it looks to wear the crown!" He saluted Caesar who stood and saluted back, playing along good-naturedly to the crowd's delight.

"Our performance takes place generations before the founding of our great city," continued Taurus, his voice becoming more theatrical by the moment, "when King Minos ruled the majestic island of Crete. The king's people were tormented by the monstrous Minotaur, a half-bull, half-man creature that ran wild."

At that, an impossibly tall and overmuscled man wearing a bull's head, his body covered in patches of mud and animal hair, ran to the edge of the stage and roared madly up at Taurus. In each hand, he carried a bloody dagger that had been molded into the shape of a sharp bull's horn.

Taurus shouted over the clamor. "But King Minos, like all good kings, was as resourceful as he was wise. He instructed the master craftsman Daedalus and his son Icarus to build an impenetrable labyrinth to imprison the Minotaur."

On cue, a man with a long gray beard accompanied by a strong youth ran up and down the wooden walls of the maze, busily inspecting the boards and hammering here and there before standing back in awe of their labyrinthine creation.

As if noticing the giant maze for the first time, the costumed Minotaur turned away from Taurus's stage. Curious, he moved toward the entrance to the labyrinth and ran inside, down one long passageway and then turning to run down another. Quickly lost, he tried to backtrack but took a wrong turn and hit a dead end, roaring and throwing his hairy arms up in rage.

"Once the people of Crete were safe from the creature," said Taurus, "King Minos ordered that fourteen of the most beautiful youths in Athens, seven boys and seven girls, be sacrificed to the Minotaur."

A piercing scream went up as a naked girl no more than fifteen years old was pushed into the maze by arena slaves. Her screams attracted the Minotaur and led him back to the entrance. When the girl spotted him, she screamed louder and began to run away, down a passage. The Minotaur gave chase.

The arena slaves pushed another naked girl, then another, into the maze—"Run!" they were ordered—until seven of them were dashing down various passages. After that, the arena slaves forced seven naked young men, all perhaps fourteen or fifteen, into the maze one by one, also instructing them to run.

For several long minutes, the crowd was content to laugh at the sight of the terrified naked teenagers racing down various passages, turning corners, hitting dead ends, and even unsuccessfully trying to scale the wooden walls to avoid a run-in with the Minotaur.

A clamor of excitement rose as one young man chose to turn left, a poor choice, and found himself in the same narrow channel as the Minotaur. At the sight of the dagger-wielding beast, he yelled what sounded like *Mama!* in a foreign language, and Pomponia heard Soren's laughter mingle with that of the men around him. Again, she found herself wishing she were home, in the bath.

The Minotaur stabbed at the youth's body with his horn-shaped daggers, roaring and thumping his chest in dramatic fashion as the naked boy crumpled to the ground.

The Minotaur then turned his attention back to the maze, back to chasing the remaining teenagers.

Just when the novelty of the Minotaur and the tormented youths was starting to wear off among the spectators, Taurus gave the go-ahead for the next act. The sound of thunderous hooves and angry snorts rose from the arena floor, again piquing the crowd's interest.

Pomponia looked down to see a herd of massive black bulls—perhaps ten or twelve in total—being funneled through a chute that extended from the arena's unseen stables and into the labyrinth's entrance. Snorting with anger, the hot-blooded beasts charged down the first channel, heads down and feet kicking up behind them.

The enclosing wall and the floor of the stadium began to shake, the vibration extending up into the stands. Taurus put his hands on his head—*Blessed Jupiter, let the walls hold!* he thought—and the amphitheater's spectators jumped to their feet again.

A young foreign girl with long blond hair was the first to be trampled. She turned at the last moment, her arms crossed in front of her to cover her bare breasts, and screamed at the sight of the sweating bull bearing down upon her. The screams stopped instantly, and the beast ran on, leaving the girl's broken body to roll grotesquely several times before coming to a stop against the wooden wall.

In another section of the labyrinth, another black bull was about to charge over a boy, when the youth reached out to grab the girl fleeing ahead of him and toss her behind, into the beast's path. His efforts were for naught, as the bull trampled the two of them as easily as it trampled one.

The audience laughed at the youth's failed plan.

It went on like that for some time, until the last naked teenager had been trampled and the bulls had grown bored of the game. They slowed their pace and stomped angrily down the passageways until their handlers ushered them out of the labyrinth and back through the chute to the stables.

"Saving the bulls for another day," Livia remarked to Pomponia. "You have to give Taurus credit. He puts on a good show, but he keeps costs down. Bulls are more expensive than teenagers."

That marked intermission. The excitement and frantic shouts of the amphitheater settled into a thousand private conversations and the calls of food vendors selling salted meat, figs, and other snacks.

Pomponia stood to stretch her legs and accept a cup of wine from a passing slave. *It's about time*, she thought. *Maybe this will help get rid of my headache.*

She discreetly turned her back to the imperial balcony's finer company and drank the wine in three swallows, as if it were medicine. When she turned back around, Soren was standing right in front of her. His female companion had both her arms wrapped tightly around one of his; she reminded Pomponia of a tree snake clinging to a branch.

Soren held a meaty drumstick in his hand and spoke with a mouth full of food. "High Priestess Pomponia," he said, "my friend Aelina from Capua would like to meet you."

Who cares about your friend from Capua? thought Pomponia. She made a minimal effort to be pleasant and asked Aelina, "Do you like the games?"

"Oh, I love them, Priestess," said Aelina. "Especially when I get to watch them from Caesar's balcony! My friends in Capua will never believe it."

"Indeed," said Pomponia. She glanced over Soren's shoulder, looking for someone else she could speak with. Caesar and Tiberius were having a heated discussion with a group of senators, while the client king Herod was staring at a slave woman's backside. Livia was nowhere in sight, likely having gone to the latrine. That was a good enough reason to leave Soren's company.

"If you'll excuse me—"

"If you're wondering why Tacita isn't here," said Soren, "it's because she had to stay home with my daughter. Infants are so fragile," he said sourly. "One day they're fat and healthy, and the next . . ."

"And the next *what*?" asked Pomponia.

Soren stripped the remaining meat off the drumstick and set the bone on the refuse platter beside him. For a moment Pomponia thought he might retreat. "And the next," he said, "some calamity strikes, and they die."

"The poor little dears," said Aelina.

Pomponia sensed her cheeks redden. She held Soren's eyes as she inwardly wrestled with how to meet his threat. Appeasement? That was not in her nature. Yet she could not risk sparking Soren's vengeful disposition.

Soren had already ordered the killing of her brother. Scorpus had seen it happen on the street below his hovel in the Subura: Pomponius had been stabbed with a dagger from Soren's house. The Vestal rubbed her fingers together, still able to feel her brother's ashes and bits of bone as she had spread them on the ground, promising him vengeance.

Now, with Soren holding himself out as Calidia's real father, he had *patria potestas*. If he wanted to, he could put his fingers around the baby's neck and squeeze. He had the legal right to do so. There would be few if any questions and no punishment.

Or he could take a more subtle approach and simply starve or suffocate the child, or stage some accidental, life-threatening injury to her. The baby was not his blood. She was defenseless. Pomponia imagined her little niece sleeping sweetly in her cradle, Soren's bulk looming over her, full of impulse and rage.

The Vestal smiled graciously. She caught the attention of a slave. "Bring the medallions." The slave approached with a silver tray upon which were a number of oversized versions of the special aureus that Tiberius had commissioned for the emperor. Pomponia selected a particularly well-struck gold specimen and handed it to Aelina. "A gift for Caesar's guests," she said, "and rich proof for those disbelievers in Capua."

"How generous!" said Aelina. "Thank you, Priestess. I shall display it prominently in my home for all to see."

Soren licked the grease off his lips. "What about me, Priestess? Am I not Caesar's guest as well?"

"Oh, Soren, you don't need more gold," said Aelina. "Not after the killing you made on the sale of Anchises and Thracius. I mean no disrespect, High Priestess, but I think you may have overpaid."

"I always do," Pomponia said indulgently. "Rome should be thankful I am in charge of the sacred hearthfire and not the treasury." She waved the slave away. She wouldn't give Soren a rusted iron nail, never mind a shining gold coin that bore her own image.

Catching the last of her words, Octavian joined the conversation, Livia on his arm. "I may yet put you in charge of the treasury," he said, "for I have noticed a financial phenomenon. The less money the magistrate records in the treasury, the more marble appears in his home. We'll soon be stripping the floor in his triclinium to dress our temples."

Aelina's eyes went wide in the company of Caesar. She fidgeted with her hair and opened her mouth to say something, but Pomponia caught Soren silence her with a pinch to the arm.

A horn blew in the arena below, and Taurus returned to the stage, still dressed in his kingly attire. Most spectators in the grand oval of the amphitheater had already returned to their seats and were waiting for the second half of the main performance, but a few stragglers still looked for empty spaces in the stands, their shuffling and bumping annoying those already comfortably seated. There was nothing worse than a latecomer.

Yet, as often happened as the games wore on, those on the imperial balcony remained standing, their attention divided between the goings-on in the arena and the food, drink, and conversation around them. The games were never as good as the gossip.

Pomponia's head throbbed as the horn blew a second time and Taurus's voice rose up.

"Honored guests," he said, "fellow Romans. You may think the story of the Minotaur ends with the tragic death of those young beauties in the monster's twisted lair. But alas, tragedy knows no end. Soon, Daedalus fell out of favor with the king, and Minos trapped the craftsman and his son in the labyrinth."

The actors playing the parts of the master craftsman Daedalus and his son Icarus returned to the arena, but this time they ran into the labyrinth itself. They clung to each other in fear and crept down one narrow channel, cautiously peering around a corner and then tiptoeing down the next channel, expecting at any moment to be confronted and slain by the Minotaur.

"Can you imagine those poor souls, trapped in the prison of their own creation? Yet, the craftsman had insight. He knew the only way out"—Taurus extended an arm to the skies—"was up!"

Taurus gave the spectators a moment to applaud as a large flock of geese was released from the top tier of the amphitheater. The birds flew, honking and flapping, over the heads of the spectators, feathers falling from above.

"Daedalus had Icarus collect feathers from the birds that flew overhead. Daedalus, that resourceful craftsman of the gods, made his son a giant pair of wings and glued the feathers to them."

No sooner had the flock of geese cleared the amphitheater than figures appeared on the top tier at the far end of the stadium: a man, outfitted with oversized wings, being dragged to a large wooden catapult.

Taurus went on. "*Be wise*, Daedalus cautioned his son. *Do not fly too close to the sun lest the heat melt the glue on your wings!* But did the youth listen? Let me ask you, friends, does youth ever listen to age? Does the fool ever listen to the wise?"

To the crowd's delight, the winged man was forced into the bucket of the catapult and, a moment later, shot through the air, high over their heads. He flapped his wings and screamed, but his cries were soon drowned out by the uproarious laughter and applause of the crowd.

Finally, something they hadn't seen before! Taurus puffed out his chest with pride.

The crowd's laughter and applause rose to a clamor and shook the stadium as the winged man's trajectory quickly took a tragic downward turn. He landed with an audible thud in the sand of the arena.

But the arena workers hadn't gone through all the trouble of hauling a huge catapult onto the roof for a single shot. Another Icarus was piled into the bucket and catapulted above the heads of the spectators. After an airy arc, he too landed solidly in the sand of the amphitheater's floor.

And then another.

Before long, even the guests on the imperial balcony were paying attention, doubling over with laughter and laying bets on how far each new Icarus would fly before falling to his death.

After another couple of flying Icaruses, the novelty began to wear off. But Taurus and the catapult operators had known that would happen and were prepared. Three more catapults appeared on the top tier of the amphitheater—including one above and behind the emperor's balcony to afford Caesar the best view—and within moments Icaruses were being launched from all four directions.

Two of them collided midair. The wooden frames of their wings broke apart, sending wood shards and feathers flying into the crowd—the crowd in the lower-class section, of course. Spectators covered their heads and yelled.

Another two Icaruses looked as though they would collide, but the trajectory of one catapult was off: one winged man landed in the sand; the other landed in the stands, causing a locus of chaos. The encircling crowd burst into frenetic applause and roared for more.

The absurdity of it all distracted Pomponia from her headache, and she breathed a sigh of relief. She looked to Caesar to see how he was enjoying the show. It was exactly the kind of thing the emperor found amusing.

She heard a shout somewhere high above her. A shout of panic . . . and a strange, distant *snap*.

And then she felt the worst pain of her life.

A crushing blow to her chest, between her breasts. She found herself on the floor so quickly that she didn't even remember falling.

Pomponia blinked dazedly at the sky as a crowd of faces appeared above her, including the shocked faces of Caesar, Tiberius, and Caeso.

"Priestess," breathed Tiberius, "can you speak?"

"Yes, yes, Tiberius."

She felt Octavian take one of her arms and Tiberius the other. Gently, they helped her to her feet and sat her on a cushioned chair. Caeso took the veil off her hair and felt her head. "Did you strike your head, Priestess?" he asked.

"I did not. Stop fussing, Caeso."

Pomponia blinked to clear the haze from her eyes. It hurt to take a deep breath, but she quickly realized that Aelina had it worse.

The woman was sprawled out a few feet away, jerking in and out of consciousness as two slaves tried to wake her. Her face was white, and a goose egg was already forming on her forehead.

Only a foot away from Aelina lay the unmoving body of a feathered Icarus. Blood was seeping out of his nose.

"*Mea Dea!*" exclaimed Livia. "Priestess . . ."

Pomponia put her hands to her aching chest, looking at Livia. "Did he hit me?"

The empress shook her head.

"No," answered Caeso. His face showed a mixture of relief and revulsion. "Master Soren pushed you out of the way at the last moment."

The Vestal dropped her hands onto her lap. Every senator on the balcony was swarming Soren to praise him for his heroics.

The look of shock on Caesar's face transformed to one of rage. He nodded a silent command to his soldiers. Four or five of them marched off the balcony, no doubt to execute the culpable catapult operators on the top tier behind them.

And then as if proving that absurdity, like tragedy, has no end, Caesar left Pomponia's side to take the tray of gold medallions from the hands of a slave and pass the entire contents to Soren. "It is small payment," said the emperor, "when all of Rome owes you a debt."

*   *   *

As he sat across from the empress of Rome in her luxurious oversized lectica, Soren hoped he looked more humble than he felt.

"I hope you find good use for all that gold," Livia said to him as she cooled her face with an oval fan made of stiffened blue silk.

"That depends on your definition of *good*," he replied.

Fatigued, she tossed the fan onto the floor. "How is your friend?" she asked, more out of curiosity than concern. "Did she ever come to?"

"I don't know. I had a slave take her home. She was still thrashing about like a landed fish last I saw her."

Livia peeked around the closed curtains and sighed with irritation. Octavian probably hadn't even left the balcony yet but was rather arguing policy and legislation with those wifeless senators who had nothing better to do on a nonbusiness day.

She reclined on a large satin cushion with green and yellow stripes and eyed Soren. "You know that whole 'don't fly too close to the sun' act was Caesar's idea. It was a private gibe at my son. He sees himself as the wise Daedalus and Tiberius as the foolish Icarus."

"Perhaps not," said Soren. "Perhaps he sees Tiberius's greatness and wants to keep him on the ground."

"While he himself soars."

"Well, no man can soar forever," said Soren. A loud clatter outside the lectica made him pull back the curtain, and he smirked. "Just ask them."

Livia turned up her nose as a cart of fallen Icaruses rolled by on its way to one of the mass cremation pits on the outskirts of Rome, where they would be burned. Before the contagion, the countless corpses from the games would just be dumped into uncovered burial pits; however, Octavian's legislation now banned such lazy practices.

Behind the cart of dead Icaruses there followed a cart piled high with the carcasses of the big cats from the day's beast hunts. This was by far a more profitable cart. It was headed to the Forum Boarium, where the animals' attractive pelts and exotic meat would be stripped and sold.

At long last, a troop of senators emerged noisily from the amphitheater. They broke into smaller factions according to their interests and allegiances as Caesar walked through their midst, heading to the imperial lectica.

"I take my leave," Soren said to Livia. "But rest assured, Empress, I have not forgotten our mutual purpose." His eyes moved from one senator to the other, assessing each in turn. "I will indeed put Caesar's gold to good use."

"I know you will, Soren."

Soren stepped out of the lectica and quickly moved to the periphery of the amphitheater where a few groups of senators were gathered, still talking about policy and law and disbursements.

He straightened his back and winced as an uncomfortable sensation stabbed his stomach. He thought back to the drumstick. *Was the meat rancid?* No. It wasn't the food. It was something else, something that Soren was unaccustomed to feeling—trepidation.

Was this how Brutus had felt when he had secretly sniffed for co-conspirators in the Senate? When he and other discontented senators had first planned to assassinate Julius Caesar, had they felt a similar sensation in the pits of their stomachs? Had their hearts pounded?

They had had it easier. Julius Caesar had more enemies in the Senate than did his adopted son and heir. This Caesar was well liked by politicians, the people, and the military. This Caesar knew how to keep the senators rich, the public happy, and the soldiers busy, while at the same time achieving the impossible: peace.

The Pax Romana, the peace of Rome, was so directly attributable to this Caesar that many called it by his name—the Pax Augustus. It had created stability and prosperity for Rome as well as its provinces and client states, which had been unimaginable a generation earlier.

Who would want to see such a Caesar bleed on the Senate floor? Who would risk their life or reputation to even hint at assassination? Julius Caesar's assassins had been motivated, or at least justified, by ideals: they had claimed to be saving Rome from a tyrant. This Caesar's would-be assassins would not have so noble a reason to rally around. It would have to be personal.

Soren ignored the cramp in his gut and leveled his gaze on two senators who stood apart from the others: Murena and the younger Caepio.

Perhaps.

Caepio's family had lost a small fortune during Caesar's proscriptions years earlier, although he himself had shown just enough loyalty to Caesar to keep both his head and his assets.

Yet, here he is, shoulder to shoulder with Murena, thought Soren. *Everyone knows Murena's neck is the closest to Caesar's sword . . . His idiot son's neck has already felt it.*

Murena's eldest son, who was generally disliked to begin with, had been discovered to be one of Julia's lovers. Caesar had given him the option of suicide; however, the man had been unable to go through with it. So Caesar had lent his assistance by having him decapitated in the Forum, just steps away from the Senate doors. Soren had watched it all unfold with amusement.

Steeling himself, Soren squeezed his fist closed until the round edge of a gold medallion in his palm cut into his flesh. *Fortune favors the bold*, he told himself. He uncurled his fingers and looked down at the laurel-crowned head of Caesar.

Then he rested a hand on the chest fold of his toga, tossed the gold medallion to a beggar, and strode toward the two men.

CHAPTER VI

Impedit Ira Animum
Anger impedes the mind.

−FROM THE *DISTICHS OF CATO*

Tacita wasn't sure what had woken her. It had only been a couple of hours since she had nursed Calidia, so it probably wasn't her. She turned her head. Soren still hadn't returned to their bed.

But that was all right. When she had gotten up to feed the baby, she had peeked into Aelina's bedchamber. The woman was sleeping fitfully, but at least she was sleeping alone. She had returned home after the games without Soren. No doubt the great spectacles had tired her out, and she had left him to gamble, drink, and whore the rest of the night away on his own.

Tacita felt the familiar flare of anger and jealousy. Why would Soren take Aelina to the games instead of his own wife? Since having Calidia, Tacita hardly went anywhere. Soren had refused her a wet nurse, which had left her all but housebound. She rarely knew where he was or whom he was with.

But at least he wasn't with Aelina. With a bit of luck, the woman would start back to Capua after breakfast, maybe before Soren even got home.

Enlivened at the thought, Tacita lifted herself out of bed. A slammed door or dropped plate would help Aelina wake up early and be on her way. She wrapped a light blanket around herself and shuffled out of her room, past the door to Aelina's bedchamber, and toward the kitchen.

She heard the sound again, the same one that had woken her. This time, she knew exactly what it was: the rhythmic squeaking of the wooden bed-frame in Aelina's room. Breathlessly, she turned and tiptoed back to Aelina's door.

Please let her be screwing a slave, thought Tacita. The woman had been drooling after one of the big African slaves the day before. Maybe Soren had given her permission to use him.

But even as she silently cracked open the door and peeked into the room, Tacita knew what she would see. No matter how much she tried to convince herself otherwise, Soren never failed to disappoint her.

He was on the bottom. Aelina was straddling him, holding her long hair up as she raised and lowered herself onto him. His hands were on her breasts, and he squeezed them tightly as she gyrated.

"I'm almost there," he muttered.

At that, she lifted herself off him. He groaned in protest.

"Ask me to stay in Rome," she said.

"What?"

"You heard me," Aelina said girlishly. She dragged a fingertip down his chest. "Ask me to stay in Rome. As your guest."

"I don't care whether you stay or—"

"Fine."

Aelina leaned over to dismount, when Soren gripped her hips and held her in place. "All right." He grimaced. "You can stay."

She began to gyrate again.

Tacita closed the door, not wanting to hear her husband's groans of release or Aelina's cries of triumph.

*   *   *

It was an unscheduled day of rest at the House of the Vestals. Pomponia had risen with the dawn—and with the nagging remnants of her headache—so had sent temple slaves to spread the word to the other priestesses and the novices. If you're in bed, stay there.

She canceled the novices' classes; postponed several meetings with magistrates, merchants, and other priests; and contented herself with simply making sure those at watch in the temple kept the *ignis inexstinctus*, the eternal fire, burning.

By noon, the house was alive with carefree activity. Lucasta and Caecilia were in the temple with the eldest novice, Lauressa, all three due to be relieved soon, while just about everyone else was in the courtyard enjoying the sunshine and sweets.

Pomponia sat next to the decorative pool in the center of the garden and shielded her eyes from the sun. She tossed the last of her breakfast bread toward the base of Fabiana's marble statue in the peristyle. A crow had been waiting patiently there for quite a while, and Pomponia felt it should be rewarded for such perseverance. It broke the bread in half with its beak, swallowed one portion, and flew off with the rest.

The chief Vestal felt a smile form on her face at the sound of the novices' wild laughter. The girls were lined up before Thracius, each waiting for her turn to be spun by the arms, around and around, to the point of disabling dizziness.

Anchises was supervising. "No more than six spins," he kept saying to Thracius. "You'll make them sick."

But the retired boxer paid him no heed and kept spinning until he himself wobbled unsteadily and fell back onto the grass, nearly landing in a rosebush. The girls piled on top of him.

At first, the young novices had been afraid of Thracius and the disfiguring burn scars that covered his arms and legs. Now he had to sneak through the house barefoot to avoid being set upon by them.

Another shriek of laughter, and Pomponia realized something pleasant: her headache was finally gone. Even better, when she looked up, Quintina was approaching from the portico holding the baby Calidia in her arms. Tacita trailed behind—without Soren.

A silent message—*Can you believe this?*—passed in glances between Pomponia, Quintina, and Anchises. Pomponia stood up to greet Tacita, and the younger Vestal held out the sleeping baby for her inspection.

A few of the novices scurried over to see the baby, then just as quickly grew bored and darted back to Thracius, demanding another spin. Only the novice Longina remained. She poked at Calidia, prompting the baby to squirm and wake.

"Go now, Longina," said Quintina.

The novice ran back to the action, racing another young girl to the front of Thracius's line. As Longina began to lose ground, she stuck out her leg and the other girl tripped over it, landing on her stomach.

Quintina felt herself clutch Calidia more tightly out of frustration and eased off. "I will speak to her," she said to Pomponia, but the chief Vestal's eyes were fixed on her little niece.

"Her eyes . . ." said Pomponia. She stopped. *Her eyes look just like Pomponius's.* She brushed aside a mosquito that tried to land on Calidia's soft cheek. "Her eyes are a very pretty brown." The baby squinted in the sun and squirmed in Quintina's arms. "Let's go inside," Pomponia suggested.

They moved through the peristyle and into the triclinium, blinking sunspots out of their eyes and settling onto the couches.

"If I may speak honestly, sister," Quintina said to Tacita, "I am surprised to see you here without your husband."

"He doesn't know I'm here."

Pomponia raised her eyebrows. "Tacita, is that wise?"

"Probably not."

Quintina gently passed the baby to Pomponia. "Sister," she said firmly, "inflaming your husband's anger threatens your child as much as yourself."

"There is a woman here from Capua," Tacita blurted out angrily. "He couples with her right under my nose!"

Pomponia swallowed her disgust. She had always found the petty jealousies and maneuverings of married women exhausting. That was especially so when they were married to men like Soren. Shouldn't such women be delighted their husbands were coupling elsewhere? She tried to sound sympathetic. "I saw her," she said, "at the games. She suffered an injury during a performance."

"Well, she's recovered now," said Tacita. "Soren has allowed her to stay indefinitely in our home."

"How will he react when he learns you were here?" asked Quintina.

"You should see her," continued Tacita. "She walks around like she's his wife and I'm not. She tells the slaves what to make for supper, she has ordered some trees to be removed from the—"

"Sister," said Quintina, "when Soren learns you came here without him, without his permission, what will he do? Is there any chance he will hurt you or Calidia?"

"I doubt he will hurt me. He is too busy with Aelina."

Quintina tucked her veil behind her ears. *I don't care whether he hurts you*, she thought. "Is there any chance he will hurt Calidia?"

As if feeling the increasing tension in Pomponia's arms, Calidia began to squawk. Pomponia stood and placed the baby in Tacita's arms. Still fuming at the thought of her husband's betrayal, Tacita slipped an arm out of her dress to expose her breast and put Calidia to it.

"Why do you not have a wet nurse?" asked Quintina.

"I don't know. Soren won't let me have one." Her voice softened. "He cares for his daughter and prefers that I feed her."

"*His* daughter?"

"Quintina," said Pomponia, "take care."

Quintina looked at the high priestess and then back at Tacita. "I think you are becoming as foolish as our mother was," she said, her anger boiling over. "Did you know that Mother did not have a wet nurse when you were born? Father refused her one. That way, he could go wherever he wanted, and she was trapped at home."

"Soren loves me. It is Aelina who is the problem—"

"He hates you, Tacita. He hates you the same way that our father hated our mother. Tell me, does he also beat you?"

"Of course not!"

"If he hasn't yet, he will." Quintina's face was scarlet. "I remember the sight of our mother lying on the floor after receiving our father's fist. Do you not remember?"

Pomponia thought of Quintus.

She thought of that night long ago when he had gripped her arm and kissed her mouth. She thought of the times he had spoken tenderly to her at the stables during those early days when Quintina was still a novice and learning to ride. She thought of the night in the Regia when he had of-fered his own blood to Mars to protect her.

Yet, his darker nature was never truly hidden. He could be critical and controlling. He loved her, but if the Fates had spun a different thread and they had married, would his darkness have fallen upon her the way it had fallen upon Valeria? Not wanting such thoughts to taint her memory of him, Pomponia spoke up.

"Tacita," she said steadily, "the House of the Vestals has always served as a sanctuary for those in danger. Stay with us. You and Calidia will be safe, and you will want for nothing."

"Stay here? In a house with a bunch of women, instead of at home with my husband?" Tacita scoffed and looked around the luxurious fres-coed room as if it had suddenly transformed into a public latrine. "I mean no offense, Priestess, but if you'd ever been with a man, you'd know that that is a very undesirable thought."

Quintina jumped to her feet as if about to strike her sister, but Pom-ponia gripped her arm and pulled her back down onto the couch. She spoke levelly to Tacita. "You must forgive your sister," she said. "She wor-ries about you and her niece. The offer to stay with us stands if you change your mind."

*   *   *

Aelina was reclining on a couch in the triclinium when Tacita returned home with the baby. The uninvited houseguest wore an expectant smirk, and Tacita was about to ask her what was so amusing when she heard a solid *thud* in her ear—or rather in her head.

The pain registered a moment later. A throbbing, aching pain deep in her skull. Her ear burned from the impact, and her vision was black. When it returned, she was shocked to find herself on the floor, behind the couch. Aelina was kneeling up on the couch and looking down at her, the grin still on her face.

She heard a muffled sound—Calidia crying. Not a regular cry, but a guttural, gagging type of cry that Tacita had never heard her make before.

She opened her eyes wide and scanned the room, trying to see where the baby was.

Calidia was lying under the table against the wall. The force of the impact had knocked her out of her mother's arms, and she had hit the floor, rolling until the wall had stopped her. *Stop crying*, willed Tacita. *You'll make him angrier!*

"Get it out of here," Soren seethed.

Wise enough to both remain silent and seize an opportunity to leave the room, Aelina leaped off the couch and bent under the table, grabbing Calidia by a foot and pulling her toward her. She lifted her up like a bag of flour and headed to the nursery.

Soren stood over Tacita and stepped on her hand until she cried out in pain. "Where were you today?"

"I went to visit my sister," said Tacita. She tried to pull her hand out from under Soren's sandal. "That hurts!"

"Just wait," said Soren. He grabbed her by the hair and dragged her out of the triclinium, toward the kitchen. As he entered, the two slaves who were preparing supper exchanged fearful glances and ran off without waiting for Soren to dismiss them.

Effortlessly, Soren tossed Tacita against the wall, face-first. Her nose made an audible crack against the brick, and she gasped before coughing up a mouthful of blood. A thick red stream ran over her chin, down the front of her stola. She slid down the wall to sit on the floor and put her hand to her nose.

"Soren," she pleaded, "I am sorry. I meant no disrespect. I was only angry because of Aelina."

Soren crouched down in front of her. "Was Priestess Pomponia there?"

Tacita nodded.

"What did you talk about? What did you tell her?"

"Nothing, I swear it. We talked about . . . we talked about . . ."

"Did you talk about me?"

A pause. "No . . ."

Soren raked his fingers through his hair. "Did you talk about me?" he asked again.

Tacita swallowed a mouthful of blood, tasting the iron and trying to breathe through the throbbing pain in her nose. Her stomach churned, and her heart hurt from pounding so hard in her chest. She reached out to touch Soren's arm. "I would never speak ill of you, no matter what they say."

"And what did they say?"

"They are worried you will injure me or Calidia," said Tacita. "I told them you would never do such a thing." She swallowed another nauseating mouthful of blood and wiped the tears from her eyes.

"Does that bitch not remember that I saved her life not two days ago? Did she speak of that?"

"No."

"Did you remind her of it?"

"I did not know of it," said Tacita. "You took Aelina to the games, not me."

Soren's eyes narrowed. The ropey scar around his neck seemed to swell and pulse with rage. "Did they question you about who fathered Calidia?"

"They know who, Soren," said Tacita. "It is exactly how you wanted it. But I did not confirm it. I have always said you are her father."

"You can never say it was Pomponius," said Soren. "If you admit it, they will go to Caesar. They are waiting for the right time."

"I will never say it. You must believe me, Soren. I am loyal to you, not to them."

"Prove it."

"Do I not prove it every day?"

Soren turned his head and spat on the floor before pushing himself to his feet. He loomed over her and then leaned down to clasp her by the shoulders and lift her to her feet, his fingers digging painfully into her body. She trembled as he took her hand and pulled her toward the open fire of the oven.

"Scaevola thrust his hand into the fire to prove his worth," said Soren. "We'll see if you're as serious as he."

Tacita's breath caught in her chest. She searched for the right words to pacify him, to reassure him that her devotion was steadfast. But it was no use. Soren was not a man of words. He was a man of action.

Tacita offered a silent prayer to the gods, whichever god was listening. *Please, make it end quickly. Make him believe me. Make him pull my hand out right away.*

Without giving herself another moment to think about it—each moment of delay only increased her own dread and Soren's anger—Tacita inhaled deeply and put her hand in the fire.

The pain was instantaneous, beyond anything she had experienced before or imagined possible. It was a grotesque pain, and even through the blinding agony, she could smell the burning of her own flesh, and she knew that her body would be changed forever.

She howled in pain yet kept her hand in the fire. The strength to do so did not come from loyalty or conviction. It came from her fear of death. Tacita knew the moment she withdrew her hand, Soren would kill her. She kept that thought in her mind, forced it to remain, through every moment of the torture.

"Take it out," said Soren.

Tacita lifted her hand out of the flames. She tried not to look at it, but out of the corner of her eye she saw the blistered and charred flesh, the curled black stumps that used to be her smooth, pretty fingers, and the spots that still glowed red with fire. The shocking pain seemed to expand with every moment, boundless and ever-changing.

Soren put his hand on the back of her head and pulled her toward him, placing a kiss on her forehead.

"I believe you," he said.

CHAPTER VII

Miseram Pacem Vel Bello Bene Mutari
Even war is better than a miserable peace.

–TACITUS

Priestess,

Your vineyard here in Tivoli has produced excellent wine this season. It is better than the last two years. I was speaking with your neighbor Ennius, and he says the preharvesting I recommended last year is producing an excellent yield for him as well. I must admit I am pleased with myself. Our secret guest is critical of my canopying practices, but you must not listen to anything he says. His mastery lies in drinking the wine, not growing it.

I must tell you that he is every bit as insufferable as your slave Anchises warned us. I remind him daily of the baths in the slave quarters, but to my grief he rarely makes use of them. He smells like a horse at all times.

And therein lies what seems to be his one good quality. He is a re-markable horseman. He has arranged a breeding program with several stables in the region, and I am confident your stables will be even more profitable than the vineyard. Word has gotten out about his farrier skills as well, and we sometimes have townspeople coming by for his services, although you must not concern yourself. He is no longer a Roman. He is Egyptian.

He has even taken to the Egyptian gods. At first, I thought he was mocking me, but now he prays to Isis as often as I do. He wears his linen skirt like a native and goes bald or wears his wig. I did fashion a better one for him, such was his complaining of the itch from the wool one.

He has also adopted my accent, which again I initially thought was in jest. Yet the transformation is not inconceivable. My former queen, Cleopatra, was of Greek lineage and yet was as Egyptian as myself. I mention this so that when we next see you, you are not surprised to find you have two Egyptian servants instead of one, even though I remain the more appealing.

Your faithful Ankhu

Pomponia sat back in the cushioned chair at her desk and laughed softly at the mental image of Ankhu's ward, the outlaw Roman charioteer, following the noble Egyptian around like an unwanted, unwashed double. The absurdity of Scorpus's transformation seemed to slightly ease the anxiety of the situation.

More important, it was a credible cover story. Although Soren continued to move about with bodyguards—including a huge ex-gladiator who rarely left his side—and still had a price on the outlaw's head, the official manhunt for the charioteer had been called off amid rumors of his death while on the run. He was yesterday's news.

Pomponia burned the papyrus scroll in the flame of the candle at her desk, letting the ash fall into a polished silver bowl. Picking up her stylus, she wrote back to Ankhu: "Send some wine, and keep a close eye on our guest."

She rolled up the papyrus and fastened it with her red wax seal—an image of the sacred hearth with S SAC POMPONIA VM written below—and then put it in the basket for her Tivoli messenger.

She sorted through the rest of the scrolls, which spread from one end of her desk to the other, and selected one from Carthage.

She broke Nona's Vestal seal and smiled nostalgically at the elder priestess's handwriting. It told of more good news.

Nona and Sabina hadn't simply calmed the waters after the barbarian attack on Vesta's temple in the important Roman province. Their arrival and their efforts had turned a moderately successful temple into a thriving one. Caesar would be pleased.

Yet as important as the temple's success was to Rome, Pomponia was relieved to know that both Nona and Sabina were truly happy with their new posting. She had worried they would be homesick for Rome. Even during her time in nearby Tivoli, barely a day's ride from Rome, Pomponia had often missed the Eternal City. Not so with Nona and Sabina. They both openly preferred the metropolis of Carthage to the Caput Mundi. Pomponia felt a twinge of envy. And curiosity. She had never traveled farther than Tivoli and would likely never do so.

She said a quiet prayer of gratitude to the goddess and moved on to the next scroll. As her mind registered the seal, her eyes moved briefly to her closed door and then back to the scroll—it was from Despina. How had she overlooked it?

Her thoughts landed heavily on Soren. Ever since his thinly veiled threat against her little niece, Pomponia was constantly having to remind herself to focus on the task at hand and to resist falling into distractingly dark thoughts. It was beginning to affect her work.

She broke Despina's seal and read the scroll.

High Priestess Pomponia,

Caesar's health remains improved, but he still suffers from coughing fits each morning that rack his entire body. Musa has sent for a special tonic from Greece, one derived from a type of flower that only grows on an island there. He says it worked well for Caesar before, so he will try it again. Musa was so upset by the emperor's coughing fit this morning that he nearly broke down in tears, and Caesar ended up consoling him.

I have information for you, Priestess, although it comes to me secondhand from a slave in the house of Tiberius. It concerns the activities of Tiberius the other night, after the games had ended and after the emperor and empress had returned home. Normally I would dismiss it as gossip, but I know you are prudently assessing his nature, so I will convey what I have heard.

I am told that Tiberius and King Herod remained on the imperial balcony well into the night, even after the last of the spectators had left and the amphitheater workers had cleaned much of the stadium. They were drinking to excess and were having a number of the slaves perform sexual acts on one another. I have written to you previously about this being Tiberius's habit.

Herod was very interested in the story of the Minotaur and the labyrinth, and had found the performance where the youths were trampled in the maze to be quite entertaining.

Tiberius told him more of the story . . . that according to legend, the Greek god Poseidon sent King Minos a great bull for sacrifice, but the king defied him and kept the bull alive. As punishment, Poseidon made Minos's wife, Pasiphae, fall in love with the bull, and the Minotaur was the product of their perverse union.

Herod was fascinated by this story. He asked to see the amphitheater's stables so that he could get a better look at the bulls that had been used in the show, so impressive were the beasts. Tiberius took him, and they continued to drink in the stables.

Herod had the idea of making a slave girl act out the story on a bull. Tiberius found this amusing, so he ordered a girl to do it. She protested, but he told her that if she put on a good show, she could have her freedom.

The girl crept into a stall and began to fellate a bull as it slept. The animal did not respond, but Tiberius and Herod were greatly aroused by this and had slaves fellate them as they watched.

Eventually, Tiberius grew tired and was ready to go. He told the girl she could stop, but Herod said, "No, it must penetrate you." He ordered the girl to have intercourse with the bull.

At that, Tiberius cuffed Herod on the head and said, "A Jew cannot command a Roman woman. Did you not hear me? She is a freedwoman." Herod apologized, but Tiberius ignored him, and that was the end of the evening.

Pomponia stopped reading to a take a sip of wine. She curled up her nose. The wine was pleasant enough. It was the thought of Herod that was distasteful. She wasn't alone in her dislike of him. Maecenas could not tolerate him at all, and Caesar was losing what patience he once had. Few senators would dine with him or invite him to their home. Only Agrippa had had any real care for the man, and that was born more from their shared passion for elaborate building projects than anything else.

The truth was, Herod just couldn't shake his bad history. After gaining advancement through his father's artful politics with Rome, he had misstepped after the assassination of Julius Caesar by foolishly supporting his friend Marc Antony instead of Octavian. After Octavian's victory at Actium, Herod had come crawling, promising to pay a mighty tribute and levy great taxes on Judea for Rome if he could maintain his kingship. So far, he had proven capable and kept his side of the bargain. Rome got richer, and so did Herod. He even got to play king when he came to Rome, sitting on the imperial balcony with his benefactors, who balanced reports of his increasing paranoia against his effectiveness as a ruler.

Yet, it wasn't just his history that made Pomponia dislike Herod. It was also his religiousness or, rather, his lack of it. Herod and his people prayed to a single male god. Of all the religions Pomponia knew of, theirs was the strangest. It was impossible to have a god without a goddess. The very idea was as inconceivable as it was unnatural. Jupiter without Juno? Mars without Venus? Herod's religion had no priestesses either.

As strange, Herod claimed that his god allowed men to have multiple wives, something both the gods and the laws of Rome forbade. Pomponia's cynical side suspected it all had less to do with the natural balance of divinity and more to do with the banal desires of mortal men. How women in Judea permitted such insult to themselves and their daughters was beyond her.

Pomponia willed her irritation with Herod into submission. After all, she suspected he did not represent the best part of Judea any more than Tiberius or Soren represented the best part of Rome. All had proven cruel in their own ways. Power often had that effect on men. She finished her wine and picked the scroll back up to read the rest of Despina's letter.

My last matter concerns the man named Soren, the very one who
pushed you out of the path of the falling Icarus. He spoke at length to

the empress after the games, privately, in the imperial lectica. It is not the first time I have seen them speak privately, and it seems that they are growing closer.

I do not know the nature of their business, but I will try to find out. I do know that they have been exchanging letters without Caesar's knowledge, but I regret that I do not know their contents. The empress writes them alone in her chamber and seals them herself, without the use of her regular scribe. I will continue to inform you of what I learn.

Despina

Pomponia felt her heart skip a beat. Soren and Livia? What in the world could those two be discussing behind the closed curtains of a lectica? Her two worst enemies—meeting in secret. A cold sweat formed on her forehead, and she wiped it away with her veil.

What were they saying to each other? What was their purpose? What was in their letters?

The unanswered questions made her stomach churn with a nauseating blend of anxiety and anger. She was almost glad for the knock on her office door. It forced her to snap out of her spiraling thoughts.

"One moment," she called.

She burned Despina's scroll in the flame of a candle, dropping the ash into the already full silver bowl on her desk. These days, her illicit correspondence seemed to leave more ashes than the sacred fire.

"Come in."

The door opened, and Anchises slipped his head into her office. "Priestess," he said, "there is a messenger here from little Varinia's house. Her mother has just given birth but is not expected to survive the day. Varinia's father has sent for her."

"*Juno cum ea sit,*" Pomponia said with a sigh. May Juno be with her. "Where is Varinia now?"

"She is in the study with Priestess Caecilia."

Pomponia pushed her chair back from her desk. "Tell Thracius that he will be escorting Varinia home immediately. I will fetch her."

"Yes, Priestess."

Pomponia walked quickly out of her office and to the novices' study. She rapped gently on the door and opened it to find Caecilia in mid-sentence.

"I am sorry to interrupt, sister," said Pomponia. "Varinia, come with me."

The little girl was sitting diligently at her desk and looked up, alarmed to hear the Vestalis Maxima call her name. Pomponia could read the thoughts going through her mind: *Am I in trouble? No . . . it is Mother . . .*

She seemed to delay for a moment, as if trying to fend off the inevitable, but then stood and joined Pomponia in the colonnade outside the study.

Pomponia took her hand and led her down the stairs, turning to walk through the garden instead of through the house.

"Is my mother dead?" the novice asked.

"No," said Pomponia. "She has delivered a child. You will see whether you have a little brother or sister."

"Is she all right?"

"Thracius will take you to her right now," said the priestess.

Varinia broke into tears. "I do not want my mother to leave."

Pomponia stopped before the row of Vestal statues that lined the length of the peristyle. She gripped the girl's hand affectionately. "Look at these statues of our sisters, Varinia. These women all served the goddess before us. And there"—she pointed to the single male statue—"is King Numa Pompilius, who established our order all those centuries ago. Did you know that he was an ancestor of mine? Walk along the Via Sacra to the Rostra and the Senate house, and whose faces will you see in marble? Romulus, Camillus, Pompey the Great, Julius Caesar." She kissed the girl on the top of the head. "This is Rome. No one ever really leaves."

Pomponia knew her words were no comfort. Not now. But they held the girl's spirit up long enough for Thracius to ready a lectica and come to collect her.

"Little rosebud," the boxer said as he lifted her up, "we'll go do this together, shall we?"

The novice put her head on his shoulder, and he carried her out of the garden. In that moment, Pomponia didn't care how much she had over-paid for him.

Pomponia stood alone in the courtyard. Despite the busy midday hour, she could barely hear a sound from the Forum just beyond the walls of the Vestals' house. It was almost eerily quiet. She stood before the statue of Fabiana and folded her arms.

Her thoughts moved from one dark place to another, like a black wolf slipping through the night.

Her own mother's death in childbirth and her brother Pomponius's murder. The outlaw Scorpus living in her villa in Tivoli. Quintina's hatred of her sister, Tacita. Caesar's chronically frail health and Tiberius's appointment as his heir. Worst of all, Livia's and Soren's private machinations and Soren's power over the life of Pomponius's daughter.

Calidia, the only blood connection that she and Quintus would ever share: her niece, his granddaughter. She could still hear Soren's words: *One day they're fat and healthy, and the next some calamity strikes, and they die.*

She felt the now familiar grip of anxiety and anger tightening around her chest. As she looked up at the expressionless marble face of Fabiana, she realized something: this was the first time in her life she felt truly helpless.

As if mocking her dismal state, a chorus of carefree voices entered the garden. The novices were taking a break from their studies. They gathered in the area behind her, some sticking their fingers in the pool to tickle the fish, and others drinking the honey lemon water the slaves had set out for them.

One of them skipped over to stand beside her and looked up at the statue of Fabiana. It was Longina. The girl took a step forward, just a bit closer to the statue than was generally respectful, so that she was standing on the exact spot where Pomponia had buried the little white dog Perseus.

The girl pointed up at Fabiana's stone face. "She looks kind of chubby," she said.

"*Vesta, da mihi vires!*" exclaimed Pomponia. Vesta, give me strength!

To the wide-eyed disbelief of the other novices, the Vestalis Maxima grabbed Longina by the neck of her tunica and dragged her unceremoniously out of the garden, through the peristyle, and into the house. Pomponia pulled her straight through toward the atrium.

"Open the bloody doors!" she called out.

Caeso and Publius, who had been chatting idly in the atrium, dove toward the doors and opened them wide.

Pomponia dragged Longina through the atrium and into the vestibule, ignoring the girl's cries and not stopping until she had passed through the ornate red doors of the House of the Vestals.

Still clutching the novice's tunica, Pomponia swung hard and tossed the girl outside onto the busy street of the Via Sacra. She landed at the feet of two passing senators who, quickly deciding it was best to mind their own business, stepped over her and kept going.

Teeth clenched, Pomponia turned to Caeso. "Take her home."

"Yes, my lady," said Caeso.

Pomponia stormed back into the house, leaving Caeso on the street to dispose of the ex-novice. She gripped one of the doors and pulled it closed as Publius closed the other.

The doors were locked, and Pomponia, suddenly feeling very drained, stepped back into the atrium and sat on the edge of the *impluvium*.

Outside, she heard Longina cry out. "Priestess, my father will kill me!"

I don't care, thought the Vestal. *I have enough children to worry about.*

CHAPTER VIII

Etiam Stultis Acuit Ingenium Fames
Hunger sharpens even the wits of fools.

−PHAEDRUS

THE ISLAND OF PANDATERIA

Julia had been accused of many things in her life, but excessive modesty wasn't one of them. Nonetheless, she found it felt subversive to walk around in the open, in the middle of the day, without any clothes on.

It had been days since she had worn a tunica or even wrapped a palla or blanket around herself. At first, she had felt every change in temperature however small. Now, her body had adapted. Whether it was a cool gust of wind or a spray of cold water from the sea, she barely noticed.

"I'm as naked as you, Phoenix," she said to the flightless seagull who now waddled behind her wherever she went. He even slept on the floor of her hut at night. To the emperor's daughter, the hut was a hovel. To a crippled seagull, it was a palace.

Julia stepped carefully along the rocky edge of the island until she reached the sandy shore where the ugly little man left wooden boxes of fresh water and food. He had come the day before, pried off the lid for her, and promptly paddled away.

She knelt down and looked into the box. Amphorae of fresh water. Bread wrapped in cloth. Some figs. She bit into a fig and threw the other half to Phoenix, who nearly fell onto his broken wing in his haste to reach it.

"I used to feel that way about wine," Julia mused. Phoenix looked at her sideways, opening his beak the way he always did when she spoke to him.

She piled the contents of the box on the sand beside her and then moved to the large boulder several feet away. Tucked under one corner was a flat, smooth stone. She brought it back to the wooden box and pushed the tip through the tight slats of wood, leveraging her weight until she had popped off each plank in turn.

Next, she took the bread out of the cloth and placed each of the nails from the box in the center of the square fabric, wrapping it up and tying the edges to secure it.

Finally, she loaded her arms with the wood planks and carried them and the cloth package of nails along the shoreline, to a rocky section of Pandateria that the ugly little man could not see when approaching or departing the island.

For months she had been stripping her supply boxes of their best planks of wood and arranging them into a remarkably solid raft. Now she set about securing them together with the bent nails she had also pillaged from the supply boxes, hammering them in with a heavy piece of scrap metal—it looked like a fragment of an old anchor—that she had found on the shore.

Pleased with her work, Julia wiped her forehead with her arm and stood back to look at the raft. It was nicely squared off and about as long as the couch she used to recline on in her father's library but twice as wide.

"You are no stranger to the sea, Phoenix," she said. "Will it hold?"

The seagull opened his beak and flapped his good wing. His broken wing flopped miserably beside him.

"You're right," said Julia, looking out at the rough waves on the water. "The sea is an unfriendly place."

She walked naked back to the sandy part of shore, wading waist-high into the water to grab the edge of the fish netting the man had left for her. She dragged it behind her and tossed it onto the beach. A bucketful of small fish flopped hopelessly within the netting, sunlight reflecting off their iridescent silver scales.

Phoenix descended on the captive fish like Zeus's eagle descending on Prometheus, his beak tearing into their flesh. His appetite nullified the last of his reservations about getting too close to Julia, and he hopped over her legs and arms, continuing to feast even while she struggled to untangle the netting.

"This will work well," she said. "I'll wrap it around the corners of the raft. For extra reinforcement. What do you think?"

Phoenix gobbled a fish, nodding his head to help it slide down his throat.

"Good," said Julia.

She swung the net over her shoulder and began to drag it back toward the rocky section of the shore and the raft, when a sudden, hot pain stabbed into the bottom of her bare foot.

Julia shrieked and fell onto her side. She grabbed her ankle and cranked her leg to look at the sole of her left foot—and the head of the rusty nail that protruded from it.

"*Futuo!*" She clenched her jaw in pain and sobbed, squeezing her ankle. Phoenix waddled this way and that on the sand, unhappy with his patroness's dramatics.

Julia bit her lip. It had to be done, and the longer she waited the worse it would be.

She slipped her fingernails under the head of the nail and pulled slowly, watching in agonizing horror as the shaft—*How long could it be?*—emerged from the sole of her foot bit by bit, seeming to strike every nerve in its bloody egress.

Finally, the nail emerged completely, and blood gushed out of the hole. Hot flares of pain shot along the bottom of her foot and up the sides of her leg before settling into an excruciating throb.

Julia looked around for something to press against the wound to stop the bleeding but remembered she had left the cloth from the bread on the other shore. She instinctively reached for her palla but then cursed her nakedness and resorted to pressing the heel of her hand against the wound to try to stop the flow.

As she sat dejectedly on the sand, bent over and gripping her foot, trying to breathe through the pulsating pain, Phoenix appeared before her. He looked at her sideways and sat down, doing his best to position his broken wing in a way that caused him the least amount of discomfort.

Julia knew exactly how he felt.

CHAPTER IX

Corruptissima Republica, Plurimae Leges
The more corrupt the state, the more laws.

−TACITUS

ROME

The interior of the Tabularium was alive with the work it was built to do—specifically, tabulating the taxes due and payable to the Roman treasury by every citizen, noncitizen, landowner, business, and province in the Roman Empire.

Almost everything was taxed, from property to prostitutes, livestock to olives. If you lived in it, walked on it, grew it, ate it, or had sex with it, you probably had to pay some kind of tax on it.

Still, it used to be worse, especially for those in the provinces. The dreaded *publicani*—tax collectors hired by Rome to extract taxes by any means—were only slightly less dreaded than the plague. If they were tasked with collecting one thousand five hundred sesterces from a landowner, what stopped them from submitting two thousand to the state and keeping five hundred for themselves? Nothing.

Yet the tax reforms under Augustus and Agrippa, aided greatly by Tiberius, had managed to quash the worst of the publican corruption. The emperor had made taxation less burdensome and fairer. But no one was lining up to thank him. Taxpayers within and outside Rome still complained, still pointed to abuses, still paid with one hand while making an obscene gesture with the other.

Those who calculated the taxes—quaestors, magistrates, and other tax officials—weren't generally any happier than those who owed them. They lamented that, on top of having to pay taxes themselves, their wages weren't nearly high enough to compensate them for the insults they suffered from their neighbors or people at parties who learned what they did for a living.

Pomponia sat at a large desk in an office on the Tabularium's top floor. On either side of her sat a quaestor and the priest Laelius. Across from her sat Caesar and Tiberius. The five of them had barely moved since dawn, having spent the morning scrutinizing the magistrate's lengthy report on the interest and taxes collected by various temples in the empire.

With the work now breaking for lunch, Pomponia stood up to stretch her spine. The four men quickly rose, partly out of respect and partly to relieve their own aching backs.

The five of them walked downstairs and out the columned portico into the fresh air. A short distance away, a group of disgruntled freedmen were standing behind a line of soldiers. When they saw Caesar, they sprang to angry life.

"Caesar!" one called out. "I protest the freedman tax! I protest the freedman tax!"

They all joined in.

Octavian held his arms out to his sides. "Protest in front of the Senate, then," he said. "It is they who will not revoke it."

"We did protest in front of the Senate," the man shouted back. "They told us to come here!"

The soldiers moved the protesters back farther as Caesar and his companions walked by. "That freedman tax is a bad one," said Tiberius. "The slave owner is taxed when he frees a man, and then the freedman is taxed also? If I may be so bold, Caesar, you should revoke it regardless what the Senate wants."

"The tax is excessive," said Octavian.

"*Boni pastoris est tondere pecus, non deglubere,*" replied Tiberius. A good shepherd shears his flock, not flays them.

Caesar put his hand on Tiberius's shoulder. "You grow wiser by the day," he said. Pomponia wasn't sure whether he was sincere or not.

As Laelius and the quaestor excused themselves to leave on other business, Tiberius spoke. "I am meeting Mother for lunch. Will either of you be accompanying me?"

"I will lunch at the House of the Vestals," said Octavian.

Pomponia discreetly eyed the scribe who followed behind her. *Run ahead. Have the cook prepare something.*

"Shall we walk or take my lectica, Caesar?" Pomponia asked.

"Caesar, you may want to take a lectica," answered a voice that instantly made Pomponia's chest tighten. Soren emerged from the Tabularium behind them. He was carrying an armful of wax tablets, and the two scribes trailing him were carrying baskets of what looked like rolled-up maps. He nodded deferentially to Caesar and Tiberius, ignoring Pomponia. "Looks like rain."

For a moment, the Vestal felt the same stab of disrespect she had felt years ago when Quintus would acknowledge everyone but her. But those slights were for a different reason. Quintus was trying to hide his love for her. Soren was trying to hide his hate.

They all glanced up at the gray clouds forming overhead, moving and bulging to the sound of a low rumble. The wind was picking up too.

"It might blow over," said Caesar.

"Maybe, but we could use the rain," replied Tiberius. "Soren, come with me to Caesar's home for lunch. Mother and I will look at the maps." He turned to Pomponia. "The Senate has allocated villas to Priestesses Nona and Sabina. I will show you their location once I've approved them."

"That is very generous," said Pomponia. "They will be honored."

"Priestess," Tiberius said curiously, "where is your freedman Ankhu these days? I was going to have him accompany my men to Carthage."

Pomponia looked up, pretending to study the clouds. *He's in Tivoli, hiding the condemned charioteer Scorpus, the one who gave your friend that nasty scar around his neck.* "He is caring for my vineyards in Tivoli," she said casually. "I shall send for him at once."

"No, not at all," said Tiberius. "It is no matter."

Octavian began to walk ahead, either impatient with the chatter or simply wanting to beat the rain. "Let's walk," he said to Pomponia.

"Yes, Caesar."

Tiberius and Soren took their leave, while Pomponia fell into step beside Octavian. His lictors walked ahead of them, and a number of soldiers, including Caeso and Publius, followed a few steps behind. The soldiers' eyes scrutinized the faces and movements of passersby for any sign of mischief.

Caesar quickened his step, and his companions responded by doing the same as they all descended a broad gold-inlaid marble staircase into the Forum and passed by the wide columns of the Temple of Saturn. They followed the street along the length of the massive Basilica Julia on their right, its two tiers of ongoing arches extending before them, leading to the Temple of Vesta.

"Does something trouble you, Caesar?" asked Pomponia. He seemed suddenly distracted.

The low rumble of the storm clouds gathered into a loud roar and clash of thunder. Wind whipped at their clothing. In the distance, a flash of lightning flared through the darkening clouds. Pomponia jumped and then laughed at herself, her smile fading as Octavian gripped her arm tightly.

His face was white and drawn, his eyes looking upward in stark terror, as if he alone were witnessing Jupiter emerge from the black clouds and descend to earth in all his terrible, shining glory.

She took his hands and steadied him. Raising her voice to be heard, she said, "Caesar, what is it? Are you unwell?"

Another flash of lightning and clash of thunder, this time even closer and louder. Rain began to fall in thick, heavy drops. It fell sporadically at first but then gained momentum and fell steadily until Pomponia's bare arms were dripping. She let go of Octavian and began to unfasten the small palla wrapped around her waist.

But then she stopped in mid-action as slowly, unbelievably, Caesar began to drop to his knees before her.

"Caesar!" Pomponia lowered herself to kneel and put her hands on the sides of his head, studying his face. "Are you unwell?" she repeated.

He shook his head. And then Pomponia remembered.

Caesar never allowed himself to be exposed to the sky during a storm. Even during public festivals or sacrifices, he quickly took shelter. It was a paranoia that had originated during his youth while he was on military campaign, something Octavian had never excelled at during the best of times.

As Agrippa had told the story to Pomponia, he and Octavian had been marching in an open field during a storm, when the man directly in front of Octavian had been struck down by a bolt of lightning.

The strike had killed the man, a slave, instantly. He had been left lying on the ground, burned and smoking like an animal on a sacrificial altar. The men around him, including Octavian and Agrippa, had been momentarily blinded and deafened.

When their senses returned, Agrippa had nervously laughed it off. Not so Octavian. Deeply superstitious, he had taken it as a sign from Jupiter and had offered daily to the god for months afterward. The paranoia had persisted and, now that Pomponia thought about it, recent quips from Livia suggested it was worsening with age. She could not have imagined it had become this crippling, though. She silently chastised herself for not insisting they take her lectica. It had been waiting just outside the Tabularium.

Her veil and hair now drenched with rain, she looked up. Caesar's lictors and guards were staring at him in disbelief, wondering what to do.

"I'll mind him," said the Vestal. She pointed to the people standing in the shelter of the basilica's arcade and staring openmouthed at the emperor. "We don't need an audience. Get rid of them."

Caesar's men began to disperse the crowd as Publius and Caeso remained alert and close by, their sharpened daggers drawn as they unexpectedly found themselves the sole guardians of both the Vestalis Maxima and the emperor of Rome.

Pomponia turned back to Octavian. "Let's take shelter," she said. He didn't respond. "Caesar," she said, now shouting to be heard over the growing booms of thunder and crashing of rain on the cobblestone. "Can you move into the basilica?"

Octavian looked at her, blinking away the rain that now fell in thick sheets. "Give me a moment, Pomponia," he said.

"Vesta watches us," she said, trying to give him something else to focus on. "Look, the temple is just there, you can see the smoke from the sacred fire."

Octavian followed her eyes. Down the Via Sacra, a portion of the domed roof of the Temple of Vesta was visible behind the columns of the Temple of Castor and Pollux, puffs of smoke showing as a light haze in the downpour, the roof's special drainage efficiently funneling away the rain so that not a drop fell into the temple's sanctum to threaten the fire.

"Yes," he said but did not move.

"We must get you to shelter," said Pomponia. "Musa says you cannot take a chill. The rain is cold."

Pomponia took his hands and began to stand, gently pulling him onto his feet. He stood helpless, so she continued to pull him, this time toward the cover of the basilica's arcade. If she could get him that far, they could slip inside and find a heated room.

They had made it two or three steps when a shockingly loud bolt of lightning cracked behind them. Pomponia wondered whether it had struck something, perhaps the Rostra or one of the statues that stood outside the Temple of Saturn.

Mala Fortuna, she thought. *That will not help.*

Caesar's chest expanded as he took a deep breath. He kept walking, though. "We are nearly there," said the Vestal. Pomponia couldn't help but admire him. The fear was real, but so was the will to overcome it. Octavian didn't rule the world by accident.

But then, as if reminding her who really ruled the world, another bolt struck the earth, this time in front of them, closer to Vesta's temple.

For one disorienting moment, Pomponia could hear nothing at all, but then the rumble of thunder above and the crashing of the rain on the cobblestone returned. The smell of ozone filled her nostrils. It grew noticeably darker, and a chill came over her. She looked toward the temple.

Was it her imagination, or did the roof look somehow different through the downpour?

A wet cold enveloped her feet, and she looked down. The water was rising before her eyes, now almost to her ankles.

The Forum was flooding.

To her horror, the rainfall was overwhelming the drains that emptied into the Cloaca Maxima and ultimately into the Tiber River—that included the drain between the Basilica Julia and the Temple of Vesta.

"Caesar," she said more emphatically, "we must move into the basilica. I must return to the temple."

He didn't move. Murky brown water and floating twigs flowed rapidly past his legs. His toga flapped in the gale—a gale that whistled and screamed as it wound its way through the wind tunnels created by the long colonnades and densely packed buildings in the Forum.

Pomponia called out to Caeso and Publius, who quickly appeared beside her. "Move him into the basilica!"

"Priestess?" asked Publius. Surely she didn't expect him and Caeso to lay their hands on the emperor without his permission.

"Do it now," she insisted.

The Vestal's guards exchanged brief glances before each took one of Caesar's arms and carried him through an arch of the basilica's arcade and into the shelter of the covered colonnade, dragging his sandals through the rising floodwaters as if he were a drunk they were clearing from the street and not a man who could order their crucifixion.

Pomponia followed and then ran ahead, deeper into the basilica. She pointed to a magistrate who was at work behind a desk, seemingly oblivious to the torrential downpour and the drama unfolding just outside the basilica. "You!" she commanded. "The emperor needs warmth."

The man stood up so fast upon seeing both the Vestalis Maxima and the emperor materialize in his workspace that a pile of wax tablets tumbled to the floor. Still gripping his stylus, he came out from behind his desk. "Caesar," he said with a bow, "this way."

Caeso and Publius half dragged, half walked Caesar across the marble floor and through an arched doorway that led into a small but richly decorated law office. The magistrate rushed to a fireplace and stoked the dying fire within. He placed two logs and kindling on top, and it crackled to life.

Pomponia felt a hammer of panic. What was happening at the temple? She had to get to the sacred fire.

The magistrate pulled a chair closer to the fireplace, and Caeso and

Publius sat Octavian upon it. Pomponia stood shivering at his side. "I must go now, Caesar. It is my duty."

"Your duty is to me," he said sharply. "Stay."

Pomponia recognized the look of fear on his face. She had seen the same look on her own face when she recently caught a reflection of herself in the shining metal of the bowl on her office desk, the one now filled with the ash of burned secret scrolls.

It wasn't just fear of the storm. It was all of it. The burden of authority and the chronic, sickening dread of making a mistake. The knowledge that despite their smiles, not everyone was a friend and that there was always a dagger hidden somewhere.

For Octavian, it was the fear of assassination. Of suffering the same fate as his divine father, Julius Caesar, the man whose basilica—the Basilica Julia—he now took shelter in. Caesar had accomplished great things and was revered by many. Yet the physicians who had examined the dictator's body had revealed a sobering fact. Of the twenty-three stab wounds he had suffered, only one had been fatal. In the end, that's all it took. A single blade.

For Pomponia, it was the fear of *damnatio*, of failing in her religious duties, of being condemned to the Evil Field and buried alive on a false accusation of *incestum*, or of seeing one of her sisters so condemned. It was the fear of Soren. His star was on the rise as his friendship with Tiberius grew, and the higher he rose, the greater her fall could be.

Another sharp crack of lightning, another roll of shaking thunder. Even from deep inside the basilica, even through the pounding of the rain, Pomponia could hear a crash from somewhere outside. Did it come from the area of the temple? It could have.

Caeso and Publius heard it too. Caeso put his hands on his head and swore under his breath, overcome with frustration, battling his own impatience.

"What in Juno's ass are you doing loitering in here?" Livia strode into the small room with her guards, all of them soaking wet. She pointed to Caeso. "Take the priestess to the temple." Her eyes landed on Octavian, hunched over in the chair before the fire, and her voice softened. "I will tend to Caesar." She walked to him and knelt at his feet. "Octavian," she said tenderly. "I have brought your tonic from home. Let us sit by this little fire and drink together."

Pomponia moved toward the arched door, wringing the water out of her palla. She pulled her veil off her matted hair and dropped it on the floor. Before she left, she looked back at Livia. The empress mouthed a silent "*Gratias tibi.*" Thank you.

Together, Pomponia and her two guards slipped out of the basilica and back into the full force of the storm outside. All three of them looked around, shocked. In the few minutes they had been in the basilica, the floodwaters had risen to the level of their knees.

Publius waded over to Pomponia. "I will carry you," he shouted above the wind and thunder.

"Don't be foolish," she shouted back. "It will be faster if I walk." She lifted her stola to her knees so she could move more freely and then followed behind the guards, letting the bulk of their bodies shield her from the worst of the oncoming wind.

She looked ahead and squinted, trying to catch a glimpse of the temple, but between the violence of the wind and the debris flying in it—sharp leaves, chunks of roof tile, and what felt like hail moving sideways instead of coming straight down—she could not keep her eyes open wide enough.

Yet as they fought their way closer, Pomponia realized that her greatest fear was unfolding before her eyes.

The first thing she saw was the thick figure of Thracius in a group of twelve or fifteen soldiers in the area before the temple, all of them working frantically to unclog the vital drain that emptied into the Cloaca Maxima. Anchises was there too, dragging some kind of long tool through the water and grasping at a submerged object.

The floodwaters were so deep in this area of the Forum that the men were taking turns diving under the water to try to clear the drain. Each diver had a rope tied around his waist in case the drain suddenly cleared. If that happened, he would be instantly sucked into the Cloaca Maxima and his colleagues would have to pull him back quickly, fighting against a deluge of raging water, before he drowned.

But the second thing Pomponia saw was even worse: the roof of the Temple of Vesta had completely collapsed.

The sacred fire was out.

*   *   *

At first, it had seemed to Quintina that the clouds would blow over and the storm would miss them altogether. But now as she stood in the courtyard of the House of the Vestals and looked up into the open sky, she could see a mass of black clouds rolling in, moving with the unstoppable aggression of an invading army about to do battle in the heavens.

Oh well, she thought. *We need the rain.*

She sat on the marble edge of the pool and studied the wax tablet in her hand. Since Nona's move to the temple in Carthage, Quintina had taken over many of the mill duties, constantly doing inventory and increasing the stockpile to ensure there were always enough sacred wafers to perform the many religious rituals that Rome, a city of a million people, required.

A raindrop fell on her hand, and she brushed it off to keep reading and writing: flour, salt, pure spring water, oven and millstone maintenance, distribution protocol, the religious schedule for the coming months . . . Another raindrop. She closed the wax tablet. She might as well go in to her office.

A sharp rumble of thunder and a far-off flash of lightning made Quintina and the two slaves who were pruning the rosebushes behind her jump. They exchanged amused smiles. Quintina walked over to inspect their work. "Scrub the columns on the second-floor colonnade when you're finished here."

"Yes, Domina," said one of the slaves.

Another flash of lightning, closer this time, followed a few moments later by a long rumble of thunder that was loud and deep enough to feel almost physical.

The storm was moving in unusually fast. It had an ominous presence to it, a certain force that Quintina didn't like. She handed the wax tablet to one of the slaves. "Take this to my office."

Seeing Lucasta emerge from the area of the *tablinum*, Quintina waved at her. "I don't like the looks of this storm," she said.

"Nor do I," said the other Vestal, her neck craned to look at the blackening sky.

"I'm sure they're already doing it," Quintina continued, "but can you or Marcella double-check that Thracius and his men are clearing the drainage system on the temple's roof?"

"Yes, sister."

Lucasta left just as heavy drops of rain began to fall more frequently. Quintina had barely walked the width of the garden before her feet were wet in her sandals.

She instinctively raised her shoulders as the loudest crack of lightning she could ever remember hearing jolted the earth. Waves of thunder followed.

That was close, she thought. *Did it strike the Rostra?*

Ignoring the hard, heavy rain that now fell as a constant sheet of water, Quintina sprinted across the rest of the already flooding courtyard and up the multistory staircase to reach the high rooftop terrace of the House of the Vestals. She ran to the edge and looked out over the Forum.

Her stomach sank. The flash flood had nearly cleared the Forum of people, and the streets were already rivers of muddy water and debris. She looked in the direction of the Rostra—had the tall Aquila been knocked over? She couldn't be certain. The pelting rain and wind were so violent that she could not see clearly.

She wiped the rain from her eyes and looked at the roof of the Temple of Vesta just as the top of a ladder moved away from it. That was good. It meant the men had inspected the drainage system.

But her relief was short-lived as a jagged line of white electricity snaked down from a black cloud above. It struck the temple's roof and erupted in a blinding flare of white light and noise.

"*Mea Dea!*" Quintina cried out. She gripped the balustrade and blinked to clear the spots from her eyes, waiting for her vision to return. When it did, a wave of dizziness washed over her. There was no mistaking what she saw. The domed roof of the temple had been damaged.

Gathering the bottom of her stola, Quintina bolted across the terrace and down the staircase, through the House of the Vestals and into the atrium. Reaching the vestibule, she tried to open a door but felt resistance. She pushed harder. The door opened to the street and a flood of murky, frigid water gushed over her feet to flow quickly into the house, streaming toward the atrium. She gasped aloud from the shock and cold.

She waded outside, where the floodwaters had already risen above her knees. She looked over her left shoulder and blinked up at the temple's bronze roof. The damage looked even worse from below.

Eight or nine soldiers—including Quintina's personal guards, Gaius and Marcus—were scaling the side of the temple on ladders, trying to reinforce the roof and repair the drainage system before the temple's sanctum took on water.

Thracius and Anchises, along with another group of soldiers carrying tools and ropes, hurried to the temple and looked up at the men working on it. Quintina stood beside Thracius, gripping his tunica to steady herself against the raging water and torrential wind. He put his arm around her and shouted up to the men.

"How bad is it?"

"It's bad," Gaius shouted down. "But we can't take any more weight up here. Stay down there, and clear the drain!"

Anchises waded through the water to Quintina. "Where is the Vestalis Maxima?"

"She's at the Tabularium," Quintina sputtered through the rain.

Thracius let go of the priestess and spoke to Anchises. "We have to go." The two of them moved off, trudging through the water with the rest of the soldiers toward the drain of the Cloaca Maxima.

Quintina stared at their backs as they left, praying to the goddess for Pomponia to appear further down the Via Sacra. She had never faced a crisis on her own, let alone something this sudden and serious.

Not only did her prayers go unanswered—Pomponia was nowhere to be seen—but the gods threw down a new problem for her. Hail. Hail the size of her fist. It pelted the roof of the House of the Vestals with a relentless *bang bang*, sending chunks of tile flying, and making

Quintina shriek and cover her head with her arms as she darted toward the temple.

She flew up the steps, subconsciously noting that the floodwaters had risen as high as the second one. If the men didn't clear the drain soon, the temple would flood. No doubt the waters were already spreading throughout the lower-lying house. Even in her haste, Quintina knew that Cossinia would at this very moment be inspecting the vaults, instructing the slaves to gather any scrolls on the lower level and directing the novices to move the stores of sacred wafers out of the mills to higher ground.

Quintina opened one of the temple doors and nearly tumbled into the sanctum. Caecilia and Lucretia were on watch and were standing before the sacred fire which, thankfully, was burning as strong as ever. Caecilia was uttering a soft prayer to Vesta, while Lucretia was making an offering into the flame.

"Is the roof badly damaged?" Lucretia asked. She pointed up. "Look there, you can see a section is not sitting properly."

"Yes," said Quintina, "I worry it may collapse. The vaults are waterproof so the wills and documents will be safe, as will the Palladium. But we will need to move the sacred fire. We will take it to the Shrine of Vesta at Caesar's home."

As stones of hail pounded the roof of the temple—*pop pop*—Lucretia knelt down to pile kindling into a basket for transport. She felt wetness against her knees and drew in a quick breath. Water was spreading across the floor, leaking from the roof. The drainage system was failing.

A dreadful *thump* sounded above them, and all three Vestals looked up to see the roof shift and a virtual waterfall pour into the temple. They barely had time to comprehend that when a large section of the roof collapsed on top of them in an avalanche of weight, water, wind, and sound.

Lucretia cried out. Her head was free, but both of her arms were trapped under a twisted pile of bronze and heavy slabs of marble. Caecilia heaved a piece of bronze off her own body and limped through the rubble to reach her, trying not to slip as the rain continued to fall. Blood was pouring down her left leg.

Quintina opened her eyes. Her back was cold and wet from the rain, but her midsection was hot: she was surprised to find herself lying on top of the bronze bowl of the sacred fire, her body shielding a low, struggling flame—it was all that had survived the fury of the roof's collapse—from the worst of the downpour.

She raised her head and looked around. The temple's round cella was littered with metal and stone debris. The marble pedestal of the hearth was smashed to pieces. She had no idea how the bronze bowl had come to be below her.

Quintina called out to Caecilia. "Never mind Lucretia for now. I must move the fire to the shrine. Can you find the kindling?"

Kneeling at Lucretia's side, Caecilia slipped her arm between slabs of rubble and through shards of a shattered terracotta *culullus*, searching for the basket of kindling somewhere below. Her arm came out bleeding. "I can't get to it." She cast her eyes desperately around the wreckage, wiping the rain from her eyes with a bloody arm. "I can't see any wood or kindling, nothing at all!"

Quintina looked up at the remaining section of bronze roof hanging perilously above them, and then looked at the closed doors of the temple, wanting nothing more than to see Pomponia burst through them.

The doors opened—but it wasn't Pomponia. It was Quintina's guards, followed by Caecilia's and Lucretia's. The men took one look at the devastation within and entered the sanctum without waiting for permission, navigating their way through sharp, slippery rubble toward their charges.

Quintina looked down at the fading fire in the bronze bowl. "There is no choice," she called to the other Vestals. "I will go as fast as I can." She went to grasp the bowl's handles but found they were both broken off. With no other option, she put her bare arms around the bronze bowl and lifted, feeling the smooth skin on her forearms and hands burn from the heat.

"*Vesta, permitte hanc actionem,*" she said.

"Wait," Lucretia cried out as her guards struggled to free her from the rubble. She was staring at a tipped-over basket near the doors. "Cossinia's toys," she said.

"Yes, that will work," Quintina replied. Doing her best to cover the fire with her body, she moved toward the overturned basket. Near it lay a piece of smooth wood partially carved into the shape of either a wolf or a dog. It was Cossinia's occasional pastime while on watch—making dolls and toys for the Vestals' little nieces and nephews.

It would have to do. Quintina hunched over the bowl and gently placed the wooden dog on the dying fire. Ignoring the hot pain, she used her fingers to brush embers on top. The fire was burning. But even in the best of conditions, it wouldn't burn for long.

"Get your shields," she instructed Gaius and Marcus.

The guards understood immediately. As Gaius stood over her, Marcus ran back outside the temple and returned seconds later with two military shields that boasted the proud red and gold design of the Roman legions—wings of an eagle and Jupiter's thunderbolt.

Quintina stood, still holding the bronze firebowl in her arms, as her guards lifted their shields over her head to shelter her and the sacred flame from the rain; the rectangular, convex shape of the shields was perfect for the task, but Quintina stopped herself from indulging in any feeling of relief. There was a long way to go.

"We will take the Palatine ramp to Caesar's home," she shouted to her guards.

Under the sheltering canopy of the two shields, Quintina carried the fire out of the temple—hearing the hail bounce off the shields above her—and into the House of the Vestals.

"Kindling!" she called out, but not a single priestess or novice, not even a slave, was in sight. She kept running, straight to the vestibule that opened to the Palatine ramp.

Although vaulted and covered by an arched roof, sections of the ramp's walls contained latticework that allowed air to flow through the passageway in the hot summer months. As the Vestal carried the bronze firebowl up the ramp, her guards held their shields on either side of her to protect her, and the fire, from the gusting wind that moved through the latticework.

Quintina looked into the bowl. The fire was still burning, but not as strongly. "We need to move faster," she said.

"Priestess," said Gaius, "can we not burn the flame in the House of the Vestals? Why must we go to Caesar's home?"

"The eternal flame can only be housed in a sacred space. Our house is a domestic space. The Shrine of Vesta at Caesar's home has been consecrated. The high priestess and the Pontifex Maximus blessed it themselves. Next to the temple, it is the holiest place in Rome for Vesta's fire."

The breathless explanation renewed the guard's resolve, and he quickened his step. Quintina, already at a near run, had to move even faster along the incline to keep up with him. She did so carefully, watching her step as much as the fire. She did not want to spill the sacred embers at the feet of a frantic priestess and two soldiers. She did not want to be the priestess who let the eternal flame die.

If she did, they would all die.

Perhaps Caesar and the Senate would spare Cossinia, Marcella, and Lucasta, but Caecilia and Lucretia were on watch. They, and Quintina, would be condemned. So would their guards.

And Pomponia? Who knew what fate would await her? Caesar felt deep friendship for her, but he was also deeply religious. If he felt the goddess needed to be appeased, he would sacrifice Pomponia. Regardless of the circumstances, she was the chief Vestal. All problems began and ended with her.

Worst of all, what horrors would be unleashed on Rome itself if the Vestals violated the Pax Deorum and lost the protection of their goddess?

The Vestals' fate would be no worse than the fate of the men, women, and children of a godforsaken Rome—slavery, plague, civil war. Such fears had been bred into Quintina, into all Romans, over generations of invasion and warfare. Rome's pact with the gods was necessary for the protection and perpetuity of the Eternal City.

As they reached the top of the Palatine ramp and arrived within the fortified walls of Caesar's complex, Quintina's guards again lifted their shields over their heads. Although much of the grounds were covered with arched walkways, one of which led to Tiberius's new and ever-expanding home, they had to pass through Caesar's gardens before they would arrive at Vesta's shrine.

Quintina ran along the path, walled on both sides by towering cypress trees and thick shrubs. On any other day, this familiar winding section of the imperial estate would be relaxing and lovely. Today, it felt like the Minotaur's labyrinth. But instead of being pursued by a monstrous creature, she was being pursued by the realization that the fire in her arms was almost out. All that remained alive in the bowl were a handful of embers and a piece of the toy dog's wooden hindquarters.

She looked up and, through the biting rain, saw the tall columns of the Temple of Apollo in the distance. Caesar had dedicated it to the god of healing after Apollo had spared him from the contagion. The columns were a welcome sight. It meant they were almost at Vesta's shrine.

Soon, they reached a cleared space enclosed by an iron fence. Within were the ruins of the hut of Romulus—large blocks of stone arranged in a circle, and a thatched roof. Rome's founder had lived in this very spot on the Palatine Hill, and it was no coincidence that the emperor, Rome's new Romulus, had built his home close to it.

At the entrance gate to the hut stood a life-size bronze statue of the Lupa, the she-wolf that had nursed the twins Romulus and Remus after they were taken from their mother, the Vestal Rhea Silvia. Quintina glanced at the wolf's face—fierce, protective, determined.

Then she looked down at the fire and dropped to her knees.

A single red ember was all that remained.

With the rain pelting down on the shields above her, Quintina gently set the firebowl on the ground. She fumbled frantically with her stola, reaching for the tunica underneath. Using all of her strength—and abandoning all modesty in the presence of her male guards—she tore a dry section of fabric from the undergarment.

Holding her breath, Quintina touched the edge of the fabric to the ember. It smoked and hesitated, but then caught. A path of red began to climb up the side of the torn linen. She placed the fabric in a small heap in the bowl and the fire flared. *It worked.* But it would only do so for a few brief moments, not long enough to reach Vesta's shrine.

She heard the sound of heavy footfalls in the rain and the voices of men. One of them was Tiberius. Quintina looked up into his face and saw his expression transform from one of detached confusion to terrified comprehension.

"*Attat!*" he exclaimed and shouted to the men around him. "Run ahead and open the doors to the shrine!"

As the other men scrambled to the circular Shrine of Vesta, Tiberius looked around in panic—what could burn? The trees and vegetation were soaked. He eyed the thatched roof of Romulus's hut, but that too was rain-soaked. Just about everything else was made of metal or marble.

Everything but the base upon which sat the Lupa. It was made of wood.

Tiberius tore at the ornate molding on the statue's base with such force and desperation that his fingers bled. Finally, a piece snapped off.

He dried it as best he could using an inside fold of his toga and then broke it in half, the sharp edges of the molding cutting deep into his palms. He dropped to his knees beside Quintina. She took the smooth wood from his hands and set it tenderly on the fire, whispering a prayer to the goddess.

Tiberius put his bloody palms up in supplication and also prayed. "*Vesta Mater*," he said, "*Magna Dea*, this unsullied priestess honors you, Caesar honors you, Rome honors you . . ."

The fire flickered. Quintina leaned over so that her face was nearly touching the wood molding and whispered another prayer to the fire, letting her breath stir the embers. A loud crack. And then another. The fire was regaining strength, its flames reaching around the ornamental wood, embracing and consuming it at the same time.

She met eyes with Tiberius: he looked like a man staring Pluto in the face. "It still burns," she said.

He leaned over and kissed her hands. "Blessed priestess," he said. Quintina could hear the tremble in his voice.

The Vestal stood up. Her hands were shaking, but she gripped the bronze bowl and proceeded under the shields of her guards. Tiberius followed behind. The men who had been with him slowly knelt as she continued past them to the shrine.

Like Vesta's temple in the Forum, Caesar's shrine to Vesta was round, made of white marble, and had a bronze domed roof with an oculus in the center that was open to the sky. Unlike the current temple in the Forum, however, a replica statue of the Palladium sat atop the shrine: Octavian had brought it back from the ancient city of Troy when he had visited a few years earlier. Yet to Quintina, the most important difference between the two structures was that the drainage system of the shrine's roof had managed to keep its cella dry.

Not able to accompany Quintina inside, Gaius and Marcus waited at the base of the steps with the other men, including Tiberius, as she stepped inside the shelter of the shrine. To her relief, neither the encircling wall nor the white and black mosaic floor had a trace of moisture.

She carried the firebowl to the round pedestal that stood toward the back of the shrine and placed it snugly within its marble cradle on top. Quickly, she selected several strips of thin kindling—*Had dry wood ever felt so divine?*—from a basket and moved back to the fire.

Carefully, and with a murmured prayer, she laid the strips of kindling on top of each other in a circular pattern so that the wood resembled the shining orb of the sun, the source of Vesta's energy and of all life.

It was an ancient pattern that only full Vestal priestesses knew and that was only used in the most desperate of times: when the goddess's patience had been tested by a violation of the Pax Deorum. Quintina hoped that Pomponia would approve.

The goddess seemed to. Her sacred fire cracked and roared. Strong flames explored the wood and radiated heat outward to fill the shrine with her divine warmth.

Outside the shrine, Quintina could hear the men's voices. Then other voices. Women. She took the few steps to the door and nearly fell into tears at the sight of her rain-soaked sisters Cossinia and Marcella running toward her. Their eyes were pleading for information.

"*Vestam laudo,*" she called out from the top step. "It did not go out. It still burns."

Tiberius, Quintina's guards, and the rest of the men at the base of the steps broke into a loud cheer and began to congratulate each other as if they had all shared equally in the preserving of the flame and the saving of Rome.

Cossinia and Marcella ran up the steps and into the sanctum. Cossinia headed directly to the hearth fire, but Marcella gingerly took Quintina's wrists between her fingers and inspected them.

"Quintina," she said, "you are badly burned."

Tiberius and the other men stared up at Quintina; the Vestal's palms and inner arms were blistered from the heat of carrying the bronze bowl.

The rain-soaked men cheered again at the Vestal's courage; however, Quintina did not feel courageous. She felt like crying. She felt sick. She raced down the steps of the shrine and leaned over a flower bed, her wet veil clinging to her face and her stomach contracting.

And then the Vestal Virgin who had saved Rome from all manner of death and destruction vomited into Caesar's roses.

CHAPTER X

Periculosior Casus ab Alto
A fall from on high is more dangerous.

–ROMAN PROVERB

THE ISLAND OF PANDATERIA

"Julia, come down from that tree. You are to meet your stepmother today. She has a son about your age. His name is Tiberius."

Julia let go of the branch she was holding and landed on her feet. She took her father's hand. "Aunt Octavia was going to take me to play with the novices today at the House of the Vestals."

"There will be time for that later. Let's put you in a clean tunica, shall we?"

"Yes, Father."

"You must not call me Father *any longer, Julia. You must call me* Caesar *now."*

Julia lowered her eyes. Her father led her into her bedchamber . . . but something was wrong. She rushed to the doll cradle by the wall.

"Caesar! Look! They have cut the heads off all my little dolls."

"We had no other choice," said her new stepmother.

"You are too old to be playing with dolls," added the child Tiberius. "Look at this." He opened his hand to show Julia a black spider that flopped around in his palm. He had pulled six of its legs off. "Mother and I will do the same to you one day."

Julia woke with a gasp. Was it a dream or another hallucination? She turned over on her sweat-soaked straw mattress and looked at the rough wall of her hut.

The biggest spider she had ever seen—it was nearly as big as the wall itself—sat there expectantly, waiting for her to see it. When she did, it somehow dragged itself across the wall with only two legs and slipped out the closed door of the hut.

She was glad it was gone, but it had left its remaining legs stacked up against the wall. One by one, they began to move until all six of them were slithering around the dirt floor under her bed like long black snakes.

She forced herself to sit up in her bed. "It's not real," she said to Phoenix. He opened his beak in agreement. When she looked back down, the spider legs were gone.

"I dreamed of my babies," Julia told the seagull. "The little emperor that never was. He is dead. Murdered. But the other still lives. Her name is Agrippina."

The harsh wind from the storm outside whistled and howled around the hut, rattling the flimsy walls and door. Rain dripped down from the ceiling, and a sudden loud thunderclap made Phoenix flap his good wing in surprise. He settled back down.

"Jupiter throws thunderbolts at our door," Julia said to him. She clutched the thin woolen blanket and wrapped it tightly around her shoulders. "I am so cold, Phoenix. I would start a fire, but I think I would freeze to death before I could gather the wood. Anyway, it will be too wet to burn."

Shivering, she reached down to pull the blanket off her left foot. Thick yellow pus was seeping through the cloth that she had wound around the top and sole of her foot. The swelling had spread: her leg was hard and puffy nearly to the knee, and there was a strange rash. She held the back of her hand against her swollen ankle. It was hot to the touch.

"I have to look at it, don't I, Phoenix?"

The gull opened his beak.

Julia inhaled and began to unwind the cloth. Her hand flew up to cover her nose and mouth from the stench. Her heart thudded with dread at the sight, and she found herself sobbing.

She had seen a wound like this before. It was on a young slave boy that Tiberius had dragged home from the market as a plaything. The creature spoke not a word of Latin but was so quick to learn that Caesar had complimented him. The next day, Tiberius, petty even then, ordered the boy to run barefoot over a pile of broken glass.

Not long after that, the boy's foot had become abscessed, and he had fallen into a feverish stupor. Musa had treated him as Julia and Tiberius watched in morbid fascination.

Her cheeks red with fever and wet with tears, Julia closed her eyes and tried to remember what Musa had done. He had soaked the boy's foot in hot water and then cut the bottom of it, behind the big toe, with a scalpel. He had then squeezed the foot, causing the pus to gush out of the wound like mud belching out of a sewer.

There was nothing in the hut to soak her foot in, but it would have to be cut anyway. Shaking almost violently now, both from the cold of the fireless hut and from the chill caused by her own raging fever, Julia forced herself to drop the blanket from her shoulders and stand up.

The throbbing in her foot intensified as her blood drained downward. She put her hand on the wall to steady herself as a wave of dizziness washed over her. Once the worst of it had passed, she hopped on one foot to the brazier in the corner of the hut. She grasped the bread knife on top and hopped back to the bed.

She moved quickly, knowing it had to be done and not giving herself time to think her way out of it. Grasping her left foot, she twisted it sole-up and, using her right hand, brought the blade of the knife across the abscess.

But the blade was jagged and worn, sharp only in sections. It left a line of shredded skin and blood on the bottom of her foot but did not lance the abscess. She let the pain and frustration escape through a long, low cry that made Phoenix tilt his head in mild interest.

Julia threw herself back onto the mattress. She dropped the knife to the dirt floor and put her hands over her face. "I don't want to die here," she said. She pounded her fists on the mattress. "How could he do this to me? He commands armies, but he cannot see how his own wife commands him? He preaches piety to the people but abandons his daughter? He is a fool and a hypocrite!"

Exhausted, she let more tears come. "I am sorry, Agrippa," she said to the ceiling, her teeth chattering from cold. "I am sorry I killed you and our little doll." Her sobs morphed into a sad laugh. "But I will tell you that in person soon enough."

CHAPTER XI

Necessitas Ultimum et Maximum Telum Est
Necessity is the last and greatest weapon.

–LIVY

ROME

The state accolades and public gathering in the Roman Forum had all the energy, color, and pomp of a military triumph. It *was* a triumph of sorts. A triumph of duty, of devotion. Of what it meant to be a Roman.

Red banners with *SPQR* emblazoned in gold hung down from the capitals of vibrantly colored marble columns and from the painted arches of long, multitiered arcades.

The Aquila, which had been knocked down by lightning during the storm, had been replaced to again soar above the Rostra, and the relief carvings that decorated the sides of the great speakers' platform had been washed to a shine. Red and white rose petals covered the freshly scrubbed cobblestone of the Via Sacra from the sacred area of Vesta to the doors of the Senate house and across to the Rostra.

Behind the high doors of the Curia, the Vestal Virgin Quintina had spent the early-morning hours being honored by Caesar and a full house of senators for her heroic piety in the face of natural disaster.

With the senatorial ceremony over, Quintina was led out of the Senate house and across the decorative pavement to the Rostra. She was dressed in a fine white pleated stola and palla, and she wore the red woolen head-band and crimson-bordered white *suffibulum* veil of the Vestal. Citizens of all ages called out her name and threw flowers at her feet.

The Vestal ascended the Rostra to stand between Caesar and Tiberius. Tiberius wore a purple-bordered white toga, while Caesar had donned the emperor's solid deep purple.

Behind her stood Gaius and Marcus, dressed in their best Roman armor—formed and embossed leather cuirasses, red-crested helmets, and scarlet capes pinned at the shoulders with gold fibulae. They each held a legionary shield. On the far left side of the Rostra stood the priestesses Pomponia and Cossinia.

Tiberius held out his arms and stepped forward to address the crowd of spectators below. As he did, soldiers wound through the gathering, looking for any troublemakers, drunks, or prostitutes they could arrest or at least give a decent beating to.

"Friends and fellow Romans," said Tiberius, "the Senate and the people of Rome honor the Virgo Vestalis Quintina Vedia, daughter of Quintus Vedius Tacitus and kin to the heroic Vestal Virgin Tacita of long ago."

Tiberius indulged a few moments of cheering and then raised his arms for silence again. "Is it not in this priestess's very blood to uphold the Pax Deorum and protect Rome, even at great pain to herself? We have seen that indeed it is." He nodded a silent instruction to Pomponia, and the chief Vestal removed the palla around Quintina's shoulders.

Tiberius took Quintina by the wrists and held up her arms to the crowd. The burns and blisters along the skin of her inner arms and palms glistened in the sunlight, Tiberius having instructed Musa to remove the dressings for the ceremony.

"As the roof of Vesta's temple collapsed," said Tiberius, "your faithful priestess held the sacred flame's scalding bronze firebowl in her arms, sacrificing her own young flesh to protect yours. Even as her skin burned, even as the rain fell, she escaped to the sanctified Shrine of Vesta on the Palatine Hill. And do you know how she did this? Under the Eagle!"

At that, Quintina's guards raised their red shields to proudly display the golden Eagle wings upon them. They then lifted the shields over their heads, showing the crowd how they had sheltered the Vestal from the rain.

In an exuberant burst of Roman patriotism, the gathering of citizens before the Rostra applauded and chanted the soldiers' names. *Gaius! Gaius! Marcus! Marcus!*

By now, the two soldiers were folk heroes. Well-to-do fathers considered them as marriage material for their daughters. People painted their names on the firewall behind the Forum of Augustus. It was even rumored that Taurus was dreaming up a dramatic reenactment of their exploits for the amphitheater.

"This Vestal," continued Tiberius, "was as much a soldier that day as a priestess. Like the legendary Vestal Aemilia who revived the *viva flamma* by burning her own headdress, the Vestal Quintina saved the dying fire by tearing the clothing from her own inviolate body to nourish its sacred embers. Even as the roof of Vesta's temple lay in ruins, even as the Eagle on the Rostra fell to the ground, even as Jupiter tested our mettle with his thunderbolts, Vesta's eternal flame burned on in the shrine. Caesar, the Senate, and the people of Rome are thus still favored by all the gods!"

With the applause and chants—which now alternated between the names of the guards and the name of the priestess—reaching their peak, Tiberius stepped to the edge of the Rostra and shouted, "Hail, Caesar!"

As the chants shifted to hailing Caesar, Octavian stepped forward, and Tiberius, deferring to the greater man, stepped back.

Octavian raised his arms in greeting and then dove his hands into a large coffer on a wide pedestal. His hands emerged full of coins. He tossed them into the crowd below.

The guards in charge of crowd control perked up—this is when things tended to get interesting.

With those in the crowd now more focused on scrambling for coin than applauding their saviors, a small army of lictors and legionary soldiers escorted Quintina down from the Rostra and to her waiting lectica. Caesar and Tiberius returned to the Senate house.

Pomponia and Cossinia met Quintina at the lectica. Both put a string of flowers around the younger Vestal's neck. Her expression was appropriately demure, but her face was flushed from being the focus of the day's attention.

And there was more to come. Rome loved to revel in its own heroism, and the story of the Vestal who burned her own tunica to keep the sacred flame alive would no doubt become legend. It was a great reason to have a party, and Quintina and Pomponia were to attend an elaborate one later that evening at the home of Tiberius.

"You do your ancestors proud," said Cossinia.

"Even your father would have smiled today," Pomponia added. She straightened Quintina's veil affectionately. "Sister Cossinia will accompany you back home. Musa is there, so he can dress your burns again. Make sure he uses water from the Spring of Juturna to clean them. I will follow shortly. Session is about to open, and I must speak of the matter before the Senate."

"Yes, Pomponia."

Quintina and Cossinia stepped into the lectica, and the high priestess stood watching as the temple slaves lifted it off the flower-strewn cobblestone and began to carry it back to the House of the Vestals, people bowing or kneeling to the priestesses as it passed by.

Now to more unpleasant business.

As senators filed past her to enter the Curia, Pomponia gazed up at the square marble-clad building, her eyes resting on the golden statue of the goddess Victory that stood on the high triangle of the pediment above the tall doors.

Now that Quintina had been honored in the Senate—the gods knew she deserved it—Pomponia was to stand before the same senatorial body to face questions, perhaps even accusations, about the roof's collapse and the stewardship of the sacred fire.

Would she face disciplinary action, or would she simply suffer an upbraiding? In the past, chief Vestals who had allowed misfortune to fall upon the temple had all been penalized in some way. In the worst cases, they had been doomed to the Evil Field. In others, they had endured the humiliation of being demoted or having the Palladium removed from their care in the temple and kept—presumably under better guard—in the Shrine of Vesta on the Palatine Hill. Time would soon tell what awaited her.

Pomponia joined the procession of senators passing through the great doors to enter the oblong space of the high-ceilinged Curia. As she always did when entering the Senate house, she noted the dramatic change in acoustics. That was by design. Caesar had restored the building according to the sound-amplifying specifications of the famous architect Vitruvius.

The senators loved it. It made whatever they said sound much more impressive than it actually was.

Pomponia checked herself. No point starting out in that tone.

She moved across the decorative porphyry-tiled floor toward a senior senator by the name of Tulio, a man she knew was sympathetic to her position. He ushered her deeper into the rectangular chamber of the Senate to sit beside himself and a number of other senators who all offered their hushed support.

"Do not let certain bastards find a way to blame you for anything," said Tulio, as he threw a sideways glance at Senators Murena and Caepio, who sat on the other side of the chamber. The other men nodded in emphatic agreement.

Pomponia felt her throat go dry. Had she not seen Soren cozying up to those very senators as of late? She thought about asking a scribe for water but did not. It might betray her nerves. Instead, she folded her hands in her lap and cursed herself for letting Soren develop yet another secret alliance right under her nose.

As it always did, the shuffling and murmuring of the large gathering of senators—rows of them against both long walls—began to naturally subside, signaling that session was about to convene. The praetor stood and opened his mouth to speak.

But then in a rather dramatically timed moment, Laelius, the high priest of Mars, strode into the Senate chamber as if he commanded it, followed by the high priest of Jupiter and the chief augur. All three men looked as indignant and cheerless as Pomponia had ever seen them. They disregarded the praetor and spoke directly to Caesar.

"Caesar," Laelius said and bowed, "as representatives of the religious collegia of Rome, we offer our support to our sister the Vestalis Maxima and request to be in attendance."

Senator Murena spoke out. "Why do you offer your support? The high priestess has not been accused of anything."

Laelius raised an eyebrow. "Senate has not started," he said.

"The priests may attend," said Caesar.

The praetor cleared his throat and put his hand on a fold of his toga. "I call Senate into session."

After reading a list of absentee senators' names and their accompanying excuses—"my wife is ill," "my house caught fire," "my daughter is marrying," and so on—to Caesar and Tiberius, the praetor addressed the Senate as a whole.

"For the benefit of the people of Rome, the first matter for discussion is the recent roof collapse of the Temple of Vesta. According to the docket, Senator Murena has the floor."

Murena stood up and raised his chin. "We thank the high priests of Jupiter and Mars for being here," he said. "I am sure we were all dazzled by their theatrical entrance. But we stand on the rich floor of the Senate, not the ramshackle planks of an actor's stage. I will remind our devoted priests that there is no room for grandstanding in the Roman Senate."

"Look who speaks!" shouted an unseen senator, and the chamber burst into laughter.

"Order!" shouted the praetor.

"High Priestess Pomponia," said Murena, "where were you when the rain began?"

Pomponia met his eyes. The abruptness of his question raised her ire, but she remained seated and answered matter-of-factly. "I was at work in the Tabularium."

"Were you aware of the rain?"

"I became aware of it."

"Why did you not immediately return to the temple?"

"Senator Murena," said Pomponia, "I do not raise the hem of my stola and dash for the temple every time it rains. Nonetheless, when I realized there was a danger of flooding, which as you all know happened very quickly, I immediately began to make my way back."

"You must have heard the lightning strike the Rostra. Why did you not arrive at the temple sooner? Could you not have moved more quickly?"

"I was delayed."

"What delayed you?"

"There was a great deal of debris on the street, in the water, that made it difficult to pass."

The senator cocked his head in an exaggerated way that suggested he didn't quite believe her explanation. "What kind of debris?"

"Branches, roof tiles, but mostly the water itself. It was windy, and the current of the floodwater was very strong. I had to fight against it the whole way."

"Was there anything else that delayed you? Any person or circumstance?"

Pomponia sat up straighter. *He knows about Caesar's episode during the storm.* "No, Senator Murena, nothing else. I can assure the Senate that I traveled as quickly as I could under the circumstances."

"So it was only the water that delayed you," pressed Murena. "Nothing or no one else?"

"It was only the storm, Senator. Nothing else."

"Did you not see—"

The praetor spoke up. "The priestess has answered the question, Senator Murena. Move on."

The senator nodded to the praetor's authority. "When you finally arrived at the temple," he said to Pomponia, "what did you find?"

"I found two badly injured priestesses in the debris." ·

"And what of the roof?" asked Murena.

"A large section of the roof was collapsed."

"I see," said Murena. "When was the last time you had the roof inspected? What is your protocol for maintenance?"

Pomponia stood up. "Your line of questioning betrays your ignorance, Murena," she said sharply, dispensing with the formality of his title. Ignoring him, she spoke to the rest of the Senate. "Think, gentlemen, of the goddess's discontent to know that funds allocated to strengthening her temple and protecting it from floodwaters were secretly channeled to the neighborhood of certain senators."

A low murmur ran through the rows of seated senators.

Tiberius leaned forward, placing his hands on his knees. "What do you mean, Priestess?"

"Shortly after the crisis at Vesta's temple in Carthage," began Pomponia, "Caesar ordered that eight million sesterces be allocated to the expansion of the Cloaca Maxima and other structures under the sacred area of Vesta. That included improvements to the major drain of the Cloaca Maxima in the area, the very drain that failed during the flood. It also included reinforcements of the related drainage network, including the temple's roof. Yet work was never completed. I had my scribe investigate where the monies went. He discovered documents in the Tabularium that indicate a number of senators, all of whom found better things to do today than attend this sitting, diverted those funds to sewer upgrades on their own streets."

The murmur grew louder, more disapproving.

"Esteemed senators," said Pomponia, "if you were at this moment to walk to a particular street on the Esquiline, you would find the best decorated sewers in all Rome. I myself would not be surprised to find them gilded with treasury gold and inlaid with the finest Parian marble."

The murmurs of disapproval morphed into laughter.

Pomponia continued. "Who knew the excrement that flows from the latrines of certain senators was so illustrious? It must be so, since these wise senators felt it was more worthy of public funds than the sacred fire!"

The laughter grew loud and heavy, reverberating within the acoustics of the rectangular chamber.

"Order!" the praetor called out.

Murena shouted over the din. "Priestess, perhaps your scribe's research is not as reliable as you think. Scribes make mistakes."

"I hope this one has not, Murena," replied Pomponia, "since you sold him to me with all manner of praise."

The praetor again called for order amid a boisterous uproar of laughter, but this time it took Tiberius standing up to restore calm.

Caepio, who had been seated beside Murena, stood up to speak. "When will the sacred flame return to the temple?" he asked Pomponia.

"No later than the ides," she answered. "It will be done according to rites, with the goddess's approval."

"How can you be sure?" asked Caepio.

"If one priestess was able to secure the goddess's approval in a torrential downpour with half of Rome's sewage assaulting her and both of her hands on fire, I am certain our order can handle the task. I have kept the goddess's favor for over thirty years, Senator Caepio. I was learning my duties while you were still mewling for your mother's milk. If you have lost confidence in my capacity, you may make a motion to have me—"

A chorus of angry noes rose up in a resounding flourish. Someone threw a stylus at Caepio's head: the young upstart was making few friends in a Senate full of middle-aged and old men.

"The Senate will not hear such a motion," said Caesar. He sat back in his curule chair, irritated. "That is enough of this nonsense. Priestess Pomponia, rest assured the treasury funds will be redirected to the drainage network of the area sacred to Vesta. I will personally see to it this time. You may sit down."

"*Gratias tibi ago*, Caesar," said Pomponia. She sat down.

"There is no need for further debate," said Caesar. "This matter is closed. However, I wish to raise another—it is one of decorum." He looked squarely at Murena. "When our holy priests entered this chamber, Senator Murena, you chastised them for their etiquette. You accused them of grandstanding. Yet, you dare to stand before Caesar, before the noble senators in this great chamber, with a face as bearded as a goat? Without the decency of a clean-shaven face?"

"Hear, hear!" agreed the senators.

Murena faltered at the wave of criticism and bowed deeply. "I offer my heartfelt apologies to Caesar and the Senate," he said. "I have a lively mistress. She causes me to oversleep." He smiled broadly, hoping the ribald humor would summon some solidarity among the senators.

Caesar contorted his face as though a sour odor had settled around him. "You have as much discretion as your son did," he said.

The Senate chamber fell silent.

Someone coughed.

It was awkward, horribly awkward, and terrifying.

"I make a motion," said Caesar, "that Senator Murena's country house in Ostia be demolished as punishment for his disrespect to this body."

The praetor stood. "All in favor of the motion?"

Not surprisingly, it was unanimous.

Everyone agreed with Caesar.

CHAPTER XII

Saepius Locutum, Numquam Me Tacuisse Paenitet
I have often regretted my speech, but never my silence.

—PUBLILIUS SYRUS

The last time Anchises was at the grand house of Tiberius was after the dedication of the Temple of Mars Ultor in the Forum of Augustus. He had sung for Rome's elite in Tiberius's triclinium and then again in the garden. Everyone had been smiling. Everyone had congratulated him on his performance.

But he had been sick inside.

Sick with worry and longing for Thracius. Sick with hunger and hopelessness, worn down by the chronic dread and despair that came with being owned by the abusive Soren.

Now as the empress once again led him into her son's triclinium, the faces that smiled at him seemed less threatening, more human. But they hadn't changed. He had. And it was all because of the priestess.

He and Thracius had been reunited. They lived together in the comfortable slave quarters of the House of the Vestals, and although the priestess kept saying she would find them other accommodations, Anchises suspected she was in no hurry to do so. He had become her confidant, and both he and her freedman Ankhu were as protective of their Vestal as Vesta herself was of Rome.

Thracius had as much purpose. When he wasn't being ambushed by the novice priestesses, he was teaching the soldiers that guarded the temple how to box. They thought of him as something of a sports legend. His burns may have made him less appealing to some women, but they had won him the machismo admiration of men.

Even now, in the home of Caesar's heir, Thracius was surrounded by noblemen inspecting his scars, debating the merits of recent boxing matches in the amphitheater, and asking his opinion on the best new boxers to bet on in Rome. While he did not box any longer, he remained a performance slave. Or perhaps *celebrity slave* was a more apt description. Either way, he and Anchises were the renowned Apollo's Pair, and Priestess Pomponia knew that people wanted to see them together.

In many ways, life had come full circle, and they lived much as they had under their first master, Lucius Bassus. Bassus had always taken them to parties where they had eaten fine food, enjoyed good wine, and mingled with society's elite. He had always treated them well. The slave auction that saw Thracius and Anchises sold to Soren—well, that had not unfolded the way their former master had intended. He was not to blame.

Yet, despite the good life, he and Thracius were still property. They were slaves. But as Anchises looked around the triclinium, he found himself philosophizing: *Who wasn't?*

His mistress, although High Priestess of Rome, had been summoned by the Senate no differently than a slave being summoned by her master. And the Senate itself? Was that not just a gathering of Caesar's wealthier slaves in good togas?

The same could be said of Rome's nobility. They owned property and land, but Caesar owned them. Every well-dressed, bejeweled woman in Rome was slave to her husband, who in turn was slave to Caesar. All were slaves to Caesar. All citizens, all soldiers, all freedmen across the vast expanse of the Roman Empire. Caesar was master to every single one of them.

The empress Livia—Caesar's most beloved slave—led Anchises to his performer's platform in the center of the triclinium.

"My dear friends and family," she said, "thank you for being with us here at the home of my son. Tonight, we rejoice that Vesta's divine fire stills burns in the heart of the Caput Mundi. We give our praise and gratitude to our sacrosanct priestesses, whose blessed order has served the goddess since the days of Rome's founding. We honor our Vestalis Maxima, whose instruction has shaped vigilant priestesses who perform their duties with precision and, as we have seen, even at great pain to themselves. We show our affection to Priestess Quintina, for her resourcefulness and piety."

A round of affectionate applause.

Livia looked lovingly across the dining room at Octavian, who sat regally but relaxed on a long scarlet and gold couch. "But most of all," she continued, "we thank the gods for our emperor, son of the divine Julius Caesar, for his clemency and wisdom in the rule of our empire and in the care he has taken for its eternal glory. For this crisis has also revealed the caliber of Caesar's chosen heir, Tiberius. As our Vestal priestess and her heroic guards protected the sacred flame under the worst conditions imaginable, Tiberius assumed the duty of his divine appointment to assist." Livia raised her wine cup to salute Tiberius and Quintina.

Rome's elite clapped again and toasted the heir and the priestess.

Livia lowered her cup and again looked admiringly at Octavian. "For decades, Caesar Augustus and High Priestess Pomponia have fulfilled their respective duties to Rome. Our hearts and minds are at ease that the union of Caesar and Vestal is as perpetual as the eternal fire, as the Eternal City itself. It is as our founding father—Romulus, who looks down on us as the divine Quirinus—decreed."

A final flourish of patriotic cheers and applause.

Livia put her hand on Anchises's shoulder. "Now, my dear friends and family, I give you the virtuoso Anchises."

Those standing against the far walls of the triclinium or lingering in the colonnade moved closer to hear and see the renowned singer better. More guests filed in from the library and garden. It had been months since he had performed in Rome.

As Livia moved away, Anchises called the lyre player to his side. "The last time I had the privilege of performing in this fine home before Caesar and his esteemed guests," he began, "I sang in celebration of Mars, the avenging god. Tonight, I sing in celebration of Vesta, the protecting goddess." He waited as the customary clapping subsided, then put a hand to his chest and bowed deeply. "Dear friends, twice did I beg Caesar's poet,

Virgil, to release a few lines of his epic so I could sing them to you, and twice did he refuse me, the second time with words I shall not share." Anchises paused until the swell of laughter subsided. "Yet, the world is too magnificent for only one poet, is it not? The younger Ovid has therefore written words in honor of our emperor, and if I may say, in honor also of our devoted Priestess Quintina, the timeless fire, and the timeless city itself. I will sing those words for you now." Anchises stepped onto his low platform, nodded for the lyre player to begin, and sang.

Pomponia listened to one chorus of Anchises's singing—he sang of the waves and the flow of time—and then she slipped through the room to where the crowd was sparser. His voice had a way of bringing whatever emotions she was feeling to the surface, and she couldn't risk that right now. Not with her emotions vacillating between angst and anger, worry and weariness.

And certainly not with Soren glaring at her over the rim of his wine cup.

She gravitated as casually as she could toward Caesar's couch, hoping he would call her over. Maecenas had joined him, and the two of them were talking under their breath as a magistrate was trying to push yet another scroll under Caesar's nose. When Caesar saw Pomponia, he gestured to her. She sat on an adjacent couch.

"Your slave Anchises is as stellar as ever, Priestess," said Maecenas. "I wonder if I might borrow him on the kalends. I have the misfortune of having to host a party for my brother-in-law's inheritance. Personally, I won't be celebrating. The man will be even more intolerable when he has money."

"By all means, Maecenas," said Pomponia. "He is at your disposal. Thracius as well. I'll send some wine from my vineyard in Tivoli along with them. It will help build your tolerance."

"Please do." He pointed his chin at Anchises, who continued to sing. "Ovid's lyrics sung with that voice? It wouldn't sound better in Elysium." He set his empty wine cup on a tray and accepted a fresh full one from a slave. "Ovid is more forthcoming with his work than is Virgil," he continued. "The lyrics you hear today are from an epic poem he is writing called *Metamorphoses*. It is a long way from being finished—Virgil will be finished sooner, which is its own breed of miracle—but Ovid's poem will tell our history from creation to the divinity of Julius Caesar."

Octavian sniffed loudly. "I like Virgil better," he said. "Ovid talks too much. I've never trusted men who talk too much."

"I challenge that, Caesar," said Tiberius. He appeared at Octavian's shoulder and looked down at him good-naturedly. "You once told me that you prefer men who speak over men who whisper. So men who speak excessively must be the most desirable of all, no?"

Octavian looked up at the ceiling in thought. "You touch on philosophy, Tiberius," he said. "For that we must consult the Greeks. *Mēdén ágan.* Nothing in excess."

Pomponia laughed with the men, but her laughter caught in her throat as Soren sauntered up to Caesar's couch as if by imperial invitation. The Vestal expected one of Caesar's scribes to subtly usher him away, but Tiberius greeted him before that could happen.

"Ah, Soren," he said affably, "I do not see your wife here tonight."

"Young mothers," Soren said dismissively. "It is difficult to pull them away from their whelps. Tiberius, might I have a word?"

Tiberius glanced down at Caesar, who nodded his permission for him and Soren to leave. Once the two men had moved on, Octavian spoke to Maecenas. "Livia must be in the garden. I will join her. You may discuss that matter with the priestess now."

"Yes, Caesar."

Octavian rose from the couch. As he exited the triclinium for the courtyard, Maecenas leaned in closer to Pomponia. "Caesar wishes to thank you for your discretion in the Senate house today."

"Caesar need not thank me for doing my duty," said Pomponia.

"Nonetheless, he wishes to reward your fidelity, especially in the wake of Senator Murena's questioning. Is there something the emperor can provide you? Another villa perhaps? Or perhaps . . ."

Pomponia brushed her veil off her face. "Come now, Maecenas."

"Or perhaps I can use this occasion to enlist your help with another matter."

"I'm listening."

"I know Octavian," Maecenas said seriously. "Privately, he worries about his daughter, yet he cannot relax the terms of her banishment or even write to her. It would be seen as a concession."

"Yes," said Pomponia, "but the people wouldn't care. They have always been forgiving of Julia."

"You and I know that," said Maecenas, "but Octavian does not believe it. He rejects any action that might come across as weak or as condoning her immorality. He says fire will mix with water before he forgives her—his words. I have tried to improve Julia's condition by providing a more comfortable residence on Pandateria. Caesar feigned reluctance, yet soon approved. But then . . ."

"Livia talked him out of it," finished Pomponia.

Maecenas leaned back on the couch. "The estrangement is taking its toll on him. It amplifies his other anxieties and weakens his health. The incident during the storm was just one example."

"It doesn't help that the general is gone."

"Agrippa was Octavian's second self. It wouldn't have mattered how poorly Julia treated him: Agrippa would never have permitted her exile. He cared for Octavian. He would not have let him grow so distant from his only daughter." Maecenas scratched his scalp in frustration. "Caesar and I have been friends for many years, but I have never been able to speak to him the way that Agrippa did. Agrippa would simply insist that Julia return, and it would be so. I have to proceed more politically. I must help Caesar make it look like he is doing a favor for someone else."

"What will you do?"

"I will tell him that you are worried about Julia's well-being in exile and that it would bring you comfort if he would consider receiving a letter from her."

"Livia will never allow it. She would build Julia a thousand houses before she'd permit a single letter."

"I'll say that you have asked for his discretion as he considers it," said Maecenas. "He will then feel justified in keeping it from her. I think part of him is looking for an excuse to do that."

"When Livia finds out, she'll turn like a wolf sprung from a trap."

"She hasn't managed to bite you yet," Maecenas said with a grin. When Pomponia didn't respond, he raised an eyebrow. "Oh?"

"It was not a serious bite," said the priestess. "She disposed of a slave I was once quite fond of."

"You speak of Medousa," said Maecenas. "I suspected as much."

"Your suspicions are more reliable than most people's facts, Maecenas. Do as you see best. Caesar is fortunate to have your counsel," she said and then added, "and your friendship."

Maecenas chuckled and looked at his wife, Terentia. Draped in a rich yellow dress with an emerald-embroidered palla, she was hanging flirtatiously off the arm of a young magistrate who was probably half her age. "Caesar and I have reconciled any personal differences we had," he said. "I hope it will remain so."

Somehow sensing that the intimate conversation between the Vestal and her husband concerned her, Terentia unfastened herself from the young magistrate and glided to the couch.

"High Priestess," she said cordially, "I left an offering for the goddess near the temple this morning."

"Thank you, Lady Terentia," said Pomponia. "We hope to move the sacred fire back to the temple very soon."

"How long will the roof repairs take?" asked Terentia.

"Only days," Pomponia answered. "The component parts of the roof exist in duplicate. They just need to be fitted together and secured. With some improvements, of course. The empress has commissioned a bronze statue of Vesta to stand at the apex. Fabiana once told me there was one up there when she was a child. I don't know why it was ever removed." She looked over Terentia's shoulder where Quintina was subtly trying to find an escape route from an elderly augur who had managed to corner her. "Poor Priestess Quintina. I should go rescue her."

Terentia grimaced. "It's Pythius," she said. "I will go with you. It will take two."

The two women left Maecenas to join Quintina. Instead of leaving the women to socialize, however, the old augur lingered.

Terentia hooked her arm around his. "Pythius, I have heard a rumor that you have written the most fascinating book on the auspices. Is that true?"

"It is," he replied, beaming. "I have a whole chapter on divination practices in the old Alba Longa. And I have just started work on my next book. It is on the *Libri Fulgurales* of the Etruscans . . . how to divine lightning strikes in different sections of the sky."

"No! That is my particular area of fascination. Let us indulge in some seasoned dormice, and you can tell me all about it."

As Terentia led Pythius toward an elaborate food table on the other side of the triclinium, Pomponia made a mental note to send the woman a gift for her self-sacrifice.

"Let's go into the courtyard," she said to Quintina.

The two Vestals strolled leisurely out of the oversized but still crowded dining room and into the openness of the garden and the refreshing night air.

Quintina looked up into the dark sky: a glowing, white full moon hung heavy above them. "Oh, this is better." She arranged her palla around her shoulders, careful to not brush against the bandages that wound around her forearms.

The lyre player had relocated to the side of a pool in the garden, and the sound of his pleasant music mixed with the cheerful chatter of the many conversations within the large courtyard.

Pomponia spotted Anchises and Thracius conversing with Livia and two of Caesar's generals who had recently returned to Rome after campaigns in Noricum and Germania. One of the generals was comparing scars with the boxer.

"Caesar seeks to expand the empire," Pomponia said to Quintina. "I do not know where it will end."

Quintina was still looking up. She pointed to the moon. "Maybe there."

"Maecenas told me that Caesar has commissioned a statue of you," said Pomponia. "We will put it in the peristyle next to the statue of your ancestor, Priestess Tacita. I remember when your father first brought you to my office. I took you into the garden and showed it to you. You picked a rose and placed it at the base. Your father was so angry. He thought you were too bold."

Quintina said nothing, but tears began to flow down her cheeks. "When Tacita faced the Gaul in the temple all those years ago . . . what do you think she was feeling?"

"I don't know. Perhaps a sense of duty. Resolve."

"I don't think so, Pomponia. I think she was terrified beyond words. I think she could feel death pursuing her, shaking the ground and about to crush her from behind . . . like those black bulls that ran down the slaves in Taurus's labyrinth."

"You showed great courage, Quintina."

"I did not feel courageous. I did not feel the presence of the goddess. I felt desperation, and that is all. Perhaps I am not as pious as you think. All I could think about was what would happen if the fire went out. I would be buried alive, as would Caecilia and Lucretia, and probably you too. And I love all of you so much. I love you more than I love the goddess herself . . ."

"That is all right, Quintina. The goddess does not ask that you love her above all. The immortals are not so vain. You need only uphold the Pax Deorum, to keep her fire burning, and you did that."

"If Tiberius had not appeared, the fire would have gone out."

"But he did appear. And now all is well."

"You should have seen him," said Quintina. "He was as terrified as I was. His hands were shaking when he stripped the wood off the Lupa's statue. I think we have underestimated him and his devotion to Rome."

"Perhaps," said Pomponia. "But we have not underestimated his devotion to Mallonia. The poor woman! Look how she darts like a mouse, this way and that, behind this column and that chair as he sneaks up on her with silent cat paws."

Quintina laughed and dried her eyes, relaxing. "You will have noticed that Soren is here. Not with Tacita of course, but with that woman from Capua again."

"Her name is Aelina. Anchises says it was she who sold Scorpus to Soren in the first place."

"Scorpus . . . oh yes, the slave charioteer who tried to kill him."

Pomponia nodded her head and silently cursed herself. How could she speak so carelessly? Quintina knew nothing about Scorpus or how she was harboring the fugitive in Tivoli. She was searching for a way to quickly change the subject, when Livia joined them. Like the Vestals, she was also watching Tiberius's almost comedic stalking of Mallonia.

"Yes, you may laugh," she said to Pomponia. "My son insists on making himself the object of ridicule."

"That is not so, Lady Livia," replied Pomponia. "Priestess Quintina was just telling me of Tiberius's resourcefulness during the crisis of the storm. She says his conviction helped preserve the sacred flame. And I myself have seen the burden of duty that he shares with Caesar. Not since Agrippa has Caesar had such support in the day-to-day management of the empire."

"Yes," said Livia, "he has many excellent qualities." In a rare moment of vulnerability, she added, "But also a few vices."

"What man does not?" asked Pomponia.

"No man that I know," said Livia. She clucked her tongue. "I must do something about his infatuation with Lady Mallonia."

Pomponia nodded slightly to Quintina, and the younger Vestal excused herself to mingle with others in the garden.

"What have you tried so far?"

"I've told Tiberius that he looks the fool when he chases an ugly widow twice his age. He will lose whatever authority and regard he is building for himself in the Senate."

"It is pointless to warn the love-struck," said Pomponia. Returning the gesture of Livia's openness, she added, "You will recall that I had a similar problem not long ago. The problem was only resolved when the temptation was removed."

"Shall I tie weights around Mallonia's ankles and throw her in the Tiber?"

The quip almost made Pomponia laugh out loud. It had to be the wine. She was indulging herself more than usual. It offered a blessed respite from the stress of the last few days. "Why not start with something more civilized? Offer her a villa outside of Rome."

"Why? The woman is rich. She would buy her own villa if she wanted one."

"She may not be as rich as you think. I have heard that her husband left more of their estate to Caesar than is generally known. On top of that, her daughter's recent dowry was significant."

Livia emptied her wine cup in a less than regal swallow. "I'm not surprised. The girl got her looks from her mother."

"Find out where she vacations. Or where she has family. Buy her a villa there." Pomponia tipped her cup toward Mallonia who had slipped behind a column in the peristyle to avoid Tiberius. "She's spent half the party hiding behind furniture to avoid him. Perhaps she's eager to leave Rome and just needs the means."

"I'll try it. It can't hurt."

Pomponia thought about using the moment's spirit of mutuality to question Livia about her association with Soren and especially about what Soren might be up to. She decided against it. Regardless of what Livia would say, if anything, she would only be revealing what Soren wanted her to reveal.

"Empress Livia," said a voice behind them, "and Priestess Pomponia."

"Lady Aelina," said Pomponia. She took a step back. "Perhaps I should not stand too close to you. The last time I did, I was almost crushed by a winged man."

"There is another way to look at that," Aelina said sprightly. "Any bodies that fall from the sky will land on me, not you."

"How long will you be staying in Rome?" Livia asked Aelina in a tone that suggested she didn't really care. "You are a houseguest of Soren, no?"

"I am," replied Aelina. "I would like to stay as long as I am welcome, or at least as long as my presence does not upset Soren's wife. Priestess Pomponia, if I may ask—are there strained relations between the priestess Quintina and her sister, Tacita?"

Pomponia almost choked on her wine at the woman's impudence. Before she could answer, Livia spoke up. "I don't know what is acceptable these days among the pottage-fed simpletons in Capua," she said, "but questioning a superior lady about personal issues is considered most uncouth in Rome."

"Priestess, I am so sorry," said Aelina. "I meant no disrespect. It was only my concern for my host that made me wonder."

So, thought Pomponia, *Soren keeps all the women in his life in the dark, including you.*

"Why are you concerned about Soren?" asked Livia. "I am his friend. Is there something I should know?"

Pomponia pretended to be distracted by Anchises's spontaneous burst of song by the pool. It disguised the fact that she was listening with open ears to the women's conversation: Livia was doing her work for her.

"Oh, Soren is a complicated man," said Aelina, the first traces of a slur forming at the beginning of her words. "If you ask me, he and his wife are not well suited. He is most dedicated to serving your son Tiberius, though. The man barely speaks, but when he does, it is of Tiberius. Oh, look—it is Apollo's Pair. Come here, boys! Anchises! I say, Anchises, come here!"

The matrons surrounding Anchises complained softly at the interruption as the virtuoso's eyes landed on Aelina. He remembered the face from Capua: the vapid and chronically adulterous wife of the well-liked nobleman Mettius, Scorpus's former owner. Anchises had long suspected that Aelina had sold Scorpus and his woman, Cassandra, to Soren despite the wishes of her late husband. Distracted, the singer apologized to the women around him and moved to stand beside Pomponia.

"Lady Aelina," he said civilly. "What brings you to Rome?"

"Oh, Apollo's Pair," she said, either ignoring or not hearing his question. "I was always such a fan. I was so disappointed when I heard that Soren sold you—no offense, Priestess. But I was hoping that when I came to Rome"—she winked at Anchises—"I might ask Soren to let me borrow that big man of yours for an evening. Tell me, where is he? If you're here, he must be too." Her eyes hungrily scanned the garden until she saw Thracius. He was standing under a tall torch, the flickering light making his scars look even more disfiguring. She turned up her nose. "Ew, what happened to your sexier half, Anchises? He looks like the morning firewood!"

"Gods," Livia muttered. She rolled her eyes at Pomponia and left.

Aelina leaned in to Anchises, who pulled back to avoid the wine on her breath. "Look at you, living the fine life in Rome. You always had the talent to sing for the emperor, that much is certain."

"How gracious of you to say, Lady Aelina," said Anchises.

"I have a secret to tell you, Anchises," Aelina continued. "It is I that you have to thank for your good fortune." She poked at his chest with a bent finger.

"How so?"

She put her finger to her lip. "If it weren't for me, you and Thracius would still be in Capua."

Pomponia sensed Anchises's body tense. His expression turned to stone. "How so?" he asked again.

"Soren wanted to buy you," she whispered, "but he didn't know how much to bid. I managed to sweet-talk Manius into revealing his bid." She pressed her lips together, waiting for Anchises to laugh. Or thank her. Or both. "Don't you understand?" She poked his chest again. "That's the only reason Soren won the auction . . . because he knew how much to bid. Isn't that hilarious?"

Anchises's nostrils flared. His voice deep and loud, he stepped closer to Aelina. "You wretched cun—"

"Anchises!" said Pomponia.

Aelina's eyes went wide with surprise and confusion: *Was Anchises the virtuoso just about to call me a* cunnus?

Catching the edge of rage in his partner's voice, Thracius quickly joined the group. He put his hand on Anchises's back. "What is the matter?" he asked.

"Anchises felt unwell for a moment," Pomponia replied. "I think he is composing himself now, though." She squeezed the singer's hand, hard.

Anchises felt a throat-clamping hatred rise up in him. He had lived like a starving sewer rat in Soren's dark, dank basement for what seemed like an eternity. Soren's violations and his own loneliness were like suffering from a disease with no end and no cure. He had existed in a constant state of fear, anxiety, and pain, worried that at any moment Soren would kill him or order Thracius to be killed. There were times when things were so bad that he had almost wished it so.

And Thracius. Anchises's lover had been imprisoned in the *ludus*, existing in just as much protracted uncertainty, abuse, and helplessness as Anchises. Like him, he had more than once succumbed to the despair of a hopeless life and the belief that they would never be together again.

It was Soren's fault, yes, but now Anchises knew that it had all started with Aelina. Aelina, that insipid, tedious excuse for a woman, who aspired to be nothing more in life than Soren's unpaid whore.

Thracius patted Anchises on the back. "Let's go inside and sit down. Maybe take some water?"

"Yes, Anchises," said Pomponia. "Go inside now."

Aelina rocked on her feet. "How'd you get those burns, Thracius?" she asked.

"Oh, don't feel sorry for him." Soren suddenly shouldered into the conversation and leaned in to Aelina. "Thracius now guards a house of virgins. What man wouldn't revel in that posting? Charred or not, Rome has been good to him."

"Excuse us," said Pomponia. She gripped Anchises's arm, urging him to follow her.

"And Anchises . . ." Soren licked the wine off his lips and then smiled at the singer as if they shared a dirty secret. Which of course they did. "Anchises has had his pleasures too."

The singer suddenly felt fixed to the floor. He lowered his eyes. He couldn't bear to look at anyone—not the priestess, not Aelina, not Soren. And especially not Thracius.

At first, the boxer seemed not to have heard Soren's words. He seemed stuck on the idea that Anchises was unwell, most likely from too much wine or rich food. But then slowly, almost as an afterthought, he processed the words, and the weight of realization fell upon him.

The boxer looked at Anchises, then at Soren, then back at Anchises, his expression oscillating between hatred for his former owner and sadness at his partner's hidden indignity being revealed so publicly.

"I almost forgot to tell you the good news," Soren said jovially to Pomponia, changing the subject but still enjoying the anguish on the faces of his former slaves. "Apparently we are going to be neighbors."

Pomponia clung to her composure. "What do you mean?"

"The villa next to yours in Tivoli came up for sale. I am sending Aelina to finish the documents on my behalf. Tiberius needs my assistance here in Rome, so I can't step away."

Aelina smiled excitedly, as if it must be the best news the priestess had heard in ages.

"Normally, I wouldn't have been able to afford such an extravagance," said Soren, "but the gold I received from Caesar and your purchase of Apollo's Pair have left me with more coin than I know how to spend."

Anchises's arm slipped out of Pomponia's grip and came up fast. "I will—"

But before Anchises's fist could land on Soren, Thracius did what he did best. He knocked Anchises out cold with one clean, quick jab that was so smooth, so skilled, the virtuoso simply slumped downward as if he had silently succumbed to the wine. Thracius caught him.

"Take him out through the *posticum*," said Pomponia. "Not through the house. Wait for me in my lectica."

Amused, Soren stepped back as Thracius supported Anchises—already groggily returning to consciousness—and walked him out of the courtyard. Only a few people noticed: they laughed and raised their cups to Anchises as if congratulating him on managing to enjoy the evening and Caesar's exceptional wine to their fullest.

"A word to the wise, Priestess," said Soren. "I wouldn't invest too much in your slaves, especially ones with such volatile dispositions. It doesn't matter how attached you are to them. You may one day find them attached to a crossbeam just outside the Esquiline Gate."

Pomponia shrugged off Soren's bold reference to his bed slave's crucifixion. Gods, when would the man let it go? "You know how artist types are," she said. "They're always keen to give a performance of one kind or another."

Excusing herself with an indifferent smile, she left Soren and Aelina's company and returned to the louder, more crowded triclinium. She grabbed the arm of the first slave she saw. "I'm leaving. Have my litter brought around."

"Yes, High Priestess."

Careful to appear unhurried while at the same time avoiding eye contact with anyone who might draw her into another conversation, Pomponia proceeded to the atrium of Tiberius's home and then out the portico to the open air.

Her lectica—one of her larger ones—appeared almost instantly, carried on the shoulders of eight robust litter-bearers and accompanied by Caeso and Publius. Both guards had smirks on their faces, having just poked their heads into the lectica to find an uncharacteristically impaired Anchises. The *lecticarii* set it down, and Caeso opened the curtain for Pomponia to step inside. She pulled the curtain closed behind her and sat opposite Anchises and Thracius.

"You foolish man," she chastised Anchises. "I don't care if he buggered you every night before his bath and twice on the kalends. It is done. You know what he can still do if pushed."

Anchises clutched his head and leaned forward. "*Futuo*," he swore. He sat back up. Even in the dim light of the oil lamps that illuminated the interior of the lectica, Pomponia could see a bruise forming on the side of his head.

She looked at Thracius, startled at the murderous glint in his eyes. She had come to see him as a man who spun children in the garden, not a man who used to routinely bludgeon men to death. She thought for a moment of all the unfortunate opponents who must have seen that same glint before being dispatched to the underworld.

"I want to kill him," the boxer seethed.

"Do you, now?" she asked. "Well, he can only die so many times, and others have already spoken." She threw herself back onto a cushion.

"We need Scorpus," said Anchises.

"Scorpus? Scorpus thinks he's Ramses reborn and spends his days drinking my wine and riding my horses."

"Maybe," said Anchises. "But don't underestimate him. He can—"

"We need *Ankhu*," Pomponia interrupted bitterly. She fidgeted with her veil and then pulled it off her head in frustration. Her face softened into something resembling her usual self. "I haven't heard from him in weeks," she revealed. "The last messenger I sent to Tivoli never returned. I don't even know if he made it to my villa at all, or if Ankhu even received the last message I sent."

"Why did you not tell us this earlier?" Anchises asked.

"I don't know. With everything else going on, I just kept telling myself that a message would come tomorrow and then the tomorrow after that." She put her face in her hands. "I didn't want to tell you I was worried. Hearing myself say it aloud would make it too real. And now with Soren buying the property next to mine? It cannot be a coincidence . . . can it?"

Anchises slid forward and took her hands in his. "Priestess," he said, "what was in the last letter you wrote to Ankhu? How much did you reveal? Did you mention Scorpus by name?"

"That's the worst part," whispered Pomponia. "I can't remember."

"I will leave for Tivoli in the morning," said Thracius.

"Yes." Pomponia nodded. "You can both go. Find out what's going on. I also want you to instruct Ankhu to buy the property next to mine. Tell him to offer whatever it takes."

*   *   *

"You should not be here, Quintina."

"Why not, sister?" Quintina stood in the atrium of Soren's home, critiquing its frescoes and scanning the death masks of his ancestors that hung over his *lararium*. She dragged her fingertips through the water of the impluvium. "This water is dirty." Shaking the water off her fingers, she studied Tacita's bandaged hand with interest. "It seems we are both recovering. What happened to you?"

"I burned myself," said Tacita. "In the kitchen."

"What were you doing in the kitchen? You have a house full of slaves. Look, there is one now, peeking around the corner."

Tacita spun around. "Leave us!" she shouted at the horse-toothed slave.

"So, not only does your husband bind you to the house," Quintina said quietly, "but he also places spies within it? I can see why you love him so. He thinks of everything."

"He will be upset that you came here unannounced."

"Why? What is so wrong with one sister visiting another? I only wish to see my little niece. How is she?"

"She is fine," said Tacita. "But you need to go. You cannot be here when he gets home."

"I wouldn't worry about that. He won't be home for a while. He was having too much fun with Lady Aelina."

"Aelina was there? At Tiberius's house?"

"Indeed," said Quintina. "I saw her speaking with the emperor and the empress. She had on the most beautiful dress, and every time I saw her, she was tasting some new delicacy. She is very sociable, you know. I wouldn't be surprised if many there tonight assumed that she was Soren's wife. I mean, you are never seen."

"Why would they think she is Soren's wife? Did they seem . . ."

"Familiar with each other? Yes. And then some." Quintina sat on the edge of the impluvium. "But that cannot come as a surprise to you. Soren does not strike me as the kind of man who bothers to hide his affairs. It is always that way with men who hate their wives."

"He does not hate me, Quintina. You do not understand him like I do. Strong men like Soren are not always comfortable showing their emotions lest they appear weak."

"Oh, sister," Quintina said with a sigh. "You mistake his disdain for complexity. It is the same lie that all ill-treated wives tell themselves."

"What would you know of being a wife, Quintina? The closest you ever came to a man was Septimus, and he was no more loyal to you than Soren is to me." She crossed her arms in front of her, hiding her bandaged hand in her palla. "Ask me how I know that," she said bitingly.

Quintina called upon the goddess to help her control the sudden swell of hatred she felt for her sister, to help her swallow and not speak the vicious words forming on her tongue. She put her hands on her knees and let out a carefree laugh.

"Look at us," she said. "We are like Romulus and Remus in sister form. But we can choose a happier path than they." She stood up and faced Tacita, looking first at her own bandaged arms and then her sister's wrapped hand. "We are sisters in blood, but I wish us to be sisters in friendship too. I know I speak harshly of Soren. But I watch him eat and drink at Caesar's home with another woman on his arm, and I know it should be you. You are the sister of a Vestal Virgin of Rome. You should be at all the great parties, not some mousy woman from Capua."

"It *should* be me. I do not know why he treats me so."

"Yes, you do," said Quintina. "We both do. The child is not his."

Tacita said nothing.

Quintina forced herself to proceed slowly. To linger on those things that mattered most to Tacita.

"You used to have a turquoise dress," she said. "It had purple glass beading. Do you still have it? How I would have loved to show off my beautiful sister this evening to Rome's most noble people." She gently took Tacita's hands in her own. "You were always a woman that men desired. And you know the best way to inflame a man's fading desire . . ."

"Jealousy," said Tacita.

Quintina nodded soberly. "I think you can marry much better than Soren. But if you are determined to make him want you again, he needs to feel some of the jealousy that you now feel."

"How can I do that? I am always home with Calidia."

"You must think long-term," said Quintina. "If you were to admit the child was not his—"

"He would kill me if I did that! He wants her."

"What a man wants is as changeable as the clouds on a windy day. He may have wanted her at one time, who knows why, but now he doesn't care. His friendship with Tiberius has presented him with new opportunities and changed his priorities. He has become an important man, an adviser to the next Caesar. And from what I saw tonight, he wants a beautiful woman on his arm, not a fading beauty at home suckling another man's child like a sow in a barn. He will never want you again if this continues."

"I love him," said Tacita. She pulled her hands away from Quintina and covered her eyes as she wept. "I love him more than anything, but you are right. He acts like he hates me." She looked at her bandaged hand. "His temper is worse than ever. What you say is true. Calidia's father is—"

"Wait, sister," said Quintina. "There is no going back once you say it. But I can promise you one thing. Once you admit the child's true parentage, any anger he shows will quickly fade to relief." She touched Tacita's hair affectionately. "And a renewed desire for you. I suspect that Soren will try to have his own child with you very soon. He will want a son."

Tacita's eyes lit up. "I would love to give him a son."

"I am certain there is nothing he would want more. Men have extra love for wives who bear them sons. Imagine if he could be free of another man's daughter and instead have his own son? He would be a different man. He would be a devoted husband."

"And Calidia? What will happen to her? Our uncle will not want her."

I'm amazed you thought to ask, thought Quintina. "We can work out the details later, but she is welcome to stay in the House of the Vestals as long as necessary. You should come and stay with us too. Let Soren miss you for a few days."

"What if he forgets about me?"

Quintina laughed. "You know that is not how men work. A man spends far more time thinking about the woman who is *not* in his bed than the one who is."

"I am younger than Aelina. Prettier too."

"And more refined," Quintina added. "Aelina made a fool of herself in front of the empress. Soren won't put himself in that position again. He needs a wife who will impress Lady Livia. You are from a great family, and I have told few people this, but I will be the next Vestalis Maxima of Rome. The empress will value that relationship. You will have it all. Youth, beauty, nobility, and connections. Soren only needs to be unburdened of the child and to feel the pain of your absence for a few days, and then you will have him too. He will soon realize that he needs you."

"And that he loves me."

"That too. You can start over with him."

A hushed sound from around the corner, beyond the atrium, caught the attention of both women. Soren's spies had returned.

"I will leave now," whispered Quintina. "But I will have a temple slave hide just down the street. Later tonight, when you've had time to think it through, write me a letter. Tell me everything. Throw the scroll onto the street. My slave will bring it to me."

"I will tell you now."

"Take a little wine," said Quintina, "and then do it. I want you to be at peace with your decision."

Quintina kissed her sister on the cheek before she could say anything else. She didn't want Tacita to just say the words. She needed them in writing.

"I will fix this," she said as she walked out of Soren's atrium to her waiting guards. "Trust me."

CHAPTER XIII

Iupiter in Caelis, Caesar Regit Omnia Terris
Jupiter rules the heavens, Caesar all the earth.

−VIRGIL

THE ISLAND OF PANDATERIA

Using a bread knife to try and slice the abscess on the bottom of her foot had been a stupid idea. It hadn't worked.

Neither had praying to Apollo. She had pleaded with the god of healing, had promised to offer whatever she could find on the island to him, but he had not come to her aid. He was probably too busy protecting her father's fragile health and accepting his lavish offerings of great bulls, round pigs, meaty goats, and fattened sheep.

All Julia had to offer were spiders and fish. She had thought for a moment about offering Phoenix, but he had seemed to read her mind and had disappeared for a whole day. When he had come back, she had assured him that she wouldn't have gone through with it.

Yet not all the gods had forsaken her. Her favorite god, the one she was perhaps the friendliest with, had taken mercy on her and had healed her through trickery.

Bacchus, the god of wine, had come to her in a hallucination. He had stood by the little brazier in her hut, so tall and magnificent that the roof had lifted right off, and his vine-crowned head had disappeared into the storm clouds above. He had waved the clouds aside and looked down at her, his laughter coming out as thunderclaps that shook the ground and rattled the walls. He had said something to her in a booming, foreign voice that she could not understand—who could understand the gods?—and then he had left by a single massive step that had taken him far out into the sea.

Julia had sat up in bed, terrified and amazed, to find that Bacchus had left a full cup of wine on the brazier. She had been so overcome by the sight of the red wine sloshing over the rim that she had stood up quickly, putting all her weight on her abscessed foot. The pressure had caused the abscess to burst open on the spot. The pus had lain as a rank pool of thick yellow fluid for days, until her fever abated and she felt well enough to clean it up.

Now the wound on her foot had cleared. So had her head.

The skies had cleared too; however, what they revealed on the shoreline had made her sit on the rocks and cry for half a day. The storm had torn the planks off her raft and scattered them in all directions, even out into the water. It had been no small feat to gather them all again and restart the labor of nailing and binding them together.

But she had made good use of the extra days on the island. Her visit from the god had inspired her to be more pious. To understand the true nature of the gods.

"In Rome," she said to Phoenix as she knelt on the sand and wound rope around the corner of her raft, "the gods are made of marble or bronze. They are everywhere. You would be awestruck to see them, Phoenix, such are their size and beauty."

The seagull wobbled closer and opened his beak.

"Their statues are much taller than even the tallest man." She pointed to a tree behind them. "Some of them are as tall as the trees and more splendid than you can imagine. When you look up at them, you are filled with fidelity and wonder. Their faces are so serene and sure. They are gods, so what would perturb them?"

Julia finished securing one side of the raft. She stood up to gather more rope and found she had been kneeling on a large black insect. She picked it up with two fingers and tossed it to Phoenix. He nibbled it with his beak, then let it drop to the sand. He was either too immersed in his patroness's story to eat or he now preferred her bread to bugs.

"When you pray to the gods, you can see the power in their eyes," she continued. "Will they answer your prayers? Sometimes. But even when they do, it is rarely in the way you think. That is why you must be very particular when you ask, and even then, they will mostly do as they please. They do not always have mercy, but they always have a sense of humor." She knelt in the sand again and looked seriously at Phoenix. "That is the greatest thing to fear about them, because the things they find funny are not the things we find funny."

Julia finished securing the other side with rope and then sat cross-legged to study the finished raft. The boards were tight, and the whole structure was solid. It would float.

She looked at Phoenix. "I have seen Neptune's great statue in the Forum, his eyes as green as the sea and his hair wild with sea serpents. Red crabs crawl in his mighty beard, and his trident is so gold it hurts the eyes to look at it on a sunny day." She opened her arms to the sea before her. "And yet I never truly saw Neptune until I came to this place. When I look out at the water, I can see his fleshy back until the horizon. I can hear his words in the crash of the waves. I can smell and taste his salty hair in the sea spray." She turned her head to look at the fire she had made nearby. "It is the same with all the gods. In the Forum, Vesta's temple is as beautiful as the goddess. Great columns of the finest marble encircle the sacred fire. But the goddess is on our island as well, Phoenix. We don't have columns to build around her fire, but we have placed the finest stones we could find around it. And do you know what? I don't think I have ever heard a fire crackle as loudly as this one. That is why you and I have been able to make a home here."

Julia stood and looked up at the shining sun, shielding her eyes from the glare. "The sun god Apollo always watches us with one of his great eyes during the day." She walked away from her raft and toward the small square cage she had constructed from scraps of wood, rusty nails, and rope. "Apollo is also the god of travelers," she said to Phoenix. "I pray that he will protect us on our journey."

She bent down to pick up the gull. He flapped his good wing in protest but then quickly settled. He had accepted his transformation from wild seabird to crippled pet some time ago. Gently, Julia put him inside the cage and then carried it to the raft. She secured it with rope.

Again, she looked out to the sea. She squinted in the direction from which the ugly little man always came, but she could not see any land. It had to be the right way, though. All she had to do was paddle until she reached a shore or was spotted by a passing ship. Anything was better than waiting to die on this island.

The sky on this particular morning was favorable for a journey, so she loaded a wooden box of freshwater amphorae, bread, dried fish for Phoenix, and blankets onto her raft.

With one last look back at the island of her exile, Julia pushed the raft away from the shore and scrambled on top, onto her knees. The water came through to soak her legs, but the raft stayed afloat. She pushed it further away from the shore with a long stick.

Phoenix flicked his beak back and forth. He cocked his head upward to look at the blue sky above and then down to look at the blue water below. He fluffed his feathers with excitement.

"My father has his faults," Julia said to him, "but he has always done his duty to the gods. That is why he is still Caesar. I cannot fault him for banishing me. I see now that my sacrilege left him with no other choice. But now I am ready to do what the gods of Rome demand of Caesar's daughter."

The raft hesitated for a moment in the shallower waters of the shore, but Julia dug her stick into the sandy seafloor harder, and the raft shifted and moved along freely.

Within moments, the stick could no longer reach the bottom. She withdrew it from the water, laid it on the surface of the raft, and grabbed the wide plank of wood lying next to Phoenix's cage.

And then she began to paddle into the open sea, a strong wind at her back, in the direction of the morning sun.

CHAPTER XIV

Venter Praecepta Non Audit
The stomach does not hear advice.

−SENECA

TIVOLI

For Scorpus the Titan—now Scorpus the Egyptian—seeing Apollo's Pair together, dressed in fine tunicas and looking spoiled as ever, was like going back in time. Back to his former life in Capua. A life where he was a star charioteer and Cassandra was still alive.

As Thracius and Anchises walked into the stable, Scorpus could almost picture his beloved Cassandra walking with them. She had always liked them. The sudden memory of her made his eyes moisten, and he wiped his brow with his arm, pretending to be clearing away the sweat.

"*Salve*, Scorpus," said Thracius. He did not comment on Scorpus's changed appearance. Anchises had warned him of it in advance, but he still couldn't help but be surprised. Scorpus looked like a man who had been broken and was slowly putting himself back together again. Perhaps they all did. "We must be playthings of the gods to find ourselves meeting again like this." He extended a muscled arm to Scorpus. "We grieved at Cassandra's fate."

Scorpus grasped Thracius's arm. "You have also suffered, brother," he said. "And from the same disease."

Ankhu clapped his hands together. Enough of the reunion chatter. The priestess must have sent Thracius and Anchises to Tivoli for a reason. "What news from Rome?" he asked Anchises.

"The priestess wonders why you have not written to her as of late."

"I responded to the last letter I received from her," said Ankhu. "That was over a month ago."

Anchises furrowed his brow. "She has written more recently. It is possible the last letter she sent was intercepted."

"By Soren?" asked Scorpus.

"In the worst case, yes," said Anchises.

"What about the messenger, Sextus?" asked Ankhu.

"He hasn't reported to the priestess," Anchises replied. "And since you're asking the question, I'll assume you haven't seen him either."

Ankhu shook his head. "The last time I saw him, he was on his horse heading to Rome with a scroll. I will tell you this, though: Sextus is a very capable slave and quite incorruptible. He would not have betrayed the priestess to Soren, at least not voluntarily. Nor did he know Scorpus's true identity." Ankhu walked deeper into the stable, opened a gate, and grasped the halter of a tall white horse. "I will ride out along the Via Tiburtina and find out what I can. You stay here." He looked at Anchises and Thracius. "Eat. Rest. You will start back for Rome as soon as I return."

Ankhu walked his horse into the open, finished saddling it, and mounted. He rode off quickly without another word and without looking back.

Scorpus watched him leave and then turned to Anchises and Thracius. "We should not delay any longer," he said. "I don't know what the priestess is waiting for. I could kill Soren on the street tomorrow. Even Ankhu knows I'm right, but the man doesn't have the balls to cross his mistress. And look at you, Thracius. I can tell by your face that you agree with me."

"Soren is no fool," said Anchises. "Whether or not he has read the priestess's letter, whether or not he has confirmation that you live, he nonetheless takes constant precautions. If he isn't in the company of Tiberius's guards, he is being trailed by his own bodyguard slaves. Anyway, killing him is only half the priestess's problem. She must have the child's true parentage legally recognized if she is to adopt her. Soren has to be alive for that."

"What do we care of the child?" asked Scorpus. He stared at Anchises.

"That day we spoke in secret in the market, after the priestess had bought you . . . you said we could trust her, that she would know what to do and that she hated Soren as much as we did. You told me about Thracius's burns, which by the way are even more revolting than you described, and you vowed vengeance. Now you talk of children?" He grabbed the fabric of Anchises's tunica. "Perhaps fine living has sapped whatever manhood you had."

It was a good two or three minutes until Scorpus began to regain consciousness. Anchises was kneeling beside him as he lay sprawled on the ground, Thracius angrily pacing a few steps away, shaking the sting from his fist.

"Wake up, you idiot," said Anchises.

The charioteer sat up and rubbed his head. He tried to get his legs under him, but it took Anchises's help to get him to his feet again.

"Let's go into the kitchen," said Scorpus, dazed but trying to appear coherent. "I'm supposed to feed you."

The three of them walked toward Pomponia's country home which, as Anchises and Thracius had expected, was nearly as opulent as the House of the Vestals, with a sprawling but well-tended, colorful garden and an octagonal pool with low marble statues of birds and fish all around it.

The Vestal had lived here during her years of service at the temple in Tivoli, and Anchises knew that she had at one time considered retiring here with Quintina's father. She had revealed the secret to him on one of their intimate evening walks through the Forum. As far as Anchises knew, he was the only man other than Ankhu that the priestess had trusted enough to tell.

Instead of entering the home through the colonnaded front portico, Scorpus, in what seemed like an uncharacteristic act of humility, entered through the slave door. It opened near the kitchen, where a female slave was dismembering some kind of small animal and dropping its parts into a boiling pot on the brick oven. She looked at Scorpus, and he jabbed his thumb at their guests.

The three men sat around an oblong wooden table as the slave set food and drink out for them: pork, olives, cheese, bread, and wine. When she was done, Scorpus pointed to the door, and she left.

"This wine is delicious," said Anchises through a full mouth.

"Thank you," said Scorpus.

"He compliments the wine," said Thracius, "not you."

"Let off, Thracius," scolded Anchises.

The singer emptied his wine cup and then reached across the table for the spouted amphora of wine to refill it. Scorpus pointed at the scar on Anchises's forearm.

"You used to have Bassus's tattoo there, no?"

"You know I did," Anchises answered. "And you know who removed it. Why must you instigate?"

"Cassandra was crucified."

Thracius shifted his eyes to Scorpus but said nothing. Anchises pushed himself back in his chair. "We know."

"And my friend Pomponius was murdered. Both of their deaths are on me." Scorpus pulled off his Egyptian wig to reveal his smoothly shaved head.

Anchises stared into his cup. He couldn't deny that it was Scorpus's impetuous rescue attempt that had triggered the servile law and resulted in the crucifixion of Soren's entire household of slaves, including Cassandra.

Unexpectedly, Thracius broke the silence. "I can see how you would think that." He stuffed a handful of black olives in his mouth, tonguing for the pits and then picking them out of his mouth as he spoke. "I wanted to escape from the ludus and free Anchises. I didn't want to think about what Soren was doing to him, yet it was the only thing I could think about. One of the guards"—he glanced at Anchises and then back at Scorpus—"one of the guards, he was maybe sixteen, he liked to be my boy while I was there. I told him we would run off together if he helped me break out."

"You never told me this," said Anchises.

"I'm telling you now," Thracius replied. "One night, he got the other guards drunk and brought the key to my cell. He opened it. I didn't know my way out, especially not in the dark, so I let him lead me. We made it to the second gate before we got caught." He chewed soberly at the memory. "Don't ask me why, but I didn't take so much as a single lash for it. But the boy . . ."

"What happened to him?" prompted Scorpus.

"They hung him by his wrists from the ceiling, just outside my cell."

Thracius spat out the last olive seed. "Then they flayed him alive. His skin came off in four big pieces, right to the muscle. He was just red meat hanging there. He didn't look any different from a cow shank hanging in the market with the flies crawling all over it. I stayed on my knees and prayed to Pluto to take him sooner. I don't know if it did any good. He lived about an hour."

Anchises pressed his palms into the tabletop, processing what he was hearing. Scorpus rested his elbows on the table to hear more.

Thracius took another handful of olives and continued. "Was it my fault he was killed? I didn't want him to die. I liked him well enough." He leaned across the table until he was nearly nose-to-nose with Scorpus. "But the Fates cut his thread, not me. The guards in the ludus skinned him, not me. I'm not to blame. It's the same with Cassandra and your friend Pomponius. It is only the Fates and Soren's cruelty that are to blame."

The men sat for a long time in silence, Scorpus ruminating on Thracius's words. Pomponia's wine was much-needed medicine, and one by one, they each put their heads down on the table and fell fast asleep where they sat.

They were awoken hours later by Ankhu's return. He walked straight to the brick oven and pulled a piece of meat from the pot on it, talking while he ate.

"What do you want first," he asked, "the good news or the bad news?"

"The bad," said Scorpus.

"Sextus is dead."

Scorpus muttered an obscenity. "What's the good news?"

"Soren didn't do it." Ankhu waved a meaty bone at Scorpus. "When we first left Rome through the Porta Tiburtina, do you remember that toothless soldier who warned us about a gang of marauders around the Altar to Proserpina?"

Scorpus thought back. "He said they were hiding in a herd of sheep."

Ankhu nodded. "Well, it looks like they grazed on our messenger." When no one acknowledged his cleverness, he went on. "I spoke to a legionary posted near the altar. He told me that after they'd killed all but one of the bandits, the last one started talking. He led them to a big pit into which they'd been rolling their victims after they robbed them. The soldier took me to it. I found Sextus in it."

"How can you be sure it was him?" asked Scorpus.

Ankhu looked at the meat in his hand as if it had suddenly turned rancid. "He's looked better, but it was him. I could see his ownership tattoo and his clubfoot. The man couldn't walk in a straight line to save his life, but he could ride a horse like Bellerophon on the back of Pegasus. It's too bad."

"That's a measure of relief," said Anchises. "But what about the scroll?"

"The scroll had the seal of the Vestalis Maxima on it," said Ankhu. "Anyone caught with it illegally, whether the seal was broken or not, would be executed. I'd bet the bandits either burned it or buried it just to get rid of it. With the recent rains, it would be illegible by now, even if someone did find it."

Thracius stood up. "I'll go ready the horses," he said to Anchises. He left the kitchen and exited the house through the slave door, heading back to the stable.

Ankhu sighed and leaned against the wall. He raised his eyebrows at Scorpus in an expression that said, *Go do something. I want to talk to Anchises alone.* Scorpus put his wig on his head, straightened his linen skirt, and left the two men to speak in private.

"What are you really thinking?" Anchises asked Ankhu.

"There's every reason to feel reassured," said Ankhu. "These kinds of things happen on the road."

"But?"

"But I hate not knowing what became of the scroll." The Egyptian sat down tiredly beside Anchises and wiped his greasy fingers on a cloth.

"You'll hate this even more," said Anchises. "Soren plans to buy the property next to this villa." Anchises put his hand out to calm Ankhu, who was already halfway out of his chair. "The priestess wants you to purchase the property for her first. She says to offer whatever you must."

"*Insanos Deos!*" Ankhu said groaningly. "The man is possessed."

Anchises lowered his voice. "He's sending his mistress to buy the estate for him. Her name is Aelina. She's a miserable excuse for a woman and the widow of Scorpus's previous owner. When her husband died, she sold Scorpus and Cassandra to Soren."

"Scorpus is not so unlike Soren," said Ankhu. "Both are possessed by the spirit of vengeance. I will tell you, Anchises, that I love Priestess Pomponia. I consider it my duty to protect her, and I would give my life for her."

"I know you would."

"She trusts you," Ankhu continued, "so I trust you. But I do not trust Scorpus, and I will protect my mistress even if it means disobeying her."

"You're talking about killing Scorpus, aren't you?"

"It's what I wanted to do the first time I laid eyes on the man," said the Egyptian. "I know you have a history with him, and I know that he has suffered unjustly. But my loyalty is to the priestess. I need to know that you feel the same way. That you would do whatever it takes to protect her."

"You can be assured that I would."

Ankhu squeezed Anchises's shoulder in solidarity. "Let's hope it doesn't come to that. Now, let's finish our business so you can set out. Come with me."

The men continued to talk quietly as Ankhu led Anchises deeper into Pomponia's luxurious home and into a large study, much larger even than the Vestal's office in Rome. Its high walls were painted a deep blue and decorated with beautifully intricate frescoes depicting the signs of the zodiac.

Two signs in particular stood out to Anchises. The first was Virgo—the Virgin. The sixth sign of the zodiac, it happened to parallel the six Vestal Virgins that guarded the sacred fire.

The second sign that now held special meaning to him was Gemini—the heroic twins Castor and Pollux. Their temple stood only steps away from Vesta's temple in the Forum. It was his favorite temple to walk past on his nightly strolls with the priestess.

"I painted these murals," said Ankhu, noticing Anchises's interest. "I also painted the Egyptian zodiac in the library. Next time you are here, I will show you." He stood on a stool and reached up to pull a curled map out of a pigeonhole shelf, then rolled it open on Pomponia's desk. It was a map of the Vestal's villa and surrounding properties.

Anchises put his finger on the map. "This is the one he is going to purchase."

"Not if I can help it," said Ankhu. He studied the map silently, thoughts flying through his head. Finally, he rolled it back up. "Let's get you on the road," he said.

They walked purposefully back through the house and out the slave door, arriving at the stable just as Thracius was double-checking his horse's throatlatch. Scorpus was doing the same for Anchises's horse.

Thracius and Anchises mounted their horses as Scorpus moved to stand beside Ankhu. "May the gods go with you," said the charioteer.

"I don't know what gods you mean anymore," Thracius said good-humoredly. "Roman or Egyptian?"

"It doesn't matter," replied Scorpus. "They probably aren't listening anyway."

Satisfied they had mended the worst of their wounds, Thracius grinned down at Scorpus before quickly turning his horse and taking it to a quick canter back to the road at the edge of Pomponia's property. Anchises followed closely behind.

There was plenty of light left, and although they were both tired, they could still make it to Rome. The priestess would be wondering and worrying. That was worse than them being tired.

They rode in silence for nearly a mile, the only sounds being the chirping of birds and the clip-clopping of their horses' hooves on the Via Tiburtina.

The whole while, Anchises had fixed his eyes on the back of Thracius's head. Finally, he forced himself to ask the question that had been burning inside him for hours.

"Why did you never tell me about the boy?" he shouted ahead to Thracius.

"What boy?" Thracius called back to him.

"The boy in the ludus."

The boxer chuckled. "You're not the only one who can put on a performance," he said. He turned his head to look back at Anchises. "There was no boy."

CHAPTER XV

Et Sceleratis Sol Oritur
The sun shines even on the wicked.

—SENECA

ROME

The carved and gold-inlaid wooden doors of Caesar's library opened from the inside and Tiberius stepped into the antechamber, where Soren was waiting. Soren quickly stood.

"Come in," said Tiberius.

Trying to control his nerves—why had Tiberius summoned him so suddenly to Caesar's home?—Soren walked rigidly across the mosaic floor.

Caesar was sitting at his desk. When he saw Soren, he shook his head. Soren set his jaw. It was just as he feared. Caesar had somehow heard the seditious rumblings of certain senators—murderous rumblings that Soren himself had started.

His mind began to work: What to say in defense? How to deny it? Should he implicate the empress, or would that only make matters worse?

"Sit," said Tiberius.

Soren sat on a couch against the wall.

"I have too often trusted the wrong men," began Tiberius.

"Sir, it is not—"

Tiberius put up his hand. "I will speak. I have too often trusted the wrong men," he began again. "I have had false friends. These were men who used their friendship with me only for their own gain, not caring about my authority or reputation as Caesar's heir." He picked a scroll off Caesar's desk and handed it to Soren.

Soren uncurled the papyrus and read:

My dear sister Quintina,

After you left, I waited up for Soren. He finally returned home but of course had Aelina with him. She does not even bother to hide her disdain for me and neither does my own husband. You are right that Aelina is a disappointment to him, though, as I heard him chastise her for drinking too much in front of the empress. He still took her to bed, however, which made me nearly tear my hair out.

It is true that the child living under his roof is not his own. She is the child of the chief Vestal's brother, Pomponius. Soren knows. At first, he wanted to raise her, but now he seems to hate me for it, and I think he hates Calidia too. He made me put my hand in the fire to prove my loyalty to him.

I want nothing more than to regain Soren's love and devotion. I dream of giving him a son, his own son, and going to all the finest parties with him. I think I should come and stay at your house for a while. It is a wise bit of advice that he needs to miss me before he can long for me again.

Do not respond to me by a letter, as Soren reads my correspondence before I do. It is best that you simply make the arrangements and send for me.

Your loving sister, Tacita

Soren gripped the papyrus so tightly that it began to tear. His hands were trembling. From what? he wondered. Fear? Rage? Shock?

Tiberius took the scroll from his hands and then placed it back on Caesar's desk. "Soren?" he said quizzically.

Soren said nothing. His fists were clenched so tightly that his knuckles blanched.

Suddenly, he felt Tiberius's hand on his shoulder. He expected the man to squeeze it, to shout for the guards, to have him dragged by the toga out of the library and to the Carcer, but none of it happened. Instead, Tiberius's hand patted him supportively.

"Priestess Quintina brought this letter to me the moment she received it from her sister," said Tiberius. He sat next to Soren on the couch. "As much as I have valued our friendship over these last months, I can see that I have nonetheless underestimated it. It appears that you have been tolerating an adulterous wife out of friendship for me, to avoid bringing any scandal to my circle." Tiberius sighed. "I mean no disrespect to your daughter, Caesar," he said to Octavian, "but it was shameful to be associated with an adulterous wife. It hurt my credibility in the Senate and with the people." He looked at Soren. "You have been raising another man's child, living with a promiscuous wife, all to spare me the embarrassment of again being associated with scandal. That is the type of man that Caesar's heir needs by his side. I will never forget the sacrifice you were willing to make for me."

Soren shook his head. Then he nodded. "It was no sacrifice," he said. He hoped the fire of hatred in his stomach, the one that burned for that traitorous little tramp Tacita, didn't show on his face.

Octavian rocked back on his chair until its wooden legs squeaked on the mosaic floor. "This kind of behavior on the part of a well-bred Roman matron is becoming all too common," he said. "I ask you, what could be a greater insult, what could be more unnatural to a man, than raising another man's child?"

Tiberius nodded in agreement, hoping Caesar wouldn't make the connection: he had largely raised Tiberius, although coldly and begrudgingly. But those days were behind them now. Mostly.

"This is why I drafted my morality legislation," Octavian continued. He tapped his finger on the armrest of his chair. "For this exact situation. Think about it. Women can be crafty. When their bellies grow with pregnancy, how can a husband know for certain whether the child inside is his?"

"He cannot know," said Tiberius. "She may say it is his, but it may in fact be his friend's. Or his brother's. Or his neighbor's."

"Or even his slave's," added Octavian. "There is no way to know. That is why women must face stiffer punishments for adultery than men. Otherwise, a man from a noble Roman family risks bastardizing his bloodline without even knowing it. Did you know that Romulus passed a law similar to mine? He knew how important it is to protect true Roman bloodlines."

Tiberius poured a cup of wine and handed it to Soren. Soren squeezed the gold cup tightly, then took a sip, another sip, and finally downed the rest of the drink in one swallow.

"That's how it's done," said Caesar. "Good man." He let his chair drop back on all four legs. "You won't take offense to this, Soren"—it was an order as much as an observation—"but your wife's behavior is of no surprise to me." He didn't say it, but Soren knew what he meant: Tacita had briefly enjoyed the celebrity of being one of Caesar's lovers.

Tiberius stood with an abruptness that indicated the meeting was over. Soren also stood.

"I've taken care of things for you," said Tiberius. "It's the least I can do to repay your loyalty. I've already had a magistrate formalize a divorce, and your former wife and her child have been removed from your home. Guardianship of the child will be transferred to the high priestess. All is being done with the greatest of discretion. You are a free man."

Tiberius escorted Soren to the doors of the library. Once there, Soren turned to face the two men. "Thank you, Tiberius." He bowed to Octavian. "Hail, Caesar."

Soren stepped into the antechamber and watched the heavy wooden doors of the library close behind him. He imagined how happy, how relieved Pomponia would be, how victorious she would feel when the baby was delivered into her arms. She would assume that he had lost his power over her.

She couldn't be more wrong, thought Soren. He stood straighter as his rage faded and the reality set in. *The next emperor of Rome just poured me a cup of wine.*

CHAPTER XVI

Dies Nefasti
The forbidden days

Pomponia knew that she could be a little on the authoritarian side. She knew that her sister Vestals were as competent, knowledgeable, and devoted to their duty as she was, but nonetheless she often found it hard to delegate or to let them do their work without oversight. The exception was the elder Nona, to whom Pomponia had always deferred. But Nona was in Carthage.

She also knew that although the novices liked her, they tended to gravitate toward other priestesses—Caecilia, Lucretia, Marcella, and especially Quintina—when they had a request they wanted a definite *yes* in answer to, whether it was asking for a second piece of honey cake or asking to participate in a rite or ritual they were not fully qualified for. They saw their chief Vestal as someone who never bent the rules.

If they only knew, she thought.

But Pomponia was proud of herself this evening for what she saw as a personal breakthrough: she had let Quintina decide when and how to move Vesta's living flame from the shrine at Caesar's home back to its true home in the Forum. And why not? Quintina had transported the fire in the worst of conditions, blending proper rites with her own panicked resourcefulness. The goddess favored her. Pomponia wasn't about to challenge that.

The way Quintina had chosen to fulfill the task said a lot about her relationship with the goddess. Instead of employing pomp or public ceremony,

Quintina had decided to make the occasion a humble, reverent, and private one between the goddess and her priestesses, including the novices.

Although Vestal rites usually took place at dawn or at midday to honor the life-giving light of the sun—Vesta's fire in the sky—Quintina had chosen twilight as the time to carry the bronze bowl that contained the sacred flame out of the shrine, through Caesar's gardens, down the Palatine ramp, through the House of the Vestals, and back into the temple.

The mild weather, abundant kindling, and the repaired handles on the firebowl all soothed the memory of that day when she had traveled the same path in the other direction—desperate, in pain, terrified.

The Forum was still and quiet, having been closed to the public hours ago. The only sounds were the Vestals' murmured prayers, the snapping of the fire, and the chirping of some sparrows hopping along the cobblestone, searching for a few more insects before settling into their nests for the night.

As Caecilia and Lucretia opened the doors to the temple, Quintina ascended the marble steps followed by Pomponia. Above them was the dome of the temple's new bronze roof, strong and lovely. Above that, the setting sun colored the sky in vast glowing swaths of orange and blue that canopied the great Roman Forum and stretched to the horizon.

Quintina and Pomponia entered the circular sanctum. It was lit by flickering oil lamps affixed to the walls and felt unusually cool without the sacred fire to heat the space.

Cossinia, Marcella, Lucasta, and twelve novice priestesses all moved to stand around the new round marble pedestal which would cradle the firebowl: the previous pedestal had been cracked beyond repair during the collapse. All held their palms up to the goddess as Caecilia and Lucretia closed the doors and joined them.

"*Vesta, permitte hanc actionem,*" said Quintina. She set the bronze bowl of fire atop the pedestal and then raised her palms as well.

Lucasta handed Pomponia a terracotta tray upon which lay very thin strips of wood that had been previously anointed. Pomponia held the tray out and each of the priestesses took a strip of the wood, setting it gently on the sacred fire in turn.

The second to last priestess to place her kindling on the fire was the novice Varinia, still recovering from the loss of her mother. Pomponia saw the wonder and reverence on the girl's face as she performed the rite. It was a sudden reminder to her that, despite the many cares and conflicts of the world, communing with Mother Vesta's divine presence offered profound comfort and peace.

Last, it was the turn of the Vestalis Maxima. Lucasta took the terracotta plate from Pomponia's hands, and the chief Vestal whispered a prayer to the goddess as she set the remaining wood strip on the hearth fire.

With Vesta's fire once again burning in the Aedes Vestae as it had for centuries, Pomponia smoothed the back of Quintina's veil. "The goddess is home," she said. "Thanks to you."

"She's not the only one we bring home this day," Quintina said, and smiled.

At that, the novice Varinia clasped her hands together and looked up at Pomponia. "May we go see little Pomponia now?"

Little Pomponia.

Formerly little Calidia.

Since the chief Vestal's lightning-strike adoption of her brother Pomponius's daughter that very morning—a special case approved by the emperor himself—the child now carried the same name as Pomponia, that being the feminized version of her family's noble name.

Pomponia rubbed Varinia's head. "Yes, please do. Let's make her feel at home."

When the novices had left the temple, Pomponia put her hands on her hips and craned her neck up to look at the new domed roof. The embossed rosettes in the bronze were a beautiful new feature, and smoke from the hearth fire was already curling up toward the oculus, slipping out to travel upward, toward the heavens. "It is even lovelier than the last one," she said.

Lucretia glanced up, her head cocked sideways. "It looks heavier than the last one, that's for sure," she said. "Let's hope Jupiter doesn't drop this one on me."

Pomponia gently touched Lucretia's hands. They still showed the deep but healing wounds she had received when the roof had collapsed. "He wouldn't dare."

Because Lucretia and Caecilia had been the two Vestals on watch during the storm and the roof's collapse, Pomponia felt it would best please the goddess if they were the two priestesses to perform the first watch under the new roof. It would bring a sense of consistency and completion to their duties.

And so the other priestesses filed out of the temple and back into the house, dispersing to attend to their other duties, visit the new baby in the house, or simply rest before their own watches.

Quintina waited at the bottom of the steps for Pomponia. "Are you coming to see our niece?"

"Nothing could stop me. But I'll let the crowd thin out first," she said as she smiled broadly. She pointed over Quintina's shoulder to where Anchises was waiting for her. "I will take my walk with Anchises and then meet you inside."

"I wish we could have her to ourselves," said Quintina. "Without Tacita around, I mean." Her voice took on an irritable tone at the thought of her sister. "Maybe I'll have one of the slaves lock her in her room."

"She will be gone soon enough," said Pomponia. "I have a few nurses for us to interview. Once you and I agree on one, I can make other arrangements for Tacita."

"Like what?"

"Leave it to me," said Pomponia. "I'll see you inside."

Pomponia joined Anchises where he stood leaning against a low iron and marble railing that ran around part of the Regia. He was staring up into the darkening sky, watching the smoke billow out of the temple's opening and wisp away.

"The sunset colors make for an auspicious evening, don't you think?" she asked.

"Orange and blue," replied Anchises. "The colors of fire." He pushed himself off the railing, and they began their evening walk as they often did, strolling along the cobblestone toward the Temple of Julius Caesar, as the color overhead started to fade into the dark, starry canopy of the night sky. After they had walked far enough to ensure privacy, he turned to her with a knowing look. "You can relax now."

She let her shoulders drop, but a loud sound of metal on metal made both of them jump, and they turned to see a group of ten or twelve workmen huddled around the entrance to the Cloaca Maxima near the Temple of Castor and Pollux, hammering away at something. Although the men had been ordered to stop working while the Vestals brought the sacred flame home, they were now back at it. They worked around the clock, in the heat of the day and then by torchlight at night.

"Gods, I wish that were done," said Pomponia. "It'll keep the baby up."

"It keeps old people like us up," Anchises replied. "Little Pomponia would sleep through the ascension of Romulus. But it isn't the sound that's been troubling you."

"No, it isn't."

Anchises offered his arm, and Pomponia hooked hers around it. She had dreamed for months of bringing her niece home to live under the loving protection of herself and Quintina. She had found her thoughts flying off, fantasizing about claiming the child as her own adopted kin and calling her by her true name of Pomponia. She had imagined, again and again, the moment that she could fulfill her vow to Vesta and raise the girl to serve the goddess.

But the truth and the unexpected way it had all come about had shattered the perfect fantasy. The occasion of her niece's homecoming was not colored with the joy or relief that she had always assumed it would be. Her ongoing uncertainties and conflict with Soren had caused what should have been a monumental event in her life to seem somehow anticlimactic and unfinished.

And unsettling.

Soren would be as mad as the Minotaur.

"I know Quintina thought she was doing the right thing," said Pomponia. "I just wish she had consulted me. I almost cannot believe she didn't."

"She was trying to surprise you," said Anchises. "And please you."

"I know, but it's not like her to take such action without talking to me."

"She's always lived in your shadow. That's changing now. She was the one who took action, on her own, to save the fire. Perhaps it's emboldened her to act more independently. Did you not have to do the same when Fabiana was chief Vestal?"

"Yes, but things are more complicated now."

"Quintina didn't know that," said Anchises. "She has no idea that Soren has been any kind of personal threat to you. Nor does she know about Scorpus. As far as she knows, the only issue was getting Tacita to admit the baby's true father. To her, that problem is now solved."

"Solving that problem is like cutting off the Hydra's head," said Pomponia. "Two more will grow back in its place. Soren will be looking for a way to retaliate."

"And we will deal with that when the time comes," Anchises replied. "Like Hercules, we'll cut off all the heads and singe the stumps."

They strolled along the cobblestone of the torch-lined street with the arches of the two-story Basilica Aemilia on their right. The basilica's guards called out friendly hellos, and they returned them, as they did almost every night. They kept walking, past the Lacus Curtius on their left and the Curia on their right, toward the Rostra and the golden Eagle that perched high above and gazed down on the Forum with the confidence and splendor of a god.

Pomponia stopped walking and folded her arms in front of her. She looked up at the Capitoline Hill above them and the great temples that seemed to hang in the sky. The greatest of these was the Temple of Jupiter Optimus Maximus, its colossal columns and crowning statue of Jupiter riding in a four-horse chariot illuminated by firebowls that burned below. Within the temple were massive cellae dedicated to the god's wife, Juno, and his daughter Minerva, the three of them making up the Capitoline Triad.

Pomponia chewed her lip as she gazed up. "I know there's probably nothing to worry about," she said to Anchises. "From what Ankhu said, my messenger Sextus really was killed by bandits. It is likely the letter is no more."

"But . . ." prompted Anchises.

"But I wish I knew for sure."

Anchises instinctively looked around himself. Although they were alone, he still lowered his voice. "Ankhu is a wise man. Maybe we should do what he advises and kill Scorpus. Give Soren what he wants so that—"

"Scorpus saw the face of my brother's killer," Pomponia interrupted. "He's the only one who can identify him."

"I knew you'd say that," said Anchises. "Here's what I can't figure out, though. If Soren does know you're harboring Scorpus, why hasn't he just had Tiberius send some *legionarii* to arrest him? Scorpus is still a fugitive. He could capture him and disgrace you at the same time."

"Soren knows that if he goes to Tiberius, I'll go to Caesar and accuse him of killing my brother," said Pomponia. "Then Caesar will order an official investigation . . ." She shook her head. "No, he doesn't want that kind of attention right now. After this whole scandal with Tacita, he can't afford any more personal drama if he wants to stay close to Tiberius. If he does know, he'll wait until he's in a better position before he does anything."

"Well, whether he knows about Scorpus or not, you're correct that he will seek some kind of retribution. He will think you were behind his divorce from Tacita."

"He hated Tacita," said Pomponia, "and no doubt he hated the baby too. Now that they're gone and he's an important man in Tiberius's circle, maybe he'll be content with that."

Anchises pictured himself sitting in his squalid little room in Soren's basement. He remembered well the dread of hearing his former master's angry footfalls on the dirt floor and the way the slaves all scattered and fell silent. "Maybe," he said, unconvinced.

They began to walk again, soon passing the Rostra and stopping in front of an unusual round monument. It was an old structure, even for the Forum, and had been rebuilt and restored many times. For the last several months, the monument had been hidden by scaffolding, but now Anchises could get a good look at its most recent form. It had a barrel-like base of multitone green marble and a domed roof made of rare sky-blue marble tiles. At its apex was a golden orb, upon which stood a statue of Romulus.

"This is the Umbilicus Urbis," said Pomponia. "It's the navel of Rome." She gestured to the nearby Milliarium Aureum, the Golden Milestone. "All roads in the empire lead here." She took a few more steps and pointed to a low door in the monument's round base. "Right through that door is the Mundus, an underground pit covered with a stone. When Romulus founded Rome, he welcomed people from different tribes. Each would throw a handful of soil from their homeland into it so that Rome would be home to all. The best fruits of the season were also thrown in as sacrifice to the gods of the harvest, who live below the earth, where the seeds take root. There is a shrine down there now."

"Can we go inside?" asked Anchises.

"Even if you could, you would not want to," said Pomponia. "The Mundus is the gate to the underworld. Only priests of Pluto, and sometimes the priestesses of Proserpina and Ceres, are permitted to enter." She pulled her palla around herself. "Priestesses of Vesta are certainly not allowed." She gave him a humorless smile. "Which is fine with us. Vestals are never eager to go underground."

"What a dreary place," said Anchises.

"Not so," said Pomponia. "The Mundus reminds us that life and death are just two parts of the same monument. At some point, we all pass through the door."

Fireflies flitted in the space around them, making it look as starry as the sky above. "Our evenings always take a philosophical turn, don't they?" Anchises said wryly.

"Oh, it gets better," Pomponia continued. "Three times a year, we have a ritual where the Mundus is opened. That allows the spirits of the dead to enter the living world. It is forbidden to do official business on these days. People won't marry or travel or even couple, lest a woman conceive. It's bad luck."

"Well, we don't need any bad luck," said Anchises. The mention of dark spirits and looming misfortune had suddenly turned his thoughts back to Soren and the trepidation of what might happen next. How would Soren respond to losing custody of the child? Had he read Pomponia's letter? Did he know about Scorpus? If so, when and how would he strike?

The singer looked at Pomponia's face and could see by the flickering light of the torches that she was thinking the same thing.

The waiting was the hardest part.

"Take heart, Anchises," said Pomponia. "We won't have to wait long to see what Soren has in store for us."

"Why do you say that?"

The Vestal gazed thoughtfully at the door to the Mundus. "Because the gate to hell opens tomorrow."

CHAPTER XVII

Ex Africa Semper Aliquid Novi
There is always something new out of Africa.

—PLINY THE ELDER

It was the only Roman religious ritual that was performed during the dead of night: the thrice-yearly opening of the Mundus.

Despite the ceremony being held at *media nox*—midnight—a black canopy had been erected over the monument of the Umbilicus Urbis and the Mundus that lay below it. Hades was dark, much darker than even the darkest night, and so the priests of Pluto were careful to ease the journey of those spirits who emerged from the underworld. Perhaps the gesture would please the god of death.

Pluto. The most disliked god, and yet the only one who was assured to personally appear in the life of every mortal. But when? And how? Would he take a father first or his son? It was those uncertainties more than the certainty of death itself that seemed to weigh on most people. To make matters worse, there was no bartering with this god.

In fact, only one being had ever managed to negotiate with Pluto, and that being was herself a goddess: Ceres, the goddess of grain and the harvest. And she was a strong negotiator indeed.

Every Roman knew the story. It happened long ago when Ceres's daughter, the lovely Proserpina, was walking through a field of flowers on a sunny day. It was all sun then, for there were no dark seasons.

Pluto saw her, fell in love with her, and abducted her. He took her to the underworld to rule by his side as his queen.

But neither the mother nor the daughter cared for the appointment. Distraught and grief-stricken at the abduction of her daughter, Ceres went to Jupiter. "Order Pluto to release my daughter," she demanded. "If you do not, I will forbid the fields to bloom. There will be famine. Humans and animals will die, and you will have no one to honor you, no one to sacrifice to you."

At first, Jupiter did not listen. But as the months went by, the earth fell into winter, and the crops withered. People and animals despaired and died. So the father of the gods reconsidered. He spoke to Pluto and told him of Ceres's actions. The god of the underworld relented. Sort of.

It was agreed that Proserpina would live in the upper world with her mother for part of the year: this became the spring and summer, when Ceres rejoiced and filled the fields with vibrant life.

But for the rest of the year, Proserpina would rule with her husband as queen of the underworld: that time became autumn and winter, when Ceres wept, and the land became as dreary as she.

Pomponia stood well back from the door to the Mundus and gripped a torch that burned with the sacred fire of Vesta, Pluto's divine sister. Octavian stood next to her in his capacity as Pontifex Maximus, draped in his priestly toga. Like Pomponia and the other priests present, he performed his duties *capite velato*, with his head covered.

Caeso, Publius, and eight centurions formed two lines of five men each in front of the pontiffs, symbolically ready to defend them from whatever evil spirits emerged.

Before them, three priests of Pluto stood with their heads down near the door to the Mundus, murmuring incantations to the dark gods. The priestesses of Proserpina and Ceres, as well as a number of officials, stood nearby. Although the Forum itself was closed to the public, people outside its stone walls prayed softly to the spirits of departed loved ones, hoping to commune with them once the underworld was opened.

A meaty black pig with flowers wrapped around its belly—a pretty gift for Proserpina—was led to Pomponia. As were all sacrificial animals, it was tame and content. Caesar held the priestess's torch while she crumbled a sacred wafer over the animal's head. "*Vesta te purificat.*"

The pig lifted its head and tried to nibble Pomponia's stola, but a priest of Pluto pulled the animal away, back to the Mundus.

As one priest held the pig, another approached the entrance to the Mundus, careful not to trip in the dark over the low marble altar that sat just before it. He slipped a large key into the thick wooden door and unlocked it with an audible *clunk*.

It was a sound that those present had heard countless times and at countless doors. And yet the sound at this particular door was somehow different.

The priest entered the Mundus, moving aside the stone that covered the underground cavity. He emerged again and took two steps back, allowing the spirits to exit the underworld. He stepped back also to avoid the strange smell that always emanated from the Mundus when it was opened: a foul smell that the priests said was the breath of Cerberus, the three-headed dog that guarded the entrance to Hades.

After several moments, the priest stepped forward again and spoke into the Mundus. "Illustrious king, whose realm waits below the firm and solid ground, home to all. Mighty Pluto, all-receiver, whose domain brings forth death and rebirth, permit your faithful priests to offer this sacrifice."

At that, the black pig was led to the low marble altar near the door. As it had been trained to do, it stepped onto the altar and stood waiting for its reward, which on this occasion, came swiftly in the form of a slit throat. The animal collapsed, and the priests quickly maneuvered its head so that its blood drained down into the shrine of the Mundus.

The priests murmured more secret words to accompany the rites and then turned to the Pontifex Maximus, nodding.

It was now time for everyone except the priests of Pluto to leave; it was the task of the three remaining priests to descend into the underground shrine and clean the blood once enough of it had streamed down. They would remain at the Mundus throughout the night and the coming day, during which time the door would be left open.

It would only be the following evening, at the moment of sunset, that the priests of Pluto would set a bowl of pomegranate seeds by the entrance to entice the dark spirits back inside, and then close the door to again seal the world below from the world above.

As the gathering dispersed, Pomponia headed back to her lectica, which was waiting for her just by the Golden Milestone. A number of other lecticae were also waiting, including those of Tiberius and Soren. Tiberius waved a friendly good night to her as he stepped into his, but her chest tightened to see the senators Murena and Caepio stepping into Soren's.

She slowed her step as she passed by to see whether anyone else was with them. Just then, Soren emerged from the darkness behind her. How had she not sensed he was on her heels?

"Priestess Pomponia," he said. He stood solidly beside her, compelling her to stop as well.

Caeso walked over from her waiting lectica. He hadn't trusted Soren since that first day the man had come to the House of the Vestals to plead for his bed slave's life. The Vestal's guard was on edge whenever the man was near Pomponia.

Soren eyed Caeso smugly. He lifted his chin and spoke to Pomponia. "A word in private, Priestess?"

"I'm afraid I cannot allow that," Caeso asserted.

The look of smugness on Soren's face only intensified. He knew what Pomponia would say.

"It's all right, Caeso," said Pomponia. She began to walk along the street to a more private spot, but Soren walked toward her lectica.

"Let's speak in here," he said.

Caeso put his hand on the dagger at his side. "Absolutely not," he said. It wasn't just the danger of what might happen behind the closed curtains that troubled the guard, it was also the appearance of impropriety. That was just as dangerous to the Vestal. "You may speak outside," he said to Soren.

Pomponia looked around. Caesar and Tiberius had left, as had almost everyone else. The only people who remained were the priests of Pluto by the Mundus and the senators in Soren's lectica.

The priests were not a problem. They would not think twice of the chief Vestal consulting with Tiberius's right-hand man. But the senators in Soren's lectica were another matter. Their sudden friendship with Soren, and by extension Livia, gave her stomach-churning anxiety. They could not be trusted.

Yet she had little choice. Turning Soren away was even riskier than speaking with him. She strode to her lectica, pulled the curtain back herself, and stepped inside. "Come in," she said to Soren.

"Priestess," said Caeso, "I must—"

"Stand guard," snapped Pomponia. "Do your job."

The guard pressed his lips together and moved to join Publius, who seemed as irritated as he about the situation. Caeso fixed his eyes on the lectica as Soren stepped in and closed the curtain behind him. Publius continued to scan the quiet Forum for any threats.

Soren sat across from Pomponia and examined the dim interior of the Vestal's lectica. He said nothing but tapped on one of the fading oil lamps affixed to an interior wall and its flame flared up again. Pomponia wished it hadn't. She didn't care to see his face any clearer.

"What is your business, Soren?" she asked.

He leaned back to emphasize that he was in no hurry. "I had a very good sleep last night," he said. "It's quiet in the house without that bloody baby crying."

"She sleeps well enough in our house."

"I know what is in your letters," Soren said bluntly. "You place too much trust in slave messengers, Pomponia."

Even as she felt herself break into a cold sweat at the revelation, even as she felt herself bristle at the impious use of her name, Pomponia began to run through her options.

How soon could she send Anchises and Thracius to Ankhu with orders to kill the outlaw Scorpus? Or is that what Soren was waiting for her to do? Would he ambush Anchises and Thracius on the way there? Did he have spies in Tivoli watching Ankhu and Scorpus right now? For all she knew, Soren's men were closing in on them this moment. She had to find a way to warn Ankhu.

Not yet sure how to respond, she chose what was always the safest path and said nothing at all, but merely raised her eyebrows as if he were wasting her time.

Soren tongued his bottom lip as he studied her. Boldly, he let his eyes move up and down her body, spreading his legs slightly. He could feel himself becoming aroused. He looked down between his legs to see if there was any evidence, but the Vestal refused to follow his eyes.

"I don't know what you think you're doing," said Pomponia, "but it is not just my life that you put at risk. It is your own as well." She glanced at the curtains. "All it would take is one of my guards to open that curtain and see you like this . . ."

Soren leaned forward and gripped Pomponia's hands. "Then, if I am to be condemned, I might as well make it worth it."

Pomponia fought the instinct to pull her hands back. Soren's grip was too tight, and the attempt would only amplify her weakness.

"Your information is not as dangerous to me as you think," she said.

"No?" Soren laughed.

It was the laugh that made Pomponia rethink what was happening. It was the laugh that made her realize she was wrong.

He wasn't talking about the letters between her and Ankhu.

He was talking about the letters between her and Despina.

Soren knew about the letters that she and Caesar's slave had been exchanging for years: the letters that revealed to Pomponia the details of every private conversation, every adviser's meeting, every family conflict, and every sordid coupling that happened in the house of Caesar since the death of Medousa, when Despina had taken over the auburn-haired slave's secret duty.

And that was worse than any scandal about an escaped slave. That was indefensible. The future played out before her in a single heartbeat. She had known Octavian long enough to be certain of what he would do.

First, he would have her stripped naked, tied to a post in front of the Rostra, and scourged to within a breath of her life. Then he would have her put in a box, bound and gagged, and carried off to the Campus Sceleratus, the Evil Field, where she would be forced to descend into the black pit. Buried alive.

None of it would matter. Not her long friendship with him or her years of service to Rome. Not the way she had sacrificed Vestal tradition to give him Marc Antony's will. Not her loyalty to him in the Senate. None of it would save her. He would kill her.

He would kill the Vestals who served under her too: her beloved Quintina, Lucretia, Caecilia, Marcella, and Cossinia. Octavian would not know whom he could trust, so he would kill all of them at once, dispatching soldiers to kill Sabina and Nona in Carthage before they'd even received word of what had happened. The Vestals in Tivoli wouldn't be safe either. He would replace all of them with novices.

He would kill little Pomponia too. He would order her to be taken to the woods and abandoned, left to die a slow death of exposure or a violent death at the fangs of wolves.

The alliances she had made since her days as a novice would be meaningless. No senator, no priest would stand with her. Not even Maecenas would help her. He would not be as surprised as Caesar. Perhaps he suspected Despina was her spy; however, he would not intercede for Pomponia as he had for Julia. He would recognize the futility of trying to assuage Caesar's anger and sense of betrayal, and he would instead agree with him.

Yes, condemn her. Condemn them all.

And after he had condemned her body, Octavian would condemn her memory. He would melt down the coins that bore her image, destroy the inscriptions and documents that bore her name, and remove any trace of her from history. It would be like she had never existed at all.

Pomponia noticed that her hands had begun to tremble. She tried to pull them away from Soren, but he held them more tightly and leaned forward, so close to her that she could feel his breath on her face. She stopped resisting. When she did, he loosened his grip and instead began to caress her hands.

"Tell me, Pomponia," he said softly into her ear. "Has a man ever touched you like this before?" His hand moved under her palla to stroke the soft skin of her inner arm.

One man had touched her that way before. Quintus, the night he had held her by the arm and pressed his lips against hers. How she wished he were here. He would have opened Soren's throat and spat in the pool of blood. But he was gone, and she was alone.

"Do you not fear the gods?" she asked Soren.

He looked at her as if the matter had never occurred to him before. He seemed to consider it. "Why would I?" he asked. "They have done much worse."

"What do you want? More gold?"

Again, the same expression of mild bafflement. Soren shook his head. "I don't know," he said. And then with more certainty, "But I will give it some thought and let you know."

He released his grip on her. Raising his arms, he brushed her veil off her shoulders and then again let his eyes move over her body in a way that made her want to run home and scrub her flesh raw in the bath. "*Vale*, Priestess," he said as he stepped out of the lectica and slid the curtain closed behind him.

Almost immediately, the curtain opened again. Pomponia tensed but then bit her lip to stifle a sob as Anchises stepped inside and sat across from her.

"What in the name of the gods was Soren doing in here with you?" he asked. "Caeso and Publius are near violence with each other over what to do!"

Pomponia dropped her face into her hands. "He knows, Anchises."

The singer reached out to pat her knee. "We suspected as much," he said. "I will go to Tivoli and see Ankhu. We will deal with Scorpus. Ankhu is already prepared to—"

"It's not Scorpus," cried Pomponia. She looked at Anchises, her eyes stark with fear. "He knows about *Despina*."

Anchises looked at the floor so that Pomponia could not see the alarm in his eyes. He moved to sit beside her and put his arm around her shoulders. Yes, this was much worse. He searched his mind for some words of reassurance but found none.

Suddenly, Pomponia pushed herself back from him. "Why did you come out here? Is something wrong?"

Anchises pressed the heels of his hands into his eyes. "A messenger has just arrived from Carthage."

"Carthage? At this hour? Gods, what now?"

"I am sorry to tell you this. Priestess Nona has died. She was on watch in the temple when she collapsed."

Pomponia stared at the flame of the oil lamp on the wall, not sure of what she felt. Sadness? Relief? At least Nona would never know how Pomponia had failed as Vestalis Maxima. At least she had died with dignity by the sacred fire, not by a soldier's sword or in the black pit. Perhaps Vesta was already dispensing the justice she felt each of her priestesses deserved.

Anchises poked his head outside. "Take us home," he called out. A moment later the lectica rose, and the litter-bearers began the short journey back to the temple.

The virtuoso wiped the tears from the Vestal's eyes and the sweat from his brow.

Outside in the stillness of the night, he could hear the priests of Pluto murmuring prayers to keep the dark spirits of the underworld at bay.

So far, they are doing a terrible job, he thought.

CHAPTER XVIII

Amicus Magis Necessarius Quam Ignis aut Aqua
Friendship is more necessary than fire or water.

−PLUTARCH

THE ISLAND OF PANDATERIA

The panic of drowning was one thing. But the reflex to breathe and the horrifying thought of doing so while submerged was another. Julia tried to move her arms and legs, praying that somehow, some way, she would suddenly acquire the skill of swimming before her body compelled her to inhale.

Not only did her prayers go unanswered, but her arms and legs suddenly felt as heavy as the marble statues of the gods that she was praying to.

A hot fist of pain tightened in her chest as she sank farther below the surface of the water. She opened her eyes. A school of dotted fish was moving toward her, but it suddenly shifted direction as one massive aquatic entity to move under her feet, swimming through the sea below her no differently than a flock of starlings would fly through the sky above.

She tried again to move her stone arms but only her fingers responded. Something solid brushed against the bottom of her feet—a large fish—and she felt her legs spasm in response.

Even through the panic, she knew she could not stop it any longer: her heart beat even faster as, against her will, her body inhaled the water, sucking it in, desperate for air but only filling her lungs with a thick, burning, salty fluid. The awareness of it was even more grotesque than the feeling.

Her spine convulsed, and she found herself looking up. Sunlight was streaming through the surface of the water, dimmer and more distant with every passing moment. Phoenix's cage was up there too, empty and half-sunken. She thought she saw a flash of a pink, webbed foot.

Poor Phoenix! He will drown too!

The guilt flared and then settled into a strange calm. She was just about to sink into it when a sharp pain pulled at her head.

The ugly little man had a tight grip on her long hair. He pulled on it hard until her head broke through the surface of the water. She felt him heave her body out of the sea, and she landed with a watery thud on the bottom of his boat. He pulled himself out of the water and knelt, soaking wet, in front of her.

He was shouting something at her and shaking her shoulders. Julia rolled onto her side and coughed, coughed from some deep part of her lungs, and retched up mouthful after mouthful of seawater, sputum, and finally vomit. She felt a warm stream of urine run down her legs.

She gasped for air and felt her lungs expand to take it in, the pleasure of the breath overwhelming the pain in her lungs. She gripped the side of the ugly little man's boat and pointed to the faltering seagull.

The man reached into the water and grabbed Phoenix by his broken wing, tossing him into the boat. The gull made a croaking type of cry as he landed by Julia's head and tried to get his feet under him. If Julia weren't so weak, she would have pushed the ugly little man overboard and knocked him out with his own paddle.

Then again, he had just saved both of them from drowning.

He put his hand on her shoulder. "Domina, are you all right?"

She tried to respond, to say that she wasn't necessarily all right but at least she was alive, but every sound came out as a cough.

The man pulled the cork out of a canteen and passed it to her. "Do you need some water?"

His stupidity made Julia cough even more. *Do I look like I need more water?*

Eventually, her coughing subsided. She leaned over and touched Phoenix's head. He puffed his feathers and opened his beak.

Julia looked over at the ugly little man. "Thank you," she said.

"Thank your great father, Domina," he replied. "He bade me to return early this month."

"Why?"

The man moved two paddles aside to reveal the ornately carved African blackwood box underneath them. It was too costly and rare an item to belong in his dilapidated boat.

"Caesar sends supplies for you to write to him."

Julia pushed herself onto her knees and crawled over to the box. Her father's favorite imperial seal—the head of Alexander the Great—was inlaid with ivory and turquoise on the lid, and the familiar sight made her chest tighten with emotion and ache all over again.

She wondered who had interceded on her behalf. Her mother? Scribonia would have tried but not succeeded. She was no match for Livia. Quintina? No. She would have wanted to, but she would have been overruled by the Vestalis Maxima. Maecenas? Yes. Maecenas would have acted in Agrippa's absence. He was also the person most likely to have found a way around Livia.

As the ugly little man navigated them back to her island, Julia tried to remember a time when she had spoken a kind word or been friendly to Maecenas. She had always taken her father's advisers for granted, always seen them as old men her father had befriended as a child.

She had fought her marriage to Agrippa and then been a wretch of a wife to him, and she had barely restrained her ridicule of Maecenas when his adulterous wife was coupling—to the knowledge of everyone in Rome—with Caesar.

Despite that, he had risked it all to try to initiate some kind of reconciliation between her and her father. When Livia found out—and she would—there would be consequences. No one knew that better than Maecenas.

Julia made a vow to herself. If she ever stood before him again, she would wrap her arms around him and thank him.

That thought sparked another. It had been a long time since she had wrapped her arms around a man. Any man. Thoughts of Maecenas faded as memories of her favorite lover, a wealthy landowner named Sempronius, returned. The man was outstanding. She had spent many nights mentally reliving their time together: how he moved, how he sounded and felt. The things he did to her.

Sighing, she lowered her head and whispered to the seagull who now sat contentedly on her lap. "We've risen from the sea like your namesake rose from the ashes." She stroked his back. "Thank you, Phoenix."

CHAPTER XIX

Dolendi Modus Non Est Timendi
There is a limit to suffering, but not to fear.

—PLINY THE YOUNGER

ROME

Soren had known her secret for four days now.

For four long days and three longer nights, Pomponia had lived with a sickening feeling in her stomach. At times, it felt like hunger—that would be expected as she'd barely eaten—but whenever she swallowed food, it threatened to come back up again. She felt a tight band of stress wrap around her chest and upper back, and her head ached constantly.

Her lack of sleep was catching up to her too. Moving through the light of day felt no different from moving through the haze of night.

But she smiled through it all and acted like nothing was out of the ordinary. What choice did she have?

Around her, horns and pipes played lively music. People laughed and conversed, children shrieked with excitement, prostitutes openly searched for clients, and vendors shouted out whatever food, drink, or trinkets they were selling, smiling at those who purchased and spitting at the sandals of those who didn't.

Pomponia's leg muscles burned as she climbed the steps that led up to the canopied terrace that had been erected high above the man-made lake in the Campus Martius. She sighed from the effort and stopped for a rest, turning to look down at the massive body of water below.

Only a couple of weeks ago, the area was nothing more than a deep natural valley; however, after days of water being diverted into it from the nearby Tiber River, and thanks to the brightly painted stone and mortar border that encircled the massive oval-like a ring of rocky shore, it was now a lake.

Even the waterfowl believed it. A motley collection of ring-necked and tufted ducks quacked and swam languidly in the center of the lake, avoiding the stone shore, where children tried to throw either bread or rocks at them, depending on their nature.

All around and seated on hundreds of spectator stands built just for the occasion, tens of thousands of people had gathered to watch the *nau-machia Augusti*—the naval games of Augustus. Many of them had come from nearby towns and even more distant parts of the empire, such was the promise of Caesar's great spectacle.

At each end of the lake were full-size warships: two opposing fleets of triremes, giant galleys propelled by three rows of oarsmen. Their square sails hung down from high masts as hundreds of men, many in armor, moved about the deck in preparation for the impending mock naval battle.

Not that the *mock* part mattered, for these men were not actors but rather slaves, criminals, rabble-rousers, and prisoners of war who were being forced to fight. Their deaths would provide something almost as valuable as military victory—public entertainment.

Pomponia began to ascend the steps again with Caeso and Publius. As she moved, people leaned over the railings with extended arms to offer her gifts: embroidered fabrics, ivory statuettes, and jewelry for her and the other priestesses, and carved dolls and animals for the novices.

She accepted these gifts graciously, offering each person a quick blessing and then passing the item to the slaves behind her to bring back to the House of the Vestals.

But the experience was tainted. Now, every interaction and conversation she had with anyone—whether a temple slave, a faithful citizen, or Caesar himself—was corrupted with the same thought: *What if they knew?*

What if they knew that their Vestalis Maxima had been spying on their emperor for years? It would be the greatest scandal to strike Rome in recent history. Her name and the Vestal order itself would descend into mockery. It was unlikely the order would ever fully recover the respect or reverence of the people, and it would certainly be stripped of its independence and power.

As if pouring salt in the wounding thoughts, Caesar greeted her at the top of the steps as she arrived on the covered and lavishly decorated imperial viewing terrace.

Behind him, Anchises was singing to the empress and a number of other noblewomen, as well as the usual collection of magistrates, senators, and priests. Virgil and Maecenas were there too, enjoying the private performance.

Of more interest to Pomponia was the trio leaning against the far railing of the terrace: Soren, Tiberius, and Quintina, all laughing at some anecdote of Tiberius's. Quintina cast Pomponia a look: *Don't worry about Soren. He's behaving himself.* She pointed to the other side of the terrace and grinned. There, Thracius was pretending to drop a young novice over the edge while the other girls laughed and dared him to do it.

Pomponia tried to smile back, but the carefree pleasures of others only seemed to amplify her own feelings of peril. She bowed to Octavian, tried to ignore the presence of Soren in her peripheral vision, and gestured to the blue sky. "It is a good day to go to war, Caesar."

"Ha!" he said. He looked down at the lake and the warships readying for battle. "It is to be a reenactment of my victory at Actium."

Livia approached and hooked her arm around his. "Yes, what else?" she said lightly. "Although you have so many victories to celebrate, my love. The return of the Eagle from those stubborn Parthians for one. Would that not make for patriotic theater?"

"Maybe next month," said Octavian. He kissed her on the cheek and moved off to join Tiberius, while Livia led Pomponia to two cushioned chairs near the balustrade at the front of the terrace. Once they were seated, she cast the Vestal a sardonic look. "Actium," she mused. "He will never stop milking that goat."

A serving slave appeared with a tray of wine and cool cucumber water. Livia took wine, Pomponia water. The empress regarded her. "You look tired, Lady Pomponia. Are you well?"

Pomponia sipped the water. "I am a bit tired, now that you mention it."

"You knew Priestess Nona since you were a child. Such losses can upset the body's humors."

"Yes." The Vestal took another sip.

"I was sorry to hear of her crossing," Livia continued. "She was from another time, don't you think?"

"In many ways, yes," said Pomponia. "She cared nothing of public ceremony and even less of politics. When Julius Caesar was dictator, Nona used to insist on taking watch in the temple whenever he would come by so that she didn't have to consult with him."

"We are thankful this Caesar has a more politic Vestal to rely upon," said Livia.

Pomponia went to take another sip, but her glass was empty. Livia's words were spoken in sincerity, but that only made them sting all the more.

They also made her think of the many times that Fabiana and Nona had encouraged her to avoid falling into political tangles and to instead focus only on her duties to the sacred fire and the goddess. It was only now that Pomponia fully understood how sagacious that advice had been.

Despina appeared before Pomponia and Livia. She took the empty cup from the Vestal's hand. "May I get you another, Priestess?"

"No, Despina."

Pomponia glanced at the slave's earrings. Good. They were the right ones.

After Soren had revealed his terrible knowledge to her four days earlier, Pomponia had returned to her office to retrieve a single earring from her desk drawer. It was one of Despina's earrings, gold with a Greek meander pattern and a red garnet stone. It had been in the Vestal's drawer for ten years. She had wrapped it in silk and sent a messenger to bring it to Despina, saying that she had found it in the courtyard and thought it belonged to Caesar's house slave.

But of course it wasn't just an earring. It was a message. *Do not send any more letters.*

Despina had responded by wearing the complete pair. *I understand. I will wait for further instructions.*

Performance horns blared. Gradually, the thousands of spectators, as well as the elite gathering under the imperial canopy, took to their seats. Quintina sat beside Pomponia with Maecenas's wife, Terentia, with Lady Mallonia and the novices filling the rest of the row. Although Roman women were normally free to sit with men, they often preferred the company of other women at social events.

Across from them, the men waited for Caesar to sit before taking their own seats. Tiberius sat beside Caesar, his gaze drifting across the terrace to look longingly at Mallonia. As always, Soren had the seat next to Tiberius. He bowed to Livia and sat down.

At the very rear of the terrace were Anchises and Thracius, whose back-row seating gave them the benefit of relative privacy along with an unobstructed view of the lake below; however, it also gave them an unobstructed view of the back of Soren's head.

Thracius took Anchises's hand. "The gods bless us today," he said. "We have food in our bellies, and we are together." He eyed Soren. "So don't give me a reason to knock you out again."

"I will do my best," Anchises replied. His partner had a remarkable ability to suppress, or at least delay, his own anger. It was a skill he'd put to good use in the boxing ring. Since coming to Rome, he had also learned to accept moments of happiness when they came. It was he, Anchises, who these days could never stop worrying, never stop projecting his fears into the future and living them a thousand times before they actually took form.

Thracius reached behind himself to take a cup of wine from a table and handed it to Anchises. "Whatever else may happen to us in this life, today we drink the same wine as Caesar. Don't spoil the taste with worry. Bacchus will take issue."

Anchises drank. "It is good wine," he said. "And good advice."

As the clamor and chatter of the spectators' voices subsided, one voice rose up. Taurus. He stood on a raised platform in the water about forty feet from shore. The small boat that had transported him waited nearby. He faced the emperor's terrace.

"Great Caesar," he called out, and then extended his arms and turned to address the seated crowds, "my fellow Romans! Today, our beloved emperor,

Caesar Augustus, presents a naumachia to rival even those of his divine father, Julius Caesar, whose mighty naval games were held near this very spot."

As always, the name Julius Caesar sparked a frenzy of cheers and applause. Many in the crowd had attended Julius Caesar's naumachia, which the dictator had put on decades earlier to celebrate his defeat of the Roman general Pompey the Great. The nostalgia, as much as the epic name, was rousing. Taurus waited for the commotion to abate and then continued.

"Today, the emperor Caesar Augustus, father of our country, celebrates with his people his victory upon the Ionian Sea over the forces of the fallen general Marc Antony and Queen Cleopatra of Egypt!"

On flawless cue, two massive lead galleys raised their sails. Hundreds of oarsmen rowed in perfect unison, propelling the long, slender hulls of the ships toward each other and then maneuvering so that they faced each other. The respective fleets of each galley moved weightily through the water to line up alongside them.

On the bow of one lead ship was a massive figurehead of Mars. Two imposing men dressed as Roman soldiers stood on the prow and surveyed the scene. One wore the crested helmet of a Roman general, the other a crown of laurels. The crowd jumped to their feet and cheered as they recognized the portrayals—General Agrippa and the young Octavian Caesar.

The bow of the opposing ship boasted the figurehead of a golden cobra, its red eyes reflecting in the sunlight. As it closed in, the crowd's cheers turned to shouted obscenities, for on its prow stood a bulky figure wearing the linen skirt of an Egyptian but the iron breastplate of a Roman soldier. It was Marc Antony. Next to him was Queen Cleopatra. A golden snake wound around one of her arms.

At the sight of her, Octavian sat up straight. Even from a distance, he could tell the resemblance was shocking: the lithe figure, the dark hair pulled into a bun, the black-lined eyes, and the golden diadem on her head.

"It is amazing," he said to Tiberius. He waved a soldier over. "Make sure she isn't killed. I want to see her afterward."

"Yes, Caesar." The soldier quickly left the terrace.

On the platform in the water, Taurus was still shouting to the crowd, detailing Caesar and Agrippa's naval victory and reiterating that the emperor had paid for the naumachia from his own purse rather than Rome's treasury, when people in the crowd began to take to their feet and cry out in warning.

Taurus turned just in time to see two warships about to collide behind him, so close that the long, protruding oars of one ship threatened to knock him into the water.

He shrieked and hopped down into the small boat beside him. The oarsman clutched the back of Taurus's toga to prevent him from falling into the lake and then began to hurriedly row toward shore to the tune of the crowd's laughter. The guests on the imperial terrace drained their wine cups and joined in the laughter as horns blared.

On the lake below, it was now all-out war.

Shouts of "Brace for impact! Brace for impact!" flew up from the soldier-packed decks of both galley ships as they collided in a noisy explosion of wood, sails, metal, and men. Almost immediately, the hull of one of Antony's ships began to take on water and list.

The rowers, who were chained to their posts, began to scream and claw at their ankles to free themselves from their shackles. Most couldn't. As the heavy planks and bolts they were chained to sank below the water, they too were slowly and mercilessly dragged under to sink to the bottom of the lake.

Others had a more jarring experience. As their ship was struck again and broke apart, they were flung to the end of their leg chains. The force of the sudden stop ripped the feet of many from their legs.

Despite the chaos and the speed at which the ship was going down, a few men succeeded in removing their shackles. They clambered through and over the listing vessel, grasping onto whatever they could to remain above the water.

Yet it only delayed the inevitable, as one of Caesar's ships came alongside the listing galley and a row of archers on its deck began to shoot arrows at the desperate men, impaling some to the wood of the broken hull and sending others tumbling into the sea even as they clutched the arrows sticking out of their chests.

More shouts went up as the remaining ships in both fleets closed in on the battle. "Ramming speed! Ramming speed!" Plumes of water flew high into the air as the ships met with unexpected force and sound.

To add to the destruction, catapults on the decks of the opposing ships launched heavy stones from one vessel to the other, leaving behind giant holes and causing four ships—three of Antony's and one of Caesar's—to list to the point of tipping over, sending men, arms, and equipment flying.

Mock soldiers in armor jumped into the water and began to swim desperately for shore. Most were unable to swim more than a few feet without succumbing to the weight of their iron gear and drowning. Those who managed to free themselves from their armor didn't fare much better, as archers perched on the shore shot arrows at any man swimming toward the walls.

The crowd was happy to help by pointing at those who succeeded in avoiding the keen eyes of the archers. They stomped their feet and cried out, "Over there! There's one you missed!"

As a last line of defense, a perimeter of soldiers armed with long spears ran to impale the relative few who made it to the artificial shore.

Despite the mayhem and destruction, one suspiciously lucky galley ship seemed to have escaped serious damage—the lead Roman galley upon the prow of which proudly stood the look-alikes of Caesar and Agrippa. The two men directed soldiers this way and that, and shouted for the archers to let fly their arrows at the enemy in piercing flocks of death.

As ships sank all around them, as the sound of clanging metal and snapping wood rang out, as the cries of dying and desperate men filled the air, the actor Agrippa signaled to the catapult operators on the deck of his ship. A moment later, a flurry of fiery projectiles began to rain down upon the ship of Antony and Cleopatra. The ropes and fabric of the sails burst into flames, and fire spread along the tall mast as if it were a piece of dry kindling.

The actor Antony ran from one end of his ship to the other, screaming first at his rowers and then his soldiers until a huge piece of burning sail broke off and floated down to land on top of him. He twisted and turned under the burning sail, his shrieks of pain so sharp and loud that they could be heard even as the mast itself cracked in half and plummeted to the deck of the ship.

As the audience let out a collective gasp, one of the broken, jagged ends of the mast swung haphazardly from gnarled and smoking ropes. After a few suspenseful moments, it broke free and landed directly on top of the mock general who was still screaming and flailing under the burning sail. His antics ended abruptly.

The crowd leaped to their feet in boisterous applause and laughter. Taurus thanked the gods. Even he couldn't have executed such a perfectly timed touch.

Soon, the Egyptian galley was an inferno on water. The Cleopatra look-alike scrambled onto the cobra prow—the only part of the galley that wasn't engulfed in flames—and clung to it as the rest of the ship disintegrated, littering the surface of the water with splintered wood that floated outward to mix with the debris of other sunken or sinking ships.

A small boat appeared below the prow, and the soldier who had taken Caesar's instruction to keep the mock queen alive shouted up to her. "Jump down! I'll catch you!"

She ignored him. Dying by fire or drowning was no doubt a better and faster death than whatever the Roman soldier intended to do to her.

The soldier looked up at her, irritated. Caesar and half of Rome were watching this skinny Greek slave defy him. He reached up and grabbed her ankle. With one yank, she fell hard and landed with a *thump* in the middle of the little boat.

But the woman's resemblance to Cleopatra wasn't limited to her appearance. She scrambled to her knees and, to the shock of the Roman spectators, delivered a stinging slap across the face of the soldier. Taken aback, he barely caught her in time as she tried to jump over the side of the boat back into the water.

Still not relenting, she bit his hand. He answered with a sharp blow to her head, one that subdued her but didn't knock her out completely. Caesar wanted her undamaged. The slave Cleopatra fell backward and glared hatefully at the Roman spectators who were still on their feet, laughing and clapping at her performance.

There was laughter on the imperial terrace too, although not everyone joined in. Octavian didn't find it funny at all. The whole thing reminded him of the real Cleopatra's defiance and the way she had committed suicide before he could parade her in his triumph.

Pomponia wasn't laughing either. She had too much on her mind to be entertained. She feigned amusement, but that was the best she could do. The drawn expression on Quintina's face didn't help. The anguished drownings of countless men had no doubt revived memories of Septimus's horrific drowning. It was a death that Quintina wrongly blamed on her sister, Tacita.

Yet another secret, thought Pomponia.

And finally, Anchises. Like Pomponia, he was too preoccupied with Soren's threats to lose himself in the joy of spectacle. Then again, this wasn't the type of spectacle that he tended to enjoy anyway. The mock Cleopatra was a Greek slave, like him. Judging from her behavior, she had not been a slave for very long and was not about to accept her new status without a fight.

On the lake below, it was clear that the forces of General Agrippa and Octavian Caesar had won the battle that would win the war. Nevertheless, the watery slaughter continued.

Catapults launched more flaming projectiles at the hulls of enemy ships, and archers shot at those men who either fell or jumped into the water. Soldiers from Caesar's fleet leaped onto the decks of Antony's ships and ran to the rowers who, still chained to their posts, were as easy to slay as animals caught in foot traps.

Yet, as they usually did around this time in a performance, Rome's elite began to bore of the amusements below and instead became more interested in the food, drink, and conversation around them.

Caesar was questioning Tiberius and two other senators about the possible expansion of an aqueduct south of the city, while Soren excused himself to stretch his legs. He hadn't taken more than a few steps when Terentia floated up to him.

"My, you are everywhere these days," she said.

Soren didn't answer but continued to the edge of the terrace and leaned on the railing to look out at the tens of thousands of spectators around the lake below.

Terentia tucked herself in next to him. "There must be something special about you," she said, pressing her shoulder into his. "Tiberius and the empress seem to think you can do no wrong."

Soren looked at Terentia sideways, unimpressed. She shifted on her feet awkwardly, not knowing how to proceed and feeling a bit foolish. Most men played along. Most men enjoyed being close to Rome's most beautiful woman.

But Soren wasn't most men. Not only was he accustomed to beautiful women throwing themselves at him, he also knew that the empress's eyes were watching his every move. Terentia was her husband's former mistress, and there was no way Soren was going to show her any flattery in front of Livia. Women did not respond positively to that kind of thing.

Terentia fidgeted with her bracelet and then lifted two cups of wine from the tray of a passing slave. She held one out to Soren. Still he did nothing. Realizing that defeat was inevitable and further attempts would only be more embarrassing, Terentia turned and left.

A moment later, she was replaced by Livia. This time, Soren stood up straight and offered a deferential nod. "Empress," he said, "you are looking well."

"That is unlikely," said Livia. "I've spent the morning being eaten alive by the mosquitoes infesting this swamp of Tiber runoff that my husband wants us to believe is the Ionian Sea."

"You look no worse for it," Soren insisted.

Livia turned her body to rest against the railing with her hip. She glanced across the terrace at Caesar, who was still deep in conversation with Tiberius, and then looked expectantly at Soren.

"Our matter is proceeding," he said.

Livia turned again to survey the mass of spectators. "All of these people," she said contemplatively, "and every last one of them has that one person they would remove from their lives if they could . . . that one person who is standing in the way of what they want."

"Or what they deserve," said Soren.

"Yes," Livia agreed. She spoke softly but with confidence. "And my son deserves to be emperor."

"I could not agree more, Empress."

Livia took a step closer to him. "Then, make it happen, Soren, while I'm still young enough to properly thank you."

Soren felt a flush of arousal. Livia was still a very appealing woman, but it was more than that. She was Tiberius's mother and Caesar's wife. Those kinds of connections, the ones he knew would antagonize other men, always made it better.

In fact, antagonism itself was his greatest source of arousal. As he watched Livia move on, his eyes landed on the chief Vestal. She had been uncharacteristically reserved during the spectacle. Others assumed it was her grief at the recent loss of the old priestess Nona in Carthage. Soren knew better.

Pomponia met his stare and stood. For a moment, Soren thought she might approach him—he welcomed it—but instead she made a quick round of goodbyes and signaled for her guards to escort her off the terrace. Soren felt his groin stir and began to think about what slave he would have when he got home.

Toward the back of the terrace, Anchises noticed Pomponia's departure. "Let's go," he said to Thracius. When the boxer pointed at the novices, he added, "The girls will ride home with Priestess Quintina."

With the wine and the gossip now flowing freely on the terrace, Anchises and Thracius navigated their way through the gathering as quietly as they could to avoid capturing Soren's attention. They descended the steps to the pavement below.

For a moment, Anchises considered walking back to the House of the Vestals. The exercise might clear his head; however, he and the famous burn-scarred boxer were now too easily recognized in Rome for that. They didn't get far before the first drunken man slapped Thracius good-naturedly on the back and then jabbed his finger at Anchises.

"Come on," he slurred. "I hear you sing like Orpheus. Why not sing my wife here a song? It's our anniversary. Ten years married today."

"What a happy woman she must be," said Anchises. "But I am not permitted."

The singer grabbed Thracius's tunica sleeve and pulled him to a small, open space where the horse-drawn carriage the priestess had given them for their personal use was waiting. He instructed the driver to head home and then closed the curtains, shutting out the sights—although regrettably not the sounds or smells—of the thick, moving crowd that was packed shoulder to shoulder in this area of the Campus Martius.

They rode mostly without speaking until the streets of the Campus Martius turned into the fine cobblestone of the Roman Forum and the Via Sacra before the House of the Vestals.

Anchises exited the carriage first and was greeted by Caeso and Publius. "We only just arrived ourselves," Caeso said to him. "The priestess went straight to her office. I do not mean to advise you, but she seemed ill tempered."

"I will leave her be," said Anchises. "Thank you for the warning."

The guard nodded as Anchises and Thracius entered through the ornate front doors of the Vestals' home, as the chief Vestal had given them permission to do.

They moved through the atrium and along the cool marble floor to their private room. Although located in the slave quarters of the expansive home, it was only slightly less opulent than the rest of the residence, having previously been the bedchamber of the chief Vestal's first and favored body slave, Medousa.

Thracius let himself drop onto the bed. Anchises lay down next to him. The boxer could tell by his partner's silence, by the heavy pattern of his breathing, that thoughts of Soren were consuming him. He reached down for Anchises's hand and squeezed it.

"The Fates are on our side," he whispered into Anchises's ear. "They always have been. Perhaps they have forgotten us at times, but then something reminds them, and they send us good fortune again. Why worry when such forces favor us?"

Anchises stared at the ceiling. "It is not just us that I worry about. The priestess . . ."

"She has been good to us," said Thracius. "I care for her and especially for my girls. But she may be handling Soren the wrong way. There are men you can dance around in the ring, and then there are those you should just knock out as soon as you can."

"She has her reasons for her approach. There are things she has told me that—"

"It doesn't matter how many secrets she tells you, she is not your friend. She is your owner." Thracius pushed himself up onto one elbow and looked down at Anchises. "It has always been just the two of us, and it always will be. We need not fight all of her battles with Soren." He ran his fingers through Anchises's hair affectionately. "We must only survive our own."

CHAPTER XX

Si Vis Pacem, Para Bellum
If you want peace, prepare for war.

—A ROMAN ADAGE

Octavian sat on the edge of his four-post canopied bed as a slave crouched at his feet and unfastened his sandals. He felt tired but pleased. People would be talking about his naval games for years. They were far more extravagant and well-attended than Julius Caesar's had been; even men who had been at the earlier games had said so.

The slave at his feet carried his sandals away at the same time as Despina opened the door to his bedchamber. Behind her was the slave Cleopatra. She had been bathed and dressed in a white dress with heavy gold embroidery. The fabric clung to her body.

Despina directed the slave to stand before the emperor and then adjusted one of the gold beads on the woman's fine linen dress. "Caesar, I remember the queen," said Despina. "The resemblance is striking."

Octavian leaned back on his arms. "Where did you find her?"

"The slave market in the Forum. The Graecostadium. The finer Greek slaves are still sold there. One of the traders I know spotted her and contacted me. I knew the naval battle was being planned, so I bought her for Taurus to use. She cost a bit more than—"

"Worth every sesterce."

"Shall I remain or step outside, Caesar?"

"As you wish, Despina."

Despina bowed to her master and then turned to the slave, speaking in Greek. *"Poíei hōs ekéleusá se."* Do as I told you.

As the slave woman lowered herself onto her knees in front of Caesar, Despina walked out of the bedchamber and closed the door behind her.

The look-alike queen put her hands on the neckline of her dress and pulled downward to expose the curve of her breasts. She spoke only in Greek, the language that the Egyptian pharaoh—herself of Greek lineage—often spoke.

"Kleopátra hē basílissa éleon hiketeúei." Queen Cleopatra begs Caesar for mercy.

Octavian stood and looked down at her in thought. After he had won the battle at Actium, Cleopatra had offered herself sexually to him. He had refused her desperate advances: to succumb to her would have made him look as weak as Antony.

Yet secretly, he was curious to have her as Julius Caesar had. How had she managed to seduce two Roman men? Were her coupling skills so pleasurable? He had intended to find out when the time was right, but the conniving wench had robbed him of that opportunity too. His fists tightened in frustration at the memory.

"Eléou tunchánousin hoi eléou áxioi mónoi," Octavian replied in Greek. Mercy is only for the deserving.

He closed his eyes and pictured the real Cleopatra: the air of superiority in her movements, the smugness in her smile, the condescension in her voice. And then without really planning to, he struck the slave on the head.

She gasped and fell onto her side. Sobbing, she pushed herself back onto her knees. *"Kleopátra hē basílissa éleon hiketeúei,"* she repeated.

Octavian steadied his breathing. It was rare for him to show violence toward a woman, even a slave woman. But his hatred for Cleopatra, for her defiance of him and of Rome, and especially for being the vessel that brought that bastard Caesarion into the world—it all affected him in a very different way. It was personal.

And that, too, was rare for Octavian, who had always prided himself on his cool objectivity. On never being consumed by a personal grudge the way that Marc Antony had. That, more than any infatuation with a foreign queen, had been the general's downfall.

That's not to say that Octavian's politics couldn't get personal. After Actium, Maecenas had initiated a smear campaign to discredit the famed queen. He spread the rumor that Cleopatra had fellated one hundred Roman soldiers in a single night. Octavian never thought anyone would actually believe it, but as Julius Caesar was fond of saying, men believe what they want to believe.

Yet the thought of the Egyptian queen on her knees inflamed his desire, and Octavian sat back down on the edge of the bed. He spread his legs and lifted his toga, suddenly wishing that Despina had stayed to help him out of it. Still, he'd manage.

The slave girl pulled back her head and glared up at him. A look in her eyes made Octavian suddenly wonder whether he was missing something. "Do you speak any Latin?" he asked her.

"I speak Greek, Latin, and Punic fluently," she answered bluntly. The tears were gone.

"What is your parentage?"

"My father is Greek, and my mother is Carthaginian." She cocked her head. "At least, they were those things. They may be dead by now."

If the statement was meant to invoke sympathy, it failed. Few things could be more irrelevant to Caesar than a slave's tale of woe.

"Stand up and remove your dress," said Octavian.

The woman stood up and took two steps backward. She stared at Octavian, then lifted her chin and said, "I am not a slave."

Octavian laughed. "You were bought with coin. If not a slave, what are you, then?"

"Your prisoner."

"Remove your dress."

Again, the woman only looked at him defiantly. Octavian stood and reached toward the low marble table at the foot of the bed where Livia kept a slave whip. He clutched its handle. The slave opened her mouth to protest, but as the flesh-splitting lash cut into her side, only a cry of pain came out.

Her breath came in irregular gulps, and she stifled a sob. Trying to retain some dignity even in defeat, she glared icily at Caesar, using her hatred of him as an anchor as she slipped the dress off her shoulders and let it fall to the floor. Her arms instinctively moved to cover her bare breasts, but then she saw the amusement in her captor's eyes. She let her arms drop to her sides.

Now that's the Cleopatra I remember, thought Octavian. He sat down again on the edge of the bed and waited. This time, the slave queen performed as instructed.

Outside Caesar's bedroom door, Despina leaned against the warm wall—the house's hypocaust system ran behind the walls as well as under the floors—and absently watched a small beetle scurrying across the floor tiles.

As always, it was her duty to wait until Caesar was finished with whatever bed slave was his current fancy and then ensure the girl returned to her quarters. That was especially important when it came to new slaves, like this one, who didn't know what was expected of them afterward.

She rested her head against the wall. Normally, this was the type of thing that she would include in her regular letters to the Vestalis Maxima, but . . . Despina toyed with one of her earrings and tried not to think the worst. She couldn't help it, though. Had someone learned of their correspondence? The empress? Caesar's wife had seemed distracted lately. Preoccupied.

Despina stood up straight as she heard the empress's voice barking at a slave. A moment later Livia appeared, walking tiredly toward Octavian's bedchamber with a small cup in her hand.

Despina bowed. "Good evening, Domina."

"He has that slave Cleopatra in there, doesn't he?" asked Livia.

"Yes, Domina."

Livia all but spat on the closed door. "Of course he does," she muttered. The Naumachia Augusti might have been a victorious day for Caesar, but for Caesar's wife, it had struck a double blow of defeat.

First, Livia had seen the letter from Julia on Octavian's desk in his library. The letter had started with the words "Dearest Father, your loving daughter begs the forgiveness of Rome's emperor, its Senate, and its people." That's as far as Livia had gotten before she had heard Octavian approach and had to stop reading.

Second, the slut slave Cleopatra. During the spectacle, no fewer than ten men had commented to her on the mock queen's amazing resemblance to the real queen. It had become so unbearable that Livia had secretly vowed to cuff the next person—senator or priest—who mentioned it and then blame the outburst on the wine.

Livia had known then and there that this Cleopatra would survive Actium and land in Caesar's bed. The only thing Octavian loved more than enacting sexual morality legislation was enacting immoral sexual fantasies. Frightened virgins, captive queens, women who carried another man's child—Octavian could never resist a good story in bed.

To make matters worse, Livia knew when one of her husband's fantasies had the potential to become a real threat. And the slave Cleopatra, with that inscrutable air about her, was such a fantasy.

"How long has she been in there?" Livia asked Despina.

"Not long, Domina. I suspect it will be some time yet."

Livia passed Despina the cup in her hand. "When he is finished with her, take her back to the slave quarters and give her this drink."

"Yes, Domina."

"Don't drink it yourself, Despina. And don't let Caesar or anyone else drink it either. It is for this slave only. Do you understand?"

"Perfectly, Domina."

"If Caesar asks for me, tell him I have gone to Tiberius's house for the evening. I have business there."

A cry of protest sounded from the other side of the door. The crack of a whip on flesh. Livia stared at the closed door and fumed. It sounded like Octavian was having a good time.

But her anger settled, found purpose, as she remembered who was waiting for her at Tiberius's house: Soren.

She walked thoughtfully to the atrium, where a slave wrapped a woolen palla around her shoulders. "I will walk alone to Tiberius's house," she informed the slave. The grounds between the home of Augustus and

Tiberius were walled, fortified, and well guarded. A personal escort was not necessary. Plus she wanted the solitude. She had a lot to think about.

The night air was just cool enough to be refreshing as Livia wound through the lush green gardens toward her son's house, the house of Caesar's heir. Larger and more luxurious than Octavian's, Tiberius's house struck her as far more suited to a Caesar.

It made her wonder: What kind of Caesar would Tiberius be? How would he differ from Octavian? How would the Senate and the people regard him, and how would he choose to use his limitless power?

He was competent enough, that much was certain. When it came to senatorial, political, military, or religious matters, he was always informed, fair-minded, and respected. In fact, many people, including herself, had been surprised by just how faithfully he now fulfilled his duties to Rome and how humbly he was willing to learn those duties from Octavian.

But he was not without his flaws. Livia knew about some of his perversions. The things he made children do to him in the bath. The way he instructed his slaves to couple in front of him. His obsession with Mallonia. There was also the incident at the amphitheater, the one where he had instructed a slave girl to fellate a bull. That was not his perversion, though, so much as the client king Herod's. Tiberius's depravities were child's play next to Herod's.

They were also no worse than Octavian's.

The great Caesar Augustus. The man had transformed Rome from a scrapping republic to an unconquerable empire. And yet this same man had a penchant for deflowering virgins, openly coupling with the wives of his closest friends, and engaging in sexual fantasy with women like the whore slave Cleopatra, whom he was at this very moment defeating and defiling on their marriage bed.

As she walked in the dark, Livia's thoughts floated erratically, landing on this memory and that, on this present humiliation and then a past one. The pretty little bed slave Octavian had impregnated and left her to dispose of. The countless wide-eyed Vestal-like innocents he had plied and left her to usher away. Terentia, the haughty wife of Maecenas, whom he had forced her to compete with in that humiliating beauty pageant.

And worst of all, that back-biting young slut Tacita, who had shared their bed and whose soft hands Livia could still feel moving over her breasts, violating her body and her dignity.

Her shoulders now tense with her rising emotion, she entered the glowing light and warmth of Tiberius's atrium and was greeted by a house slave. "Empress," he said, bowing, "Master Tiberius is currently . . ." The slave inwardly debated what to say.

"Let me guess," said Livia. "He's in his bedchamber with a woman. Or two."

"Yes. Apologies, Domina. Master Soren is here, though."

"Take me to him."

"At once, Domina."

Livia unwrapped the heavy palla from her shoulders as the slave led her into the large triclinium. Soren was sitting upright on one of the several couches that had been arranged to facilitate conversation. He held a cup of wine in one hand and a wax tablet in the other.

"I'm glad to see someone in the house of our next Caesar is working," Livia said.

Soren stood and smiled. "Tiberius retired only moments ago," he said. "He will regret having missed you."

"No man regrets having missed his mother," said Livia. "But this is better anyway. It will give us a chance to speak in private." She waved away the two slaves who stood behind the couch, and they exited the dining room.

"Sit, Empress," said Soren. "Can I pour you some wine?"

Livia took the wine cup that was already in Soren's hand and put it to her lips. She reclined on a couch. Soren did the same, positioning himself so that their faces were nearly touching.

Soren knew what she wanted. "I have been consulting at length with Senators Murena and Caepio," he said in an intimate whisper. "We have a plan."

Livia felt a flutter in her stomach. Anticipation? Fear? Dread? She wasn't sure. It was one thing to think and talk about conspiring against Octavian. It was something else entirely to know that others were involved, that a plan for his assassination—the word itself was shocking—had been formulated and would soon be in motion.

She was suddenly surprised to find herself weeping. Despite all the humiliations she had suffered during her marriage to Octavian, she could not deny that she loved him. They had never shared a child, no, but they had shared a life for over twenty years. The passage of time, if nothing else, had forced feelings of affection into her heart.

But she could not let those feelings stand in the way of what had to be done. Tiberius had to be emperor. She could not take any chances, not now that Julia was writing to her father. Livia could just imagine her words: *Oh my dear father, great Caesar, Tiberius is a cruel man . . . He assaulted me . . . He speaks against you in private . . .*

It would only be a matter of time until those planted words sprouted doubt in Octavian and he changed his will. He could not live to do so.

Soren wiped the tears off her cheek. "Tiberius doesn't know the details," he whispered. "And you have done enough. You do not need to know them either. We are all agreed it will be better this way. Better for him and for you." He lowered his head. "There is something you should know, though. It concerns Lady Mallonia."

Livia drained her wine.

"As you know, she was the wife of my late brother, who died of the contagion. She and I have strained relations. She is the woman that Tiberius has in his bedchamber this evening. He had me call on her and bring her here."

"That woman," breathed Livia. "Why is she still in Rome? I offered her a villa outside the city, anywhere she wanted."

"Mallonia's family has lived in Rome for generations. She is a proud woman."

"Not too proud to couple with a man half her age."

Soren rubbed his chin. "I do not believe she does so voluntarily," he said. "There was violence involved."

Livia let her empty wine cup fall to the floor and lay back on the couch. She put her hand over her mouth and muffled a frustrated "*Futuo.*"

"I do not know how Mallonia will respond," Soren continued. "I will speak to her about keeping the matter private."

"She must do so," said Livia. "The last thing we need right now is a hysterical noblewoman accusing Tiberius of rape."

Soren nodded. "I will do what I can." He raised himself on one elbow so that he was above Livia's face, looking down at her. "Remember, Empress," he said soothingly, "soon we will not need to worry about such things. Soon we will answer to no one."

CHAPTER XXI

Et Mala Sunt Vicina Bonis
There are bad qualities that are close to good.

–OVID

TIVOLI

Aelina hated to travel. Yes, it was a relatively short journey between Rome and Tivoli, and she was in the comfort of Soren's carriage. But she still hated it.

The boredom. The jerky movements of the horses that either woke her up or caused her to spill her wine. The squabbles between travelers along the Via Tiburtina, especially on those stretches that were being expanded or repaired: *Move your cart! No, you move your carriage! Hurry up or let us pass! Why are your horses so slow? Make way for foot travelers! By order of Caesar and the Senate, move aside for the mail cart!*

She lay back on the fine fabric within the carriage and let her palms move over the space where Soren usually sat. She felt a little tingle at the thought of him. It was obvious that he cared for her more deeply than he let on. He had trusted her to inspect and purchase property in Tivoli for him, and he had ensured her safety by sending two of his strongest slaves to accompany her.

And now that he was free of that annoying young strumpet of a wife—how wonderful to know that child was not his!—anything was possible, even marriage. Aelina would do whatever it took to make that happen.

She sighed contentedly at the thought and stretched her arm to pull back the curtain. "How much longer?" she called out to the man holding the horses' reins.

"Not long now, Domina," he answered. "The road is less busy now, so we will make better time."

She pulled the curtain closed. The fool had been saying that since they had passed the Altar to Proserpina. Then again, Aelina knew she shouldn't complain. They had been warned about bandits in the area but, happily, their trip had been peaceful.

A scream shattered that peace. Aelina sat up, startled. Another scream and then the sound of a grunt and a tumble. *Did the driver just fall onto the road? It certainly sounded like that.*

She gripped the curtain—should she open it? She wanted to see what all the commotion was. The screams had multiplied and been joined by a clashing of swords. The carriage jerked back and forth as the horses reacted to whatever was happening around them.

But then peace returned. The shouts and sword clashes stopped, the horses calmed, and the carriage sat unmoving.

Aelina held her breath and opened the curtain.

An Egyptian man was standing immediately outside the carriage. He smiled when he saw her. She thought about smiling back, but before she could, she felt his huge hands clamp down on her hair. He pulled her out of the carriage to land heavily, painfully, on her knees on the cobblestone.

"You can take the coin," she whimpered.

The Egyptian laughed. His grip on her hair tightened, and he dragged her over the cobblestone and into the ditch alongside the road. But he didn't stop there. He kept dragging her toward the woods. In the moment before the thick trees obscured her vision, Aelina saw the bodies of the horseman and Soren's two slaves sprawled on the road.

She cried out. "Stop! The money is hidden under the carriage! I will show you." But he didn't stop. He didn't even seem to be listening to her. Aelina grunted and tried to twist out of his grip. "Do you not speak Latin? I am not carrying the coin!"

Aelina reached up to try and pry the Egyptian bandit's fingers off her hair, but he was too strong. She shrieked as he jerked her body forward violently, bouncing her over a hard tree root and then dragging her over the sharp branches, needlelike thorns, and jagged rocks of the forest floor. She heard a rip as the fabric of her expensive tunica tore. Thistles stabbed the bare skin of her legs.

"What are you doing?" she shouted. "Are you deaf? The money is in the carriage!"

The man's grip on her hair tightened again, this time making Aelina fear that he would rip her hair right off her scalp. How ugly she would look to Soren then! She slapped at his hands and dug her nails into them.

And then she found herself flying through the air. She landed against the solid boards of a wooden wall and blinked.

She got up on her knees and looked around. She was in some kind of a shack. Metal hooks, animal traps, and dirty knives hung from the ceiling. Dried deerskins were nailed to the walls, and the floor was streaked with old bloodstains. The door closed, blocking out all light except that which came through a single small window.

The Egyptian stood in front of her, so tall that his head nearly touched the roof. She had never seen a man so tall. Not since—no. That was impossible. That man looked nothing like *this* man.

The Egyptian pulled off his wig and rubbed his shaved head. "Hello, Domina."

Aelina fell back. The voice. She recognized the voice. Slowly, the features fell into place; they were a bit more sunken than they used to be, perhaps darker, and obscured by cosmetics, but the voice pulled all the pieces together.

"Scorpus?" she asked.

"Scorpus the Titan," he corrected.

Aelina had a sudden vision of herself as Scorpus saw her: kneeling on the ground, with a torn dress and disheveled hair. She raised her hands to tuck clumps of wayward hair back into place. Deciding she needed to assert her authority—she was the master, he the slave—she spoke sharply. "Help me up at once."

Her decision was the wrong one. Scorpus kicked her in the stomach. She wretched and gagged, coughing up her stomach's contents: the bread and olives she had been snacking on since the last milestone.

Aelina decided to try another approach. "I can take you to Soren," she sputtered. "I can sneak you into his house . . . You can kill him."

Scorpus cocked his head. "You always were a traitorous little slut, weren't you, Aelina? Mettius deserved better. What I do to you today, I do for him as well as for me." He sniffed. "And for Cassandra."

"Who is Cassandra?"

If there was any small part of Scorpus that was still unsure about whether he would go through with it, it was gone now. He took a step toward Aelina, grabbed her by the neck, and lifted her off the ground. She slapped at his hands and kicked furiously, but it was pointless. The Titan towered over her as large and wild and undefeatable as Hercules possessed by Hera's wrath.

Scorpus slammed Aelina's back against the wall. He turned his body to hold her in place as he reached for a hammer and one of four long, thick rusty nails that he had previously placed in a sack that hung on the wall.

With an efficiency that almost suggested he had done this before, he extended her left arm and pinned it against the wall: he placed the tip of the nail against her inner wrist and drove the nail through the flesh, ligament, and bones in one hard, fast blow.

A violent spasm shook Aelina's body, and she let out a loud, gasping scream. She pounded Scorpus's back with her free hand and tried to kick him away, but his weight was immovable. Still screaming, she tried to pull her bloody wrist off the nail, but he had hammered the nail's head at an angle so her wrist could not slip off.

Scorpus took a second nail from the sack on the wall and twisted his body to keep her in place. He extended her right arm and hammered the nail's shank through her wrist, again bending the head so there was no way she could pull herself free. This time, Aelina's scream was more gasping than loud. The pain and the position made it impossible to get any real volume.

Scorpus took a step back to inspect his work. Aelina stood open-armed and openmouthed, taking shallow breaths, her eyes pleading with him to stop. Blood coursed down the wall from both her wrists.

His eyes moved down to her legs. Her position—with her back against the wall instead of hanging on a cross—meant he couldn't nail her ankles in the proper way. He would have to improvise.

Still holding the hammer, he took another nail from the sack. Aelina groaned in protest and mumbled something. Tears plastered her cheeks and streamed down her neck, soaking the neck of her tunica. Scorpus knelt and pressed the back of her left lower leg flat against the wall. He held the tip of the nail against her knee and pressed it into the flesh. He wanted Aelina to know what was coming. Her groans grew more pitiful, more desperate.

"Stop," she managed to exhale. "Please don't, please . . ."

Scorpus pounded the nail through her knee. Her kneecap shifted grotesquely to one side, as if it were trying to somehow leap out of her leg. He angled the nail to secure it.

Aelina's moans and whimpers were barely audible now. Every short breath, every small movement on her part felt like the nail going in anew. The pain had immobilized her.

"Almost done, Domina," said Scorpus.

He hammered the final nail through her right knee.

Scorpus stood up and unhooked a rag from the wall. Wiping the blood off his hands, he again stepped back to review his work. Something was missing. Ah, yes. Of course.

He gripped the neckline of her tunica and pulled, ripping the fabric in half to expose her bare body. Her dress hung at her sides like a worn tunica on an old scarecrow.

Scorpus stared at her nakedness and laughed. "Something just occurred to me," he said. "I'm probably the only man from Capua who has never seen you naked." He ran his hands over her breasts and then squeezed hard, very hard, until they burned bright red. "It was worth the wait," he said.

And then he sat on a stool in front of her and stared into her face. It was a face contorted with an agony and terror that was beyond anything he had ever seen during all his years on the racetrack or in the amphitheater.

"I speak truthfully, Domina," he said. "You are the most beautiful sight I have ever seen. With your permission, I am going to sit here and watch you die."

CHAPTER XXII

Arx Tarpeia Capitoli Proxima
The Tarpeian Rock is near the Capitoline.

−A ROMAN MAXIM

ROME

Standing before the hearth inside the temple, Pomponia placed her hands over the goddess's eternal flame. As the heat radiated into her palms, she let her head drop back on her shoulders and watched wisps of sacred smoke—the goddess's breath—slip out the oculus in the new bronze roof.

On the other side of the marble hearth, the Vestal Quintina sat at a small but pretty desk that she had positioned under one of the larger oil lamps affixed to the circular wall of the temple; such was the Vestals' workload that the desk was a welcome new addition. She had a wax tablet in one hand and a stylus in the other. She was deep in thought.

So was Pomponia. After checking that Quintina was immersed in her work, Pomponia dipped her fingers into the top of her tunica and pulled out a lock of dark hair. Quintus's hair. She held it between her fingers, this last piece of him.

It was her most valued possession, more valued than even the intaglio ring with the Vestal seal he had given her as a would-be wedding ring. It was far more valuable to her than her country villas, fine jewelry, and the sacks of gold coins that were locked away in her personal treasury in the House of the Vestals.

But the more valued the sacrifice, the greater the chance that Vesta would honor it. That is how the gods worked. Pomponia gently placed Quintus's lock of hair in the fire.

Vesta Aeterna, she prayed silently, *mother and protector of Rome, your humble priestess asks for your protection against the man named Soren Calidius Pavo. If you grant it, I will commission an obelisk, which I am told the Egyptians build to honor the rays of the sun, to you and to Caesar Augustus, the emperor who has so richly honored your name and your temple. I give this item that is precious to me so that you will make it so.*

The flames delicately folded themselves over and around the lock of hair, consuming it entirely so all that remained of Quintus was a spot of ash in the eternal fire.

Perhaps this would be one last way he could protect her.

One of the temple's bronze doors opened, and Cossinia stepped inside. She placed a piece of kindling onto the fire and stood beside Pomponia, wondering how to broach the subject on her mind.

Pomponia spoke first. "I could not have made it through Tuccia's death, and all the ordeals that followed, without you," she said. "It's been one crisis after another. The contagion, General Agrippa's death, the attack on the temple in Africa, the flood and the collapse of the roof, imperial scandals and exile . . . you've even seen your chief Vestal crushed by Icarus falling from the sky. I know what you are going to ask, and I cannot blame you for wanting to serve the goddess in a less temperamental place."

Cossinia laughed, but her voice was sincere. "It has been an honor and a privilege to serve in Rome alongside you and my sisters," she said, "but I am homesick for the temple in Tivoli."

"I know," Pomponia replied. "I have already kept you much longer than we anticipated. You have my permission to return home whenever you wish."

"I think I will do so soon, Pomponia. My niece is with child . . . I would like to be there."

"Then, I will adjust the docket and the watches this evening. Go home, Cossinia. Tomorrow. You have earned it. Anyway, we will visit often when I am at my villa." She laughed. "You will return to Tivoli a celebrity, nay? You are the Vestal whose toy dog carving kept Rome's sacred fire burning in a crisis."

"Clearly you have not heard the latest telling of the story," said Cossinia. "The religious collegia have decreed it was a carving of a wolf, not a dog."

Pomponia nodded, amused. "That does sound more epic."

"Lucasta is joining me on watch," said Cossinia, "but she will be a while yet. She is just finishing up a lesson in the novices' study."

"I am fine to wait," said Quintina. "I have to get through these notes anyway." She scribbled something on her wax tablet and added, "I like the wolf story better too." She glanced up and tapped her stylus on the desk. "But it was a dog."

Pomponia smiled a farewell and exited the temple to step outside into the mild air of the early evening.

As he often was, Anchises was waiting for her at the bottom of the temple's steps. He was carrying little Pomponia in his arms.

"Hello, Priestess," he said, holding up one of the baby's hands to Pomponia.

The Vestal took the child's hand and kissed it. "How is my sweet niece today?" she asked. The baby flashed a gummy smile and squawked happily at her aunt. Pomponia felt her heart grow degrees warmer.

"There is news from Maecenas," said Anchises.

"Gods," exhaled Pomponia. "What is it?"

"Nothing that concerns you directly, although I was saddened to hear of it. The emperor's poet, Virgil, has died."

"Oh, Anchises, I am sorry to hear that," said Pomponia. "I know you had a friendship of sorts with him."

"Of sorts, yes," replied Anchises. "I had hoped to sing more of his verses. They are as beautiful as anything ever written. Now I shall never get the chance."

"But I thought his poem was complete?"

"It is," said Anchises. "But he was not happy with the final verses and so left instructions in his will for the poem to be burned in its entirety."

"Caesar will never allow it," said Pomponia. "He will order it performed, regardless. You will sing Virgil yet."

Anchises considered this. "You know Caesar well," he said.

"Too well," replied the Vestal. "That's the problem."

Caeso and Publius opened the doors to the House of the Vestals for Pomponia and Anchises. They passed into the atrium, where little Pomponia's wet nurse took the baby from Anchises's arms. They wandered slowly through the house and into the peristyle of the courtyard.

Anchises stopped abruptly. Pomponia retraced a few steps to stand beside him.

"Not again," said the singer.

They watched unseen as Tacita eyed Thracius kneeling on the grass in the courtyard. He was pulling weeds out of a rosebush. She pinched her cheeks for color and then glided up to him as innocently as one of the novices he cared for.

Pomponia whispered, "I suspect it's precisely that kind of nonsense that my brother fell for."

"He may not be her last victim either," Anchises grumbled. "Just watch."

Playfully, Tacita tapped Thracius on the shoulder. He looked up at her. "Yes?"

"Oh, I do not need anything," she said. "I am just wondering why you are doing the gardeners' work for them?"

"I am doing the work that needs to be done," said Thracius.

"But what a waste of your talents!"

"I care not for my talents."

"I hear they are quite . . . diverse," said Tacita.

Thracius stood up. Tacita positioned herself in front of him and reached out to touch the burns of his arms. "We are the same," she said, looking sadly at his burns and then at her own. "Tell me, Thracius, do you still have sensation where the scars are?" She traced her fingertips along the boxer's thick forearm.

Anchises tensed. It was hard to watch. He knew that Thracius had always enjoyed coupling with women as well as with men, but it had been a long time since he had done so. And Tacita, despite her burn-scarred hand, was still very lovely.

The singer leaned toward Pomponia. "It is like this every day now," he said. "I think Tacita's true form is a snake. She no sooner slithers out of one hole than she's seeking another."

"I have a plan in motion to get rid of her," said Pomponia. "Another day or two at the most, Anchises. Be patient. Meanwhile, you have reminded me of something I wanted to show you. Come."

Pomponia led Anchises back into the house toward the main kitchen. Several slaves were chatting idly in the kitchen: two were butchering a dead pig on a large wooden table, while the others were cleaning the walls and brick ovens.

"Leave us," said Pomponia. The slaves quickly exited the kitchen. When she was certain they were gone, she took a burning candle off the table and led him through the pantry.

"Everyone was told they were expanding the sewer under this section of the house," she said. "That is partly true." She ran her palm along the brick wall until she found a certain tiny chink in the brickwork. She pushed it, and a small, secret door popped open.

"Magic," said Anchises.

"Engineering," Pomponia replied. She pushed the door aside and squeezed through, Anchises following with difficulty behind her. He put his head through the doorway first and then twisted his shoulders and body to maneuver himself through.

Pomponia closed the door behind them and knelt down. By the light of the candle, she felt along the floor tiles for a hidden handle: she pulled it upward and another secret door opened, this one leading underground.

Anchises knelt beside her and peered down into the darkness. In the dim light, he could make out a ladder that went straight down. He turned to the priestess.

"Vestals don't like going underground," she said humorlessly.

Still holding the candle, she spun on her knees and lowered one leg into the hole. Her foot found the first rung of the ladder and she moved downward. Anchises followed her, proceeding by feel.

He reached the bottom of the ladder and stood beside her as she moved the candle before them to show him the space: a narrow dirt tunnel that snaked into the darkness.

"It's an escape tunnel," she said. "It's narrow so that women can get through it quickly but not men, especially not men in armor."

A clump of loose dirt rained down on Anchises. "Will they be paving it?"

"No. It will be left like this. If we need to escape, the guards can collapse the entrance once we're through so no one can follow us."

Holding the candle before her, Pomponia led Anchises through the narrow tunnel. The singer did his best to avoid scraping the walls of the tunnel but couldn't help leaving trails of dirt in his wake.

They walked through the tunnel, at times having to duck their heads and turn sideways to slip through the dirt-lined passageway, until Anchises could make out the sound of rushing water. A few more steps and they arrived at a more open juncture, where sewage from the Palatine Hill flowed past them like a thick, rancid river, heading toward the main line, the Cloaca Maxima.

Pomponia covered her mouth with her veil to filter the smell. Anchises put his mouth in the crook of his elbow.

"If we needed to escape," she shouted over the noisy waters, "we could follow the sewer to any number of exit points in Rome. We could emerge out of almost any drain."

"Like the rats," said Anchises.

"Like the rats," echoed Pomponia. "Or we could follow the Cloaca Maxima all the way to where it empties into the Tiber. It would depend on what kind of crisis we were facing and where we'd dispatched guards to collect us." She held the candle out to the left, where the sewage was flowing down from the Palatine. "We could also walk up the sewer straight to a drain at Caesar's house." She gestured to the narrow stone walkway built into the curved wall of the sewer: it ran adjacent to the flowing wastewater. "We wouldn't even have to get our stolas dirty."

"Well, thank the gods for that."

"I read about tunnels like this in the archives," Pomponia continued. "After the attack on the temple in Carthage, I wanted to restore them. Quintina's ordeal convinced me too. We don't need any more frantic Vestals running through the pouring rain trying to keep the flame alight." She pointed to nowhere in particular down the tunnel and then the sewer. "There will be gates and kindling placed throughout. As long as Caesar's improvements to the infrastructure hold and the sewers don't back up, it should work."

"Who knows about this?" asked Anchises.

"Caesar and Maecenas, two imperial engineers, and the two of us."

"What about the men who dug it?"

"*Mortui silent*," said Pomponia. Dead men don't talk.

"And the other priestesses?"

"I'll show them once everything is completed. The novices won't be informed, though, just in case I feel the need to throw any more of them out onto the street."

Anchises smirked. "Let's get out of here."

They backtracked to the kitchen, and Pomponia made sure to seal the hidden doors in the tile floor and brick wall before returning the candle to the butcher's table.

"Shall we take a more refreshing walk outside?" asked Anchises. "The Forum should be secured and clear by now."

But Pomponia was distracted. Anchises felt it too. The unsettling experience of being underground and the circumstances that required the building of the escape tunnel in the first place—the threat of invasion or some kind of catastrophic crisis—had cast a pall over their moods.

It was a sobering reminder that, despite how insulated and privileged their lives seemed, it could all collapse around them within moments, like a dirt tunnel. Soren could make it happen.

"Let's clean up," said Pomponia, "and then meet out front. I'll have a carriage brought round. I have something else in mind."

*   *   *

Pomponia had never been to the Evil Field at night.

In fact, she had rarely been there even in the day. There just wasn't much need for it. The last time she had visited was ten years ago, after Tuccia had been absolved. She had left on the ground an oil lamp that burned with the sacred flame to honor the priestesses who had been wrongly condemned.

She stepped out of the horse-drawn carriage into the dark night and carried a lamp with a thick flame across the small grassy field to the black marble block that sealed the entrance to the pit. A single line was engraved upon it: *Damnatae Vestalium Virginum.*

The condemned Vestal Virgins.

She sat on the grass and placed her palm on the cool marble. Anchises sat beside her.

"Fabiana knew one of the priestesses down there," said Pomponia. "Or at least whose bones are down there. She was a young Vestal named Licinia. She was falsely condemned and later absolved . . . not that the absolution did her any good."

"How many Vestals have been buried here?" asked Anchises.

"No one knows for sure. The archives say that Priestess Tarpeia was the first, though. Her bones have been buried here for over seven hundred years."

"Tarpeia as in the Tarpeian Rock? The cliff that traitors are thrown off?"

Pomponia nodded. "Tarpeia was one of the earliest Vestal priestesses who served during the founding years of Rome. She was the daughter of Spurius Tarpeius, the commander of the citadel on the Capitoline Hill. It is said that she opened the gates of the city to the Sabine army in exchange for gold jewelry, but once the invaders entered Rome, she was crushed by their shields as they fell from the cliff above." Pomponia shrugged. "But who knows the real story."

"You have reason to doubt the account?"

"The accusation against Tuccia opened my eyes," said Pomponia. "The annals list the names of condemned Vestals: Pinaria, Oppia, Sextilia, Floronia. Considering how many Vestals served through the centuries, very few were condemned. But of those who were, how many were innocent? How many were falsely accused so that some incompetent general or greedy landowner or crooked senator could advance himself or absolve himself of some wrongdoing? For all we know, Tarpeius betrayed his people and then blamed it on his daughter."

"Domina," said Anchises, "who made the accusation against Priestess Tuccia?"

"Lady Claudia. She was Livia's sister."

"I did not know the empress had a sister. What happened to her?"

"I had her killed," Pomponia said as she traced her finger along the letters engraved in the marble. "I had Ankhu abduct her from her villa. She was sold as a slave. Eventually she was fed to the lions in a second-rate arena in Africa."

Pomponia turned to see Anchises's reaction. The expression on his face—eyebrows raised in surprise, mouth open—made her giggle. The giggle turned into a laugh. "My slave Medousa used to give me that same face." The laughed subsided. "How I miss her."

"I am a poor substitute," said Anchises.

"You are no substitute at all," Pomponia replied. "You are more than that. You are an authentic friend to me."

"Thracius and I have never been happier, Domina."

"I doubt that is true, but it is good of you to say so. If I am brought down by Soren, I will do my best to ensure your safety."

"You will not be brought down."

Pomponia leaned on Anchises's shoulder and exhaled. Behind her in the darkness, she could hear the horses snort and pull at the long grass.

She sighed again. "There is an old saying: *Arx Tarpeia Capitoli proxima.* It means that it is easy to fall from a place of high power." Pomponia pulled her palla tighter around her shoulders. "Nowhere is that more true than in Rome."

*   *   *

Dawn had not yet broken, and all was still in the House of the Vestals. Varinia and the other novices were tucked away in their beds, sleeping peacefully. So were Quintina, Caecilia, Lucretia, and Cossinia: Marcella and Lucasta were on watch in the temple with the eldest novice, Lauressa, who was close to becoming a full Vestal herself.

Pomponia was awake in bed, staring at the ceiling. In the fireplace against the far wall of her bedchamber, the last embers of a fire were burning. It was enough to warm the room. She focused on relaxing her shoulders, willing herself to sink into the bed and catch a few more moments of sleep, but her thoughts were jumping between yesterday's duties and today's.

After returning from the Evil Field with Anchises the night before, she had stayed up late to adjust the docket and watches so that Cossinia was free to leave for Tivoli in the morning.

After that, she had written letters to Sabina and the religious collegia in Carthage, approving the sketches for a statue of the long-serving Vestal which would stand in a treed grove in the forum in Carthage. From everything Sabina had written to Pomponia, it seemed the people in Carthage were brokenhearted at the loss of Nona. Pomponia knew how they felt.

She closed her eyes and listened to the first soft chirpings of birds outside the window of her bedchamber. It was soothing.

For a moment. Then it was interrupted by the loud voices of men somewhere beyond her door. They were coming from far away but still inside the house.

Even as her stomach sank with a now familiar feeling of dread, Pomponia kicked off the covers and dressed quickly, pulling a tunica over her head and wrapping a palla around her shoulders.

She hurried out of her room and rushed downstairs toward the atrium, her bare feet absorbing the coolness of the orange and white mosaic floor until she nearly ran into Caeso's chest.

"What in the name of the gods is going on?" she asked.

Although she was already imagining the worst. She was expecting to see Caesar or the high priest Laelius marching toward her, stern-faced and accusatory.

Her memory flew back to that night the Pontifex Maximus and soldiers had stormed into the House of the Vestals. She would never forget Lepidus's stricken face and his trembling words: *Priestess Pomponia, it is my most grievous duty, but I must tell you that an accusation of incestum has been made against the Vestal order.*

She pushed the old memory out of her mind. She had new problems to solve.

As the other Vestals joined her, their faces as worried and searching as hers, Caeso straightened his iron breastplate and struggled with a leather strap. He, too, had been woken from sleep—the night guards were still on duty—and had donned his armor in a hurry.

"Some of Tiberius's men are in the atrium," he said. "Soldiers. They are demanding Lady Tacita."

"Why me?" exclaimed Tacita.

Pomponia and the other Vestals jumped at the outburst. None of them had heard Tacita approach. Like them, she stood wide-eyed, barefoot, and disheveled from slumber.

"Why me?" she asked again, this time her voice louder and more frightened.

Pomponia nodded at Caeso. *Tell us what you know.*

"Lady Tacita is charged with adultery against her former husband, Soren Calidius Pavo, and indecency contrary to the *lex Julia de adulteriis.*"

Tacita shook her head, confused. "The lex what? What is that?" When no one answered, she looked at Quintina. "You promised me safe refuge here from Soren!" She turned to Pomponia. "You are the Vestalis Maxima! Tell them that you have offered me sanctuary, and they will have no choice but to leave me alone."

Pomponia looked at Caeso. "Give her to Tiberius's men. I withdraw the order of sanctuary."

"Priestess!" Tacita lunged for Pomponia's palla, but Caeso intercepted by wrapping his arm around her throat. He dragged her effortlessly toward the atrium where the men had been instructed to wait.

The shock of the experience now having subsided, Caecilia folded her arms across her chest. "Will she get a trial?"

"Why trouble the courts?" Pomponia answered. "She is guilty."

Caecilia shrugged. *Whatever you say. I don't care either way.*

It was a sentiment the others shared. There wasn't a priestess, novice, guard, or slave in the House of the Vestals who had been impressed with Tacita's presence. Whether she was falsely pitying a Vestal's virginity, flirting with the male slaves, or striking the kitchen staff, she had managed to offend everyone during her short stay. No one was upset to see her dragged across the floor like a sack of useless offal.

Caecilia and Lucretia turned to go back to their bedchambers. As Cossinia did the same, she put her hand on Pomponia's shoulder. "It is good I return to Tivoli today. My heart cannot take much more Roman excitement."

"I'm tempted to come with you," Pomponia replied, "so don't be alarmed if you find me hiding under the cushions in your carriage."

Cossinia laughed and departed. Once Pomponia and Quintina were alone, Quintina leaned against the wall. "Where will they take her?"

"To the Subura. She'll be stripped of her citizenship and sold as a prostitute to one of the brothels. It's a discretionary penalty under Caesar's new morality legislation. I fully expect the Senate will challenge the law at some point, but not for Tacita. It's hard to believe," said the high priestess, "but when it comes to Tacita, we all want the same thing. You and me, Livia, Caesar, Tiberius—even Soren. Everyone will be happy to see her live as a *probrosa*."

Quintina felt a smile form on her face as she pictured her sister, Tacita, pinned down on a dirty mattress by some grunting, filthy man. The smile wasn't conscious; it just arose from some deeper part of her. "It is the most justice Septimus will ever receive," she said.

Pomponia leaned against the wall next to her. She found it hard to look Quintina in the eye when she spoke of Septimus.

"It is some justice for Pomponius too," she said. "Although I still hope to offer him more."

Quintina let her smile spread. "Justice can wait," she said. "Let's go check on our niece. She grows more adorable every morning."

CHAPTER XXIII

Saepe Nihil Inimicus Homini Quam Sibi Ipse
A man is often his own worst enemy.

—CICERO

TIVOLI

Ankhu clutched the handle of his piercing ax so hard that his knuckles went white. He had never been so angry in his life. Scorpus the Titan, Scorpus the Fool, had been missing for two days, and Ankhu knew exactly where he had gone.

To find Aelina, his former owner and Soren's current plaything, and kill her.

Yet Ankhu wasn't angry at Scorpus. He was angry with himself, at his own indiscretion. No doubt Scorpus had overheard him and Anchises discussing Aelina's trip to Tivoli, and no doubt he had, from that moment forward, planned to exact the type of impulsive, emotional, doomed vengeance that he seemed to excel in.

He was angry at his own indecision too. Why had he not acted months ago? Why had he not followed his instinct and killed Scorpus? He could have told his mistress that the rogue charioteer had run off, that he had taken coin from the house and a horse from the stable and simply left. She would have believed it. Probably.

He sat fuming, crouched behind stacks of hay and supplies in an empty horse stall in the back of the priestess's large stable. He had a feeling that Scorpus would return tonight.

The man would unsaddle his horse, bathe it—though regrettably not himself—drink an amphora or two of the priestess's wine, and pass out in the corner of his horse's stall. He then would awake in the morning and complain for hours about his hangover.

I will spare him the trouble of that, thought Ankhu.

The Egyptian heard movement outside the stable. One of the doors creaked open, and a slant of light from the full silver moon illuminated the rows of stalls. A stabled horse neighed softly and shifted on its legs. Another whinnied and clopped, irritated by the interruption.

The sound of human footsteps moved deeper into the stable. Ankhu knew the location and pitch of every squeaky, creaking, loose plank of the floor. It's how he knew when Scorpus was standing immediately outside the empty stall he was crouching in.

The Egyptian sprang to his feet and raised his ax high in the air—the Titan was as tall as Cronus—and brought it down on the man's skull with expert precision, despite the fact that, for some inexplicable reason, Scorpus seemed two feet shorter than he had been two days earlier.

The man collapsed, and Ankhu wrenched the blade out of his skull. He stepped back and squinted in the darkness. The dead man at his feet wasn't Scorpus.

The floor planks creaked again, more loudly this time, and Ankhu looked up. He took a measured step back as the silhouettes of three very large men appeared in the stable's doorway, all of them holding weapons that he could not quite make out in the moonlight.

"There he is!" one of them yelled. "And the bastard's already killed Pontius!"

They all rushed toward him at once.

Ankhu leaped over the low wall that led to the adjacent stall and unfastened its door to emerge several steps behind the men who were now spinning around trying to find him. It only took them a moment to spot him. Ankhu thought about making a run for it—he needed to get help from the house—but there wasn't enough distance between him and the assassins to make that a viable option.

Worse, two more large men suddenly appeared in the entrance, blocking it off and trapping him between them and the original three at the back of the stable.

The Egyptian unhooked a long bullwhip from the wall and cracked it hard at one who was running toward him from the doorway. The man's hands went up to his throat, and he fell forward. The other lunged to the side.

Ankhu swung the whip around to where the three to his rear were also advancing. The whip caught one man across the eyes, instantly blinding him, causing him to shriek in pain and run directly into a wooden post. "I can't see!" he screamed, panic-stricken. "Iuppiter, help me, help me!"

At the sound of the man's piercing screams, one of his companions turned and stabbed him in the ear. Useless was bad enough, but annoying was intolerable. The blinded man fell to the floor, dead before his body hit the ground.

The two remaining men at the back of the stable darted toward Ankhu. The Egyptian could see their weapons clearly now. The one who had stabbed the blinded man held a short gladius; the other held a long sword.

Ankhu dropped the whip. It was useless with the men so close to him. Instead, he dove for the latch on the stall next to him, swinging the door open. It provided a brief but bulky barrier between him and them, but more important, it freed a particularly belligerent black stallion who charged out of his stall, snorting angrily at all the ruckus and looking for someone to blame.

The horse saw Ankhu, decided he wasn't at fault, and instead kicked out his hind legs with such force that the attackers on the other side of the door were sent flying. The one with the gladius got up as quickly as he had fallen, but the other remained where he was, unconscious.

The horse reared, kicking his front legs wildly in the air. He came down hard, lowered his head, and charged through the one open door, into the night. The man closest flattened himself against the wall to avoid being crushed.

That left one unconscious intruder and one each in front of and behind Ankhu.

Unfortunately, the two who remained on the attack were not only the best trained but also the most familiar with each other's fighting styles. They were adept at working in unison and had killed countless targets together; after all, splitting one sack of coin was better than having no sack at all.

They closed in on Ankhu from both sides. Their calm confidence, the way they glanced at each other to communicate some secret strategy, caused him a rare moment of hesitation. It cost him.

The assassins attacked with such swift skill that the Egyptian couldn't quite tell how they had gotten so close to him. He stopped trying to figure it out and instead fought on instinct alone.

As one man brought down his sword, Ankhu raised the handle of his ax to block it and then kicked his legs out from under him. The man fell onto his back.

That thug momentarily down, Ankhu spun to face the other. He swung his ax upward: the blade slipped between the assassin's legs to land squarely between them, lodging deep in his genitals. The man screamed in agony and stumbled into an empty stall. He reached out to grab a metal hook on the wall to try and stop himself from falling but slipped on the pool of blood forming at his feet and tumbled forward. He sputtered an obscenity that was cut short as his forehead landed squarely on the hook. He hung silently from it, his arms dangling loose at his sides.

Ankhu blinked at him for a fraction of a second. That was all the time the other assassin needed. Still lying on his back, he swung his sword at the Egyptian's legs.

Ankhu's left leg came off at the knee.

He fell, landing only an arm's length away from the assassin. Peripherally, he saw his lower leg slide across the floor and come to a stop with a *thump* against a stall door. He rolled onto his back and forced himself to sit up, at the same time lifting his ax over his head and bringing it down on the assassin's arm, chopping it in half.

The Egyptian lifted his weapon again and brought the blade down on the man's jaw. He raised his ax and repeated the action. The assassin made a gurgling sound and tried to reach for his jaw with his one remaining hand, but the blood pouring out of his mouth was too much. He drowned in the red flood.

Ankhu fell onto his back and sucked in a deep breath of air. He refused to acknowledge the shocking pain. Or the horror of it. He forced the image of his amputated leg out of his mind and rolled over.

He managed to push himself onto his hands and knees—or at least one knee. He wasn't exactly sure what was happening with the other and couldn't bring himself to look. Exhausted, he tried to crawl along the stable floor; however, he could not keep his balance and soon collapsed. He pressed his nose into the floor and breathed.

If he could get into the open and call to one of the bigger male house slaves before the one remaining assassin regained consciousness, he could still make it.

He extended his right arm in front of him and clutched a raised plank to drag his body forward. It worked once, twice, a third time, bringing him closer to the open door. But when he tried to drag himself forward a fourth time, his body wouldn't move. He seemed to be stuck to the ground.

Puzzled, Ankhu slid his hand under his chest and down his torso— until he felt solid metal. He blinked, trying to put it all together. He felt no pain. Yet there was no other explanation.

He had been impaled from above. The assassin's sword had gone clean through his back to sink into the wood planks of the floor, pinning him in place.

He felt a flare of panic: *How will I warn the priestess?*

And then, thanks to merciful Isis, he felt nothing at all.

CHAPTER XXIV

Ingenium Mala Saepe Movent
Misfortune often stirs genius.

−OVID

ROME

A prostitute who worked in the new Domus Tauri—the House of the Bull—in Rome's Subura district could be said to be making the best of a bad situation.

The Domus Tauri was one of the cleaner brothels in the Subura. It was owned and operated by a former slave of Tiberius who had apparently earned her freedom by fellating a bull for him and King Herod of Judea.

Afterward, Tiberius had given her some coin to invest in her future as a freedwoman, and she had been wise enough to know the one thing that was guaranteed to turn bronze into gold: sex.

She had also recognized the profitability of celebrity. Instead of trying to hide her sordid past as a bull's fellatrix, she marketed it. She changed her name to Pasiphae, the woman who fell in love with the bull of Poseidon, and made sure that all her prostitutes, female and male alike, similarly adopted erotic personas. Even the name of her establishment, the House of the Bull, was expert marketing: it promoted her persona while flattering the potency of its male clientele.

Venus herself could not have created a more successful brothel. During the short time it had been in business, the Domus Tauri had become the premier brothel for senators, patrician men, and priests who could afford the high-quality prostitutes and sensationalized sexual experiences it offered. Some even kept a favored woman or man there for their exclusive use. For a prostitute, that was about as good as life could get.

Unfortunately for Tacita, she had not been sold to the Domus Tauri. She had been sold to a lower-class *lupanarium* that didn't even warrant having its own name. It was just the corner brothel where you could get essentially the same services for a quarter of the price. And instead of being managed by a business-savvy freedwoman who took great care of her inventory, it was run by a one-armed old Greek man who spent more time on top of his prostitutes than their clients did.

Tacita stood in a cold bucket of water and tried to clean the Greek's filth off of her. Out of her. She looked down and cringed at the brown water running down her legs. The cloth she used was so dirty she might have been better off not trying to clean herself at all.

"It's no use," she heard a voice say to her.

Tacita looked up to a see a woman not much older than herself staring at the brown cloth with an upturned nose.

"Do you have a better idea?"

"I always have a better idea," said the woman. "That's why I just bought you."

Tacita blinked, not understanding.

"Gods," muttered the woman, "I hope you're not simple." She motioned for Tacita to step out of the bucket. "I'm Pasiphae. You're going to work in my brothel instead."

"Pasiphae . . ." said Tacita. "Do you mean the Domus Tauri?"

"Ah, you've heard of it. Good. It will better suit your background." Pasiphae handed Tacita a clean tunica. No longer concerned with modesty, Tacita wriggled out of the stained one she was wearing and pulled the fresh one over her head. The new owner waved her forward. "Let's head home. You can bathe there."

As they left the street of the nameless lupanarium and walked toward the slightly better yet still loud and bustling street of the Domus Tauri, Tacita did her best to keep up with her new mistress while also trying to avoid stepping on the garbage, and sometimes the feces, smeared along the cobblestone.

Pasiphae looked at the grimy, calloused bare feet of her newest acquisition. "We'll get you into a decent pair of sandals. You'll tear a man's back to shreds if you wrap those around him."

Tacita regarded her feet with disgust—they used to be so soft and pretty—then looked at Pasiphae. "Why did you purchase me? Your brothel is quite famous, and I don't—"

"You screwed Caesar, didn't you?"

"Yes."

"Did you suck him too?"

"Yes."

Pasiphae stopped in the middle of the street, seemingly oblivious to the streams of people who moved past, bumping into her with their elbows or the large baskets they carried.

"A man will part with silver to screw a woman that Caesar has had," she said. "He'll part with gold to be sucked by her. They like to pretend their cocks are as important as his." She crossed her arms in front of her chest and smiled. "I remember you, you know. You were at a party at the house of Tiberius. I served you wine."

Tacita scraped something foul off the bottom of her foot. "Yes," she said, "and look at me now."

"In time you can earn your freedom, as I did."

"I know how you earned your freedom. I think I'd rather be a slave."

"That's because you haven't been one long enough. You haven't even had real customers yet."

"Maybe not, but that pig who owns the lupanarium has already taken me by force several times."

"Your concept of force will change once you have paying clients," said Pasiphae. She started off again as Tacita followed. "The Greek took it easy on you. He didn't want to damage the goods. But a man who parts with a denarius in the brothels is determined to get his money's worth. You will soon see the difference."

They walked until they reached the thick wooden door of the Domus Tauri. Pasiphae gripped the iron ring affixed to it and knocked. A moment later, the door cracked open, and a well-muscled man wearing a tarnished soldier's breastplate peeked out suspiciously before nodding at Pasiphae and opening the door wider.

"The place is guarded by ex-legionaries," Pasiphae said as she led Tacita through the vestibule and into the well-decorated atrium. "If a client wants you to do something he didn't pay for in advance, just shout out. One of these big boys here will come to collect. But don't worry, that doesn't happen often. We cater to a higher-class crowd for the most part."

Tacita could tell. Despite the domus's modest Subura exterior, the interior was surprisingly comfortable. An attractive male slave sat at a desk in the corner, counting coins and jotting notes down on a tablet. On the wall behind him were ten or twelve small paintings of naked couples in different sexual positions and acts.

"It works the same way here as it does in any lupanarium," said Pasiphae. "Usually I'll negotiate with your clients and collect payment, but if I'm not around, it'll be up to you. If a client comes in, always discuss what he wants to do in advance. Some just prefer to point to the picture. Then Philo here will add up the costs, and he'll pay." She looked sternly at Tacita. "The client always pays first. No freebies, no favors. If you get lucky and a man of means wants to hire you exclusively, we'll move you into one of the *insulae* on the second floor. For now, you will live in your workroom."

Tacita followed the owner deeper into the brothel and down a narrow hallway. Oil lamps hung from the low ceiling to cast shadows in the windowless space. The smell of sweet incense was powerful, although not quite powerful enough to completely mask the pungent smell of sex.

Small rooms lined each side of the hallway like stalls in a stable. Tacita tried to ignore the moans, grunts, and rhythmic slapping together of bodies. She avoided looking at the shadows that moved behind the closed curtains: silhouettes of arms and legs intertwined and moving.

She still could not believe that her life had come to this.

She was still trying to understand how it had happened. Exactly when had it all started to go wrong? How long had Quintina been scheming to make her confess Calidia's true parentage? Why had Soren agreed to the divorce without a fight? Was it because of Aelina? Or had he just been using her all along?

To make matters worse, Tacita had no idea how she was going to maneuver her way back to freedom, back to wealth and status. But she would think of something. With all the time she was spending on her back lately, she had plenty of time to think.

The largest of the prostitutes' workrooms was located at the far end of the hallway. Instead of a curtain, it boasted the prestige of a heavy wooden door with a white marble plaque on it. When she was close enough to read the inscription, Tacita sniggered. *Caesaris Meretrix*, she read. Caesar's Courtesan.

"See?" said Pasiphae. "All it takes is an idea." She opened the door and they stepped inside. The room was spacious enough to be comfortable, with a good bed, rich linen, fine furnishings, colorful frescoes, and a basin of fresh water. Several beautiful tunicas and stolas hung from a wardrobe in the corner.

"Oh, this is much better," said Tacita. She moved across the room and sat on the soft bed. "Thank you."

Pasiphae barked an exuberant laugh. "I didn't do it for you, foolish girl. I did it for the customers. So they can play Caesar for a while. Now pretty yourself up. When I send a customer in to you, be sure to call him *Caesar* or *Emperor*. Put on a show, or you'll be back to scrubbing yourself in a bucket of brown water and short hairs." She laughed again and left the room, closing the door behind her.

Tacita lay back on the bed. It wasn't Soren's bed. It wasn't Caesar's either. It wasn't even the bed she had been given in the House of the Vestals.

For the time being, however, it was a way to make the best of a bad situation.

CHAPTER XXV

Historia Magistra Vitae Est
History is the teacher of life.

—CICERO

Pomponia had never been one to physically lose her cool. Yet, she couldn't stop herself from throwing half the items on her desk—cups, an amphora, sealing wax sticks, styli, and wax tablets—against the wall.

The young male slave that had just arrived from her villa in Tivoli ducked and moved aside to avoid being struck. She had not reacted well to the news that Ankhu's decapitated body had been found on the stable floor, surrounded by the bodies of five assassins sent to kill him.

Weakened from her outburst and emotionally drained from the shock and grief of her friend's murder, Pomponia collapsed into the chair in her office. She pressed the back of her head against the wall.

The slave waited for her to speak.

"What else do you know?" Pomponia asked him.

"Ankhu's kinsman, the horseman, returned home later that morning, and he—"

"Do you mean he was *gone*?"

"Yes, Domina. He was gone for two days. None of us knew where. Ankhu was very angry and went into the stable with his ax to wait for him. We were all certain he was going to kill him."

"When Scor—" Pomponia corrected herself. "When his kinsman returned, what did he do?"

"He saw Ankhu's body in the stable and went mad. He crushed the skulls of the other dead men with a shovel and cut off their genitals. We were all fearful of him. Then he went into the house and took a great deal of coin from Ankhu's quarters. Some of the male slaves tried to stop him, but he overpowered them. After that, he took two horses—the black one he likes and another one loaded with enough supplies for a long journey— and raced off."

"Think," said Pomponia. "Is there anything else? Did he say where he was going?"

"No, Domina, but he took his Egyptian papers with him."

Pomponia noticed another stylus rolling across her desk and threw it against the wall. It was then that she noticed Anchises and Thracius standing just inside her doorway. The singer rubbed his face. The boxer pounded the wall with a fist.

The Vestal felt her head throb with angry regret. She had waited too long and been too contemplative, too complacent, in the face of Soren's aggression. If she had acted long ago with her usual confidence and decisiveness, Soren would have been dead long ago. And Ankhu would be alive today.

Instead, her longtime friend, the man who had so loyally served Quintus and carried the letters between them from Alexandria to Rome and back again, was lying headless on a stable floor.

Instead, she was being held hostage by Soren's threats as his power under Tiberius continued to grow and as his troubling friendship with Livia continued to deepen.

The Vestal exhaled and walked behind her desk to open a drawer. There was the chink of coin as she dropped several gold pieces into a small pouch. She handed the pouch to the boy.

"Go to the Shrine of Isis in the Campus Martius," she said to him. "Pay a priest to accompany you back to Tivoli. Egyptian funeral rites are different from ours." Pomponia remembered how religiously Ankhu had taken care of Quintus's body, and she spoke quickly to hide the quaver in her voice. "Ankhu must be sent to the afterlife in the proper way." She turned to Thracius. "Go with him. See if you can find . . . see if you can find his head."

"Yes, Domina," said Thracius. "Come with me," he ordered the young slave, who dutifully followed him out of the office.

Anchises peered out the doorway to watch them walk down the colonnaded corridor. He moved to Pomponia's desk and put his hands on the edge, leaning toward her on the other side. "I suspect it would be pointless to tell you it isn't your fault."

"Wholly pointless."

"I am sorry. Ankhu was a good man."

Pomponia closed her desk drawer. She stood up straight and tucked some stray hair behind her ear. "I am late. I need to teach a lesson to the novices."

"I will tell Lucretia that you have too much work and cannot attend today."

"No, I will go." Pomponia smoothed her veil and moved out from behind her desk. "I either stay busy and purposeful or stay in here and weep all day." She rolled a private thought around in her mind. *The gods know I've done enough of that.*

"We will make an offering for Ankhu when you return," said Anchises.

"Yes. I won't be long."

Pomponia left her office. Her footsteps echoed off the marble walls as she neared the novices' study, the lonely sound amplifying her sense of isolation and the unnerving feeling that she was vulnerable, exposed to some silent predator lurking in the shadows.

In the study, the windows were open and sunlight streamed into the room, illuminating the scroll-filled shelves that lined the rich orange walls and marble plaques that bore the names of the Vestal Virgins.

Pomponia noted that a new name had been inscribed on a plaque—vv · nona—but stopped herself from thinking about it any further. Now was not the time.

At the front of the room, Lucretia spoke to the girls, who sat studiously in rows of desks. "The Vestalis Maxima will be teaching you a lesson while I attend to some other matters," she told the class. As she quickly tidied her desk, she frowned at Pomponia. "Are you all right?" she asked under her breath.

There was no point lying or denying it. Ankhu was well known and well liked by everyone in Pomponia's life—they would all find out soon enough. "Ankhu was killed at my villa in Tivoli," she whispered. "Bandits."

"That is awful!" Lucretia exclaimed softly. "I am so sorry. I know he was very dear to you. Why don't you go rest? I will stay."

"No," said Pomponia. "I need to keep busy. For now, at least."

Lucretia affectionately smoothed the side of Pomponia's veil. "I will pray for him," she said. "And I will just be in my office if you change your mind and want to rest. Just send one of the novices to fetch me."

"I will. Thank you, sister."

Once Lucretia had left the study, Pomponia stood in front of the class. Unconcerned with whatever the two Vestals were whispering about, the novices had fallen into energetic chatter. They stopped when Pomponia clapped her hands together. Her eyes fell first on Varinia, the young girl whose mother had recently died, before acknowledging each student in turn.

"As Vestal Virgins, you will be counted among the great custodians of Rome," she began. "Yet even the greatest Vestals in history were just ordinary women. They felt worry and fear and sadness. They had hopes and disappointments. They had people in their lives whom they loved, and people they hated. They had friends and enemies. Yet unlike other women, unlike wives and mothers, a Vestal must never fall into self-indulgence. She must never let her worries or her enemies disable her. She must always act in those ways that Mother Vesta and that Rome itself deems proper for a priestess. That is especially so during times of trouble or threat."

The novice Lauressa sat up straighter. Pomponia knew why. The girl was about to become a full Vestal herself. The things she was learning today were the things she would be expected to teach the novices tomorrow.

"Each of you will grow to be a woman who has troubles of her own," said Pomponia. "Perhaps you will face a crisis with the temple or the order, or perhaps you will face a personal crisis. When this happens, it is wise to look to the past and to follow the *exempla maiorum*. The ways of our ancestors. Their lives are our history, and history is always the best adviser."

Pomponia walked to one of the shelves and ran her palm along the hundreds of scrolls it contained. She pulled one out and held it up to the class. "You all know the story of the Vestal Tacita and the Gaul. You have walked by her statue in the courtyard a thousand times. When the invading Gallic army overtook the Forum and cut down every Roman they saw, like a farmer scything stalks of wheat, our sister Tacita faced her enemies instead of running from them. She performed her sacred duties to the very end and accepted her fate with dignity. So did our senators and great noblemen." Pomponia slipped the scroll back into its proper place and then sat on a high stool at the front of the study. "But it may surprise you to know that not all of our soldiers behaved with the same conviction."

A few of the novices exchanged curious looks with one another. None of them had ever heard the high priestess speak of Rome's soldiers in anything but the highest of terms.

"The Gauls didn't just attack the Forum," Pomponia continued. "They attacked the Capitoline Hill too, led by their leader Brennus—remember that name. The city's soldiers tried to defend the temples of Jupiter and Juno, but in those days, nearly four centuries ago now, not all soldiers were well-trained or organized. Many were simple family men and their sons. Some had never before wielded a sword. Sadly, they were no match for the invading army, whether in numbers or strategy, so they fortified themselves in the temples. Brennus and the Gauls besieged the Capitoline Hill for months until the Roman soldiers in the temples began to die of starvation. The rest of Rome was no better off. Most of the army was off fighting elsewhere, and although people prayed that the soldiers would hear of the invasion and return, after months of being held prisoner in their own city, they began to lose hope. Word spread that the Gauls had broken into the temple vaults, libraries, and Senate and burned every scroll they could find, forever erasing the history of our earliest days. Even Vesta's temple was violated, and many ancient customs from the *Vestales Albanae*—including those passed down by Rome's first high priestess, Amata—were lost."

Pomponia took a deep breath and leaned forward. "So, the soldiers who were captive in the temples, who were starving in them, offered to pay a ransom to the Gauls if they would leave Rome. It was an act of desperation and fear but also an act of shame. The Gauls demanded one thousand pounds of gold and, alas, the Roman soldiers agreed. They stripped the gold off the temples, took jewelry from the homes of citizens, emptied the treasury, and even melted down the statues of the gods."

A collective gasp of disbelief from the class.

The Vestal narrowed her eyes. "But you will learn, novices, what happens when you subordinate yourself to the enemy. For even though the ransom was excessive, the Gauls wanted more. More than gold. They wanted to strip the Romans of their power and dignity just as the gold had been stripped from the temples. So they openly falsified the scales so that no matter how much gold the Romans placed upon them, it was never enough. Finally, the Romans complained that they had no more to give. There was not one gold bead left in all of Rome. At that, Brennus laughed. He put his heavy sword on the scale to show that even more gold was needed and then he said these words, which you will remember: *Vae victis!* For Brennus knew at that moment that he had truly conquered Rome. Not just its people or its temples, but its spirit."

Several of the novices shook their heads in anger. The story could not end like this. They would not accept it.

Pomponia looked at their faces. They were so innocent, so eager to be emboldened and so determined to see good triumph over evil. As she told the story, she felt her own indignation and resolve strengthen alongside theirs.

"Yet one Roman soldier would not accept this. Despite the odds, he managed to escape the Temple of Jupiter and slip through the Gallic army that surrounded it. He rode six horses to death in his desperation to reach the army of the Roman general Marcus Furius Camillus. When he told the general those words Brennus had spoken—'Woe to the conquered!'—Camillus clenched his fists in rage.

"Camillus gathered his men and the men of other Roman generals. They descended on Rome and swept through the Gallic army on the Capitoline Hill like a mighty storm. Their horses' hooves shook the ground like rolling thunder, and their swords struck down the Gauls like bolts of lightning."

The novices clapped.

"When the Gauls were defeated, Camillus dragged Brennus before the Roman troops and made him kneel before them. He had his soldiers set all the bags of gold ransom, more than one thousand pounds' worth, beside Brennus. And then Camillus withdrew his sword and cut off the Gaul's head. As Brennus's head fell onto the ground of the Capitoline Hill, General Camillus shouted these words to his soldiers: '*Non auro, sed ferro, recuperanda est patria!*'" Not by gold, but by iron is the nation to be saved!

"I love this story," said Varinia.

Pomponia put her hands on her lap and smiled warmly at the girl. "It is a good story," she said. "But it is an even better lesson. You must never surrender to the enemy, no matter what. It is an affront to all the gods and goddesses. It is an insult to those who founded Rome and who have fought and died for it."

"What happened next?" asked another girl.

"The great Roman army and the legions happened next," said Pomponia. Her voice sounded clearer, more confident, even to herself. "The people, the soldiers, and the Senate of Rome vowed that they would never again kneel before the enemy. They would never allow themselves to be a conquered people. So, they created the army as we know it today. They organized it into proper units of command, with the finest armor and weapons. They cataloged its tactics and changed the way it functioned and fought. That is why we have professional soldiers who are paid well and trained even better. That is why Rome is the conqueror, not the conquered." She spoke to herself as much as the novices. "And that is why every Vestal Virgin must face her enemies with an iron will."

*   *   *

The female house slave at Soren's feet was frantically trying to mop up the blood before it spread to the rich carpet in front of the couch. She glared impatiently at the two male slaves beside her as they struggled to pick up the dead man from the floor. He was big and heavy, and it took a few attempts for them to get a good grip on the dead weight. Finally, they shuffled off with the corpse, one of them supporting it under the arms, the other by the legs.

Soren wiped his hands on his white toga, leaving blotches of blood that almost made it appear as if he had been stabbed rather than the man who was presently being hauled out of the triclinium.

He set his bloody dagger on a table and strode angrily back to the basket, nearly stepping on the hands of the slave who was still cleaning the floor. She pulled her hands out of the way. Once he had passed, she hunched over again to scrub the stains, while nervously watching her master out of the corner of her eye.

Sneering, Soren again looked into the basket. The bald head that stared lifelessly up at him was not Scorpus the Titan.

The idiots that he had sent to kill Scorpus, despite all their assassination training, had targeted the wrong man. They had reported following Scorpus, who had very convincingly disguised himself as an Egyptian, into a hunting shack in the woods along the Via Tiburtina. They had staked it out for a full day and night, and then, when Scorpus exited the shack, they had found Aelina dead inside, naked and nailed to the wall.

The image made Soren's heart beat a little faster. It wasn't the loss of Aelina. He had sent her to Tivoli as a way to draw out Scorpus, and he knew she would never return. That was fine. Frankly, it was pleasant. What disturbed him was the brutality of the way Scorpus had killed her. He hadn't just slit her throat or crushed her skull. He had taken his time and relished the revenge.

If that's how Scorpus chose to kill a woman whose worst crime against him was vapid stupidity, what creative, vengeful execution did he have in mind for him?

And how had Scorpus evaded the assassins? Had he seen Soren's men watching the Vestal's villa? Had he known all along that it was his trained men, not simple bandits, who had killed the messenger Sextus? When had he decided to dress as an Egyptian as cover? It was that kind of resourcefulness that troubled Soren the most.

That and the fact that the head in the basket belonged to the Vestal Pomponia's favorite freedman. There was a chance, however remote, that his murder could reignite her vengeful spirit despite Soren's threats to reveal her secret letters to Caesar.

The idea of the Vestal and the Titan working together would not help

Soren sleep well at night. Subconsciously, his hand moved up to his throat. He ran his fingers over the ropey scar that ran around it. That had been close. Too close. He would have to start taking more precautions. His bodyguard Gibbosus had already suggested he build an escape hatch of sorts in the bottom of his lectica so he could make a surreptitious getaway if Scorpus or anyone else attacked in public. He had also recommended a number of security measures for Soren's home. They were practical ideas, but what he really needed was a political solution to his problems.

Soren clenched his jaw. He needed allies so powerful that no one—not even the Vestalis Maxima—could touch him. He needed the high ground so that he could strike at those below with impunity.

He needed Tiberius to be emperor of Rome.

CHAPTER XXVI

Nemo Repente Fuit Turpissimus
No one ever became fully wicked at all once.

—JUVENAL

Pomponia was distracted as she entered the temple for her early-morning watch. She couldn't say it was the first death she had ordered. It probably wouldn't be the last either. But it was the one that weighed most heavily on her conscience.

Yes, Despina was just a slave. But still. She had been kind to Medousa when Caesar had taken her into his household. And his bed. As Octavian's closest and longest-serving slave, she had used her own position to ensure the young Greek beauty maintained a higher status, one that protected her from Livia's petty abuses. Not her poison, though. Pomponia couldn't fault her for that.

After Medousa's death, Despina had taken her place as Pomponia's spy in the house of Caesar. She had begun to see Livia's true nature—ambitious, insecure, ruthless—and it worried her. Despina had known Octavian since the day he was born. She had seen him emerge from his mother, Atia, wrinkled and crying. She had fed him, bathed him, even scolded him. She had brought him pudding as a boy and wine as a man, had seen him apply himself to his childhood studies and ascend the Rostra as the emperor of Rome.

And she needed the same thing that Pomponia did: someone she could trust, someone resourceful, someone whose well-being was tied to

Octavian's well-being in the same way that hers was. And so their hidden alliance, their secret letters, had begun.

Pomponia knelt at the base of the marble pedestal on the mosaic floor of the temple. In one arm, she held a *futile*, the special vessel that held the spring water used every morning to clean the hearth. She dipped a cloth inside and began to wash the pedestal.

She could not put the futile down: its wide mouth and narrow base made it pointless to try. It would just tip over. And that was for a reason. The water used to purify Vesta's hearth and temple had to be uncorrupted. It was collected from the cleanest springs and carried in futiles which could never be set on the ground.

As a girl, Pomponia had done what all novices had done and still did. She had tried to find a work-around. She had tried to balance the futile at this angle or that, tried to lean it against something—but no matter what she tried, it was inevitable. The water spilled out.

She felt that way now. No matter how many options she considered, no matter how many times she tried to think of a different way, it was pointless. Despina could not live. Now that Soren knew of their secret correspondence, it was just too risky. If Soren went public with his information, Despina would be interrogated—tortured—until she confessed. It was damaging enough that he might possess one or more of their letters as proof. A living, talking Despina would make things even worse.

Her task finished, she gave the futile to a young novice who skipped happily out of the temple. Pomponia looked down at her hands. Despite having used the purifying waters of the Spring of Egeria to wash the pedestal, her hands just didn't feel clean. She placed a consecrated strip of wood into the sacred fire. A novice had carved the words *Fides et Vesta*—Faith and Vesta—into it. Fides, the goddess of fidelity and trust, of honoring one's friendships and relationships. To Pomponia, it seemed a bitter burning.

Quintina appeared at her shoulder. "It was an old tradition I read about in the archives," she said, referring to the words carved into the wood. "I thought we should bring it back on a more regular basis. I was going to speak to you about it."

"It is a good idea," Pomponia replied. "And not forbidden in the *libri pontificales*." She looked at Quintina. "But I am still Vestalis Maxima. Do not overstep."

Quintina's jaw dropped. "I meant no disrespect."

"It is disrespectful whether you meant it or not."

"Pomponia . . ."

"You cannot simply implement an old custom into our daily rites on a whim, Quintina. Care must be taken. Did you study which words are permitted to enter the sacred fire? Is there a catalog in the archives, or must we create one?"

Quintina hesitated. "I am not sure."

"Which are *certa verba*? Which are *concepta verba*? Where is precision required? Where are adaptations permitted?"

"You are correct. It was too hasty." Quintina moved to a basket of kindling and began to pull out the wood strips that the novices had carved into. "I am sorry. I did not consider all of the consequences." She set the carved pieces aside. "I did not mean to overstep, though. I thought you would be impressed."

Pomponia moved to the desk under one of the lamps on the wall and sat down. "You watch the fire," she said to Quintina. "I want to get some work done."

"Of course, sister."

The older Vestal picked up a scroll and started to read. Realizing she had finished half the scroll without absorbing any of the words, she read them again. Then again. But no matter how many times she read them, the only words in her mind were the ones Quintina had spoken.

I am sorry. I did not consider all of the consequences.

* * *

Thracius had never particularly liked being in the Palatine ramp. Even though the vaulted passageway was fairly wide—wide enough for Caesar to travel up and down in a small horse-drawn carriage—and even though it was designed with a high-arched ceiling and stretches of fine marble latticework to let in light and fresh air, there was something about it that reminded him of the dark, narrow, brick-lined passageways of the ludus that Soren had housed him in.

Maybe it was just a touch of claustrophobia. Or maybe it was the sense of dread that he had come to associate with such passageways. He thought he had left such feelings behind him, but as he and Anchises stood halfway up the ramp, waiting for Despina—waiting to kill Despina—he wondered whether he would ever truly be free of them.

Anchises looked over both shoulders: the ramp was clear. "There is no other way," he said quietly. "And there is no one else. Ankhu would have done it, but . . ."

"But he was murdered," said Thracius.

"The priestess will protect us."

"Like she protected her brother? It seems to me that any men who get close to her are dooming themselves." The boxer squinted to peer out one of the small squares of latticework. "I'm beginning to think we might have been better off as Soren's property."

"Oh, please."

"All my years in the ring," Thracius muttered, "and never once did I have to kill a woman. Not until this day."

Anchises exhaled out his nostrils. "You always said it was kill or be killed. Think of it like that."

"Says the man who does the watching and not the killing."

"*Shh*," said Anchises. "Someone is coming."

The two men craned their necks to see around the slight curve in the passageway as the sound of footsteps echoed off the walls. A moment later, the figure of Despina came into view. She jumped when she saw them.

"Oh, are you on your way to Caesar's?" she asked, and then realizing she was asking the obvious said, "I am just bringing some of the emperor's tonic to your kitchen. Had I known you were coming up, I would have saved myself the trip and—"

Anchises took a step back as Thracius stepped behind Despina. His right hand came up to cover her nose and mouth, while his left arm wrapped around her chest to hold her tightly against him.

She tried to twist out of his grip, to raise her arms to strike him, to lift her leg and kick him, and all of that failing, she opened her eyes wide and stared desperately at Anchises, pleading with him to save her.

But it was futile.

CHAPTER XXVII

Venit Summa Dies et Ineluctabile Tempus Dardaniae
It is come, the last day and inevitable hour for Troy.

—VIRGIL

Octavian had a headache. It had been a long day in the Senate, a day full of motions and vetoes, arguments and accusations. Even after the last of the senators had left, he and Tiberius had stayed for hours signing documents and reviewing the scribes' notes.

When he finally stepped out of the Senate house, he was surprised to find the sun had already set and the moon was out. The Forum had been cleared and secured. Torches lined the streets to cast flickering light against the monuments and columns. After a day of shouted motions and the heat of too many bodies packed in the chamber, the silence of night and the refreshing evening air were near bliss.

Tiberius felt it too. He sighed and looked up into the black, boundless star-filled sky.

Octavian spoke to the centurion soldier who stood waiting by the imperial lectica. "We will walk."

"Yes, Caesar," the soldier replied.

"I was hoping you'd say that," said Tiberius. He motioned for five or six soldiers to follow behind him and Caesar at a respectful distance. After sitting shoulder to shoulder in a chamber full of men since sunrise, they both needed a little elbow room.

They strolled leisurely past the long arcade of the Basilica Aemilia, on

their way to the Palatine ramp and their adjoining estates atop the Palatine
Hill. Caesar had been preoccupied all day with Senate business, but now
his thoughts were free to wander. Tiberius knew where they went.

"I was sorry to hear about Despina's crossing," he said. "I know she
tended to you since childhood."

Octavian nodded but said nothing. It was not proper for Caesar to
show emotion over the death of a slave.

"Does Musa know what happened to her?" asked Tiberius.

"He says it was most likely age or a hidden condition," Octavian replied. "She seemed unwell lately. Not herself. But it was not Despina's
habit to complain." Spotting two familiar figures ahead, closer to the
Temple of Vesta, Caesar quickened his step to join the priestess Pomponia
and her slave Anchises.

"*Salvete*, Caesar," greeted the priestess, "and Tiberius." Her slave bowed.

"I can see why it is your habit to take these evening walks," said Tiberius. "Very pleasant."

Caesar put his hand on Tiberius's shoulder. "I think I will walk a while
with the priestess," he said.

"Yes, Caesar."

Tiberius said his farewells, took two of the guards with him, and
headed for the base of the Palatine ramp. He was glad for the freedom. He
could walk a lot faster without Caesar, and he was anxious to climb into
the comfort of his bed, down a cup of wine, and fall asleep. He wasn't even
sure he had the energy to couple with any of his bed slaves first.

As Caesar fell into step beside Pomponia, Anchises slowed his pace to
walk behind them.

"Maecenas tells me that you have been writing to Julia," said Pomponia. "If I may say so, I was happy to hear it."

Octavian smiled. "She is greatly changed," he said. "From her letters,
I can tell she is as pious now as she was impious before."

Pomponia looked at Octavian. Even by the low light of the torches affixed to the Arch of Augustus, she could see the pride in his face, as if he
were a young father bragging about his daughter's first steps.

"I have put her in Rhegium," he continued, as they walked slowly past the columns of the Basilica Julia. "She has a fine domus and an allowance, but do you know what?"

"What?"

"She does not spend her allowance on excessive wine or jewelry but rather donates it to the temples in town. Is that not noble behavior for Caesar's daughter?"

"It is, Caesar."

His smile grew more indulgent. "I am told that whenever she goes into town, she carries with her a wounded seagull. She has named it Phoenix, and she lets the children feed it bits of bread and pat its head. Is that not unexpected kindness from Julia?"

"Not so unexpected," said Pomponia, "but it is good to know that she again honors the gods and her duty as Caesar's daughter. Perhaps in—"

The low but unusual sound of metal on metal made them both stop mid-step and look over their shoulders. Pomponia squinted in the darkness. By the flickering light of a torch, she saw the impossible: three figures emerging from the ground, like ghosts pulling themselves up from Hades.

"Guards!" she called out.

But it was too late. The ghosts were midway between the guards and her and Caesar. They descended on them—on Octavian—like black wolves in the night, surrounding and attacking their prey.

Before her, all was an inscrutable flurry of movement in the dark. She could hear the scraping of swords being unsheathed and the shouts of the unknown men mixed with the shouts of the advancing guards, their metal armor clanging as they ran.

Pomponia felt arms wrap around her. She clutched the man's hands but quickly recognized the gold wristbands—Anchises's. He was dragging her along the street, away from the attack.

"Keep moving!" Caeso shouted to Anchises as he and Publius ran past.

The Vestal's guards were the first to reach the assassins. Caeso nearly threw himself in the middle of the attack, using his weight to disrupt the pack's formation and the trajectory of blades.

Publius spotted Caesar in the mix of bodies, blood soaking through his toga, and covered Octavian's body with his own. As he lay with Caesar below him and the assassins above, blades sank into his back and his legs. He cried out in pain but held his position as Caesar's human shield.

As desperate to save his friend and colleague as he was to save the emperor, Caeso gripped the back of an assassin's tunica and pulled up hard, lifting the man off Publius and impaling him with his sword. He threw the man to the side and reached for another.

As the other guards arrived beside him—swords and daggers drawn, eyes wide and searching for a target—he shouted, "Caesar is under Publius! Watch where you're bloody stabbing!"

The guard closest to Caeso pulled a second man off Caesar, but the assassin managed to slip out of his grip and began to run away. Two guards gave chase, and Pomponia saw them catch up to him just in front of the Temple of Vesta. They threw him to the ground and fell on top of him, the metal of their swords gleaming in the torchlight as they repeatedly stabbed him.

That left only one man, the largest and the strongest, still on top of Publius, still stabbing wildly at the Vestal's guard, forcing his blade all the way through Publius's body to reach Caesar's below it.

Finally, Caeso and two other guards were able to heave the assassin's weight off Publius. One of the guards pulled back his dagger, aiming the blade at the man's neck.

"No, wait!" Caeso shouted. "We need one alive!"

But his cry came a moment too late. The blade sank into the assassin's neck, and thick sprays of warm blood gushed out in pulses until he stopped moving.

Caeso grasped Publius's shoulders and rolled his body off Caesar's. "I need light! More light!" As guards ran closer with torches, Caeso held his breath, dreading what he might see. He was fairly certain Publius was dead—but Caesar? He hadn't heard Caesar's voice, hadn't heard him cry out in pain or fear. Nothing.

The bloody clamor of the attack settled into a disturbing silence as Caeso knelt at Caesar's side. Pomponia lifted the bottom of her tunica and ran back to Caesar, stepping over the lifeless body of Publius to kneel on the cobblestone and lean over Octavian. She grabbed the fabric of his toga and twisted it in her hands.

"Caesar!"

His eyes were open but fixed on the sky above. She called out his name again, and he blinked as if slowly registering her presence.

"Caesar," said Caeso, "you are safe. The assassins are all killed." He grabbed the torch out of a guard's hands and held it close to Octavian, inspecting his body. "You are bleeding . . . Where are you stabbed?"

Octavian held out his hands. Both palms were bleeding, most likely from having gripped the blade of an assassin. Caeso reached out to pull Pomponia's palla off her shoulders. He tore the fabric into strips and wound them tightly around the emperor's hands to stop the bleeding.

"Help me up," said Caesar.

Caeso and another guard gripped Caesar's arms and lifted him to his feet. Octavian reached out to Pomponia, who quickly moved to his side. He put his arm around her and began limping forward, toward the Temple of the Divine Julius Caesar.

He dropped to his knees before the tall marble columns and stared up in reverence at the gilded star on the temple's pediment. Pomponia knelt beside him, and both held their palms up in prayer.

Behind her, Pomponia could hear the voices of the guards sending for reinforcements, dispatching soldiers to inform Tiberius, Livia, and senators of the assassination attempt, and surrounding the large drain of the Cloaca Maxima from which the assassins had sprung. All of their voices were loud. Relief mingled with shock.

Only one voice was low, so low that it seemed to slip under the louder voices so she could hear it. It was Caeso, begging forgiveness from the dead body of Publius.

CHAPTER XXVIII

Dis Aliter Visum
The gods thought otherwise.

−VIRGIL

Pasiphae sat on the edge of Tacita's bed in the Domus Tauri and poured them both a fresh cup of wine. As with most people in Rome, there was only one thing on their minds and only one topic to their conversation: the failed assassination attempt on Caesar. Unlike most people in Rome, however, Caesar was a man that both women had seen up close and personal.

Especially Tacita.

In fact, their conversation had segued from the more political aspects of the issue—Who would want Caesar dead and why?—to the more personal side of things.

"So, which did Caesar prefer," asked Pasiphae, "to screw or to be sucked?"

"I don't know what he did with his bed slaves or his mistresses, but he usually wanted me to suck him."

"In what position?"

"Lying down. He was usually too tired for anything else. But there was this one time . . ."

"Oooh, tell me."

"The empress joined us in bed."

Pasiphae barked out a laugh and sloshed the wine in her cup. "You are lying! The noble Lady Livia piling into bed with the likes of you? I think not."

"It is true, I swear it. I had already pleasured him, but she just showed up in his bedchamber."

"And?"

Tacita finished her wine. "He made me undress her right in front of him."

"So, you have seen the empress naked?"

"I have," said Tacita.

"What happened next?"

"He pulled her into bed and put her on top of me." Tacita set her empty wine cup on the table by her bed and then pretended to fondle her nipples. "And then he told me to play with her breasts while he penetrated her."

Both women descended into laughter.

Their hysterics were interrupted by the ringing of a bell. Pasiphae sighed happily and stood up, but Tacita scowled; she had a customer.

As Pasiphae left, Tacita quickly slipped into a fresh tunica, ran her fingers through her hair to primp it, chewed on a mint leaf to cover the smell of wine on her breath, and rubbed rose oil on her wrists and neck. Last, she blew out two of the four lamps that were burning in her room and stood with her hands behind her back; she had learned to hide her scarred hand.

She had barely finished when Pasiphae reappeared in her doorway to usher her customer inside. Tacita's mouth fell open at the sight of him.

Soren.

He stepped inside her room and closed the door behind him, cutting short Pasiphae's scripted "Welcome, and meet Caesar's favorite lover" introduction.

Tacita's heart beat faster. Was he here to rescue her? She was suddenly grateful for the few moments she had spent freshening up and smiled softly at him.

"Hello, Soren," she tested.

"Hello, Tacita," he replied.

That is a good start, she thought.

"I knew you would come eventually," she said. "I have heard that you are a big man in Tiberius's circle. Your success is all I have ever wanted . . ."

He cocked his head. "Is that why you betrayed me?"

"I was misled by my sister," she said. "She exploited the love I have for you. I was the one who was betrayed."

"Get on the bed."

"Yes," said Tacita, moving toward the bed. "Come sit by me. Let's talk."

"Men don't come to a brothel to talk."

Tacita felt her stomach flip. She had always been attracted to Soren, always ready to couple with him, and yet during their short marriage, he had rarely taken her. So, why now? Why here, in this sordid place? She knew him well enough to know that something was going on with him, something bigger than their divorce and the loss of Calidia.

It didn't matter. What did matter was that she make the most of the opportunity she had right now. She stood before him and began to remove her dress, doing so slowly to build his anticipation. Once naked, she ran her hands over her bare body.

"You are the only man I have ever truly wanted, Soren." She stepped back to lay on the bed, on her back, exposed and waiting for him. Longing for him.

He stepped to the side of the bed and looked down at her. To her delight, he dragged his fingertips down her neck, over her breasts and stomach, slipping them between her legs. She moaned and opened her legs wider for him.

He unfastened his belt and then pulled his tunica off over his head. Bending over, he pressed his body on top of hers and kissed her deeply. She could feel his tongue move against hers and, lower, his erection press against her; she reached down with one hand to push it inside her body.

He thrust into her, and she arched her back, overcome by the pleasure of him. His hand moved up to squeeze her breast, and she gasped, wrapping her legs around him, and urging him to thrust deeper. She felt his hot release and pushed her pelvis up, in painful need of her own.

He lifted himself off her.

"No, not yet," she breathed, clutching his arms to pull him back down on top of her. She needed to feel his weight, his fullness again, she needed the release of him.

He looked down at her. Just as she thought he was going to lower himself on top of her again—*Yes, please!*—he took a step back, leaving her to squirm on the bed, aching for him.

Still fully naked, he walked across the room and opened the door. Three men stepped inside. Tacita recognized them. They were three of his most revolting slaves, the ones he kept working in the garden and hidden from guests, fat and wart-covered, with toothless mouths and gummy eyes.

"Soren, no, please . . ."

He pulled his tunica over his head. As he fastened his belt, he nodded permission to his slaves. They could do as they wished with the whore.

"It hurts when something you want is taken away, Tacita," he said. Then he leaned against the wall of Caesar's fake bedchamber to make sure that he got his money's worth.

CHAPTER XXIX

Vestamque Potentem Aeternumque Adytis Effert Penetralibus Ignem
And from the holy hearth he brings forth Vesta's eternal and inviolate fire.

−FROM VIRGIL'S *AENEID*

The first reading of Virgil's epic poem, called the *Aeneid*, had been a private affair at the house of Caesar. After much practice, Pomponia's slave Anchises had recited it only to Caesar, Maecenas, Livia, and Tiberius. Caesar had wept.

The second reading was an elite invitational with important senators, magistrates and other officials, patrician couples, and members of the religious collegia in attendance. It was to be performed under and around the Arch of Augustus, just steps away from the site of Caesar's would-be assassination, and also steps away from the sacred temples the emperor credited with saving his life—the temples of Vesta and the Divine Julius Caesar.

The empress Livia stood under the arch and extended her arms to welcome the gathering. "Dear friends," she said, "our inviolate emperor, father of our country, thanks you for your prayers in the aftermath of the plot against his holy life. We come together here, in the shadow of his triumphal arch, near the temple of his divine father and the temple that contains the home fires of Rome, to honor the gods. For it can only be the gods who put such words as you will now hear into the minds of mortals." Livia gestured for Anchises to join her under the arch. "The words of the gods must be spoken with the most divine of voices," she continued. "Let us welcome Anchises the virtuoso as he recites some of Virgil's verses in honor of our founding fathers, Aeneas and Romulus; Imperator Caesar Divi Filius Augustus; and all the gods of the Roman Empire."

Anchises took a deep bow to the sound of applause, letting his smile linger for a moment on his partner, Thracius, who watched from afar. To Pomponia, Anchises had never been in better form: practiced, poised, and dressed as well as any of the noble guests in his rich red tunica and wide gold wristbands. She was proud the Vestal order could provide such talent to bring Caesar's poem to life.

The virtuoso had chosen only select passages of the epic to recite. It would have taken hours to perform the entire work, and in Anchises's experience, a little poetry went a long way. It was best to finish before the audience began disappearing to the latrines. He put his hand on his chest and began:

> *Arma virumque cano, Troiae qui primus ab oris*
> *Italiam fato profugus Laviniaque venit*
> *litora, multum ille et terris iactatus et alto*
> *vi superum, saevae memorem Iunonis ob iram,*
> *multa quoque et bello passus, dum conderet urbem*
> *inferretque deos Latio; genus unde Latinum*
> *Albanique patres atque altae moenia Romae.*
> I sing of arms and of the man, who first made way,
> A fugitive of fate, from Troy to Italy and the
>   Lavinian shores.
> He suffered storms on land and sea,
> By the force of the gods, to satisfy Juno's sleepless
>   wrath.
> Much in war he also suffered, seeking at last to
>   found the city,
> And bring his gods to Latium; whence arose the
>   Latin race,
> The Alban fathers, and the high walls of Rome.

As Anchises recited verse after verse, Pomponia grew more impressed. The poem was the story of Rome, a national epic. But it was also Caesar's story, a way to slip his rule into the history and legends of Rome: Aeneas flees burning Troy, and from his bloodline springs the Alban fathers, Rome's founder Romulus, and the great Caesars.

Pomponia's more cynical side knew as much; however, she found her throat tighten with emotion as Anchises spoke Virgil's lyrics of Vesta. After all, the sacred embers of the Trojan hearth fire now burned as an eternal fire in the heart of Rome. The second Troy.

> *Haec memorans cinerem et sopitos suscitat ignis*
> *Pergameumque Larem et canae penetralia Vestae . . .*
> On the altar of the gods of Troy, he woke the
>   smoldering embers,
> And the sleeping fire, at the shrine of venerable
>   Vesta . . .

She wiped away a tear. The poem may have been commissioned as propaganda, but Virgil's genius had elevated it beyond its purpose.

Having trimmed the poem down to a length perfectly suited to his audience, Anchises finished to a flourish of applause and, most important, before a single person had left for the latrines.

Pomponia was praising him when Livia arrived at her side. "What do you think?" she asked the priestess.

"A masterpiece," said Pomponia.

"Not the damn poem," said Livia. "Honestly, if I hear one more word about Virgil, I will join him in the grave." She pointed to the far side of the arch where Tiberius was presenting a piece of gold jewelry to Mallonia. "What do you think of that?"

"Surely he is not proposing marriage to her," said Pomponia.

"Oh, he's proposing something," Livia replied. "Maybe not marriage, but something that would turn your stomach."

"Indeed," said Pomponia. "Any news on the identity of Caesar's attackers?"

"Three Syrians," Livia replied. "The Senate has created an investigative committee. I have met with them, and I can assure you they are as incompetent as any other committee in Rome. I told them my suspicions, though."

"And those are?"

"I think Julia is behind it."

Pomponia should not have been surprised. "Julia?"

"Oh yes," said Livia. "She has the means now to communicate, and I have reason to believe she has been writing to a former lover, a man named Sempronius. He has spoken against Caesar in the past. She certainly has the motive."

The Vestal nodded. Poor Julia.

A burst of applause from the front of the Temple of the Divine Julius Caesar made both women look over. Caesar was holding a scroll and reading passages of his epic aloud.

"He thinks he's as undefeatable as Achilles now," said Livia.

"It was a vicious assault," said Pomponia. "It is remarkable that he survived."

"From all accounts, he owes that survival to your men Caeso and Publius. It is unfortunate that Publius was killed."

"They have protected me since I was a girl," replied the Vestal. "The two of them always together, my own Castor and Pollux. It will not be the same."

Pomponia braced as Soren joined them. The empress raked her eyes up and down his fine white toga, and then asked, "Where is that woman of yours these days? The stupid one from Capua."

"She's dead, Empress."

Pomponia tried not to react as Livia snorted, half in surprise, half in amusement. "Oh? How did she die?"

"She was killed by bandits on the Via Tiburtina." Soren shifted his eyes to Pomponia. "I've decided against purchasing the property next to yours in Tivoli," he said. "Seems like a bad area."

"You couldn't purchase it if you wanted to," Pomponia replied. "I've already bought it."

"Ha!" Livia said with a laugh. "Guess she doesn't want the riffraff living next door."

Pomponia could sense Soren bristle. She hoped he would excuse himself and move on, but instead it was Livia that spotted a fresh target in the gathering and left to strike.

When the two of them were alone, Soren leaned in to the Vestal. "I know you killed Despina."

Pomponia let a broad smile deflect his whispered attack. "And I know you killed my brother. And *tried* to kill Caesar."

Soren's face was rigid. Unreadable. "That is a serious accusation, Priestess."

"It's no accusation. It's the truth. And here is more truth for you. I have Scorpus the Titan on a leash, but it is one that he pulls hard against. If my grip were to slip . . ."

A trace, just a passing glimpse, of surprise on Soren's face. Pomponia bit her lip, hoping it would conceal her bluff. She had no idea where Scorpus was. He was probably still racing through the sands of Egypt on the back of her best horse, draining the last of her wine from an amphora.

"You are not the only one with a secret weapon, Priestess."

"*Secret weapon*," scoffed Pomponia. "You speak like a child playing at swords, Soren. Any war between us would be a *bellum internecinum*." A war of mutual destruction.

"You mistake me, Priestess," said Soren. "This is an age of peace." He forced his lips into an innocuous smile. The priestess and her leashed fugitive were the least of his problems right now.

Still, matters could be worse. While the assassins that he, Murena, and Caepio had hired had failed miserably, at least they were dead: the guards that Tiberius had been strategically posting around Caesar lately had been particularly incompetent, and the fools had been hasty enough to kill all of the attackers before they could be questioned.

Moreover, the empress's quick-thinking had immediately cast suspicion on Julia and one of her former lovers. Livia was certain enough that blame would stay there that she was already hinting at forming another plan against Caesar.

But that didn't mean Soren was safe. His two co-conspirators were known critics of Caesar—not his only critics, but still. They would be questioned as a matter of procedure. Eggshell men like them often cracked under the slightest pressure. He would speak to them and make sure they, like the priestess, had the right incentive to leave his name out of things. That would be easy enough. They all had wives and children.

He was forming his threats to them in his mind when Mallonia approached. "Priestess, may I have a word with you?"

Grateful for the excuse to leave, Soren stepped aside without saying goodbye to the Vestal. He raised his eyebrows knowingly at Mallonia. *She won't help you with Tiberius. No point asking.*

Once she had relative privacy with the Vestal, Mallonia glanced sideways at Tiberius. He was now speaking with Caesar in front of the Temple of Julius Caesar. "Priestess," she said, "I know you are familiar with my . . . *situation* with Tiberius."

"I am," said Pomponia. "And so are many others, including the empress. Did she not offer you a villa outside of Rome?"

"Yes, and that was very kind of her. But my family has lived in Rome for generations. I have no desire to leave."

Pomponia sighed inwardly. As a Vestal Virgin, she knew that, in Rome, one's duty came before one's desires. Why did women like Mallonia and Julia not accept the sacrifices they were expected to make?

"Things have gotten worse," continued Mallonia. "Tiberius . . . he has been forceful. As a senator's widow, I do not deserve such treatment. I am going to write to the Senate about it—"

"No," Pomponia interrupted. "Let me speak to Lady Livia on your behalf."

"Do you think she will do something about it?"

"I can guarantee it."

"Thank you, Priestess," said Mallonia.

The Vestal looked over at Soren. He was now socializing—strategizing, more likely—with Tiberius and Caesar. "Your former brother-in-law, Soren, has no official appointment to my knowledge," she said to Mallonia, "but he has nonetheless risen high in Tiberius's circle."

"How well do you know Soren?" asked Mallonia.

"Not well. Just socially. You must know him well, though."

"I used to know him quite well," said Mallonia. "When he was married to his first wife, and when my husband was still alive."

Pomponia tried to hide her surprise. "I didn't know Soren was married before Tacita."

"He was married to a woman named Dacia," said Mallonia. "He was deeply in love with her. He treated her like a queen. My husband said that he never even bedded any of his slaves, such was his fidelity to her. The marriage had a tragic ending, though."

Pomponia took a step closer to Mallonia, their intimate posture preventing anyone from interrupting their conversation. "How so?" she asked.

"Soren had been away from Rome on business, but he returned early, probably to surprise Dacia with some treasures he had bought for her. He was always buying exotic jewelry and fabrics to spoil her. Anyway, he entered his bedchamber to find her coupling in flagrante delicto with one of his slaves, a retired gladiator that he had hired to protect Dacia while he was away. He was devastated by the betrayal. He began to beat the slave, but Dacia begged him to stop, to spare him. So, unbelievably, he did. He could never say no to Dacia."

"Did he divorce her?"

"He should have, but no. He didn't even sell the slave. Dacia pleaded with him to keep him on at the house, so he did, although he forbade Dacia from having any contact with him. You can predict how long she abided by that rule. Within a week, she was coupling with the man every time Soren was out of the house. One of the other slaves finally got up the courage to tell him. So, again he came home unexpectedly, and again he found the two of them coupling in his bed. This time, Dacia told him that she and the slave were in love. The man's period of servitude to Soren was almost up, and he would soon be a freedman. She said they planned to marry and that she was already pregnant with his child."

"Gods," said Pomponia. "So, he divorced her then?"

"No. From what his slaves told me afterward, things grew quite fierce. At first Soren wept at Dacia's infidelity, but then a violence came over him. He rushed at her and put his hands around her throat. The slave—he was a retired gladiator, remember, so he was very strong—tried to pull his master off Dacia. It took a houseful of slaves to beat the man into submission and hold him down. Soren strangled Dacia to death, right there in their bed. I was told that she was naked and thrashing around, but he knelt over her, weeping even as he killed her. Then he ordered his slaves to take the gladiator into the garden and hang him from a tree, which they did."

Pomponia shook her head, astounded. "I didn't know any of this."

"Why would you?" asked Mallonia. "It is not something that Soren talks about. Most people think his wife died while with child. But it was not her husband's child, and that is not what killed her." Mallonia glanced at Soren and then looked at Pomponia. "Soren is not the man he used to be. He used to be decent—compassionate, even. But he became a different person after his wife's betrayal."

"I see . . ." Pomponia narrowed her eyes to discreetly study him: his cropped dark hair, hard face, and defensive posture. She tried to imagine him in love, being soft or kind, but could not.

Mallonia continued. "After Dacia's death, Soren found a slave who bore something of a resemblance to her. It was all very strange. He named her Dacia and had her wear Dacia's fine dresses and jewels. We were all supposed to pretend that she was the real Dacia. My husband, Pavo, refused, but Soren grew so angry that finally he relented. We played along with his fiction just to keep the peace. Although to be honest, I didn't mind. I preferred the slave Dacia to the real one. She was a sweet girl and the only one who seemed able to soothe Soren's temper. She was forever calming him and interceding for the other slaves."

Noticing what appeared to be an intense conversation between the Vestal and Lady Mallonia, and not wanting to miss anything, Livia approached. "Anything I should know about?" she interrupted.

"Hello, Empress," Mallonia said with a bow. "With your permission, I will leave the priestess and you to speak."

"By all means." When Mallonia had moved on, Livia raised her eyebrows at Pomponia. "What was that all about?"

"She says that Tiberius took her by force."

"Yes, I know," Livia said and sighed. "Why does she not leave Rome?"

"Pride, I'm assuming."

"Foolish pride."

"And troublesome. She was going to write a letter to the Senate about Tiberius's actions"—Pomponia held up her hand to silence Livia—"but I told her not to. I told her I would speak with you, and you would take action."

The empress felt a low growl of frustration escape her throat. Trying to avoid the stomach-turning sight of Tiberius making love-eyes at Mallonia by Caesar's temple, she stared at the newest engraving on the Arch of Augustus. After the failed assassination attempt on Caesar's life, the Vestal order had gifted two fine marble tablets to the arch.

The first was a beautiful tablet inscribed with the *fasti*, Rome's religious calendar. The second was the one Livia now stared at: a tablet inscribed with the names of those Roman generals—from the armies of both Caesars, father and son—who had helped the divine rulers achieve their destinies. It was a reminder to her that even though Caesar ruled alone, he didn't get there alone.

"Any advice with regard to Lady Mallonia?" she asked the Vestal.

"You don't need any advice from me," Pomponia replied. "You know what must be done. Some people . . ." She shook her head. "Some people are best dealt with swiftly and fully, as soon as they show themselves to be a problem. Delay just gives rise to further delay and complications, and always to their advantage."

"That sounds like the story of my life," muttered Livia.

CHAPTER XXX

Honori Aquilae
For the honor of the Eagle

—ROMAN MOTTO

When Caesar had asked Pomponia to lend Caeso to him, she knew he wasn't really asking and she wasn't really lending.

"You have been too generous, Priestess," said Caeso as he leaned over the balustrade of the terrace atop the House of the Vestals and looked out over the Forum. He was referring to the substantial gratuity and the house on Capri that the Vestal had given him for his years of service to her.

"Not at all," Pomponia replied. "Although the gods know when you'll have time to spend your money or see Capri. Caesar will not release you from Rome anytime soon." She rested her elbows on the balustrade and smiled at him. "That's what you get for having a good idea."

Caeso's good idea had been to replace Caesar's usual guards—a combination of privately paid bodyguards, official lictors, and regular legionaries—with an elite unit of imperial guards. The new Praetorian Guard.

This special force would be handpicked, paid handsomely, and both housed and trained in a large camp just outside the city walls. They would be skilled in everything from fighting tactics to intelligence.

In addition to protecting the emperor's house on the Palatine Hill and accompanying him wherever he went, they would also be entrusted with his most sensitive or secret missions. They would be an extension of his power—competent, discreet, and loyal. They would answer and report to no one but the emperor. As Caeso had explained to Octavian, they would be "a fleet of Agrippas."

When Octavian had heard that, he had immediately approved the elite unit and—this was the part Caeso had not expected—appointed Caeso to organize and manage its formation.

Following the assassination attempt on his life, Octavian was understandably struggling with whom to trust. After seeing the Vestal's guard literally throw himself before the swords aimed at his own heart, he knew he could trust Caeso.

"I have personally chosen your two new guards," Caeso said to Pomponia. "You can trust them as you trusted Publius and me."

The Vestal nodded.

"I shall miss this house," said Caeso. *And you, Priestess*, he thought.

"We will see each all the time," Pomponia replied. "But it will be strange to see you guarding Caesar's back instead of mine. You must forgive me if I forget and order you to fetch my lectica."

The guard laughed.

"But it is for the best," said Pomponia. "For both of us. Now that Publius is gone, it would never be the same. Caesar has given you a great responsibility, but also a great honor."

"No greater than the one I have had all these years."

Pomponia snickered. "Sentimentality? Really, Caeso, I have never seen this side of you. I hope Caesar does not know of it." She stood and embraced him. "I shall offer into the living flame for your success. Now go before you make me cry."

Caeso squeezed her tightly and then pulled away, quickly turning to walk across the terrace and descend the stairs. He strode along the peristyle and the long row of Vestal statues, wondering whether the guards who had protected these long-dead priestesses felt the same affection for their wards as he did.

He took the Palatine ramp up to Caesar's estate, stopping only briefly at the top of the hill to look back down over the House of the Vestals and the Temple of Vesta in the Forum.

Moving through the grounds and arched passageways of Caesar's estate, he reached the portico of the emperor's domus. Tiberius was just exiting, heading toward his carriage.

"*Salve*, Caeso," said Tiberius. "Congratulations on your new posting. They've already broken ground for the Praetorian barracks. I am going to see the site of the camp for myself."

"Thank you, sir," said Caeso. "It is my honor to serve under the Eagle."

Tiberius saluted the guard and then stepped into his carriage. That damn Caeso. If it weren't for him, Caesar would be ashes right now, and he would be wearing the gilded laurel wreath of the emperor of Rome.

That's what he got for listening to his mother. He had told her not to be hasty. He had warned her against pressuring his friends, men like Soren, to do her dirty work. Yes, *her* dirty work. For as much as Tiberius wanted to be Caesar, Livia wanted to be the mother of Caesar even more. Tiberius had to get her under control.

As his carriage began the journey to the site of the camp just outside the city walls, he lay back on a large, smooth cushion. Despite it all, the idea of an elite emperor's guard was a good one. He would make sure it was done right. These men would be his to command one day.

Soon, the motion of the carriage swayed his thoughts from business to pleasure. To the Lady Mallonia. To the way she pretended to resist him, to run away from him. It made him want to chase her even more.

The camp site could wait.

He opened the curtain and called out to his guards. "Take me to the home of Senator Pavo."

By the time Tiberius's litter arrived at Mallonia's home, Tiberius was already imagining how their little cat-and-mouse game would go. It excited him so much that he exited the carriage before it had even come to a full stop.

His guards rapped on the thick wooden door of the late senator's home until a young female slave opened it. Seeing Tiberius, she opened the door wider and lowered herself onto her knees.

"Master Tiberius," she said nervously, "my mistress was not expecting you."

Tiberius stepped past her and entered the home, proceeding to the atrium. The slave rushed past him to retrieve her mistress. A few moments later, Mallonia appeared, her expression a mixture of repulsion and trepidation.

"Tiberius," she said cautiously.

He stepped forward and took her hand, lifting it to his lips. He kissed it, letting his tongue swirl in her palm and staring into her eyes, but she quickly pulled her hand away.

Without waiting for an invitation, Tiberius walked into the triclinium. He reclined on one of the couches.

"Come rest by me," he said to Mallonia. He turned to the slave who had opened the door. "Wine." His eyes lingered on her pretty figure and then wandered to the two male slaves who stood by the wall waiting for instructions, their hands folded anxiously in front of them. "You have unusual slaves," he said. "They are very fair-haired."

Mallonia sat rigidly next to him. She did not respond, but as the female returned with the wine, she sent her slaves a quiet message with her eyes: *Leave us quickly.*

They turned to go, but Tiberius sat up. "Wait, come back here." He pointed to the space before him. "Stand in front of me."

The three slaves exchanged apprehensive glances and looked at their mistress. But there was nothing she could do. This was Caesar's heir. He could command their mistress, never mind her slaves. They did as they were told and moved to stand before him, their heads lowered and their arms at their sides.

Tiberius turned his head and placed a kiss on Mallonia's bare shoulder. His fingers moved down her arm, into her lap, and then pressed between her legs, urging her to open them.

"I do not consent," she said.

"You just need a little help getting warmed up," said Tiberius. He raised his hand to the slaves before him. "Take your clothes off."

Mallonia's body grew tenser. "Tiberius—"

He put his fingers to her lips to silence her. "Do it," he repeated to the slaves.

The female slave began to cry, but the young man next to her cast her a warning glance. *It will be worse if you disobey.*

Tiberius took a long draw of his wine as the three slaves disrobed to stand naked in front of him. His hand again moved to Mallonia's lap as he looked at one of the male slaves. "Touch the girl's breasts," he said. "Put your mouth on them."

"Tiberius," said Mallonia, "it is not proper. They are siblings." When he didn't respond, she tried again. "All three are related, Tiberius. Let me summon other slaves."

"No, I like these ones." He dug his fingers between Mallonia's legs. "Both of you," he said to the males, "touch her."

Tears streamed down the girl's face as the young men's hands moved over her body, over her breasts and bare stomach, down her thighs.

"That's it," said Tiberius. His voice was throatier. "Now, girl, you get on your hands and knees. And you"—he gestured to one of the naked young men—"kneel down and put your cock in her mouth."

Mallonia tried again. "Tiberius, please."

He pointed to the second brother. "You kneel behind her and penetrate her."

The girl lowered herself to the floor, now weeping openly. One of her brothers knelt in front of her. "Just do it, Lucia," he whispered. As the girl took his flaccid penis in her mouth, he pretended to respond with arousal. Her other brother did the same from behind, pretending to thrust into his sister.

"Yes, I like that," said Tiberius. He knelt up on the couch and pushed Mallonia onto her back, sliding his hands underneath her tunica. He felt between her legs and then smiled widely. "You play the virtuous matron," he said, "but I can tell that you want me."

"Stop," she said, twisting to get away from him.

Frustrated by her resistance and the awkwardness of trying to mount her on the couch, Tiberius stood up. He took Mallonia by the shoulders and pushed her roughly onto the floor beside the threesome, pulling his own tunica over his head and lifting Mallonia's tunica to her neck to reveal her bare body.

She screamed and struck at him, but he lowered his weight onto her and thrust, penetrating her while watching the slaves—both men now pretending to climax—only an arm's length away. He released quickly and his thrusts slowed.

Finally, Tiberius rolled off Mallonia's body to lie naked on the floor, on his back, his chest rising and falling as he caught his breath. The three slaves were kneeling beside him, covering their privates with their hands. The two young men stared down at their mistress. Should they do something? The young woman only wept. Tiberius reached for his tunica and stood, dressing contentedly and then finishing his cup of wine.

Mallonia sat on the floor, clutching her tunica to her bare body. "Get out of my house," she said to Tiberius.

He smiled and reached down to cup her chin in his hand. "As you wish, my love," he said. "I will send for you tonight. We will enjoy the baths at my home. I have some slaves that are very skilled at performing underwater pleasures. You will see."

For several long moments after Tiberius had left, neither Mallonia nor her slaves moved. Then slowly, trying to master the emotions she felt—violated, humiliated, hateful—Mallonia stood and dressed. She nodded to her slaves, and the three of them quietly got to their feet and shuffled out of the room to deal with their own trauma.

Mallonia straightened her tunica and combed her fingers through her tangled hair. She tightened a loose earring but, realizing the other had gone missing in the struggle, pulled the remaining one off and tossed it onto the floor.

Feeling her sense of violation and anger settle into a resolve to act, she walked toward the atrium. She would not let Tiberius get away with this. He was not fit to be the next Caesar, and she would tell the Senate as much. She didn't care what it cost her or whether they believed her or not; she had to try.

She opened the thick wooden door to her home—and found herself face-to-face with Soren.

"Going somewhere, Mallonia?" he asked.

"Where I go is none of your concern," she said. "Get out of my way."

Soren placed his hand on her chest and pushed her back into the atrium, stepping inside and closing the door behind him. "There is no magistrate or senator in Rome who will take a report against Tiberius. It is pointless."

"Then, I will go speak with the empress."

"I will save you the trip. The empress sent me here to speak with you."

"Then she knows of her son's offenses."

Soren exhaled and looked around the space. "It has been a long time since I have been in my brother's house," he said. Brushing by her, he walked into the dining room, noting the disarray of the furniture and the crumpled carpet before the couches.

Mallonia angrily followed after him. "What does the empress say?"

Soren turned to stand in front of her. "She says you are not to leave this house."

"So, I am to be a prisoner in my own home? Because her son has a perverse nature?"

"You misunderstand," said Soren. "You are not to leave this house."

Mallonia felt the blood drain from her face. "You cannot kill me, Soren. We were family."

"I have no particular wish to kill you." He withdrew a dagger from his side and held it out to her. "Take your own life."

"I will not."

"Then, I will take it for you. I will insert the blade in your chest in such a way that suicide will be assumed. The end is certain, Mallonia, just not the means." He prompted her to take the dagger. "It's between you and Pluto now. How do you want to meet him? Kicking and screaming, or with dignity?"

Mallonia held her hands out to Soren. "Do not do this, Soren. I do not want to die."

"No one wants to die, yet all do. Now come, be like Dido. End your life with honor."

Mallonia knew Soren well enough to know that he was right. She would never leave this room, not alive. The certainty of her end, the hopelessness of her situation, descended upon her, as black and heavy as death itself. She took the dagger from his hand as he stepped back and took another from his side. Just in case.

Soren moved to the table beside the couch and poured a cup of wine. He held it out to Mallonia, and she drank it to the bottom.

"It will be easier if you sit," he said.

She sat on the couch.

"Place the point of the blade here," said Soren, touching Mallonia under her breasts. "Thrust upward hard, pointing this way . . . Use force or it will hurt more."

She clutched the hilt of the dagger with both hands. And then she did what he said. Her mouth opened in shock, but a moment later, her body slumped to the side and fell onto the couch.

Soren reached down to take his dagger out of her hands. He wiped the blade off on the fabric of her tunica and then poured himself a cup of wine, sitting on the couch beside Mallonia's lifeless body to drink it. His cup empty, he poured himself another. And then another.

His brother had always been stingy with the wine.

CHAPTER XXXI

Deprendi Miserum Est
It is wretched to be found out.

−HORACE

There was something about the grunting man on top of her that struck Tacita as familiar. Senator Murena. He was a regular customer these days, but even the first time he had paid for her, she had wondered where she had seen him before.

He grunted again, finishing this time, and she patted his back. "Well done, Caesar."

He pushed himself off of her and stood up, already reaching for his tunica and sandals. Sighing with a mixture of satisfaction and exhaustion, he walked to the basin in the center of her room and splashed some water on his face.

"I hope I performed adequately for Caesar," she said. It still felt ridiculous to say such things, especially to such a lumpy old man. The real Caesar, while certainly no Apollo, at least kept himself in better form.

"Yes," said Murena. "Adequately." He tightened the belt around his tunica and left her room.

Tacita kicked her feet to free them from the twisted sheets and then got out of bed to clean herself in the basin water. She brushed her hair, rubbed fragrance behind her ears and knees, and slipped into a new tunica, this one a shimmering gold. It was a favorite of her next customer, a high-ranking magistrate named Gallus.

Pasiphae opened the door to Tacita's room just as she had finished adjusting a brooch. Gallus entered. The moment he did, a solid memory formed in Tacita's mind, and she shook an excited finger at him.

"Yes, I remember now," she said. "I remember where I have seen him before."

Gallus frowned. "What are you talking about, you foolish girl?"

"Magistrate," she said, rushing forward to clasp his hands, "I know who tried to kill Caesar."

The magistrate squinted. The girl was on the airy side, but he knew her history. She had known important people, moved in important circles. Caesar's circles.

"Who?" he asked seriously.

"Senator Murena," she answered. And then defiantly, her chin in the air, "And my former husband, Soren Calidius Pavo."

*   *   *

Anchises entered Pomponia's office without knocking. She looked up from her desk and met his wide eyes.

"Soren has been arrested," he said.

Pomponia stood up. "When?"

"A few hours ago."

"What is the charge?" she asked. She closed her eyes, not wanting to hear the words.

"The attempted assassination of Caesar."

"Gods almighty," Pomponia fumed under her breath.

Soren's arrest was unexpected; however, she could predict what would happen next. He would use his knowledge of her letters with Despina to somehow plead his way out of the charge. She wasn't quite sure exactly how yet, but it was the only leverage he had, and he would use it. Their uneasy truce, one based only on the fact that war meant mutual destruction, would be moot.

"Senators Murena and Caepio were also arrested," said Anchises.

"Where are they?" asked Pomponia.

"They are all in the Carcer. From what I could find out from the guard, the senators are already being tortured for information. Soren is being kept apart from them. Caesar and Tiberius are to meet with him later today before he, too, is interrogated."

"Then I must meet with him now," said Pomponia. "Have my lectica brought around." She paused. "And get Thracius too."

* * *

The bleak stone face of the Carcer prison loomed before Pomponia. So did the memory of Quintus. Why now? Why now, when her future seemed to be falling into a black pit, was she suddenly so overwhelmed by the past?

Medousa had been unable to hide her disapproval when Pomponia had decided to speak for Quintus after he had been imprisoned in the Carcer during the proscriptions of Octavian and Marc Antony. The slave had sulked openly, defiant and critical of her mistress's actions to the point that Pomponia had slapped her across the face. The memory felt like a slap across her own face.

But the decision to speak for Quintus had been the right one. He had been innocent, his life and property confiscated only so that Octavian and Antony could pay their troops.

The pardon had been a pivotal event in Pomponia's life. It had marked the first soft moment between her and Quintus. She had knelt on the cold, stone floor at the edge of the deep underground cell; far below, she could hear Quintus's murmured prayers. She had called down to him.

In dea confide. Trust in the goddess.

His reply had risen up to make her heart sink.

I trust you.

The pardon had also marked the beginning of her friendship and loyalty to the new Caesar. The ambitious Octavian had not released Quintus because it was the right thing to do. Rather, he had seen an opportunity to secure an alliance and accessorize his power.

It was a power that, decades later, was limitless. As the Vestalis Maxima of Rome, as Caesar's friend and ally, Pomponia had admired that power. She and the Vestal order had benefited from it.

Now she saw its underside. She saw it as others saw it, those who were not Caesar's friends or allies, those who had crossed him or spoken against him. It was a terrifying sight. No doubt Soren saw it too.

Her litter-bearers set down, and she stepped out, followed closely by Anchises. Behind her litter, Thracius and her two new guards, the ones appointed by Caeso, waited dutifully on the street. She curled her finger to Thracius.

"Come inside with me," she said.

Anchises nodded to the prison guard he had spoken to earlier—although his gold coin had done most of the talking—and the man bowed to Pomponia. He quickly ushered her and Thracius past the wide columns of the building's stark portico and into the Carcer.

By the flame of a single candle, the guard led Pomponia and Thracius deeper into the prison. The Vestal and her slave took cautious steps into the black, airless space, trying to ignore the sewer-like stench and the feeling that whatever supported the solid rock of the low roof was about to give way under its weight, like Atlas suddenly drained of strength and crushed by the weight of the world on his shoulders.

They arrived at a small stone cell. Pomponia squinted through the rust-covered bars. It took several moments for her eyes to adjust to the dim light, but then she recognized the form of Soren sitting on the floor, his back against the wall.

Thracius took the thick candle out of the guard's hands. "Leave us. We will find our way out."

As the guard receded into the blackness, Soren stood and took one step forward to reach the bars. His gaze shifted from Pomponia to Thracius, then back to Pomponia.

"So," he said to the Vestal, "Caesar has brought us both to the Carcer."

Pomponia looked past him, into the tiny stone cell. On the floor by the wall sat an amphora of wine and some figs in a bowl. That was a bad sign. Tiberius or more likely Livia had already arranged special treatment for him.

"Who is your accuser?" asked Pomponia.

"That little slut Tacita," replied Soren. "The magistrate says she remembers Senator Murena at my home, using words that implied a conspiracy against Caesar. But . . ."

"But what?"

"I am not concerned. Once I speak with Caesar, I will be able to prove my loyalty to him." He gripped the bars and brought his face close to them. "I can show Caesar that I am more loyal to him than his own chief Vestal is."

"Murena, Caepio, and Caepio's scribe were tortured by interrogators this morning," said Pomponia. "On my way here, I received word that Caepio died during interrogation. He was split open and forced to hold his own intestines. His scribe survived, but his eyes were gouged out with hot irons. He was returned to his cell and committed suicide by bashing his head against the wall. Only Murena lives. Both of his feet were amputated. Then he was forced to drink three amphorae of water and his penis was tied off. He is now begging to reveal the lead conspirator's identity but has retained enough of his wits to say that he will whisper the name into Caesar's ear only." She brought her face close to Soren's. "I wonder which one of you Caesar will speak with first?"

"Tiberius will ensure—"

"—that you are killed before you implicate him."

"The empress will intercede."

"She may try," Pomponia admitted. "Or she may not. The empress's behavior can be unpredictable, but never her motives. She will do what is in her best interests."

"Isn't that why you're here?"

"Yes," said Pomponia. "But I have taken the risk of coming to see you in person"—she glanced behind him, into the tiny cell—"instead of just sending a bowl of figs." She looked at him curiously. "Tell me, did the figs have an unusual taste to them?"

Soren licked his lips. That hadn't occurred to him.

"Nothing has changed between us," said Pomponia. "If either of us makes an accusation against the other, chaos will follow. There will be public trials and investigations . . ."

Thracius stepped in front of the bars, interrupting his mistress. "And even if you do manage to weasel your way out of it," he said bitterly, "I will find a way to personally escort you to the gates of Hades."

"I can make sure Murena is dead before my lectica makes it back to the temple," said Pomponia, "and before Caesar meets with him. Without his testimony, the only evidence against you is the vindictive rantings of your former wife."

Soren ran his tongue over his teeth. He didn't want to ask, but he had no choice. "Will you then pardon me?"

"No," said Pomponia. "I am too close to Caesar to pardon anyone even falsely accused of plotting against him. But I will have Quintina do it. She will say it is her duty to protect you from the false accusations of her troubled sister. I will also have her support the empress's suspicion that Julia may be behind the attempt against Caesar's life. You will go free." Pomponia gripped the bars of Soren's cell. "Do you understand?"

Soren moved closer and put his hands on top of hers. "I understand."

"There is one more thing," said Pomponia. "Swear to me that you will never conspire against Caesar's life again. With Julia's influence gone, Tiberius need not worry about losing his inheritance. She was the only one who posed a threat to his position."

"I swear it."

"Swear it on the soul of Dacia."

Soren glared at her spitefully. "Swear on the soul of a slave who was not worth your pardon? That is a poor oath."

"Not that Dacia."

Pomponia could see Soren's thoughts move across his face: the momentary confusion and then the realization that she knew about his dead wife.

Still holding his hands on top of hers, he stroked the back of her hands with his fingers and held her eyes. "I swear it on my wife Dacia's soul."

Pomponia pulled her hands free. She raised the bottom of her stola and turned to go, Thracius leading the way by candlelight. As they passed through the darkness of the Carcer back toward the light of the entrance, the same guard who had escorted them to Soren's cell met them in the portico.

"Do as requested," Pomponia whispered to him.

"Yes, Priestess," he said. The guard disappeared back into the Carcer, this time headed toward Senator Murena's cell.

Thracius watched him leave. "Domina, why not just have him stop at Soren's cell first?"

"You can be sure his slaves have orders to carry out if he dies in here," said Pomponia. "Right now, he's safer alive. We need to get him out of here before the empress has him killed."

Pomponia stepped into her lectica. Anchises, who had been conversing with her guards and lecticarii several steps away, returned to step in after her. He pulled the curtain closed while Thracius joined the guards behind the litter.

"Well?" asked Anchises.

She nodded unhappily. "It's done."

The lectica lifted and swayed with movement as the litter-bearers began the short journey back to the temple. Anchises sighed and leaned forward, putting his hands on his knees. "I know you do not like it, but there is no other way to keep the peace with Soren."

Pomponia rested against the cushioned side of the lectica. "That is true for now. But remember, Anchises, this is Rome. Peace only exists to prepare for war."

CHAPTER XXXII

Accerima Proximorum Odio
The hatred of relatives is the most vicious.

−TACITUS

Tacita's upscale customers at the Domus Tauri had grown bored of Caesar's courtesan. It had been a good act, a profitable one, for a few years, but it had run its course. That was especially so now that the real Caesar wasn't even in Rome at the moment. He was off in Gaul or Africa or some gods-forsaken conquered land doing whatever an emperor had to do to keep an empire together.

Pasiphae put her hands on her hips and looked around Tacita's redecorated room, nodding her head in approval at the white walls and linens and the mock sacred hearth that burned at the foot of the bed.

"From *Caesaris Meretrix* to *Virgo Vestalis*," she said. "It's good. I like it."

"You don't think we'll get shut down, do you?"

"Nah, not for a while," said Pasiphae. "Not with that holier-than-thou Caesar out of Rome. When he gets back, and if he hears of it, yes, he'll shut us down. But by then we'll have milked it for all it's worth anyway."

"That's what I was thinking," said Tacita. "And you'll be happy to hear that I already have customers on the books. Philo has been advertising me, and word is getting around."

"Very good," replied the owner. She pinched the fabric of the off-white tunica that hung from Tacita's shoulders. "Go get some coin from

Philo and head to the market. You need a proper white stola if you're going to play the part."

"Yes, Domina."

Tacita did as she was told—pressuring Philo for more coin than he was supposed to give—and then made her way through the crowded streets of the Subura to the market area. With the extra coin in her hand, she would be able to treat herself to a fine meal.

She purchased a few nice pieces of cheese and a slice of cooked pork from a vendor, paying a bit extra so that she could sit at one of the establishment's private tables and enjoy her meal in peace.

She was chewing a mouthful of deliciously seasoned pork, when a figure sat across from her.

"Hey," she said, "private table. Shove off."

"I wanted to talk to you."

Tacita looked up and dropped her shoulders. "Leave me alone, Soren."

"I tried to purchase an hour with you, but that prick Philo said I couldn't. Since when is a whore so choosy?"

"Pasiphae has banned you from the Domus Tauri. After the last time . . ." She swallowed her food, suddenly finding the taste less pleasurable.

Soren plucked a piece of her cheese off the table and pushed it into his mouth. "I've heard that you've reinvented yourself," he said. "You're playing the virgin now. Aren't you a little old for the role?"

"Vestal Virgins get old. It goes with the act."

"Does your sister know what you're doing? She'll have the magistrates pay you a visit."

"She won't care. You know the higher classes couldn't care less about what happens in the Subura."

"She wouldn't care if it were anyone else—but you? Playing the part of a whoring Vestal?" He tipped his chair back and tapped the table with his finger. "You'll be getting a visit from a magistrate by the kalends. I'd bet on it."

"Not your problem, Soren."

"Talk to Pasiphae about letting me back in the brothel. Or if not me, then at least my men. They're too hard on my female slaves."

Frowning, Tacita looked at Soren's men: four of them, his usual crew of retired gladiators who served as his bodyguards. Ever since the attack on his life by the fugitive Scorpus the Titan, he was never without them. She shook her head. "I don't want you or your pigs in the brothel. Neither do the other girls."

Soren let his chair drop forward and reached for another piece of her cheese. She slapped his hand.

"Oh well, I guess it doesn't matter."

Tacita chewed slower. "What is that supposed to mean?"

"Didn't Pasiphae tell you?"

"Tell me what?" She put down her piece of pork.

"She accepted my offer to buy you." He took the meat out of her hand and ate it. "You're hers for the rest of the lustrum, but after the census, I can take you home. You've gone from being my wife, to my whore, to my slave."

"You're lying."

"You know I'm not."

Tacita clutched the last two pieces of cheese on the table and threw them at Soren. He laughed. She stood up quickly and marched into the market, straight to the finest dress shop in the Subura.

"I need a proper stola," she said to the leather-faced woman who owned the shop. She held out four of the coins Philo had given her. "Something that's good enough to get me into the Forum Romanum."

"You'll need sandals then too," said the woman. "And a bit of gold."

"I can't afford gold."

"I have brass that will work," she said, already handing Tacita a pretty turquoise stola, a pair of sandals, and a brass necklace. "Can't tell the difference between brass and gold from a distance." Guessing Tacita's trade, she flashed a toothless grin. "Same thing goes for a whore and a proper lady."

"Can I change in your shop?"

"Sure thing, missy."

Tacita paid the owner and took her purchases into the shop, hastily changing behind a sagging curtain and ignoring the owner's greasy husband who peeked behind it. She kicked her old tunica and sandals into a pile against the wall.

She took the long route through the market, just to make sure Soren wasn't following her. Her step quickened with anger and dread—she would not survive for long under Soren's roof—as she wound her way out of the Subura and to the Forum.

As she neared its walls, she straightened her back and walked as she used to walk, casual and carefree, as if the guards who monitored the walls were below her, a well-to-do Roman woman. By the time she arrived on the street in front of the House of the Vestals, she had almost convinced herself it was true.

She approached the portico and instantly recognized two of the guards that stood outside: she couldn't remember their names, but they were her sister's guards.

"You will remember me," she said to one of them. "I am sister to Priestess Quintina. I would like to speak with her."

"We remember you, all right," said one of the guards. He grabbed her arm and began to drag her away, but the other stopped him just as Tacita opened her mouth to scream.

"Wait, let me inform the priestess," he said quietly to his partner. "It's better than making a scene. She can decide what to do." He disappeared into the house.

Tacita folded her arms and waited by the portico.

And waited.

By the time the door opened and the guard ushered her inside, her feet were near bleeding from standing in the stiff leather of her new sandals. She followed the guard through the vestibule and into the atrium, where Quintina stood waiting.

"Hello, sister," said Tacita. "It's been a long time."

"What do you want?" asked Quintina. "And make it quick, or I'll have you arrested as a runaway slave."

"I need a favor."

"You won't get one here." Quintina turned to leave.

"Soren has bought me as a slave," said Tacita. "I won't live through the first night in his house. He knows that I accused him of plotting against Caesar."

"I don't care."

"Do you care that I couple with men as a Vestal Virgin? I think I may even let my customers call me by my famous sister's name." Tacita brought her hands up to her breasts, feigning pleasure. "Oh, Quintina! That feels good. Do it harder!"

"If that's as high as you can reach in life, then feel free to do so," said Quintina. Again, she turned to leave; however, her exit was delayed by a small child who ran up to her, arms raised.

"Auntie, up!"

Tacita froze. "Is that you, Calidia?"

The little girl turned to look up at Tacita, blinking her large hazel eyes and absently scratching her cheek. "My name is Pomponia," she said. There was a sound of sandals scuffing the floor as Thracius rounded the corner into the atrium. The child shrieked with excitement and darted past him, back into the house. Thracius gave chase without even looking up to notice Tacita's presence.

Quintina looked at her sister. Despite herself, despite the fact that Tacita had caused Septimus's death, no doubt had been complicit in the death of Pomponius, and put little Pomponia's life in danger through her foolish love of Soren, the Vestal felt a wave of sadness.

They had been children together. They had played and laughed together. They had sometimes cried together too, during those times when their father was most cruel to their mother. When Quintina had been taken as a Vestal to enjoy the privileges and esteem of that duty, Tacita had been left to create her own identity in the shadow of her sister's brighter light. It could not have been easy.

Tacita stared at the empty space where the child had been. She didn't ask Quintina to bring her back or let her visit. She knew it would never happen. In all likelihood that would be the last time she would ever see her daughter so close.

"I am sorry it has come to this," said Quintina. "Go now."

"Why do you hate me so much?" asked Tacita. "I should not have coupled with Septimus, but that is no reason—"

"You didn't just couple with him," said Quintina. "You killed him. I know it was you who lied and told Caesar he was one of Julia's lovers."

Tacita's head jerked forward, and her mouth fell open. A moment later, she bent over in laughter. "Gods," she managed to say, "and you're supposed to be the smart one? It was not me who accused him."

"Who, then?"

Tacita wiped her eyes, composing herself. "I'm sorry. I honestly thought you would have figured it out by now. Who is the one person who—"

But Tacita didn't get to finish.

Quintina gasped, and her hand flew to her mouth to stifle a sob. She turned on her heel and ran out of the atrium.

CHAPTER XXXIII

*Pacis Augustae senatus pro reditu meo consacrari censuit ad
Campum Martium, in qua magistratus et sacerdotes et virgines
Vestales anniversarium sacrificium facere iussit.*
The Senate decreed, upon my return, the consecration
of an altar to Pax Augusta in the Campus Martius, and
on this altar it ordered the magistrates and priests and
Vestal Virgins to make annual sacrifice.

—FROM THE *RES GESTAE*, BY CAESAR AUGUSTUS

Vis Autem Eius ad Aras et Focos Pertinet
Her power relates to altars and hearths.

—CICERO

The gates of Janus were closed, and Rome had been at peace for decades. Internal peace, at least. There was always some uprising, some revolt, some province or conquered land that needed to be reminded who ruled the world.

That was Caesar Augustus. He had recently returned to Rome after a campaign in the western provinces and had immediately changed out of his soldier's armor and into his *princeps*'s toga to deliver his message to the Senate: the Roman Empire should remain within its current bounds.

The news, like all news, was variously received. Mothers welcomed it. Their soldier sons, those who relied on a legionary's salary and retirement land, were less enthusiastic. Still, there was always work to be had for a good man in border protection, forum and civil patrol, or in one of the empire's occupying armies. Wealthy private citizens were always hiring too.

Just as Rome had always adapted to war, it had also adapted to peace.

Peace, that utopian state personified by the goddess Pax. In honor of the emperor's return to Rome, the Senate had voted to consecrate his recently completed special altar—the Ara Pacis Augustae. The Altar of Augustan Peace.

Pomponia and Quintina, along with a small selection of Rome's elite—Caesar and Livia, Tiberius, Maecenas and Terentia, the high priests and important senators—had been invited to view the altar before its official consecration. The chief Vestal was happy to go; it was a peaceful day and perfect weather for an informal outing. Since the Senate had ordered that she and the Vestal Virgins were to make an annual sacrifice on the altar, it would also give her an opportunity to inspect the structure's layout before the first ritual. She would come to know it well.

Despite having seen more monuments and altars than she could remember, the design of the Ara Pacis—high walls with a marble altar within—impressed Pomponia. She walked around it.

Along the lower frieze of the outer walls were high-relief carvings of acanthus leaves and other vegetation, all scrolling and flowering, with birds tucked within. The altar's artists had brought in dyes and pigments from across the empire and had re-created splendidly bright scenes, the vibrant colors bringing the images to life.

Above the lower frieze was the Greek meander pattern, and above that more relief carvings and panels that proclaimed the peace, abundance, and piety of Augustus's Rome. They showed Octavian leading a sacrificial procession, his head covered in reverence to the gods and his arm extended with a *patera* for libation. Behind him followed the chief priests, senators, Agrippa, and Livia. Other exterior panels showed Mars, Lupa, and Aeneas with his son, Ascanius.

Most meaningful to Pomponia was a carving of the Vestal Virgin Rhea Silvia with her infant twin boys on her lap: Remus, reaching for his mother, and Romulus, seated in abundance and passing his mother a piece of fruit to signify his destiny as the seed of Rome.

Pomponia walked leisurely to the front of the monument. Access to the raised altar within the boundary of the high ornate walls was via steps at the rectangular structure's entrance; however, only Caesar as Pontifex

Maximus and the chief priests of Rome, including Pomponia as Vestalis Maxima, were permitted inside.

Pomponia walked up the steps, smiling as she saw a relief carving of six Vestal Virgins, herself immortalized in the lead, by the altar. It was on the smooth marble surface of this altar that the innards of the sacrificial animal would be burned as an offering to the gods. Pomponia would first purify the offerings and then Caesar would lower them into a bronze fire-bowl, where Vesta's flame would consume them, sending smoke from the altar sacrifice up to the gods.

The Vestal turned and descended the steps, meeting Livia at the base. The empress's flushed cheeks suggested she was enjoying the wine as much as the event. She snapped her fingers at a slave who quickly brought Pomponia a cup of her own.

The two women wandered several steps away from the altar. In the near distance stood a towering obelisk that Caesar had taken as a spoil of war from Egypt and Rome's engineers and astronomers had made into a solar marker to map the seasons.

Livia pointed at it. "I'll believe it when I see it," she said, "but the astronomers say that on Caesar's birthday the shadow of the obelisk will fall directly on the altar." She shrugged. "It's a nice touch, but we'll see if it works or not."

"We'll lay a bet when September draws closer," said Pomponia. She sipped her wine and smiled at the sight of her former guard Caeso. Now the Praetorian prefect of Caesar's elite emperor's guard, he too had only recently returned to Rome after accompanying Octavian on campaign. He spotted her, waved, and strode over.

Livia left them to reconnect, the Praetorian first bowing to Pomponia and then embracing her.

"You look well, Priestess," he said.

"And you look important. Such shiny armor," she teased. "I fear I did not pay you enough."

"You paid me well enough to have a home on Capri," he said with a grin, "although, as you predicted, I still haven't seen it."

"How was Caesar's health on campaign?" asked Pomponia.

"Up and down. There was one episode where we feared his fever would never abate. It took Musa's concoction a full twelve days to break it."

"What of his spirits?"

"He seemed pleased with the state of the provinces and the empire. Personally, though, he still asks about Julia. He has questioned me several times on whether I think she was responsible for the attempt on his life."

"What did you tell him?"

"I told him I couldn't rule it out. Her former lover Sempronius has spoken against both Caesar and Tiberius. He may have instigated it, perhaps thinking he would wed Julia and they would rule Rome together. It's not inconceivable. I have advised against allowing her to return to Rome. Caesar says she can stay in Rhegium instead of being sent back to Pandateria, so at least she has a domus and decent food. I will keep a close eye on her and Sempronius, though. As long as they don't have contact with each other, Julia should fare well enough."

"I see."

"But enough about Caesar," said Caeso. "How are you? And the other priestesses?"

"We are all fine," Pomponia replied. "Lucasta is so involved in her brother's career that I think she was born for politics, not the priesthood. Lucretia and Caecilia are consumed with the novices, and Marcella and Lauressa have taken over the mills. They are hardworking, but I would never tell them that one Nona accomplished more than the two of them. They have opened a shop with the bakers' guild and make the most delicious honey bread you've ever tasted. I will send some to the Praetorian barracks."

"And Sabina in Carthage?"

"That is another one who missed her calling," said Pomponia. "A good Vestal, but a better banker. That temple is made of gold, not marble. Cossinia is happy to be back in Tivoli. She and the other priestesses say they take the wine from my vineyard for libations, but the goddess does not drink that much."

Caeso laughed and looked over at Quintina. The younger Vestal was studying the reliefs on the Ara Pacis with Tiberius.

Pomponia followed his eyes. "Quintina does well," she said. "She knows Tiberius's strengths and his vices. She understands him. But she has not been herself for some time. Her sister visited our house a while back, and she has been changed ever since."

"Tacita was always trouble," said Caeso. He straightened his shoulders as they walked idly. "How are your new guards?"

"Vigilant beyond words. Although, they may soon have it easier than you and Publius did. Quintina has been asking me to approve a private passageway between the temple's sanctum and our house."

"That will be safer."

"Yes, but I think it's important for people to see us going in and out of the temple. It keeps us connected to the city."

"I would like to see the plans for the passageway," said Caeso. "I shall ask Caesar for leave to visit the House of the Vestals. Anyway, I miss the cook's dormice."

"I will look forward to it," said Pomponia. She stopped and patted his arm. "Now, you've done your duty to your former mistress," she said. "Go back to Caesar."

"Thank you, Priestess."

The Praetorian walked briskly back to his posting at Caesar's side. The sight of him and of Octavian, both looking just a little older, struck her with a nostalgia that nearly brought her to tears.

Not wanting it to get any worse, she offered her praise and fare-well to the empress and headed back to her litter, where, if she was in a crying mood, she could at least do so behind closed curtains. She stepped into the carriage, surprised to find that Quintina was already inside.

"Oh," she said, "I thought you were still looking at the altar."

"I was feeling warm," said Quintina. "I wanted to get out of the sun."

"Me too." Pomponia instructed that the carriage proceed to the House of the Vestals and then rested back comfortably. "You can dangle your feet in the *frigidarium* when we get home. That will cool you off."

Quintina pulled open a curtain and stared outside as the litter moved through the Campus Martius.

Pomponia cleared her throat. "Caeso says Caesar won't let Julia return to Rome, but she can stay in Rhegium. She will be comfortable there."

The younger Vestal's face took on a curious expression. "I can't believe that Julia and I were once best friends. It seems like a lifetime ago. Or another life altogether. I used to defend her and listen to her rail against Tiberius. And now I am loyal to him."

"You are loyal to Rome," said Pomponia.

"Tiberius will have Julia killed within the hour of Caesar's death, won't he?"

"Of course."

Quintina pulled off her veil. "And I will have helped make it happen. It's strange—is it not?—that someone you were once so close to . . . that you thought you could trust . . . That person might at any moment act against you, as I have done to Julia."

"You are doing your duty to Rome," said Pomponia. "If Julia had done hers, she would not be where she is."

"Is my duty to Rome, though? Or is it just to Tiberius? Just the other day, he was telling me about one of his patrician friends who wants his daughter to be in the order. Tiberius wants us to accept her when she comes of age, as a favor."

"There is a balance to be struck," said Pomponia, "between serving Caesar and serving Rome."

Quintina bent over to unfasten her sandals. "I have heard of Tiberius's perversions, and I expect they will only increase when he is Caesar," she said. "There will be no one to stop him. But he will be a competent-enough emperor. He understands the empire. He honors the gods. If nothing else, Rome will survive his rule."

"So will our order," added Pomponia. "As long as you do not become his vassal."

The younger Vestal tossed her sandals to the floor of the carriage and scoffed at Pomponia. "You are not one to talk, sister."

"What does that mean?"

The younger Vestal pulled her legs up off the floor, curling her body onto the cushioned bed of the carriage. "There's no need to get defensive,

Pomponia. I am just stating the facts. You were the first Vestalis Maxima in the history of our order to break the sanctity of the temple by letting Caesar take Marc Antony's will."

"Oh, Quintina," said Pomponia, "what was I supposed to do? The man was one temper tantrum away from breaking down the doors to take it himself. You forget what it was like in those days. People were starving, and he was eager for war. If Caesar had been forced to take the will through violence, we would have made an enemy instead of a friend."

"Fabiana would never have allowed it."

"No, she wouldn't have," agreed Pomponia. "She would have denied him and even tried to physically stop him. But he would have taken it anyway. And after seeing Antony's treasonous will, the people and the Senate would have quickly forgotten her noble protest. Only one person would have remembered—Caesar. He would have hated her and all of us for making him look even worse."

"Was that the first time you broke with tradition to help him?"

Pomponia pursed her lips. "Strictly speaking, yes," she said. "But before that, during the proscriptions, I had some funds sent to him so that he could pay his soldiers. The money was from the temple's safe deposits . . ."

"Oh, Pomponia."

"The men who held those accounts were already dead," Pomponia defended. "They were enemies of Rome, and Caesar was legally entitled to their fortunes."

"Did you consult with the Senate first?"

"The Senate was in disarray in those days. It was all falling apart, and I was so young . . . But I would do it again, because with or without my help, he would have become emperor." She gestured over her shoulder, back in the direction of the Ara Pacis. "If I had opposed him, do you think he would be honoring the Vestal order today by including us on his great altar? Would he have included us in his triumph or his epic, or put us on imperial coins? Would he be paving our temple in marble and our house in gold, or commissioning statues of us? There is no way. He would have reduced our funding and our pensions, and most likely our privileges as well. Our temple would have no more status or power than some stripped-down shrine to Pales in the Forum Boarium. Vesta's fire would burn half as brightly in Rome."

"All right," Quintina conceded. "Then, what about the rumors of him and virgins? You've heard them. And the stories of his banquets where guests dress like the gods—even Vesta—and he couples with them? Is there not something about that perversion that touches on this order? Yet, you have never said a thing about it, not to Caesar or the priests or the Senate."

"What Caesar does in his bedchamber is his own business," said Pomponia. She pulled open her curtain to look outside.

"You may be right about all of it," allowed Quintina. "But your support of him goes beyond duty. It is personal."

"So what if it is? I am entitled to my own friendships. It was not Vesta who pulled your father out of the pit, it was Caesar. He did it for my allegiance, and Quintus's life was worth it. And yet, the goddess still had a hand in it, for Caesar has been like a second Numa to her priestesses."

Quintina rolled onto her back and stared at the ceiling. After several moments, she said, "I know you had Septimus killed."

Pomponia exhaled. "Those are your sister's words."

"If I am speaking them, they are mine."

Pomponia unfastened her sandals and tossed them beside Quintina's. She pulled her legs up and tucked them under her body. "I did not have Septimus killed," she said tiredly. "You did."

"How can you say—"

"Septimus did not deserve his fate. But you were too much like your father, obsessed nearly to the point of harm. The empress noticed your affection for him, and she was not happy about it. From that moment on, I had no choice. It was either he die alone or both of you die and bring disgrace to the order in the process. And since you're not flying across the carriage to strike me right now, I suspect you've already figured that out."

Quintina took her upper lip in her mouth, trying not to cry. "I don't know, Pomponia," she said. "I feel like I am losing my way. I am becoming too hard-hearted." *I am becoming like you*, she thought.

Pomponia pushed herself up and moved to Quintina's bed, curling up beside her on the cushion. "During the civil war, when the grain was near gone, you used to drag pots of extra flour out of the mills to give to the people. It drove Nona mad, it left such a mess. But she could not bring herself to chastise you lest it change your soft nature. You would stand for hours in the sun, handing out bowl after bowl. I see the same kindness in our little niece Pomponia. The girl would stop Caesar's triumph to save a worm on the cobblestone."

Quintina smiled at the image. "If Julia had shown any kindness to Tiberius, maybe we wouldn't be so worried that he is going to rape half of Rome when he wears the golden laurels."

"Ah," said Pomponia, "now you speak like the next Vestalis Maxima of Rome."

Quintina rested her head against Pomponia's shoulder but said nothing.

CHAPTER XXXIV

Sacerdotem Vestalem, quae sacra faciat quae ius siet sacerdotem Vestalem facere
pro populo Romano Quiritibus, uti quae optima lege fuit, ita te, Amata, capio.
I take thee, Beloved One, as one who has met the requirements of law,
to be a priestess of Vesta, and to perform the holy rites, which is proper
for the Vestal priestesses to do for the Roman people.

—WORDS SPOKEN DURING THE RITE OF *CAPTIO*, AS RELATED BY GELLIUS

Tacita's stomach was so upset that she had vomited twice before even getting dressed. She would make the best of it, though. If living and working in the Domus Tauri these past years had taught her anything, it was how to make the best of a bad situation.

She cleaned herself in the basin in her room and then slipped into her finest clothes: the turquoise stola, cheap sandals, and brass necklace she had bought to gain entrance to the Forum and see her sister. What a waste of time that had been.

She thought back to all the times she had longed to see Soren. All the nights she had paced outside his bedchamber and wept at the sounds of pleasure that she heard through the closed door, imagining the things he was doing with Aelina or some slave and wishing that he were doing those things with her.

Now she dreaded seeing him as much as she had ever longed to see him. The best she could do was to look as pretty as possible, and maybe, just maybe, he would realize that she could still be of use to him. She had already been rehearsing the things she would say to persuade him that it wasn't her—she wasn't the one who had accused him of plotting against Caesar.

It was the magistrate Gallus. He had lied and used her because he was jealous of Soren, jealous of the stature and influence he had obtained by being so close to Caesar's heir, Tiberius. Soren would believe the story. There was nothing he loved more than an enemy, someone new to hate.

In fact, if she were really lucky—oh, it hurt just to think of it!—Soren might even manumit her and marry her again. That was the kind of boldness he liked to show.

She checked her hair and face in the polished metal mirror of her room, took a deep breath, and then opened her door to walk down the hallway, between the rows of cubicles, where the sounds and silhouettes of people having sex were ever-present.

Pasiphae had instructed her to wait in the atrium for her new master. As she stepped into the light and fresh air of the atrium, her stomach dropped to see that Soren was already there. He was bent over Philo's desk in the corner, signing a document while the slave counted the coin owed to the brothel for Tacita's purchase.

"*Salve*, Soren," she said.

"It's an auspicious day for you," he said, his back still turned to her. "You have a new owner, and your daughter is being taken as a novice Vestal."

Tacita let a pretty smile form on her lips, holding it in place for when he finally turned to face her. "I am happy for both blessings," she said.

Philo countersigned the document. "She's all yours," he said. "Actually, you have overpaid a bit . . ."

Soren stood up. "The extra is for the undertaker." He turned, took two steps to reach Tacita, and wrapped both of his hands around her throat.

Tacita's hands clamped down on his. She clawed at his fingers, but they were immovable. She felt her throat collapse, and she knew, somewhere in her panic, that even if he did let go, she would not be able to breathe again.

There was nothing she could do, nothing except stare, wide-eyed and openmouthed, into Soren's stone face as the pain and the panic faded into nothingness.

* * *

When Pomponia's long hair had been cropped short to wear the veil, she had cried. When Quintina's had been cropped, she had smiled. Their niece, Pomponia, now six years old, stood on the middle ground—concerned but not crying, smirking but not smiling—as her aunt cut her hair and placed the white veil of the novice Vestal on her head.

As a child who had grown up around Octavian, Livia, and most of Rome's elite, and who remembered living in no other home than the House of the Vestals, the captio ritual had made little impact on the younger Pomponia. When Caesar as Pontifex Maximus had held her arm to take her as a bride of Rome, she had simply trotted along beside him as if it were just another day and they were going to feed the fish in the pool, not commit the next thirty years of her life to the temple and Rome's protecting goddess.

The same was true of the evening courtyard party in the House of the Vestals, the one that followed the ceremony. To her, it was just another gathering, just more priests and magistrates and senators, just Anchises singing more of his songs and Thracius telling more of his boxing stories to Caeso and the other Praetorian guards.

As all the guests had done, the emperor and empress had marked the occasion with gifts. They had given the novice two presents. The first was one that spoke to her new status: a gold bracelet in the shape of a winding snake with lapis lazuli gemstones running down the length of its twisting back and large ruby eyes in its head. It had once adorned the arm of Queen Cleopatra of Egypt.

The second gift was one that touched more on the girl's nature: a small white puppy.

The novice Pomponia had ignored the pharaoh's gold and clutched the puppy, nuzzling her nose into the white fluff of its belly and making the creature squirm madly in an effort to lick her face. The rest of the young novices had crowded around. Never mind the emperor of Rome. There was a *puppy* in the courtyard.

Anchises had just finished a song and was cooling his throat with a cup of water by one of the pools. Pomponia joined him. It was a happy occasion, and she had to remind herself of her own rule: one cup of water for every two cups of wine.

The singer accepted a seasoned dormouse from a kitchen slave and chewed contentedly. "The cook has outdone himself," he said. He was about to take another piece of meat when the novice Pomponia ran up to him and her aunt.

"I know what I'm going to name my puppy," she said.

"Oh? What?" asked Anchises.

"Tantalus."

"Tantalus," Pomponia echoed, surprised by the girl's choice. "That is a dark name, niece. I will have to speak to Lucretia and Caecilia about their teachings."

"I didn't learn about him from Lucretia and Caecilia. Empress Livia told me about him. She said that he is the greatest of all the Greek warriors, even greater than Achilles, because he never gives up. He always keeps trying, no matter how hopeless it seems."

Overhearing the conversation from a few steps away, Quintina joined them. "That is one way to look at it," she said. She patted down the back of her niece's new white veil and looked at the elder Pomponia. "Let's go into the temple, just the three of us. No one will miss us for a few moments."

The three priestesses slipped out of the courtyard and then out of the house, turning to ascend the steps of the temple. Quintina pulled open one of the doors and smiled to Lucasta and Marcella, who were standing near the hearth. "Sisters," she said, "would you mind if we had the sanctum to ourselves for a few moments?"

"Not at all," said Lucasta. She and Marcella kissed the top of the novice Pomponia's head and exited the temple, both knowing the day held a special significance for Quintina and the Vestalis Maxima.

Quintina squeezed her niece's hand. "This is the first time the three of us have been in the temple together as sanctified priestesses. I just had a sudden feeling that I wanted to honor that." She raised her eyebrows at the elder Pomponia. "We took a winding road, but we got here. And we fulfilled our promise to the goddess."

Pomponia looked down at her niece. Whenever she looked into her hazel eyes, she had the momentary sense that her brother was looking back at her. "Your father would be proud of you today," she said. "So would your grandfather Quintus."

The three of them stood around the white marble pedestal of the sacred hearth. Pomponia reached into a basket to retrieve three pieces of special kindling made from branches of the sacred oak tree that grew by the Temple of Jupiter. She gave a piece to both the other priestesses and kept one for herself. Each had been stripped of its bark and smoothed, and each bore a different name that had been carved into its flesh—a name that each Vestal would offer to the fire so that its bearer would be blessed by the goddess.

Pomponia placed her piece in the fire first. On it was carved IMP CAES AUG. As Vestalis Maxima, it was her duty to pray for the emperor. Quintina set her kindling in the flames next. On it was carved S SAC TACITA to honor her and the novice's legendary Vestal ancestor.

Finally, the novice placed her kindling in the fire; it was carved with her own name.

But it was the elder Pomponia who felt more reverence at the sight of the sacred orange flames swirling over and consuming the name S SAC POMPONIA. It was she who felt more nostalgia as the heat of the fire radiated onto her face and the snaps and cracks of Vesta's voice resonated within the circular marble walls of the temple.

As she watched the fire take her name a second time, Pomponia could have sworn that she was a child again. She felt certain that if she looked, she would see Fabiana standing on one side of her and Nona on the other, introducing her name to the goddess and telling her that everything would be all right.

But neither Fabiana nor Nona had ever had an enemy like Soren. He had been officially cleared of any wrongdoing in the assassination attempt on Caesar, and although his star had fallen a bit in Roman society, he was determined to see it rise again. He still served at Tiberius's side, still managed to attend all the best parties and most important events.

Pomponia knew there was only one explanation: Soren had something on everyone. And one by one, he would remove them as obstacles.

During the party, she had learned that one obstacle—or perhaps more an irritant—had already been removed: Tacita. Soren had strangled her where she stood in the Domus Tauri. She hadn't survived his ownership for more than ten heartbeats.

Pomponia opened one of the temple doors and waved Lucasta and

Marcella back in. As she, Quintina, and the younger Pomponia descended the steps, she saw that Anchises was waiting for her at the bottom. Even in the darkness she could tell that his face was drawn. *Gods, what now?* she thought.

"I need a word with Anchises," Pomponia said to Quintina. "I'll be back inside soon."

"All right, sister." Quintina took her niece back into the House of the Vestals. Music, conversation, and laughter floated up from the courtyard to spread out over the otherwise empty and quiet Forum.

Pomponia joined Anchises in a private spot closer to the Temple of Julius Caesar. He stood under a torch and held a small box out to her.

"I was arranging your niece's gifts, when I found this," he said.

Pomponia took the box. It was addressed to her and had her brother's wax seal on it. She pressed her lips together and removed the lid. She looked at Anchises with wide eyes as she lifted the object out and dangled it in the air.

It was a black leather wrist cuff with a silver medallion of a scorpion in its center.

Scorpus the Titan was back in Rome.

*   *   *

It had been a week or more since Pomponia and Anchises had taken one of their evening strolls through the Forum. But the day's high emotion and the realization that Scorpus had contacted them meant the Vestal needed to walk and think. She had set out with the singer only moments after the last guest had left.

"He used my brother's seal," said Pomponia. "He must be at his house."

"Is it not staffed? Or guarded?"

"Not anymore," said Pomponia. "I didn't see the point. I just closed it up."

The Vestal stood on the dark street in front of the Lapis Niger—the Black Stone—near the Senate house. By the flickering light of the torches that lined the Via Sacra, she looked down at the pavement of solid black marble that covered the old subterranean monument. It stood in stark contrast to the white marble of the balustrade that surrounded it.

"Black seems a grim color choice for a monument so close to the Senate," said Anchises. "I thought the emperor preferred gold in this area of the Forum."

"Normally he does," Pomponia replied. She looked up at the impressive Senate house. "This area is what we used to call the Comitium," she said to Anchises. "It was the first meeting place of the Roman people and other tribes. Romulus was very proud of it, and they say he wanted his ashes to be buried here"—she pointed to the slab of black pavement—"in this spot."

"But?" Anchises prompted.

"But the gods have their own way of doing things," said Pomponia. "There are different stories, but according to a scroll in the Vestal archives, Faustulus, the shepherd who took Romulus from the she-wolf and raised him, was killed here. Mars wanted to remind Romulus that he was the son of a god, not a shepherd, so he struck the man down. Romulus buried Faustulus's ashes here, where he fell." She eyed the black marble. "There is an altar below," she said. "I have never seen it, but I'm told the Latin on the stone block is so antiquated that no one can interpret it. The priests believe it is the language Romulus used to speak with the gods, to ask that they curse anyone who disturbed the tomb." She looked at Anchises. "Next to the Evil Field, there is no more somber place in the empire. That is why many people will swear an oath on the Black Stone. If they do, you can be sure they mean what they say. It is as binding as swearing on the stone of Jupiter."

"Have you ever sworn on it?"

Pomponia knelt on the cobblestone and put her palms on the smooth black marble. "Only once," she said, moving her hands over the cool stone and feeling the spot where she had spread her brother's ashes.

CHAPTER XXXV

Non Sum Qualis Eram
I am not what I once was.

—HORACE

Pomponius's house on the Caelian Hill had always been something of a sanctuary for Scorpus. As he sat on one of his dead friend's fine couches and looked at the rich frescoes on the walls of the triclinium, he tried not to remember the sound of Pomponius's thin voice: *I'm going to die, aren't I?*

Anchises had brought bread and choice cuts of meat from the House of the Vestals, but Scorpus wasn't hungry. Even the wine, which he knew was very good, didn't sit well in his stomach. It was good to be among friends again, though—or if not friends, at least people with a shared purpose: to kill Soren.

Scorpus watched Thracius finish off the rest of the meat, while Anchises and the Vestal Pomponia spoke quietly in the corner. They returned to the couches, and the priestess sat across from him.

"Are you sure the man you've been following is the one who killed Pomponius? It's been a long time."

"It's him," said Scorpus. "His name is Gaius, but Soren calls him Gibbosus because he has a bit of a humpback. You can't tell unless his tunica is off, and don't ask me how I know that. He's a retired gladiator. He and another man barely leave Soren's side, but Gibbosus is the favorite. As far as I can tell, he's the only person Soren trusts."

Pomponia spoke to Anchises. "Assuming Soren does have one of the letters between me and Despina, you can be sure he's left instructions to release it to Caesar if he's killed."

"Soren thinks that all of his slaves are idiots," Anchises replied. "If he trusts this Gibbosus fellow, then he is the one who will have the instructions."

"Then, they have to die at the same time," said Thracius. "I could do it."

"Maybe," said Anchises. "Maybe not."

"It's too unpredictable," Pomponia agreed. "We'll have to separate them somehow."

"You find a way to take care of Gibbosus," Scorpus said to Thracius. "As for Soren, I have an idea that can make him disappear into thin air."

As they all continued to formulate a plan, Pomponia looked at Scorpus out of the corner of her eye.

She had arrived at Pomponius's house to find Scorpus still dressed as an Egyptian; however, when she had asked him how long he planned to wear Ankhu's clothes, he had quickly and quite shamelessly stripped out of them to dress in one of her brother's tunicas. It was too small on him, but at least he looked Roman again. As he had changed, she noticed the scars that ran down his back—scars she had seen him receive from Soren in the Circus Maximus when the charioteer was still defiant and wild. Now, he sat soberly across from her, listening intently to Anchises's ideas and absently scratching his cropped hair.

Scorpus felt the Vestal's gaze on him. He looked at her, realizing just how much she looked like her brother: warm brown hair, hazel eyes, soft features. With her clear skin framed by a clean white veil, she was the prettiest woman he'd seen in a while.

"Why did you come back to Rome after all this time?" she asked him. "You had a good horse and as much coin as you could carry."

Scorpus looked past her to stare at a detailed wall mural: Diana, hunting deer in a thick forest. He remembered standing in this room, full of shock and despair, shortly after Pomponius had helped him escape from his prison cart. His hands had still been stained with Ferox's blood, and he had been unable to shake the vision of having stabbed his old friend in the head to spare him the agony of another breath.

At the time, he had been filled with hate for Soren, his every thought focused on revenge. But now he thought differently. Scorpus knew that he himself was responsible for the deaths of too many good people. Cassandra. Pomponius. Ankhu.

Two of those three people had loved this priestess. Thracius and especially Anchises cared for her too. That was reason enough for him to be here. Scorpus knew that Soren was growing bolder again. Even the close call of being briefly implicated in the attempt against Caesar's life hadn't changed him. Scorpus knew why. Like him, Soren could not forget the past. He would strike again, and not just at Pomponia but at those she cared about, especially her niece: Pomponius's child, the one he had not lived long enough to hold, the one he was not there to protect.

Scorpus met the Vestal's eyes. No doubt she thought he was here for vengeance. She seemed to have a vengeful streak herself. But she was wrong. He was long past craving vengeance. All he wanted now was redemption.

The Vestal studied his face. She thought about repeating her question: *Why did you come back to Rome?* But she sensed the Titan would not answer, so she did not ask again.

CHAPTER XXXVI

Αἴθ᾽ Ὄφελον Ἄγαμός τ᾽ Ἔμεναι Ἄγονός τ᾽ Ἀπολέσθαι
Oh, to have never married and childless to die!

—AUGUSTUS, ADAPTING A LINE FROM HOMER'S *ILIAD*, AS RELATED BY SUETONIUS

Julia rolled over and put her arm across the bare chest of her lover Sempronius. She thought back to all the cold, lonely nights she had spent in that decrepit hut on Pandateria, fantasizing about the feel of his hands on her body and praying she would one day share a warm bed with him again.

He woke slowly and smiled at her, then gestured to a slave who stood by the door of the bedchamber.

"Bring me a piss pot."

The slave reached to pull a chamber pot out from under the bed as Sempronius swung his legs over the side of it. The slave held the bowl between his knees as the man urinated into it, then whisked it away as he tucked himself back under the covers with Julia.

"Your father may learn that I have been here," said Sempronius.

"My father has bigger things to worry about," Julia replied. "Like not getting killed."

"He likes to pretend he is loved by all, but it is a lie."

"He likes to pretend he is loved by his wife," said Julia. "That is the biggest lie of all."

Sempronius pushed himself onto one elbow and kissed the end of Julia's nose. "I must return to Rome soon. Maybe tomorrow or the day after . . ." He ran a fingertip over her lips.

"Oh no, Sempronius. I don't want you to go." As he stroked her lips again, she took his finger in her mouth and began to suck. She reached under the covers—yes, he was already stiffening.

"You should let me finish my thought," he said. "I must return to Rome so that I can put my affairs in order. And divorce my wife."

A smile spread across Julia's lips. She pulled him down on top of her and closed her eyes to enjoy the feel of his nakedness moving over hers, his hardness slipping between her legs. Her father's disowning, her time in exile—none of it mattered when it was like this between them. She had never had a better lover.

He had taken her for the first time on her wedding day to Agrippa. It was at the reception. He had pulled her into one of the guest latrines while everyone else was in the courtyard, and they had coupled standing up, against the wall. Later that night, when Agrippa had climbed on top of her, she had pretended he was Sempronius. It had gotten her through it.

She closed her eyes and wrapped her legs around him, feeling the heat of the sun from the bedchamber's open window warm their entwined bodies. He thrust slowly, lazily, and they climaxed together.

She opened her eyes—and gasped. A man's face was staring down at her. She recognized the face from somewhere, but the shock of the intrusion made it hard to place him. She thought harder. Yes, that was it. He was Caeso, one of the chief Vestal's guards. What could he possibly be doing in Rhegium?

"Just what do you think you're doing?" she asked, her voice rising with each word.

Caeso nodded to two men behind him—all of them were dressed in the finest legionary armor that Julia had ever seen—and they pulled Sempronius off her. They held him, naked and sweaty from their early-morning lovemaking, as Caeso pulled Julia out of bed.

She tried to grab a bedsheet to cover her nakedness, but Caeso pulled her across the room to where a tunica lay on the floor. "Put it on."

She pulled the garment over her head. "Where are you taking me? On whose orders?"

"By order of Caesar and the Senate, you will accompany me to your new domicile."

Julia looked at him in disbelief, breathing hard and trying to make sense of it all. "Am I going back to Rome?"

Caeso almost laughed. "No."

"Where are you taking her?" Sempronius demanded.

Caeso turned his head to look at the naked man, his eyes moving over him disapprovingly. "I wouldn't worry about her," he said. "You're taking a trip of your own."

CHAPTER XXXVII

Nunc Patimur Longae Pacis Mala
We are now suffering the evils of a long peace.

−JUVENAL

"Is the high priestess unwell?" Livia asked Quintina. "It is not like her to miss one of Caesar's parties."

"Not at all, Empress," replied the Vestal. "She was just feeling tired. I wouldn't be surprised if she's already asleep in her bed."

"Lucky her," said Livia. She motioned for Quintina to follow her to a private spot behind a statue of Minerva in Caesar's crowded triclinium and then peeked around it to ensure none of the other guests could overhear. "Priestess, I am glad we have a moment to speak. There has been a change in Julia's situation. I wanted to tell you before the news gets out."

"Oh?"

Livia spoke somberly. "Her lover Sempronius has been visiting her at her domus in Rhegium."

"Sempronius?" Quintina lowered her eyes. "That does not look good," she admitted. "I know that he has been critical of Caesar."

"Very critical," said Livia. "Their illicit meeting makes it even more likely that the two of them were involved in the attempt on Caesar's life. Apparently, they were planning to marry. I predict they would have tried to overthrow Caesar."

"What will happen to her now?"

"She will be moved to a more modest domus in Rhegium," said Livia.

"Her allowance will be reduced, and her slaves removed. She will also be forbidden to correspond with anyone or to venture into the town."

"And Sempronius?"

"Exiled. To Africa. He will have it worse."

"Caesar is generous to let them live at all," said Quintina, knowing it was what Pomponia would want her to say.

Livia smiled at the Vestal's response. "That is exactly what I said to Caesar. Now, if you'll excuse me, I should pretend to be interested in my other guests."

The empress strolled away from Quintina, slowly circling the guests that filled the triclinium, looking for one in particular. She spotted him. Soren. He was leaning against a red column and looking as superior as ever, waving a hand in the air and relating some anecdote that was making Tiberius snicker, and Terentia curl her lip in distaste. His bodyguard—a beast who was nearly bursting out of his tunica—stood nearby.

Livia couldn't decide whether it was safe to get close to him again. In the days following the attempt on Caesar's life, she had tried to dispose of him, but apparently the man had no taste for figs. Maybe it was for the best. He was his own species of Tantalus, resilient and, so far, loyal. She stared at him as she sipped her wine. He felt the weight of her stare and met her eyes.

Stay the course, Soren told himself. *She is warming to me again. They all are.*

He was correct. And it was all because of the emperor himself. Determined to appear fair-minded and benevolent to a man absolved of any wrongdoing against him, Caesar had made a point of associating with Soren.

As Tiberius and Terentia moved on to mingle, Soren followed Anchises's voice into the courtyard of Caesar's home. The slave was thinking far too highly of himself these days, and Soren missed no opportunity to remind him of where he really belonged—in Soren's basement, on a dirty mattress, on his knees.

He arrived in the crowded courtyard just as Anchises was finishing a song. Predictably, his wealthy fans immediately surrounded him with praise. Soren slowly navigated closer to the singer until a burst of laughter behind him made everyone turn their heads to look at Thracius.

The boxer was jabbing a finger into the chest of Soren's bodyguard Gibbosus. "Anchises," said Thracius, "would you believe this man thinks he can take me?"

"Oh, there is one in every crowd," Anchises replied. "You should know that by now, Thracius. Leave him alone."

Thracius held out his arms in a gesture of innocence. "I didn't start it. He did."

Anchises rolled his eyes. "Leave him be," he insisted.

An amused senator shouldered his way into the action. "Leave him be?" he asked Anchises. "Why? Your boy should teach this man a lesson, don't you think?"

"Senator," said Anchises, "some people never learn."

"Nonsense," Thracius countered. "Some just need to learn the hard way."

"I did nothing," Gibbosus protested. He turned to look for his master, only to see him backing out of the courtyard. Soren knew his bodyguard would never have picked a fight. Something was wrong.

Thracius grabbed the neck of Gibbosus's tunica and dragged him to an open space in the courtyard. He put his fists up. "All right, big man," he taunted. "Show us what you have."

"I don't want to fight you," said Gibbosus.

By now, a large crowd of spectators had gathered, and not one of them was in favor of a peaceful resolution. Someone shouted, "Come on, Thracius! Put him in his place."

"Yes, in his grave!" shouted someone else.

"Put your hands up," Thracius said to Gibbosus.

The bodyguard did, but only in an attempt to pacify the famous boxer. "I don't know why you—"

Thracius's punch landed on the man's jaw and sent him stumbling backward. Gibbosus's fists came up instinctively, and realizing he had no alternative, he swung at Thracius.

By now, Soren had slipped out of the courtyard and was making his way through the triclinium and to the atrium of Caesar's house. Whatever the chief Vestal's slaves were up to, he wanted to put as much distance as possible between himself and them.

He passed through the atrium and out the portico, looking ahead to the long row of guest lecticae. Seeing his, he quickened his pace even more and stepped inside.

"Let's go," he shouted to his litter-bearers. He pulled the curtain closed and sat back.

The floor moved below him, although not at all as expected.

The square wooden escape panel in the center of the floor lifted from below. Two muscular arms reached out to grab onto his lower legs. Soren tried to kick to free himself, but suddenly there was nothing to struggle against.

He found himself falling into blackness, into some kind of cool and dark pit, and didn't even have time to shout before landing heavily in water.

No, not water. It was thicker than water. As he came up and gasped for air, already gagging from the stench and his hands instinctively wiping the sludge from his eyes, he knew instantly where he was. The sewer.

The fabric of his toga soaked up the sewage to become unmanageably heavy within moments. Soren struggled to unwrap himself and finally succeeded in stripping down to his tunica. That made it easier to get his feet under him. He stood as a river of waist-high filth ran past him and looked up just in time to see a man above him, pulling the drain cover back in place and trapping them both in the darkness underground.

The man was descending the rungs of a squeaky ladder. Soren stepped back, willing his eyes to adjust to the dim light cast by the few oil lamps attached to the sides of the tunnellike sewer. He looked around, trying to get his bearings, looking for a way to escape, even as he heard the soft splash of the man joining him only steps away in the sickening brown sludge.

As his eyes finally adjusted and the man's face came into view, Soren clenched his jaw. "It all makes sense now," he said. "You down here, with the rest of the shit."

"Last time we met," Scorpus replied, "you ran away like a coward." He pointed behind Soren, into the blackness of the narrow, winding sewage canal. "Go on. I'll give you a head start."

Soren seemed to consider it, but then either his ego or his better sense prevailed, and he wagered he stood a better chance by fighting Scorpus now. That was especially so since while Scorpus had been gloating, Soren had managed to loosen a piece of sharp stone along the wall of the canal, below the level of the running sewage.

As Scorpus advanced on him, Soren bent down as if intimidated by the charioteer's attack. Just as Scorpus raised an arm to strike, Soren lifted the sharp stone and swung it hard, hoping it would make contact with some part of Scorpus's body in the dark. It did—it struck his genitals. Scorpus cursed and doubled over, his hand instinctively reaching between his legs . . . He could only feel one testicle. A severe wave of nausea and paralyzing pain washed over him.

Soren raised the stone again and brought it down on Scorpus's spine. The Titan dropped to his knees, so the flowing sewage was nearly at the level of his neck. Soren tossed the stone aside and leaped forward, gripping Scorpus by the hair and shoving his head under the sewage, leveraging his weight to hold it down.

Scorpus squeezed his eyes shut, fighting the reflex to inhale as the panic of suffocation began to overtake him. He resisted the instinct to reach up and instead searched for the dagger strapped to his leg, under his tunica. He found it.

He brought his arm up at an angle, aiming the point of the blade to where he believed Soren's chest was. It sunk into flesh, and Soren's weight came off him. Scorpus jumped up and gasped for air. He stumbled backward, wiping the sewage and black spots from his eyes.

When his vision returned, he caught a glimpse of Soren. He had pulled himself out of the river of sewage and onto the narrow stone platform that stretched along the length of the sewer's wall. Soren clutched his shoulder and ran down the dark canal in search of another drain he could escape through.

Scorpus waded to the edge of the sewage and pulled himself onto the walkway. Grimacing in pain and trying not to picture what his crushed testicle looked like, he stood and limped after Soren.

The rancid smell of human waste and rotting, liquefying solids settled in Scorpus's throat as if it were itself a thing with substance, a thing he wished he could cough up and spit out. Rats scattered and squeaked at his feet as he ran along the downward slope of the walkway.

He put one hand against the curved stone wall of the tunnel and squinted, trying to keep sight of Soren's moving body in the black distance ahead of him. The tunnel curved sharply, and Scorpus moved cautiously, peeking around the corner to make sure Soren wasn't waiting there to strike. He wasn't. Scorpus could still make out his form ahead, descending further into the tunnel like a ghost slipping into the underworld. *Facilis descensus Averno*, he thought. Easy is the descent into hell . . . That's how it felt.

He rounded another corner and looked ahead into the darkness. Yet another flare of pain burst from his groin, and he felt warm blood run down his leg to mix with the sludge already there. He wouldn't be able to go on much longer.

Soren looked back to see Scorpus falling further behind. Reinvigorated by his pursuer's faltering step, he increased his own.

But then the sound of voices in the distance made him slow down. He was just thinking of what to do—push forward or double back?—when from out of the blackness, an impossibly thick arm wrapped around his neck.

"Settle down, Soren," said Thracius. "Or I'll snap it right now."

Soren felt himself being dragged backward. He tried to use his feet to resist, but his muddy sandals only slid pathetically over the ground. Finally, Thracius released his hold around Soren's neck, but only to pin his shoulders against the cold stone of the wall.

Soren blinked to clear the stinging film from his eyes. It was brighter in this area, with more lamps on the walls. The sound of rushing sewage filled his ears. Soren knew exactly where Scorpus had shepherded him—to the part of the sewer that ran near the Temple of Vesta. Only a short distance ahead, this branch emptied into the wider, raging channel of the great Cloaca Maxima that flowed free and fast directly into the Tiber. Also a short distance ahead was the very drain from which his hired assassins, those fools who had botched Caesar's murder, had sprung.

The face of Scorpus appeared before him. And then two more faces—Anchises and, worst of all, Pomponia.

The Vestal looked at Thracius, her eyes questioning.

"Gibbosus is dead," said the boxer. "Second punch, the weakling."

The Vestal nodded soberly and then looked at Soren. She stepped closer to him, feeling spray from the river of sewage splatter onto her white stola.

"Let's get it over with," said Scorpus. He extended his arm to point the blade of his dagger at Soren's throat.

"Wait," said Thracius.

"Why?" asked Scorpus. "Because the priestess wants to do it? She's already covered in shit. No point covering her in blood too."

Scorpus's thoughts moved from the Vestal to another woman. To Cassandra. He pictured her in Soren's basement, naked and afraid. He pictured her hanging on a cross, naked and agonal. And then he pictured Pomponius, lying white-faced on the tombstone maker's table, his life-blood drizzling out of him to land on the wooden floor. His grip on the hilt of the dagger tightened until his hand went white.

Pomponia wrapped her hands around Scorpus's hand and looked into his eyes. "Give it to me," she said. Gently, she took the dagger from his grip. She held it in her hands for a long moment.

Soren could see the vengeance surfacing in her. His breathing restricted by the thick hand around his throat, he squeaked out "No!" and tried to twist away from the immovable wall of Thracius's restraint.

The fear in Soren's face seemed to invite Pomponia to act. She thrust the dagger into his stomach, slowly inching it in further until it was buried to the hilt.

Soren fought it, fought for his life. He gritted his teeth against the pain and struck at Thracius with flailing arms. Pomponia stepped back. The dagger was still buried in his abdomen: a spreading red spot appeared on his already filth-soaked tunica.

Pomponia felt Scorpus brush by her. Although his face was blanched from blood loss and the agony of his injury, he nonetheless found the strength to grab Soren by the neck of his tunica and jerk him forward, out of Thracius's grip.

Soren fell face-forward into the sewage with Scorpus jumping in immediately after him. The charioteer wrapped an arm around Soren's neck and plunged his head under the brown water. After a few moments

of Soren's pitiful thrashing, Scorpus felt the man's body convulse grotesquely. He lifted his head out of the sewage.

Thracius squatted on the platform so that he was eye level with Soren
in the river of sewage. He nodded at Scorpus.

Scorpus let go of the limp body in his arms. And then the four of
them—Pomponia, Scorpus, Anchises, and Thracius—watched Soren's
body roll in the rushing brown water until it was caught by the strong
current and swept away into the blackness.

CHAPTER XXXVIII

Ignibus Iliacis aderam, cum lapsa capillis
Decidit ante sacros lanea vitta focos.
I was by the fire of Troy, when the woolen ribbon,
having slipped from my hair, fell before the sacred hearth.

–RHEA SILVIA IN OVID'S *FASTI*

As the eternal fire of Vesta burned in its sacred hearth, the heat and snaps it emitted seemed particularly intense to Pomponia. She put her palms over the flames to feel their divinity and then turned her hands over, palms up in prayer to the goddess who had sustained and protected Rome for centuries. The goddess had sustained and protected her too.

She reached over to take a handful of loose salted flour from a terracotta bowl and sprinkled it into the sacred fire in a V pattern. The living, moving orange flames accepted the offering.

The chief Vestal had discharged Quintina a few moments early so that she could commune with the goddess privately. After everything that had happened, she wanted to give thanks alone. She felt warmth on her veil and looked up at the oculus in the domed roof as a slant of morning sunshine lit the temple's sanctum.

The doors to the temple opened, and Lucasta and Marcella entered. "*Salve*, sister," said Lucasta.

"Good morning," Pomponia replied.

After giving Lucasta and Marcella a report on how the fire had behaved during the last watch—she had read the flames and the ashes twice, and the signs were good both times—Pomponia left the temple to enter the House of the Vestals. She reached the courtyard just as Lucretia and Caecilia were ushering the novices up the stairs to the study.

As she had hoped, Caesar was also there. He had stopped to feed the fish in the pool before heading to the Senate. She waved a greeting to him.

"Caesar," she said, "do you have a moment?"

He sat on a cushioned bench by the pool and brushed a dragonfly off his purple-bordered toga before putting his hands on his knees. "It is a calm morning," he said to the Vestal.

"One that follows a stormy night," Pomponia replied.

"So, you've heard."

"News like that travels fast in Rome," said Pomponia. The news the Vestal was referring to was the body of Soren Calidius Pavo, adviser to Tiberius and one-time suspect in the assassination attempt on Caesar, having been pulled from the Tiber by sanitation workers at dawn.

Caesar nodded and sprinkled more fish food into the pool. He seemed indifferent to Soren's death. Pomponia knew he had other things on his mind—primarily the continuing exile of Julia and the backlash he was facing from the public for it. Despite some credible accusations against her and her lover Sempronius, most people didn't believe Julia would plot against her father. They felt Caesar was being too harsh. Even Maecenas had recently advised Octavian that something was needed to distract the people from the scandal and reinvigorate their admiration for him.

Pomponia steadied herself. She had to risk it. "I know who killed Soren," she said.

Octavian straightened and raised his eyebrows. "Who?"

"Scorpus the Titan."

"What? They found his body ages ago."

"They found *a* body," said Pomponia. "Not his."

"How do you know this?"

"I know this because his living, breathing body is right now having breakfast in my brother's house on the Caelian Hill." Octavian shook his head, confused. Pomponia continued. "He came to me for sanctuary. And he tells quite a story, Caesar."

"What does he say?"

Pomponia faced Caesar, her eyes earnest. "Scorpus swears that Soren was in fact plotting against you and had been for a long time. He says that Julia's lover Sempronius along with Senators Murena and Caepio were at Soren's home and that he heard them discussing an attempt on your life. Scorpus tried to gain an audience with you or Maecenas but could not. So with no other options, he did the only thing he could do. He tried to kill his master. But the attempt failed, and he went into hiding." Pomponia's voice took on a sadder tone. "Somehow, he befriended my brother, who was an admirer of his. You will remember how awed by celebrity Pomponius was. Scorpus says that he told my brother of the plot against you, but that Soren had my brother killed before he could alert me to the threat." She sighed. "He says the guilt of Pomponius's death drove him from Rome and deeper into hiding. It was only a few days ago that he returned and saw that Soren was still close to you. He took matters into his own hands—"

"And killed Soren."

"Yes. Although not without being seriously injured."

"Do you believe his story?"

"I was doubtful at first. As you know, as every Roman knows, Scorpus is a very good showman. But I do believe him, Caesar. He told me things about my brother that only a friend could have known. That is why I took the risk of giving him temporary sanctuary in Pomponius's home instead of immediately sending him to the Carcer. If he indeed acted to save your life . . ." She sighed again, letting her shoulders drop. "But now I leave the matter to your discretion."

Caesar looked up into the sky. "Scorpus the Titan, back in Rome," he said thoughtfully. "Maecenas could make good use of this right now."

Pomponia nodded, trying to appear measured. Caesar had taken the very track of thought she hoped he would.

*　*　*

Maecenas was a man with shrewd insight and many skills but one preferred policy: *panem et circenses*. Bread and circuses. He knew that whatever scandal, sacrilege, plague, or war was ravaging Rome, the people's love for Caesar could be rekindled by spectacle. And as Octavian and Pomponia had expected, he had nearly choked on his wine with the news—the *useful* news—that Scorpus the Titan was alive and suddenly in good favor.

In a single day, Maecenas had arranged for a tribunal to absolve Scorpus of the attempted murder of his former master and grant him his freedom for his self-sacrificing loyalty to the emperor. He had then ridden his horse to Taurus's house. "Get set for the comeback race of a lifetime," he had said. Taurus had nearly fainted at the news. But he had recovered quickly and immediately set out for the Circus Maximus to prepare the grand racetrack for the return of its star charioteer—and a few accompanying dramatic acts. Before sunset, newsreaders were already shouting from the Rostra and at every gate into the city: *Scorpus the Titan lives! Scorpus the Titan returns to Rome! Scorpus the Titan rides again!*

And now the great day was here.

Pomponia sat in the Vestals' private viewing box alongside Quintina and the novices Pomponia and Varinia. Pomponia did not dare leave the latter priestess at home. Missing the races was the one thing that could cloud Varinia's otherwise perennially sunny disposition. With each passing day, the girl reminded Pomponia more of Tuccia, from her eyes—they had just a hint of amber in them—to her soft heart and love of the games. And like Tuccia, Varinia had become the favored priestess of the Blue chariot team. Scorpus's team.

Behind the priestesses sat Anchises and Thracius. It was their last day in Rome. Tomorrow morning, they would head to Tivoli to live in Pomponia's country house and care for her vineyards. They didn't know it yet—wouldn't know it until they arrived in Tivoli and saw the papers waiting for them—but Pomponia had manumitted them. She wanted the moment of realization—*We are free men!*—to be a private one between them. They had earned it.

A flourish of horns, a swell of cheers, and the stamping of thousands of feet rose from the oval of the racetrack. Caesar stood at the front of his marble balcony dressed in a deep purple toga. With Livia and Tiberius standing on either side of him, he saluted his people. Shouts of *Caesar!*

Caesar! rose up so loudly that Pomponia imagined Octavian's subjects could hear his name in every corner of the empire.

Taurus stood on his platform below Caesar's balcony. He extended his arms and shouted, and though few could hear his voice above the clamor, everyone knew what he was saying.

"Emperor and Empress, blessed priestesses of Vesta, and fellow Romans, welcome! All of Rome is in the Circus today!"

Another horn sounded. The stands shook with sound and the excitement of over one hundred and fifty thousand people jumping to their feet.

Pomponia stood up to watch Scorpus's four-horse chariot burst out of the starting gate. Her heart warmed when she saw it.

Six torches, each one burning with the sacred flame of Vesta, were affixed to the sides of the ocean-blue chariot. They blazed alongside the Titan as he gripped the reins with the confidence of the sun god, as if his fiery chariot and steeds were powerful enough to pull the sun across the sky and bring light not just to Rome but to every part of the world.

EPILOGUE

Sic, Sic Juvat Ire Sub Umbras
Thus, thus, I gladly go below to the shadows.

—FROM VIRGIL'S *AENEID*

ROME, 14 CE

many years later

Octavian had always been a deeply superstitious man, so Pomponia had not been surprised when he predicted his own death. He was in the Campus Martius when an eagle landed just above the letter *A* of a temple inscription that bore Agrippa's name.

"The *A* is for Augustus," he had told her. "I will die soon."

Later that day, he had ridden in a lectica down the Palatine ramp to the House of the Vestals, where he had personally given her his *Res Gestae*, his own account of his life's accomplishments. Pomponia stored it in the temple with his last will and testament.

Soon after, he had indeed died. According to Caesar's instructions and her duty as Vestalis Maxima, following his cremation, she had divulged the contents of his will to Livia before reading it and his *Res Gestae* aloud in the Senate.

"I found Rome a city of brick," Augustus had written, "and left it a city of marble."

The ashes from his burned body were still under her nails when she had read the words. She, along with Livia and the other pontiffs, had been tasked with scooping Caesar's wet ashes from the funeral pyre and putting them in his urn. The effort had exhausted her, and she hadn't had the strength to accompany the procession to his mausoleum. Or maybe she just didn't want to go.

She didn't want to do much at all these days. She couldn't remember the last time she had been able to do a full watch in the temple. Either she grew too fatigued or one of her sisters insisted that she return to her bed to rest. Pomponia knew what they were thinking. She was going to die soon too. She didn't need an eagle to land on anything to know that.

She heard voices at the door of her bedchamber and sat up. Her niece, the Vestal Pomponia. And more voices—Quintina, with her husband, Marcus, and their children. They all kissed her on the head and fussed over her until Quintina bade the others to leave and sat beside Pomponia's bed alone.

"Have you heard the latest news?" she asked.

"Probably not," replied Pomponia. "They think I will fall over with the slightest shock."

Quintina smiled. "They don't know you like I do," she said. "It will be no shock to hear it. Julia has died. Tiberius cut off the allowance that her father had left her. She starved to death under house arrest."

Pomponia patted the back of Quintina's hand. "How are things in Tivoli?"

"As constant as the flame," said Quintina. "Nothing ever changes in Tivoli. That is why I like it so much."

"How are my vineyards?"

Quintina leaned over and lifted an amphora off the floor. "You tell me," she said, grinning, as she poured both of them a cup of wine.

Pomponia took a sip. "I would like my ashes put in the *favissa*," she said suddenly.

Quintina clenched her jaw. "Of course, sister."

The younger Pomponia appeared at the doorway. "Aunt," she said, "the empress is here to see you."

Quintina discreetly rolled her eyes at Pomponia and then touched her on the shoulder. "We will come back tonight for supper," she said. "And for more of your wine."

Quintina bowed to Livia as she left. The empress replaced the Vestal at Pomponia's side.

"You are the second person I've visited on their deathbed in as many months," said Livia. "Apparently it is the fashion these days to command a final audience."

Pomponia smiled. "I am sorry I could not make it to Caesar's bedside in time. Did he have a good death?" *You should know*, thought the Vestal. *You arranged it.*

After the eagle omen, the aged and shaken emperor had asked to see his daughter again. Pomponia knew that Livia would have no choice but to act. Only the gods knew how she had felt when she handed her husband of fifty years that bowl of figs.

"Considering it all," said Livia, "it was probably an easier death than he deserved." She raised an eyebrow at Pomponia. "May you and I be so lucky." She folded her hands in her lap. "He asked whether he had played his part well. He had me arrange his hair." Her hands moved, as if she were feeling his hair under her fingers. "And then he told me to remember our life."

The Vestal did not want to think about it any longer. "Tiberius came to see me yesterday," she said. She corrected herself. "*Caesar* came to see me. We spoke about who will replace me as Vestalis Maxima."

Livia looked at the priestess for a long moment and then glanced down. She unwrapped something from her palla and held it out to Pomponia. The Vestal narrowed her eyes as she took it—a scroll, with the broken seal of Caesar on it.

"I've been holding onto that for a long time," said Livia. "But I suppose there is no point now." She stood and walked out of the room.

The window of her bedchamber was partially closed, so Pomponia pulled a candle a little closer to read by its flame. She uncurled the scroll.

My dearest Pomponia,

You might not think it possible, but the Egyptian sun burns hotter today than it did yesterday. Were I not of such a sensible nature, I might think that a celestial event is happening and this infernal desert will soon be consumed by the sun. Between the heat and the blowing sand, I do not know how the natives tolerate it. Perhaps they are all mad. That would explain their gods.

My slave Ankhu has asked permission to begin painting the

symbols of the Egyptian zodiac that decorate the walls of Queen Cleo-patra's grand library. I think it is nonsense but will allow it. He is far more womanish than I and says you will find it appealing. It is my hope that I will be able to present the painting to you myself, as relations between Caesar and Marc Antony have soured to the point that I suspect Caesar will soon order me to return home.

Last night I dreamed that we stood by the Altar of Juno. Vesta's fire burned on top as we said our vows. I trust that you will honor your vows to me as your husband as properly as you have honored your vows to the goddess. You might need some guidance from me, as I know you have ruled yourself for many years, but I am certain you will learn and we will be happy.

Know that I still sacrifice to Mars every week for your safety and pray to Venus for your love.

Quintus

Pomponia curled the scroll back up. She dipped the edge of the old papyrus into the flame of the candle and let it burn to ash.

AFTERWORD

Writing the *Vesta Shadows* trilogy has been a long and winding endeavor, and I have had amazing help along the way. I would like to thank my literary agent Susan Raihofer, as well as my publisher and particularly my US copyeditor. I would also like to thank Dr. Joseph Tipton for his work translating Koine Greek, my dear friend Amelia Charalambopoulos for her various Greek translations, and Vanessa Wells for her help with Latin translations. Most of all, I would like to thank my husband, Don, and my son, Scott, for their brilliant contributions and inestimable patience.

At the end of each book in this series, I've given you a few images that complement and often feature in the story line and that have meaning to the larger history of the time. For this last book in the *Vesta Shadows* trilogy, I've included a photo of a favorite item in my collection: an ancient Roman coin whose reverse image is of the Vestal Virgins offering into the sacred fire, with the temple in the background.

I love this item not just because it is a rare coin and a vibrant image of the priestesses offering as sisters, but also because it provides a representation of the temple and sacred hearth. It is amazing to think that this coin was minted at a time when Vesta's fire burned in the Roman Forum. I've used this and similar images on ancient coins to describe the appearance of the sacred hearth in this series: a round marble pedestal of sorts, with what appears to be a depression in its surface, within which the fire burns, most likely in a bronze bowl. It is a simple image of a complex religion.

Someone who honored Vesta bought something with this coin—a loaf of bread, an amphora of wine, or maybe an hour with a prostitute. That person is long dead, as are the historical figures that have inspired this series—Occia, Pomponia, Tuccia, Julius Caesar, Antony, Cleopatra, Octavian, Livia, Agrippa, Scorpus, and so on. Then again, are they? Here we are, over two thousand years later, still saying their names, looking into their faces, and telling their stories. The eternal flame and the Eternal City are well named.

Because I'm the sentimental sort, I've included some material in this book and series that I find inspirational or emotionally moving. For example, I find the story of Camillus's "not by gold, but by iron" to be applause worthy. There are many parts of the Vesta religion that are incredibly powerful, rich, and beautiful. The ancients knew this, and I hope I have communicated some of the reverence they felt for Vesta's sacred flame.

Likewise, some of the quotes I've included throughout this series are words of famous personalities—Cicero, Livy, Horace, Virgil, Syrus, and others—that I find poignant and as relevant to the human condition today as they were centuries ago.

The historical elements I've included in this series, from Rome's politics to its spectacles, are those I felt best lent themselves to telling Pomponia's unique story. It's been agonizing to leave out certain events and personalities. There is so much more to tell about the Vestal Virgins and this period of ancient Rome. There are so many more political, religious, and cultural elements—some major and some minuscule—and they all intersect. The history of Rome is kind of like an R-rated soap opera that has been going on for a few thousand years: you can't talk about one person or event without going back to explain fifty other people and events, all remarkable and relevant in one way or another.

Yet this is a work of historical fiction, and I have taken some artistic license to create an original story for a general readership. I have at times adjusted or simplified complex ideas, timelines, or genealogies, including content drawn from the primary sources: Tacitus, Dio, Plutarch, etc.

When it comes to the practices and rituals of the Vestals, I've done my best to create a big picture drawn from the glimpses we have.

The *Aeneid*, the *Res Gestae Divi Augusti*, and the Ara Pacis, as you probably know, are all real surviving monuments: two literary and one marble, all having been reconstructed to varying degrees. As for the excerpt of the *Aeneid* sung by Anchises, it was inspired by the translation of Theodore C. Williams, though amended for flow. I threaded these monuments into the story because they are so integral to the time this series is set in—the Augustan Age—but also because they immortalize the eternal significance of the Vesta religion and its priestesses. From Rome's founding to its fall, Vesta is central. Her fire burned the whole time.

The religion of Vesta and the order of the Vestal Virgins are intimately connected with the founding mythology of Rome—Rhea Silvia, Romulus, the she-wolf, etc. I've included that mythology in this series, and I hope you have found it as fascinating as I do.

Yet there is nothing mythical about the importance of the Vesta religion and order as it existed. It was integral to the rise of Rome and her Caesars, and also to her history, identity, society, culture, and politics. I chose to write of this period, the late Republic to the early Empire, not only because it was a time of extreme war and extreme peace, but especially because Augustus Caesar was such an important benefactor to the Vestal order, and the eternal flame burned so brightly.

It's comforting to think that the eternal flame still burns, at least in the pages of this series and in the minds of readers like you. As Cicero said, "The life of the dead is placed in the memory of the living."

I am so happy that you have chosen to be part of that by reading this series.

Finally, I hope that you will visit DebraMayMacleod.com, where you will find more books and history on Vesta and the Vestal Virgins as well as a gallery of images from my personal collection, plus blogs, videos, and other resources.

Thank you for reading, and all the best.

DRAMATIS PERSONAE
BOOKS ONE THROUGH THREE

Aelina Wife of Mettius

Agrippa Marcus Vipsanius Agrippa, general and friend of Octavian

Agrippina Daughter of Julia and Agrippa

Anchises Slave, famous singer, and partner of Thracius

Ankhu Egyptian freedman, former slave of Quintus

Bassus Former owner of Anchises and Thracius in Capua

Brennus Gallic leader whose army invaded Rome

Brutus Senator and assassin of Julius Caesar

Caecilia Scantia Vestal priestess

Caepio Roman senator

Caeso Guard of the Vestal Pomponia

Calidia The name first given to Pomponia's niece

Cassandra Slave, intimate partner of Scorpus

Cassius Senator and assassin of Julius Caesar

Cicero Marcus Tullius Cicero, Roman orator and statesman

Cleopatra VII Philopator Queen of Egypt

Cossinia Vestal priestess from Tivoli

Dacia Bed slave of Soren; also the name of Soren's late wife

Despina Chief slave in the house of Octavian and Livia

Fabiana Former *Vestalis Maxima*, or high priestess of the Vestal order

Fabius Roman senator in prologue

Gaius Guard of the Vestal Quintina

Gibbosus Gaius Gibbosus, one of Soren's bodyguards

Herod Client king of Judea

Julia Caesaris filia Daughter of Octavian and his first wife, Scribonia

Julius Caesar Gaius Julius Caesar, Roman general and dictator

Laelius The *Flamen Martialis*, or high priest of Mars

Lauressa A novice Vestal

Lepidus Former *Pontifex Maximus*, or chief priest of Rome

Licinia Vestal priestess accused and condemned to death for *incestum* but later absolved

Livia Drusilla Wife of Octavian and empress of Rome, mother of Tiberius by her first husband

Longina Vestal novice

Lucasta Vestal priestess

Lucius Albinius Roman nobleman in prologue

Lucius Sergius Roman nobleman in prologue

Lucretia Manlia Vestal priestess

Maecenas Gaius Maecenas, close political adviser to Octavian

Mallonia Roman noblewoman and former sister-in-law of Soren

Marc Antony Roman general

Marcus Guard of the Vestal Quintina

Marcus Julius Caesar Agrippa Postumus Son of Julia and Agrippa

Manius A wealthy Roman living in Capua

Marcella Vestal priestess

Marcus Furius Camillus Legendary Roman general

Medousa Greek slave, formerly owned by the Vestal Pomponia

Mettius Owner of Scorpus the Titan in Capua, friend of Soren

Murena Roman senator

Musa Antonius Musa, Greek physician of Octavian

Nona Fonteia Vestal priestess

Octavian Great-nephew and adoptive son of Julius Caesar; Rome's first emperor, Augustus

Octavia Sister of Octavian

Ovid Renowned Roman poet, younger contemporary of Virgil

Perseus Fabiana's dog (named after the hero who slew Medusa)

Pomponia Occia Vestal priestess and successor to Fabiana as *Vestalis Maxima*

Pomponius Brother of the Vestal Pomponia

Publius Guard of the Vestal Pomponia

Quintina Vedia Vestal priestess; the elder daughter of Quintus and Valeria

Quintus Vedius Tacitus Former priest of Mars and soldier of Caesar

Sabina Vestal priestess

Scorpus the Titan Slave, famous chariot driver

Scribonia Previous wife of Octavian; mother of Julia

Sempronius Wealthy Roman, one of Julia's lovers

Septimus Young priest of Mars

Sepullius Macer Elderly magistrate

Soren Calidius Pavo Cousin of the late Vestal Tuccia and brother of the late Senator Pavo

Tacita Vedia Sister of the Vestal Quintina; the younger daughter of Quintus and Valeria

Taurus Senator and wealthy patron of the amphitheater

Terentia Wife of Maecenas

Thracius Slave, famous boxer, and partner of Anchises

Tiberius Claudius Nero Son of Livia Drusilla by her first husband of the same name

Tuccia Vestal priestess

Tullio Roman senator

Valeria Former wife of Quintus Vedius Tacitus

Varinia Vestal novice

Virgil Renowned Roman poet

ROMAN GODS, GODDESSES & MYTHICAL FIGURES

Aeneas A Trojan hero who fled the burning city and became the ancestor of Rome's founder, Romulus

Apollo The god of the sun and the arts

Athena The Greek goddess of wisdom; the Greek equivalent of Minerva

Atlas Titan who held the heavens up on his shoulders

Atrox Fortuna Goddess of fate; an aspect of the goddess Fortuna

Bacchus The god of wine

basilisk A snakelike monster

Bellerophon A Greek hero who was able to successfully ride the winged horse Pegasus

Cerberus The three-headed hound of Hades that guards the entrance to the underworld

Ceres The goddess of grain

Charon The ferryman of Hades; carries souls across the River Styx

Clementia The goddess of clemency and leniency

Clytemnestra The sister of Helen of Troy

Concordia The goddess of harmony and agreement

Cronus A Titan who ate his own children to avoid being overthrown by them

Cyclops A one-eyed monster from Homer's *Odyssey*

Diana The goddess of the hunt

Dido Queen of Carthage who committed suicide after being abandoned by Aeneas

Dis Pater A god of the underworld

Discordia The goddess of discord

Edesia The goddess of feasts

Egeria A nymph; her spring was located by the Porta Capena, and their waters were used by the Vestals for purification

Europa A woman who fell in love with Zeus, who came to her in the form of a bull

Fates Three goddesses who determine human destiny

Flora The goddess of flowers and spring

Fortuna The goddess of fortune and luck

Fortuna Virilis An aspect of Fortuna that dealt with virility; a woman might pray to her to make her husband virile so she could conceive

Gorgons Three sisters with snakes for hair; their gaze turned all who met it into stone

Hades The Greek equivalent of Pluto; also the name of the Greek underworld

harpy A terrifying mythical creature that is half bird and half woman

Helen of Troy A beautiful woman whose supposed abduction by the prince of Troy angered her husband, a Greek king, and started the Trojan War; credited with being "the face that launched a thousand ships"

Hera The Greek equivalent of Juno

Hercules A legendary hero famous for his strength

Hypnos The Greek god of sleep

Isis An Egyptian goddess

Janus The two-faced god of beginnings and endings; the Gates of Janus were the doors of the Roman Temple of Janus and were symbolically opened during times of war and closed during times of peace

Juno The wife of Jupiter; goddess of marriage

Jupiter The king of the gods; god of thunder and the sky

Justitia The personification of justice; also known as Lady Justice

Juturna The goddess of fountains, wells, and springs; the Spring of Juturna, was located in a corner of the Forum Romanum

Laocoön A Trojan priest who tried in vain to warn his people about the dangers of the Trojan horse

Luna The goddess of the moon

Lupa The she-wolf that nursed Romulus and his brother, Remus

Mars The god of war

Medea The enchantress who helped Jason and the Argonauts find the Golden Fleece

Medusa A snake-haired Gorgon; looking at her face turned people to stone

Mercury The messenger god

Midas A legendary king with the power to turn whatever he touched to gold

Minerva The goddess of wisdom

Minotaur A monster with the head of a bull and body of a man

Narcissus A vain youth who was so enchanted by his own reflection in a pool of water that he fell in and drowned

Nemean lion A giant lion with an impenetrable hide; killed by Hercules as one of his twelve labors

Nemesis The goddess of revenge

Neptune The god of the sea

nymph A female nature deity intimately connected to a particular place or thing, such as a tree or stream; nymphs usually appear as beautiful maidens

Palladium The wooden statue of Pallas Athena that Aeneas saved from Troy

Pandora A woman whose curiosity released all the evils that beset humanity, save the lack of hope

Pales A deity of shepherds, flocks, and livestock

Pegasus A white, winged horse belonging to Zeus

Penelope The wife of Ulysses

Perseus The legendary hero who slew the Gorgon Medusa

Pluto The god of Hades, the underworld

Proserpina The queen of the underworld

Quirinus An early god of Rome, likely originating as a Sabine god of war; Romulus was said to have been deified as Quirinus and was worshipped as such

Remus One of the twin sons of Rhea Silvia; brother of Romulus

Rhea Silvia A Vestal Virgin; mother, by Mars, of the twins Romulus and Remus

Romulus The legendary founder of Rome

Scaevola A Roman hero who put his hand in a fire to prove his courage

Scylla and Charybdis Two sea monsters in Homer's *Odyssey*

Spes The goddess of hope

Tantalus A figure punished after death (for stealing ambrosia and nectar from the gods) by the eternal torment of having to stand in a pool of water that would recede whenever he bent down to take a drink

Tiberinus The god of the Tiber River, often called Father Tiber

Titans A generation of gods that came before the Greek Olympian gods or the Roman *Dii Consentes*

Trojan horse A massive wooden horse presented as a gift to the besieged city of Troy by the attacking Greeks; hiding inside the horse, however, were Greek soldiers who, once the gift had passed through the gates, exited and destroyed the city

Typhon A giant, serpent-like monster from Greek mythology

Ulysses The Roman name for Odysseus, a legendary Greek king and warrior who tried for ten years to reach his homeland after the end of the Trojan War

Venus The goddess of love

Veritas The goddess of truth

Vesta The goddess of the hearth and home

Vulcan The god of fire; blacksmith of the gods

Zeus The Greek equivalent of Jupiter

GLOSSARY OF LATIN AND IMPORTANT TERMS AND PLACES

Abite! An expression: "Get lost!"

Aedes Vestae The Temple of Vesta, the sacred building that housed the sacred flame

aeterna flamma The "eternal flame" of Vesta

Aere perennius "More lasting than bronze" (Horace)

apodyterium The entrance to a bathhouse; a changing room

Aquila The Eagle of Rome

atrium The central open hall or court of a Roman home, around which were arranged on all side the house's various rooms

Attat! Latin expression of surprise, fear, etc.

augur A priest who interprets the will of the gods via the flight of birds

ave A word of greeting or farewell; when addressing more than one person, the form *avete* was used

balineum The washing or bathing room in a *domus*, often with a latrine

Black Stone The Black Stone, or *Lapis Niger* in Latin, was a mysterious and revered stone block in the Roman Forum, a monument thought to date back to the earliest period of Roman history

Bona Dea The "Good Goddess," whose rites were overseen by the Vestal Virgins

caestus The leather straps worn around the hands of boxers

calidarium A very hot bath in a bathhouse

Campus Martius The Field of Mars

Campus Sceleratus The "Evil Field," where shamed Vestals were buried alive

Capillata tree An ancient tree so named because Vestals would hang their cut hair from it—*capillata* means "hairy, or having long hair" in Latin

captio The "seizure" ceremony, where a girl is taken as a Vestal

Caput Mundi "Capital of the world," meaning Rome

Carcer The notorious structure where prisoners were incarcerated

catamite A pubescent or adolescent boy kept by a man for sexual purposes

causarius A soldier discharged after being wounded in battle

cella The part of a temple where the image of a god stood

cellae servorum The slave quarters in a *domus*

certa verba The words of a religious formula that could not be changed or adapted but had to be spoken precisely the same way every time

concepta verba The words of a religious formula that could be changed or adapted depending on the situation and purpose

chaste tree A small tree native to the Mediterranean that was considered sacred to the virginal goddess Vesta. The fruit of the chaste tree has long been believed to quell sexual desire.

Circus Maximus A large stadium in Rome that was used for chariot races, public games, mock battles, and gladiatorial combat

compluvium An opening in the roof of the atrium over the *impluvium*

cornu A type of Roman horn

crimen incesti The crime of *incestum*, where a Vestal is accused of breaking her vow of chastity *culullus* A vessel used by the Vestals and other priests, usually containing milk or wine

cunnus The female genitals; used here as a derogatory term for a woman

Curia The Senate house of Rome, located in the Roman Forum

curule chair A wooden seat upon which sat Caesar or a magistrate who held the power of imperium

decimation Type of military punishment, typically for desertion

Dii Consentes The twelve major gods and goddesses of Rome: Jupiter, Juno, Vesta, Mars, Neptune, Mercury, Diana, Ceres, Venus, Vulcan, Minerva, and Apollo

divi filius Son of the Divine Julius Caesar (i.e., Octavian)

Divus Julius The Divine Julius Caesar

Do ut des. A petition to the gods: "I give so that you will give."

Domina The deferential name a slave would use when addressing his or her female owner

Domine The deferential name a slave would use when addressing his or her male owner

domus A Roman home

dormouse [*pl.* dormice] A special type of mouse eaten as a delicacy

Elysian Fields In the afterlife, a beautiful place of rest for the good

Equus October The October Horse, annual sacrifice to Mars on the ides of October

exploratores Roman military scouts

fasces A bundle of wooden rods symbolizing a magistrate's authority; the rods may be bundled about the haft of an ax whose blade protrudes from them

Fas est et ab hoste doceri. "It is right to learn, even from one's enemies." (Ovid)

Facilis descensus Averno. "Easy is the descent to hell," a line from Virgil's *Aeneid*

fasti The calendar of religious festivals and events

fatale monstrum A "deadly monster"

favissa Underground temple depositories where sacred items no longer in use were placed; the *favissa* of the Temple of Vesta was where ashes from the sacred fire were stored

fibula A brooch or pin used to fasten clothing or a cloak; on Vestals, it secured the *suffibulum*

flabellum A fan

Flamen Dialis The high priest of Jupiter

Flamen Martialis The high priest of Mars

Flamen Quirinalis The high priest of Quirinus

Fordicidia An annual fertility festival held in mid-April

forum A public square or commercial marketplace that often included important judicial, political, historical, and religious structures

Forum Augustus New forum built by Octavian

Forum Boarium Rome's cattle and animal forum near the Tiber River

Forum of Julius Caesar A forum built by Julius Caesar near the Forum Romanum; also known as Caesar's Forum

Forum Romanum The Roman Forum was a rectangular forum in the heart of Rome which contained many official and religious buildings, as well as monuments

frigidarium The cool or cold bath in a bathhouse

futile Special vessel the Vestals used to collect spring water. The wide mouth and narrow base of the *futile* made it impossible to put down, thus keeping the water inside pure and uncorrupted.

Futuo! Literally, "I fuck"; used here as a vulgar expression

gladius A type of short sword; the primary sword of Roman foot soldiers

Gratias vobis ago, divine Jane, divina Vesta. A thank-you to the gods Janus and Vesta; this phrase was used at the end of a ritual or ceremony

haruspex [*pl.* haruspices] A person who reads the entrails of sacrificed animals

ides The middle of the month, which was considered to be the fifteenth day for "full" months and the thirteenth day for the shorter, or "hollow," ones

ignis inexstinctus The "inextinguishable fire" of Vesta

imperator The title given to a citizen, such as a magistrate or general, who held imperium (great governmental or military authority); later, this term became nearly synonymous with *emperor*

impluvium A shallow sunken pool in the atrium of a Roman house where rainwater collected

incestum The legal charge against a Vestal who was suspected of having broken her vow of chastity

in flagrante delicto "In the act of wrongdoing," especially in the act of having sex

infula The ceremonial woolen headband worn by Vestals

Insanos deos! "Insane gods!"—an exclamation of dismay, disbelief, or bewilderment

insula [*pl.* insulae] A Roman apartment block

invocationes The words spoken to call upon a deity

jure divino An expression meaning "by divine law"

jus divinum "divine law"

kalends The first day of a month

Lacus Curtius A deep and mysterious pit, chasm, or pool in the Roman Forum

lanista The manager, trainer, or owner of a gladiator or gladiatorial school

lararium A household shrine to the gods and ancestors

lectica [*pl.* lecticae] A covered or enclosed couch-like mode of transport used by the upper classes and carried on the shoulders of slaves

lecticarius [*pl.* lecticarii] A man, typically a slave, who carried a *lectica*; a litter-bearer

legionarii Legionary soldiers

lex Julia de adulteriis A law passed by Augustus that made it illegal for a noblewoman to have extramarital sex

Liberalia The annual celebration of Liber, god of wine, fertility, and freedom

libri pontificales Records, books kept by the religious collegia

lictor An officer that accompanies magistrates or important officials

litter A *lectica*; also used for a horse-drawn carriage that transported important people

ludi The public games (gladiatorial combats, beast hunts, chariot races)

ludus A gladiatorial training camp; also the singular form of *ludi*

lupanarium A brothel

Lupercalia An annual fertility festival honoring Lupa, the she-wolf that suckled Romulus and Remus

lustratio [*pl.* lustrationes] A ceremonial purification

lustrum A five-year period

lyre A stringed musical instrument not unlike a harp

maenad A follower of Bacchus; maenads were known for their wild behavior

Magna Dea A term meaning "Great Goddess"

Mala Fortuna! An exclamation meaning "Evil Fortuna!" or "Bad luck!"

manumission Release from slavery; the termination of a slave's servitude, at which point a slave becomes a freedman or freedwoman

Mare Nostrum The Roman name for the Mediterranean Sea

Mea dea! An exclamation meaning "My goddess!"

Mēdén ágan "Nothing in excess." This is not Latin but rather a transliteration of the Koine Greek μηδὲν ἄγαν. It is said that these words were inscribed on the Temple of Apollo at Delphi, and it is one of the Delphic maxims. Perhaps the most famous of these maxims is "Know thyself," which in Greek is *gnōthi seautón,* or γνῶθι σεαυτόν.

Mehercule! An exclamation meaning "By Hercules!"

Milliarium Aureum The "golden milestone" in the Roman Forum

mola salsa A ritual salted-flour mixture prepared by Vestals

Mortui silent. "The dead are silent."

naumachia A mock naval combat

ne serva **clause** A contractual provision preventing a slave from being sold into forced prostitution by his or her new master

Nemo supra legem est. "No one is above the law."

Nota res mala optima. "A known evil is best." Taken from a larger expression: *Habeas ut nactus: nota mala res optima est*—"Keep what you have, a known evil is best" (Plautus).

obstetrix A midwife

officina [*pl.* officinae] A workshop or division in the Roman mint

Paedica te! A vulgar insult: "Go fuck yourself!"

palla A woman's shawl that was worn when out of the house and which could be pulled over her head

panem et circenses Famous Latin expression meaning "bread and circuses" (i.e., things used to distract or pacify the masses), attributed to Juvenal

patera A shallow bowl that held libations

patria potestas The legal power that a man held over his household, including his wife and children

Pax Deorum The peaceful accord between humanity and the gods, which was ensured only by proper religious observance

penus The hidden innermost chamber in the Temple of Vesta, where sacred objects and important items were kept

poena cullei The "penalty of the sack" where an offender was put in a sack with animals (e.g., a snake, dog, rooster, or monkey) and drowned

Pontifex Maximus The chief priest of Rome

posticum The rear door to a Roman *domus*, often the slaves' entrance

princeps A title favored by Augustus, meaning "first one" or "first person"

probrosa A disreputable woman; a prostitute

Prosperum scelus virtus vocatur. "Successful crime is called virtue." This is part of a larger expression from Seneca the Younger's *Madness of Hercules*, which reads: *Rursus prosperum ac felix scelus virtus vocatur; sontibus parent boni, ius est in armis, opprimit leges timor.* This can be translated as "Again successful and fortunate crime is called virtue; good men obey the guilty; justice is in arms, and fear oppresses the law."

quaestio A secular tribunal

quaestor A public official; a position that could lead to a political career

Regia The building that served as the office of the Pontifex Maximus and which had been the home of the early kings

Res Gestae Divi Augusti The written account by the emperor Augustus of his accomplishments, the "things done" during his imperium; also his funerary inscription

retiarius A type of gladiator that fought with a net and trident

Rex Sacrorum A high-ranking priest

ritus Rites or ceremonies performed for a deity

Rostra A large, decorated speaker's platform in the Roman Forum

rudis A wooden sword given to a gladiator upon manumission

salve A Roman greeting; when addressing more than one person the form *salvete* was used

Sancta Sacerdos Holy priestess

scutum A type of Roman shield

secutor A type of gladiator that carried a shield and a short sword or dagger and was trained to fight a *retiarius*

seni crines A braided hairstyle worn by brides and Vestal Virgins

simpulum A long-handled ladle-like vessel that held libations

spina A low barrier wall that ran down the center of a circus. The Circus Maximus had a decorated spina with conical posts at each end, around which the horses and chariots turned.

SPQR An initialism of the phrase *Senatus Populusque Romanus*, "the Senate and the People of Rome"

S Sac An abbreviation of *Santa Sacerdos*, "Holy Priestess" (e.g., *S Sac Pomponia VM* means Holy Priestess Pomponia, Vestalis Maxima)

stola A type of dress worn by married women and Vestals

strophium A band of cloth wrapped around the breasts; an early bra

stultus A fool

subligar A type of loincloth worn by a woman

suffibulum A short ceremonial veil worn by Vestal Virgins

supplicatio A day of prayer, usually public, in thanksgiving or entreaty to the gods

Suum cuique. An expression meaning "To each his own."

tablinum The office of a Roman house, where business might be conducted

Tabularium A public office building in the Roman Forum

Tarpeian Rock A tall cliff overlooking the Forum that was used as an execution site: criminals were thrown from it

tepidarium A warm bath in a bathhouse

thermae Large public bath complexes

Tiberinalia The annual festival honoring Father Tiber, the god of the Tiber River

tibicen A player of the *tibia*, a reeded Roman pipe, a type of wind instrument

toga The traditional garment of adult male Roman citizens. The color of the toga's stripe or border denoted a man's status; for example, a reddish-purple stripe was reserved for high-status men, while a toga of solid purple could be worn only by the emperor. A dark-colored toga was worn for funerals and during periods of mourning.

toga virilis The common white or off-white woolen toga of adult male citizens

triclinium The dining room of a Roman house, furnished with couches for reclining on while eating and socializing

tunica A garment worn alone or under a toga or *stola*

Twelve Tables The very earliest laws of Rome

Vae victis. "Woe to the conquered." The words said by the Gaul Brennus after invading Rome in the fourth century BCE.

valete A Roman word of parting; "goodbye" or "farewell"

Veneralia An annual religious festival to celebrate Venus

Vesta Aeterna "Eternal Vesta"

Vesta Felix Vesta who brings good luck or fortune

Vesta Mater "Mother Vesta"

Vesta Sancta "Holy Vesta"

Vesta, permitte hanc actionem. An appeal meaning "Vesta, permit this action."

Vesta te purificat. "Vesta purifies you."

Vestalia An annual religious festival to celebrate Vesta

Vestales Albanae The Vestals of Alba Longa

Vestalis Maxima The head, or high priestess, of the Vestal order

Vestam laudo. "I praise Vesta."

Virgo Vestalis A Vestal Virgin; a priestess tasked with keeping the sacred flame of the goddess Vesta burning in the temple

vitia A mistake, especially during a religious ritual

vittae A type of ribbon or band worn in the hair; on Vestals, loops hung down over the shoulders

viva flamma The "living flame" of Vesta

Ancient Roman coin showing Vestals around the sacred hearth with temple in the background. This reverse is similar to what I envisioned on the special aureus that Tiberius has struck for Augustus. / source: author's collection]

The Gaul Brennus weighing the gold and placing his sword on the scales. By Paul
Lehugeur, 1886. / source: Public domain image, Wikimedia Commons]